HUNTED

Other books by Denise Grover Swank:

Rose Gardner Mysteries

(Humorous southern mysteries)
TWENTY-EIGHT AND A HALF WISHES
TWENTY-NINE AND A HALF REASONS (Late spring 2012)

The Chosen Series

(Paranormal thriller/romance/urban fantasy)
CHOSEN
HUNTED
SACRIFICE (Winter 2012)

On the Otherside Series

(Young adult science fiction/romance)
HERE
THERE (Late summer 2012)

HUNTED

DENISE GROVER SWANK

This book is a work of fiction. References to real people, events, establishments, organizations, or locations are intended only to provide a sense of authenticity, and are used factiously. All other characters, and all incidents and dialogue, are drawn from the author's imagination and are not to be construed as real.

Cover art and design by Laura Morrigan
Copy Editing by Jim Thomsen
Copy Proof by Regina Hirschfeld and Lissa Critz

ISBN 978-1466358287

TO Mom and Dad,
thanks for always believing in me

The Prophecy

The Chosen one will serve
The mother of the two
Elevated and Supplanter
Will battle for control
Their influence will be felt
Across the lands

The elevated one will
Conceive in the full moon
After the summer solstice
Born of great sorrow
The mother shall accept
Her Chosen One
And he will bear her mark
Protecting her until the end

CHAPTER ONE

BEADS of sweat clung to Will Davenport's forehead as he watched the house through binoculars. A gust of wind kicked up a swirl of sand that blew into his eyes and mouth.

Fucking sand. He turned and spit. He'd had enough sand to last a lifetime. When he left Iraq, he swore he'd never go back. And he hadn't, but Arizona in the end of July was too similar to suit him. His frustration mounted with every passing minute. There was absolutely no activity in the house, not that he could see, and he dreaded reporting the results.

Emma wouldn't be happy.

His intelligence had told him the group known as the Cavallo had made a safe house out of this small stucco residence in the middle of nowhere. Reports that a small blond boy had been seen here over a week ago seemed to confirm the information, but the lack of activity suggested otherwise. Not that Will was surprised. They'd probably moved Jake.

Will climbed down from the rocks and walked the short distance to his car, deciding it was time to check out the house in person. Emma was going to kill him. She begged him to scope out the location a few days ago to see if her son was here, but he had refused to leave her. She'd almost died from the gunshot wound to her thigh and, until a few days ago, she'd been deathly sick. He hated leaving her even now, but she wasn't up to withstanding the heat. Nevertheless, leaving her in the shabby motel for an extended period of time wasn't acceptable either. He wanted to confirm his suspicions and get the hell back.

Emma was a hunted woman.

Will pulled close to a low wall surrounding the yard. There was little natural cover, just sand and a few cacti. While all signs pointed to this place being deserted, he wasn't stupid enough to walk up to the front door. Grabbing his shotgun, he got out of the car and ducked behind the wall. He waited, searching for any signs of activity inside. Seeing none, he darted across the yard to the side of the stucco house. A gunshot rang out, catching him by surprise.

He hadn't expect that.

Will regrouped, considering his options. He doubted Jake was inside, but it wasn't an assumption he wanted to rely on. In fact, he hoped he was wrong. But it made sense that whoever was inside would be waiting for him. He'd made more than a few enemies in the last couple of weeks.

He clung to the side of the windowless wall, then crept to the back corner. A detached garage in the back corner of the yard looked deserted, but so had the house. With no car in plain sight, if whoever was inside had one, it had to be in the garage.

Will ran across the back yard to the dilapidated wooden outbuilding almost making it to the corner when a bullet whizzed past his head. Whoever was inside was sloppy. More confirmation that Jake wasn't here.

Will easily kicked in the door behind the garage and found a beat-up Camaro parked inside. The rest of the building was empty except for a pair of rusted metal shelves against one wall. He opened the car's passenger door and checked the glove compartment for the title and registration, without success. Groping under the seats, his fingers brushed against a gun under the driver's seat. Loaded. Will smiled. He was running low on weapons. The car might actually serve a purpose if it had air conditioning. The clunker he parked out front didn't.

Will hoped to find a container of gasoline, but the scrub brush outside proved the occupants had little need for a lawnmower. Instead, he found a small can of turpentine, some paint rags and a glass jar full of screws. He dumped out the screws, filled the jar with the turpentine, and stuffed the rags in the top.

He'd smoke them out.

Leaving the stuffy garage into the sweltering heat, he wiped the sweat from his forehead with the back of his branded arm. He couldn't get out of godforsaken Arizona fast enough. He'd had enough nightmares awakened in the last few weeks without unleashing more by playing commando in the desert.

The unsettled feeling stayed with him as he sneaked around the side of the garage and stopped at the corner. He took a deep breath and refocused, telling himself this was just another mission. Just another of the many terrorist stakeouts he'd run in Iraq. Not that he was trying to rescue the boy who branded the mark on his arm and bound him to his mother as her protector.

He spied on the house for several moments, amazed no one had come out after him. Not yet. He took a lighter out of his pocket and lit the rag, waiting for it to burn down before he threw it into the back window of the house.

"Time for happy hour," Will said.

It was a risk. There was a chance Jake was inside, but Will now doubted it. Jake was considered far too valuable to be with someone so sloppy. At this point, Will hoped merely to get information.

The fire erupted almost immediately. Will waited about thirty seconds before he ran to the side of the house and watched for the occupants to evacuate, which he presumed would be out the front door. Again, his intuition proved right. Two men in jeans and t-shirts burst out, each with a rifle in his hand.

Will fired a couple of shots into the ground next to their feet, halfway between the front door and the landscape wall. "Hold it right there or the next one's got your name on it."

They stumbled to a stop, thrusting their hands into the air.

"Drop your guns."

The rifles dropped the earth with a dull thud, barely heard over the growing crackle of the flames.

"Okay, hands behind your heads and walk slowly over to the wall, then turn around."

They shuffled forward and spun to face him, their faces pale and drawn with fear. Will hid his surprise. Teenagers. A scrawny dark-haired boy nearly six feet tall and his red-headed companion, who stood several inches shorter as well as wider. *What the hell?* He'd expected amateurs, but kids? The Cavallo had to be toying with him.

Will moved closer. "What are you little boys doing out here all alone? You a couple of latchkey kids waiting for your mommy to come home?"

The dark headed teen straightened his back and squared his shoulders, glaring at Will in defiance. His anime t-shirt stretched across his thin chest.

"What? You getting a growth spurt?" Will laughed, then lowered his voice to a growl. "You didn't answer my question. What are you boys doing out here?"

"Waiting for you." The defiant one curled his lip, accentuating the patches of hair growing unevenly under his nose.

The redheaded boy remained silent, his freckles bursting from his ashen face. His hands trembled over his head.

Will raised his eyebrows. "Do you even know who I am?"

The kid with an attitude narrowed his eyes. "I know you don't belong here."

"And what did you expect to do with me once I showed up?"

The silent teen's lip began to quiver. Will knew the answer before the other boy answered.

"Kill you."

Will leveled his shotgun, aiming for the boy's chest. A flicker of apprehension showed in his eyes before he quickly recovered. Will had to admit that the kid had balls.

"You ever kill anyone, Ponyboy? In real life, not in some video game."

Doubt flashed briefly across his face.

Will turned the gun to the redhead. His quivering had spread to his jaw. "What about you? You ever killed a man before?"

He shook his head violently.

"Yeah, that's what I thought." Will turned the barrel back to the first boy. "*Obviously*, you don't know who I am or what I'm capable of. You boys picked the wrong man to mess with." Will cocked his head to the side and glared. "Who do you work for?"

"We don't have to tell you nothin'."

Will was hot, tired, and irritated as hell. He wanted this done. Twisting his gun around, he smacked the boy in the face with his shotgun butt before the kid had a chance to react.

The teen let out a howl and hunched forward, covering his nose to staunch the flow of blood.

"You know, you're right. You don't have to tell me *nothin'*, but I can make damn sure you *want* to tell me." He turned to the other boy. Snot ran down over the kid's lip and he looked close to passing out. "I'm giving you one chance to tell me before I give you a busted nose to match. And trust me, I'm just getting started."

"He came to us at the pool hall," the boy blurted. "He told us we had to hang out here until a guy showed up... and then we were supposed to shoot him. But he told us you'd be here sooner... last week. We didn't think you were gonna show."

The dark-headed boy moaned as he stood straighter, shooting a glare toward his talkative friend.

Will kept him in the corner of his eye. "Was there ever a boy here? A little blond boy?"

The redhead's lips thinned and his eyes bugged with fear and confusion. He gave a sharp shake of his head. "No! Just us."

Will gave him a scathing glare.

"I swear to God, mister! We never saw a little boy!"

"How long you been out here?"

"A week and a half."

Will wasn't surprised. Two weeks ago, Will had beaten the shit out of Alex, the bastard who'd fathered Jake, trying to get information about the boy. As far as Emma was concerned, Alex had no claim to him after raping her six years earlier, and Will agreed. Will would have killed him two weeks ago if Emma hadn't stopped him.

The Cavallo had probably moved Jake the very same night. "And after you killed me, what were you supposed to do?"

"We were supposed to call the guy, but only when you were dead, and then he'd pay us."

"How much?"

The kid paused realizing what he was saying. His eyes widened.

"Don't be gettin' shy on me now." Will shifted his weight to one side and gave him a cocky smile. "How much?"

The boy swallowed. "Ten thousand. Five to come out, the other five when you were dead."

Will raised an eyebrow. "Is that all I'm worth? I'm insulted."

The redhead gulped while Ponyboy pinched his nose, avoiding eye contact with Will.

"I'm gonna need that number, boys."

The redhead's face wavered with uncertainty. He looked at the gun barrel, then followed it up into Will's grim face. He cleared his throat. "It's on my cell phone. In my front pocket."

"Okay, carefully remove it. You do anything stupid and I won't hesitate to shoot you."

The boy gingerly slipped his fingers into his jeans and pulled out the phone, handing it to Will.

"What's the name?"

"Smith. John Smith."

Will grinned as he flipped open the phone. "Wow, that's original." He found the number and pressed Send.

The kid's eyes widened in terror. "We weren't supposed to call him until you were dead."

"Really? Well, let's just pretend *someone's* dead." Will pressed the speaker button, the sound of ringing filling the air. The ringing stopped.

"Crescent Dry Cleaning.... Hello... Hello?"

Will flipped the phone shut. "You boys've been played." He wasn't surprised. Whoever hired them never expected them to succeed. They were meant to be an annoyance. "But now, I have a dilemma. What am I going to do with you?" Will aimed his gun at the teen with the bloody nose.

Both boys looked frightened now. They had good reason to be. Will had just wasted over a week in goddamned fucking Arizona and he was pissed as hell.

"Lucky for you, I'm feeling a bit generous today. It's hot outside and that raging fire over there," Will jerked the gun barrel in the direction of the house. "is making me hotter. But you boys look hot, too. I suggest you take off your clothes."

They stared, their gaping mouths showing their confusion.

Will waved his gun. "You heard right. Start stripping."

They lifted the hems of their shirts, eyeing Will warily.

"You boys are taking too long. I'm gettin' hotter and that means I'm gettin' crankier. This ain't a striptease. Hurry it up." He raised the butt of his shotgun higher.

They hurried to remove the rest of their clothes until they were standing in their underwear.

Will raised an eyebrow at Ponyboy. "Huh. Tweety Bird boxers. Funny, I pictured you more as a Transformers guy." He looked at the redhead and gave him a menacing stare. "The question is: how generous am I feeling right now? Make you strip naked or leave you in your tighty-whities?"

Ponyboy glared, but the other kid trembled.

"You know, I think being found wearing *that* underwear could actually be more embarrassing than being found naked. I'll let you keep them. Now where's the keys to your car?"

Ponyboy's eyes widened in horror. Obviously, it was his. Will couldn't help chuckling as he picked up the boys' jeans, and dug the keys out of the pocket. With a quick toss, the jeans flew into the kid's chest. The boy scrambled to keep from dropping them.

The corners of Will's mouth lifted in an evil grin. "Both of you boys go ahead and pick up your clothes."

They scooped up their clothing, probably hoping Will had changed his mind. Will almost felt guilty over what he was about to do.

"Now walk over to that giant bonfire and throw them in the front door." Flames burst from the opening.

Ponyboy gripped his clothing tighter. "But my cell phone 's in there…"

"You won't be making any phone calls. Something tells me they don't make pizza deliveries out here anyway. Now move."

After they threw the clothing into the fire, Will picked up their guns and slung the straps over his shoulder.

"Either of you know anything about cars?" Will asked.

The redhead nodded. "Yeah."

Ponyboy shoved his arm. "Why'd you tell—"

Will aimed the gun three feet from the boy's feet and pulled the trigger.

The kid's feet jumped off the ground and his face paled.

"Didn't your mother ever teach you it wasn't polite to shove your friends?" He jerked the gun toward the red-head. "You know where the distributor cap is?"

The redhead nodded again, his shoulders shaking from his suppressed sobs.

Will waved the barrel tip to his car. "Good, the one in this car pops right out. Take it out and hand it over."

The boy lifted the hood and pried off the cap, then he held it out to Will.

"Why, thank you," Will said as he took the part and walked sideways to the burning house, keeping the gun trained on the kids. He tossed the distributor cap into the fire. "Let's take a walk to the back of the house, boys."

He walked backward, with the teens trailing behind. The redhead openly sobbed and Ponyboy's steps seemed to be getting shorter.

"We're sorry, mister. We weren't really gonna kill you," the red-head pleaded.

"A little late for that now, don't you think?" Will stopped in front of the garage and opened the door, then the driver's door of the car.

The teens stood in front of the garage, their breaths coming in short pants.

"You boys stand right there until I drive off the property. If I see one of you even *think* about twitching your nose, I'll shoot you. Got it?"

The redhead nodded in short choppy bursts, but Ponyboy's attitude erupted. "Who the hell do you think you are?"

This kid was starting to piss him off. "I, you idiotic fool, am the man with the gun pointed right at you. Rule number one of playing with the big boys: don't piss off the man with the gun." To prove his point, Will shot the ground near the boy's feet.

Ponyboy let out yelps of fear as he jumped around.

It gave Will momentary satisfaction, knowing he'd knocked the idiot down a couple of pegs. "Next time won't be a warning."

Will climbed in the car, relieved to feel the blast of semi-cool air from the air vents. He rolled down the driver's window and pointed the gun at the boys as he rolled out of the garage.

"Are you just going to leave us here?" Ponyboy asked in a whine.

"Weren't you just about to *kill* me?"

He clamped his mouth tight.

"Besides, you just sent the world's largest smoke signal. Someone's gonna come out to investigate. But do try to be careful and not get sunburned." Will winked and drove off, watching them in the rearview mirror.

CHAPTER TWO

BANTER from a talk show on the television filled the stuffy motel room, but Emma paid no attention. She hadn't heard anything from Will in several hours and her stomach balled in nervous excitement. He had warned her not to get her hopes up, but how could she not? Desperation to get her son back consumed her every waking moment since he'd been taken over two weeks ago. She was so close now.

A rap on the door startled her from her thoughts and she jumped upright off the bed, her heart racing. She reached for the handgun that lay next to her, the cold handle giving her a small amount of confidence. Will had moved them every couple of days, trying to stay a step ahead of the two groups after them. So far, no one had found them, but they'd been at this hotel for several days. Long enough for their luck to run out. The rap turned into a familiar pattern and she lowered her gun, releasing her breath. *Will.*

When Will's face filled the peephole view, her shaky fingers fumbled with the chain and she swung the door open. His face told Emma what she feared before he even spoke.

Her eyes sank closed.

"Emma, I'm so sorry." He shut the door behind him and wrapped his arms around her.

She sucked in a ragged breath. "Had he been there?"

"I don't know. I think he might have been, but they must have moved him right after we escaped. I only found a couple of teenagers. They'd been waiting for me for about a week and a half, which coincides with right about the time Alex told us where Jake was."

Emma looked into Will's face. "What do you mean they were waiting for you? Why would they be there if Jake wasn't there?"

He grimaced before he answered, as though anticipating her reaction. "They knew I was coming and were hired to kill me."

Emma's shoulders jerked with her sharp intake of air.

"Emma, I was never in any danger. They were kids and had no idea what they were doing. The person who hired them probably thought I would kill them and be none the wiser."

Her face hardened. "Did you kill them?"

"No, even though they planned on killing me." A slow smile lifted the corners of his mouth. "But I left them a little overexposed, so hopefully they learned a valuable lesson."

"Now what? What do we do next?"

Will pressed his lips into a tight line. "Honestly, Emma, I don't know. This was my last lead."

Her stomach dropped. "You're not giving up, are you?"

"No, but I'm not sure where to go. Perhaps we need to take a different tack."

"What does that mean?"

"Instead of focusing on finding Jake, maybe we should focus on finding the people who took him."

"Isn't that the same thing?"

"Not exactly." Will walked over to the window and looked through the crack in the curtains. "I've been chasing down leads involving Jake, a very narrow net. I need to widen it to include the Cavallo, but it's going to mean doing some backtracking." He turned back to face her. "It means leaving Arizona."

"What?" Emma's voice rose in panic. She couldn't leave Arizona without Jake.

"Emma, he's not here. They moved him and I'm sure they moved him far away." Worry lines crinkled Will's forehead. "You look tired and need to sit down. You've been standing on your leg too long. In fact, you shouldn't even be out of bed."

"Will, I'm fine. I'm not that tired and it doesn't hurt that much," she protested as he led her to the edge of the mattress.

He sat beside her and took her hand. "I know how stubborn you are. You're not going to admit that you're tired, especially when it has something to do with Jake. But Emma, you were shot less than two weeks ago and you had a nasty infection that almost killed you. Twice."

She didn't need any reminder that her infection was why he took her to the Vinco Potentia compound, worried that she'd die without medical care. It was the reason he planned to leave her there as their "guest." Thankfully, he'd come to his senses and taken her with him when he escaped, but the antibiotic he had stolen ran out and the infection came back, leaving her sicker than the first time.

"Emma, you just can't bounce back from something like that. If you're not careful, you'll have a setback. You just have to accept that it's going to take a while to recover. In fact, I didn't change your bandage yesterday. Let me check it."

He reached for the hem of her dress and Emma pushed his hand away in frustration. "Will, I changed it myself."

"I know but let me look anyway."

She looked up and saw the fear lurking in his eyes. She may have been semi-unconscious most of the previous week, but there was no mistaking the love and devotion he showed her while her fever raged. He rarely left her side. Plus, she knew he still blamed himself for her getting shot in the first place. A guilt that still plagued him no matter how many times she insisted it shouldn't. She lightly kissed him on the lips. "Okay." Lifting the hem of her dress, she exposed the thick bandage taped to her leg.

"Has it been burning? How's your pain?" Will asked as he gently pulled off the gauze to reveal the wound. In two days, the skin had almost entirely filled in the hole left from the entry wound, leaving a pink dimple in her thigh.

Will's hand froze and he looked up, his eyes wide. "Emma, your leg shouldn't look like that for another month or more. How could it heal this quickly?"

"I don't know. I only know it itches like *crazy*." Just thinking about it made it itchier and she scratched the skin around the now-filled hole.

"This isn't normal. Do you always recover from injuries faster than most people?"

What was he talking about? Jake was the one with special powers. "I don't know, Will. I haven't really gotten hurt much."

Will snorted. "Really? After spending the last month with you I would've guessed otherwise."

She rolled her eyes but understood what he meant. Since she met him she'd fallen off a cliff and gotten a concussion, almost drowned in a creek, become violently nauseated when her enemies became closer in proximity, and had been shot. All in all, the month pretty much sucked.

Her hand stopped in mid-scratch. "Will, how long would it take to recover from a concussion?"

He looked confused then his face tightened. "Several days, maybe a week."

"Do you think I had a concussion after my fall?"

He nodded, and rubbed his chin. "Yeah, I don't see how you didn't. You lost consciousness after you hit your head on that rock. And then again later." He looked into her eyes and she knew he was thinking what she was.

She'd completely recovered from her concussion within a day.

He reached for her leg, tracing the circumference of the wound lightly with his finger. The gesture gave her chills but also set off a new itch attack. She scratched with a vengeance.

"Emma, this isn't normal."

What did it matter how quickly she healed? It wouldn't help get Jake back and they weren't any closer than when they started. But she knew Will well enough to know he wouldn't let it drop until he was satisfied with her answers. "Maybe I have healed more quickly in the past, but not like this."

"So you were always different, but then things changed, made you sense the Cavallo when they were getting close and you became telepathic with me."

That one had caught her by surprise. When Alex showed up in her hospital room and she called out to Will in her mind, she never expected him to answer. "And telepathic with Jake."

Will stood up and paced the floor. "Yeah, that's right, before the truck exploded and the Cavallo took Jake, you could talk to him, too."

Just the reminder of living nearly twenty-four hours thinking that her son had died in the explosion sent her reeling and she braced her arms on the mattress. Thank God he'd come to her in her dreams. "And after my dream," she said, "when he told me he was alive."

Will stopped and turned to her in disbelief. "What? Why didn't you tell me before now?"

She sat up. "It was in the woods, when you taught me how to shoot the shotgun. I talked to him then, but he said it was too dangerous to talk to me. You already didn't believe that he was alive so I knew if I told you, you'd think I was crazy."

His eyes narrowed. "Obviously, I don't think you're crazy now. You should have told me. Why haven't you asked him where he is and save us a lot of time and effort?"

"You don't think I've tried?" Did he really think she was that stupid? "I can feel him out there somewhere, but he refuses to talk to me. It's like he's built a wall to keep me out."

"Why would he do that?"

She tilted her head with a sneer. "The same reason you were going to leave me with those nut jobs in South Dakota. He thinks he's protecting me."

His jaw clenched and he ran his hand through his hair, averting his gaze. "Emma, you know I didn't want to leave you."

She shook her head. "I know, I know. We've been over this. But right or wrong, it's his reasoning too."

Will sat on the edge of the dresser, staring at the wall over Emma's head, a frown tugging his mouth. A car back fired and Will whipped around to look through the drapes into the parking lot. He turned back with a sigh, rubbing his forehead.

Emma knew he hadn't wanted to leave her in South Dakota. The Vinco Potentia had threatened to kill her if Will didn't cooperate, but it still stung. She still wasn't convinced she should rely on him completely. What would it take for him to leave her again? The past two weeks she'd had no choice, but she was almost recovered. Emma had spent her entire life taking care of herself and the last five years taking care of her son. On her own. She wasn't sure she could let someone help her now. Everyone in her life she'd ever counted on had hurt or left her. What made Will any different? At the same time, she'd promised Jake she'd stay with Will, a promise she didn't take lightly. She glanced at Will, and the trident shaped brand Jake had burned on his arm, reminding her that Will was bound to her, too.

Still, the Vinco Potentia wasn't a group to trifle with. A secret political organization founded by Columbia University graduates, it was run by powerful men used to getting what they wanted and with enough money to get it. Right now they wanted her.

Will stood, snapping her out of her reflection. "So, you're changing. Just like Jake and everything else. What's made you and Jake change?"

She raised her eyebrows. Wasn't it obvious? "You. You're the catalyst. Even Jake said so."

He shook his head. "Maybe I've started things changing, but things were freaky with Jake long before I ever showed up. And with you to a lesser extent. Alex sought you out, knew you were significant enough to…"

Her chest tightened. "Yeah, I don't need to be reminded of what Alex did."

"The point is, you were chosen yourself, long before I entered the scene. Before Jake was born and before he could see the future. If you could heal faster than normal, you've always been special."

Emma shook her head.

"Do you remember something significant happening to you when you were a kid?"

"You mean other than the parade of boyfriends my mother brought into the house and the massive quantities of alcohol they consumed? No." Her bitterness oozed through her words.

"What about your father?"

She twisted the hem of her dress in her fingers. "I never knew my father. He left long before I was born. I figured he was just another of my mother's one-night stands. She never told me when I asked."

"Does your mother have any special qualities or powers?"

"Other than her ability to consistently pick losers? No."

"Maybe your father holds the key to your and Jake's abilities. We need to find out more."

"Yeah, well good luck with that. My mother refused to tell me anything. What does it matter anyway?"

He stared into her eyes. "Emma, the Vinco Potentia wants you, not Jake. You have significance. I suspect they want you for *you* and not just the baby, otherwise why would the prophecy call you a queen? Why not just a vessel or a baby momma?"

Emma glared, not just because of his flippant remark. Her possible pregnancy wasn't a subject she was willing to discuss. The Vinco Potentia wanted the baby they believed Emma was carrying. A baby who was supposed to be Jake's enemy. Some centuries-old prophecy said that her baby would have powers equal or greater than Jake's, somehow giving the group that possessed him power to control the world.

Emma thought it was a crock of bullshit.

Will sighed. "What if your significance has something to do with one of your parents? Especially your father since you have no idea who he is. Emma, we need to talk to your mother and find out more. Where is she?"

Memories of her mother flooded her with anger and shame.

"Emma?"

She realized she must look as horrified as she felt. "That's really not a good idea."

"Why not?"

"Let's just say my mother and I didn't part on good terms and seeing me again is probably the *last* thing she wants."

Will sat next to her on the bed and took her hand. "We have to try. Maybe it will lead us closer to Jake."

She had sincere doubts talking to her mother would lead them to Jake, but Will knew which carrot to dangle. She'd do anything to find him. Even if it meant seeing her mother.

****

Will packed what few belongings they had, which wasn't much. When the Cavallo, a splinter group from the Vinco Potentia, kidnapped Jake, they'd blown up Will's truck, burning up everything he had with him as well as Emma's suitcase. Even though he'd leased his apartment under an alias, he'd hesitated going back. The people looking for them were powerful enough to sniff it out. But the little money he withdrew with his debit card the night they got away, and what the chop shop paid for the BMW he stole to escape, was running out. They needed money so it might be worth the risk. Even if they knew about his apartment, hopefully they'd stopped watching after nearly two weeks.

"Where's your mother?" Will asked. "I'd like to try to go back to my place. I can plan it into our route."

Emma hesitated long enough that Will suspected she wasn't going to tell him.

"Missouri. Joplin, Missouri. I'm sure she's still there."

Will raised his eyebrows. "You grew up in Joplin? My apartment's in Kansas City, only a couple hours north."

Emma eyed him warily before she frowned. "What a lucky coincidence."

These were things people usually discussed on a first date, not after spending several weeks together. There was so much he didn't know about her, most of which she kept guarded even after everything they'd been through together. Maybe she used it as leverage to get him to share his own secrets.

Emma lifted herself off the bed. "Will, I can help."

"Emma, I can do this. I don't need your help."

"I'm not a fucking invalid, Will. You saw my leg. I'm healed."

The exasperated tone in her voice was something he'd become well acquainted with over the last week. "I know, I just don't want you to overdo it." He pulled her into an embrace and nuzzled her neck. "I can come up with something else for you to do."

She pushed him away, but she wore a small grin. "I don't even think so."

He laughed. "Yeah, no time to do it justice anyway. Though if you'd said yes, I would've had a hard time turning you down. Come on, let's go to Missouri."

"Funny, I thought we were already in misery."

"You must be feeling better. Sarcasm *and* wit."

Will grabbed the remote off the bedside table to turn off the television, when images of a fire on the local news caught his eye. He turned up the volume.

Emma watched Will, cocking her headed in confusion.

"...the bodies of two teens were found next to the burning home. Officials won't release the cause of death, but word has leaked that the boys' deaths were unrelated to the fire."

Will tensed and tossed the remote on the bed. "We've got to go."

"Were those the two kids you—"

"Yes." Will moved to the window and looked through the slit between the cheap polyester drapes.

"But I thought you said you didn't kill them."

"I didn't."

"Then—"

He turned back to look into her strained face. "Exactly."

CHAPTER THREE

HE doubted they'd followed him here. He'd checked and double-checked to make sure he hadn't been trailed. But he was less than twenty-five miles from the burning house. Too close for comfort.

"Have you felt sick?" While her violent nausea and vomiting triggered by the close proximity of the group was a hindrance, it had saved their lives on several occasions.

"No."

"Are you sure?"

She glared. "I think you'd have noticed the uncontrollable retching."

He eased through the door, holding Emma back in the room with one hand. The rundown motel parking lot was mostly empty.

"Stay behind me and if I tell you to run, run."

"Okay."

The car was close to the door. He reached for the passenger door handle.

"That's not our car."

"It is now."

"Where did you get it?"

"I traded it in. Now get in."

She stood in front of the car with her hand on her hip checking out the vehicle. He'd come to recognize it as her defiant stance. "Do I want to know where you got it?"

"Probably not. Now get in."

"No way. You show up with a Camaro and expect me to ride shotgun. Hand over the keys."

"Emma, get in the damned car. We don't have time for this."

She held out her hand. "Exactly. Hand over the keys. You and I both know I'm a better driver than you."

His eyes narrowed. "Better driver, my ass. You just know how to street-race."

"And if the people who killed those kids find us, who better to be driving? Hand over the keys, Will."

He hated to admit she was right. While he'd love nothing more than to insist she was still recovering, he knew she was well enough to drive. He tossed the keys to her and shoved the duffle bag with their clothes and weapons in the backseat. "Then get your ass in the car," he said. "Don't just stand there waiting for someone to take a shot at you. I've had enough fun playing nursemaid."

She slid into the driver's seat, looking happier than he'd seen her in weeks.

"If I'd known all it took to turn you on was a fast car, I would have got you one ages ago." Will teased, but his nerves were shot to hell. The sooner they got out of there, the better.

"Shut up, Will."

When she pulled out of the parking lot onto the two-lane highway, Will reached for the glove compartment. "The car came with a surprise you'll be sure to like."

She raised an eyebrow.

"I finally found that Tim McGraw CD you kept asking for."

****

Emma smiled in spite of herself. Leave it to Will to take an insult she hurled at him when they first met and turn it into something bordering on sweet. As Will watched for her reaction, she wondered where she'd be if he hadn't climbed into her car mere weeks ago. It left a mixture of gratitude and irritation.

He reached over and laced his fingers through hers, sending shivers up her spine. This new Will was growing on her and that scared the shit out of her. Had she finally found a man worth taking a chance on? Emma had spent so much of her life simply surviving that she'd never had the luxury of considering happiness. Yet, there were moments with Will that teased her with its promise. Of course, she could never consider happiness without Jake. But the reality was that even once they found him, their lives would never be normal. Too many people wanted them.

Her mind wandered to the possibility of a baby. The signs were all there, though she'd never admit it to Will. This poor baby was already hunted, not even born but burdened with prophecies and expectations. Acknowledging its existence opened a door to questions she wasn't ready to face.

Emma drove for a few hours, with Will constantly checking around them for signs of being followed. When he wasn't checking, he was asking her how she felt.

"For the fifty thousandth time, Will, I'm fine."

"You've been driving for a few hours and I don't think we're being trailed. I think I should drive."

"I'm fine."

"But what if you're pregnant? You should be resting more."

She answered him with icy silence.

"You don't want to overdo it."

"I'm not discussing this," she said through gritted teeth.

"The fact that you might be pregnant might be what saves your lifes."

"Or gets me killed."

"Senator Warren is probably doing everything in his power to make sure you're not harmed."

She turned to face him then looked at the road, anger bubbling in the pit of her gut. "Is that supposed to make me feel better? Besides, we don't even know if I'm pregnant."

"That's easily figured out. All it takes is peeing on a stick."

"If you're so excited about peeing on a stick, then you do it."

"We have to talk about it sometime, Emma. If you're pregnant, it's going to become pretty obvious in a few months."

"Then I'll deal with it then."

****

They stopped in Albuquerque well past midnight, checking into a motel that had seen better days. Once they entered the room, she stood next to the bed and smiled as he set their bag on the dresser.

He turned to her with a wary grin. She'd refused to talk to him after their disagreement. "You look like you're up to trouble."

"I don't think I'll hear any complaints."

Will raised his eyebrows. "Who said I was complaining?"

Emma closed the distance between them and wrapped a hand around the back of Will's head, pulling him down. Her lips were soft and eager on his.

He broke away, his cocky smile spreading across his face. "What brought this on?"

"Do I need a reason?" She looked up at him seductively, lifting up his shirt to slide her hands lightly over his chest.

Will sucked in his breath. He wrapped an arm around her waist, pulling her body against his as he leaned down to kiss her, his mouth more demanding than hers. She moaned as weeks of pent-up frustration boiled to the surface.

"What about your leg?" he asked, breathless.

She pulled his shirt over his head. Her fingers skimmed his back and slid down to the waistband of his jeans. "What about it?"

He pulled back and looked into her eyes. "Emma, I don't want to hurt you."

A smile lifted the corners of her mouth. "My leg is fine. You won't hurt me." Her hands moved to his front and she unbuttoned his jeans.

He reached down and grabbed her hands in his own.

"Will, really, I'm fine." Emma started to tug his jeans down over his hips; his hands released hers. She looked up. "I want you." Her voice was low and seductive.

Will struggled with his conscience, but his need won out. "In that case, you're definitely overdressed." He pulled the sundress over her head. The sight of her in bra and panties made his gut tighten and his heart pound. Will's eyes strayed to the bandage on her leg. He hesitated.

Emma placed her hand on his cheek, lifting his gaze to her face. "Don't look at that. I don't even need the bandage anymore." She kissed him again then dropped her hand from his face. She stepped back and tilted her head, smiling coyly. She reached behind her back and unfastened her bra, letting it slip over her shoulders and drop to the floor.

"Look at this instead."

Will studied her face with her teasing eyes and the barest of smiles on her lips. Her long, dark hair draped over her shoulders ending at the top of her breasts. His eyes stayed there and then down to her hips and the black panties she wore. Emma stood still, watching and waiting for him.

He looked back into her face and realized he wanted her more than he had ever wanted another woman. He kicked off his jeans, pulled her into his arms, and onto the bed, surprised he remembered to be gentle with her leg. She smiled in triumph when he lay next to her.

Afterward, she lay naked beside him. Will marveled at how perfectly she fit in his life and his arms. She looked into his face with the tenderness that caught his breath weeks ago in a Kansas cornfield. His heart tripped before he smiled then leaned down to kiss her. How did he get to this place of belonging? Will trailed his fingers along her stomach. He wondered if she was pregnant, afraid to ask again, but curious to know. He looked back into her face and she read the question in his eyes.

Emma bit her lower lip, a shadow of fear crossing over her eyes before she covered it.

"Emma, you don't have to tell me anything. I know you don't want to talk about it."

"I know you want to, but I just can't."

He nodded, but wondered if there was more to it. Even though she claimed she believed he had no choice when he decided to leave her with the senator's group, he knew she didn't totally trust him. Not that he could blame her. Not when he was the one who took her to them in the first place.

"Emma, I know you had Jake alone but—"

He felt her tense and her eyes filled with the grim determination he had seen too much in their time together.

"I know you don't want to talk about the possibility of you being pregnant and we don't have to. I just want you to know that if you are, you won't do this alone. I'll be here with you and I'll do everything within my power to keep you safe."

She watched him in silence.

"Do you believe me?"

She slowly nodded her head.

Will didn't know why the possibility of a baby filled him with excitement. It wasn't planned. He and Emma weren't married, which surprised him that he even cared. Yet he couldn't deny the happiness growing in his heart.

Tears shimmered in her eyes.

"Aww, Emma, it'll be okay. Don't cry." Will pulled her close and stroked her hair.

"Are you sure?" Her voice was so quiet he barely heard it.

Will kissed the top of her head. "Yes, I'm sure."

He hated himself for lying to her.

****

Jake sat on the edge of the bed clutching his stuffed dog, watching the television. *Diego* was on, but he'd seen this episode a gazillion times. Besides, the conversation outside the door was more interesting.

The men thought he couldn't hear them. He could, not their spoken words, but the thoughts in their heads. They didn't know this; it was his secret. It got noisy sometimes, especially since it was a fairly new for him. It started only a few weeks ago. His mother had been the first.

His eyes welled with tears at the thought of her. He missed her, but he wouldn't show his weakness to the men. They were afraid of him. If they saw him cry, they might lose their fear. His mother's image appeared in his head and a tear slipped down his cheek. He had never been away from her, not since he was three. He was five now. That was a long time ago.

Jake was tempted to call to her. He'd done it once before, but the first time she called out to him, he answered her and she almost died. Somehow, the Bad Men knew how to find her after he talked to her. When she called to him many times after that, he ignored her, burying his face into his dog to cry if the men weren't around. When he went to sleep at night, he lay in bed and pretended that she lay next to him, cradling him in her arms. The hope of seeing her again made him feel better even though he had never seen it happen in his head.

The future he saw held mostly ugly things.

The men in the hall began to get nervous. That usually meant they had to enter his room or someone more important was coming. He listened closely. It was someone new. He listened to their wandering thoughts to see if it was *him,* the man who visited Jake in his dreams before they took him from his mom. Whoever it was made them even more nervous than usual.

Jake wiped the tears off his face and stared at the television, waiting. He didn't care that he still clutched his dog. It didn't matter. They were still scared of him.

The door opened and he ignored the movement. It always aggravated the person who walked in. He could hear their frustration as thoughts rattled around in each man's head, so he did it every time. It was a fun game for now.

A man walked in, stopping just inside the door. Jake watched Diego walk through the jungle looking for a lost animal. He suddenly wondered if Will was looking for him. He told his mother not to look for him, but he never told

Will not to. He quickly pushed the thought away. He never saw Will saving him either.

The man stood still, waiting for Jake to acknowledge his presence, but Jake continued watching the television. Diego was never with his mommy. Jake wondered if Diego missed his mommy, too.

Jake heard the man's frustration turn to anger, not that Jake cared. The man couldn't do anything.

"I need one of you to come in here." The man called through the still-open door.

"No fucking way. I saw what he did to Hernandez a few days ago. I'm staying outside."

Jake felt bad about Hernandez. Kind of.

The new man groaned with his voice but thought lots of bad words Jake's mommy never let him use. Jake wanted to laugh, but it would ruin the game.

The man shut the door, taking small steps toward him. Jake watched him out of the corner of his eye. He sat in an empty kitchen chair next to the bed, crossing his legs. His hands rested on his knees, lacing his fingers together.

The man waited for Jake to look at him, but Jake devoted his attention to the speedboat that Diego drove.

"Hello, Jake." His voice was calm and smooth. He didn't sound angry like he did in his head.

It wasn't *him*.

"Do you know who I am?"

Jake was already bored with the ignoring game so he shrugged his shoulders. If it wasn't *him*, what did it matter?

The man's thoughts got excited over Jake's shrug. Words and feelings twisted in his head. Jake listened, trying to sort through the mess.

"My name is Alex."

Father. Jake sat up a little taller. *His father?* Jake turned to face him.

A smile spread across the man's perfect face. "So you *do* know?"

Jake didn't answer but continued to stare. Whenever he asked his mother about his father, she always said he was somebody that didn't deserve to know him. He tried to dig deeper into the man's head to see more but found it cluttered with unimportant things. He needed to touch him.

Jake slid off the bed, his sneakered shoes making a dull thud on the wood floor. He walked the few steps to stand in front of the man and study his face. He had blond hair like Jake's, cut short and not as curly. The man's blue eyes burned into his. Jake heard the curiosity and excitement behind them.

"I want to touch you."

Alex's eyes widened. "He speaks. Touch me, huh? Okay. You won't hurt me, will you?"

A tiny smile lifted the corners of Jake's mouth and reached his hand out to the man's arm.

He made contact with an electric jolt. Alex jerked under his hand, but Jake grabbed tight. Images flooded his mind. He pushed through them searching for answers to his questions. *Will.* Will sat in front of the man at a big wooden table, wearing his bluffing grin. *Mommy?* The man talking to his mother, her face white and scared. Will hitting the man. His mother, younger, outside by a fire. His mother crying. Alex had hurt her.

Anger boiled through Jake's body. The man yelped in pain and pulled away. Burn marks appeared where Jake's fingers had been.

"You hurt my mother."

"It was a misunderstanding. I'm really sorry about that."

Jake looked into his mind. "No, you're not." Jake balled his fists, gathering power in his hands.

"Wait!" the man shouted as he jumped out of his chair and backed way. "If you hurt me, they'll kill her."

"You're lying. You need her."

"I need her, but my associates would rather have her dead. They *will* kill her if you hurt me."

"You don't know where she is."

"We found her. Will was looking for you and they followed him."

Will was looking for him? A spark of excitement ignited in the hollow pit of his chest. "I don't believe you."

Alex squatted in front of him. "Jake, you don't have to believe my words. Just touch me again and you'll know."

Jake eyed him suspiciously. He was right. He might know from reading his thoughts, but touching him would make it clear.

This time he put his hand on Alex's forehead and shut his eyes. After the electrical jolt, images appeared. So many, he had to search for the right ones. A phone call telling Alex they had been found. An e-mail with photos of Will and his mom getting into a car. Jake pulled his hand away. Alex gasped.

Jake knew that the men holding him would kill her, but Alex wanted her alive.

"You saw? You saw I want to protect your mom?"

Jake narrowed his eyes. "Yes." It was true, but he still didn't trust him.

Alex reached out, hesitating before resting his hand on Jake's shoulder. "Jake, I missed so much of your life already. I tried to find you for years, but your mother kept you well hidden. I want to get to know you. I want to get your mom so we can be a family. I bet you'd like a family, wouldn't you?"

Jake's eyes filled with tears. He probed Alex's mind and saw he spoke the truth. But what about Will? Confusion clouded Jake's thoughts.

Alex stood up and rubbed Jake's head. "Yeah, I know you do. Don't you worry. I'm going to help you get your mommy back."

CHAPTER FOUR

EMMA stood in a dark forest, a bonfire roaring in front of her. The cool, damp air clung to her back, contrasting with the heat of the blaze that warmed the front of her. Her breath came in shallow pants, her chest rising and falling while her heart beat savagely against her ribs. An undercurrent of electricity flowed along the surface of her skin, causing a tingle that rippled across her body. She wasn't frightened. She was more alive than she had ever been and she felt power, unimaginable power. Her excitement mingled with the electrical current, causing an unexpected pleasurable sensation to spread through her. She gasped in surprise and delight.

The fire called to her. Every part of her shivered with anticipation. Emma felt a presence approach from behind. It lifted the hair off the side of her neck. A soft breeze blew and the leaves of the trees rustled, whispering in the night. Stray hairs tickled her face, leaving tiny electrical jolts in their wake. Warm, soft lips moved to her neck, kissing lightly and moving up to her ear. Warm breath fanned her damp skin and a slow burn began ignite in her gut. Emma tilted her head, looking up into the leaves of the trees above her before closing her eyes.

"You are not bound to destiny." A warm, husky voice filled her ear as the mouth that spoke the words kissed her neck below her earlobe. Waves of pleasure washed through her. Every part of her yearned for more.

She didn't know who made her feel this way. She only knew it wasn't Will.

****

The next morning Will drove as Emma watched the endless sand and scrub brush. The barren land looked like her future, bleak and hopeless. The memory of her dream rushed back and she tried to stuff it back in the recesses of her mind where it belonged. It was a dream, just a dream.

Will shifted in his hand on the steering wheel. "Emma, I need to know more about your mother."

She tensed out of reflex. Thinking of her mother only added to her anxiety. "And?"

"Where did she work?"

"I'm sure she works at the same place she worked at the last twenty-five years. In housekeeping, at the hospital. My mother may have a revolving door for men, but she's a creature of habit with her job."

"So she couldn't have gotten remarried?"

Emma laughed with a snort. "No, not that she was ever married to begin with. She always said she was too much woman for just one man."

"Someone might be watching her house. It might be safer to visit her at work. What shift did she used to work?"

"Days. No weekends. Mom likes to keep her weekends free." Emma's eyes remained fixed on the passing landscape, squashing the familiar feelings of helplessness that crept in whenever she was around her mother. "What are you going to ask her?"

"About your childhood. About your father."

"What if she won't answer you?"

"There's always ways to make people tell you want you want to know."

She turned her head toward him with a blank stare. "Because that's what you used to do in the military. Find people and get information out of them." It wasn't a question, more of a statement. He told her this almost word for word what seemed like a lifetime ago. The day she was shot.

He glanced at her with guarded eyes before answering. "One of the many things I used to do. You don't need to worry about your mother. I won't hurt her. Most people don't need much coercion. You just need to find out what motivates them."

She turned back to the landscape. "Men and beer."

"What?"

"That's what motivates my mother, in that order."

Will shifted in his seat. "Then maybe we're going about this wrong."

"What do you mean?"

"If she likes men and beer, does she hang out in bars a lot?"

"Yes. She said she worked hard all week. She deserved some fun on the weekends. Once I was old enough to stay home alone, she'd go out every Friday and Saturday night."

"What was her pattern? Did she go home after work and go out later?"

Emma nodded.

"Okay, then that's our plan."

Common sense told her that seeing her mother was the best course of action, yet she couldn't shake the dread.

The little control she had left seemed to be slipping away. She wasn't in control of anything. She couldn't even get her son back on her own. The fact she didn't know anything about Will, the man whom she'd pinned all hope of finding her son on, only made her feel worse. "What did you really do before I met you?" Her words were bitter.

Will turned to her with wary eyes. "What difference does it make?"

"Because I'm trusting you with my life and I know nothing about you. Answer the question. You were a bounty hunter?"

He took a deep breath then released it. "Not exactly."

She waited and when he said nothing more, she pressed on. "Then what *exactly* did you do?"

"This and that. I used my military background for different jobs. Sometimes I escorted people to places. Sometimes they weren't so willing to go."

"Like me?"

He looked back at her and flashed the cocky smile he used when she first met him. "I don't remember you being unwilling."

She wasn't about to let him off that easy. "Only because of Jake. I never would have agreed to go with you if Jake hadn't insisted that I needed you."

The mention of Jake sobered them both. They were traveling the opposite direction of the last place he'd last been seen with no real clues to follow. Emma felt as though they were pedaling backwards.

CHAPTER FIVE

THE next evening Will and Emma pulled down a narrow road lined with older homes.

"That one, the brown one on the left." Emma pointed to a bungalow several houses down. The yard needed mowing and landscape was overgrown. Paint flaked off the weathered siding. An old Buick was parked in the driveway.

A woman with bleached-blonde hair emerged from the front door. She wore a pair of too-tight jeans and an equally tight red knit shirt. Hitching her purse on her shoulder, she slid into the front seat of the Buick.

"Speak of the devil." Emma muttered under her breath. Just the sight of her brought all the feelings of insecurity and inferiority rushing back.

"That's her?"

Emma bit her lip. "Yeah, that's her."

The car backed out of the driveway and headed the opposite direction they were parked. They followed the Buick a couple of miles before it turned into crowded parking lot. Will drove past, around the block and pulled into a space in the back.

Will turned to Emma. "You hang back and let me talk to her first."

"I know. We've been over it already."

"And no flirting with dirty old men like the last time we were in a bar," he said, bringing up the night they met.

Emma snorted. "Yeah, I think you're safe as long as you don't go flirting with waitresses with their cleavage hanging out."

"Deal." He leaned over and kissed her. "You okay?"

"I'm fine, let's get this over with."

They walked to the entrance side by side. Will stopped on the sidewalk outside the door.

"If you aren't inside within two minutes I'm coming out to get you."

"Got it."

He paused outside the entrance, hesitating. She knew he hated leaving her out here, but they couldn't risk Emma's mother seeing her yet. He leaned down and kissed her, his mouth hard and insistent. She paused before she kissed him back, matching his ardor. When he reluctantly pulled back, she searched his face, breathless.

"What was that?"

"I just wanted you to remember who you were leaving with tonight." He let go of her and winked before walking through the entrance.

She took a deep breath, trying to slow her racing heart.

"Hey baby, you waitin' for someone?"

A thin greasy-haired man sauntered toward her from the parking lot. He looked like a frequent patron, thin and pasty from too much alcohol and cigarettes and not enough food and sunlight.

Emma raised her eyebrows. "Not you," she answered, her voice hard.

"Then what are you doing out here all alone?" He moved next to her and leaned close, smelling her hair.

She narrowed her eyes in disgust and took a step away from him. "I don't think you heard me. *Not interested.*" She turned her back to him and started for the door.

His hand grabbed her shoulder in a firm grip. Emma stiffened.

"I think the lady said she wasn't interested," a deep male voice growled behind her.

Emma turned to see a dark haired man shove the drunk against the wall. The new man wasn't nearly as large as Will, but to Emma's surprise, he shoved the drunk with little effort.

"I think you owe the lady an apology," he snarled.

"That's okay, I don't need one…" Emma said, backing up slowly to the door.

The slimy guy watched her, his bulging eyes pleading for help.

"Well, I think you do," the dark-haired man said in a calm voice dripping with indifference. His lack of emotion scared her. He slammed the man again. The drunk's head bounced off the brick wall with a dull thud.

"I'm..m..m sorry," he stammered.

The dark-haired man released him, literally tossing him to the side. "Get the hell out of here."

He slunk off into the parking lot, limping past the parked cars and disappearing into an alley.

"Are you all right?" The dark-haired man's voice was low and his eyes softened as he looked her over.

Emma's heart pounded, not sure what had just happened, but sure hanging around with this guy was a bad idea."Yeah..."

"You're sure?"

Something about him seemed familiar, yet she couldn't place him.

"Are you coming or going?" His eyes were dark and piercing, as dark as his black hair.

Where did she know him from? It was there, bobbing below the surface. "I'm sorry, what?"

He laughed. "Maybe you're not all right after all. I asked if you were leaving or going inside."

She shrugged off a fuzziness that had bled into her brain. "Just because you think you rescued me doesn't mean I owe you anything." She started for the door.

He fell in step beside her. "Since you're going in, I'll escort you and make sure you aren't accosted again."

Emma could only imagine Will's reaction to her walking in with another man, especially this man. Even in the dark parking lot, she could tell he was gorgeous. She gave him a withering glare. "That's not necessary. My boyfriend is waiting for me inside."

He moved closer. "Then your boyfriend is foolish leaving you alone." In a fluid movement, he slowly moved past her and leaned into her ear. "He should be more careful." His voice was mesmerizing. He opened the door, his eyes fixed on her.

Emma walked past him, her senses dulled by the fuzziness again. She stood in the entrance and scanned the room for Will, hoping the man didn't follow behind her.

Will sat at a table in the opposite corner, a beer bottle in his hand. A woman with blond frizzy hair, leaned over the table, rubbing Will's arm. *Her mother.* Emma found a vacant table and slipped into a seat swallowing the rising unease. Will cast a quick look in her direction then gave his full attention to the woman in front of him. She knew her mother's interest in Will was all part of the plan, but seeing her draped over him made her skin crawl.

A country song droned in the background as her mother wove her magic. Will played his part well. His face serious, he bent over in what looked to be an intense discussion.

"Either you got stood up or you gave me the brushoff. I'm guessing the former since you don't have a drink in front of you."

Emma looked up, surprised to see her rescuer from outside standing next to her, now blocking her view of Will's table.

"Uh… it's complicated," She said, irritated she felt the need to explain.

He moved gracefully and sat in the chair opposite her. "I like a good story." His dark eyes twinkled.

Will's eyes widened then narrowed when he glanced her direction.

Emma peered at the man across from her. Again, she had that sense of familiarity. His slightly wavy black hair, dark eyes, and his five o'clock shadow gave him an exotic look. He was average height and slender, smaller than Will.

"Have we met before?" She tilted her head as she studied him, her voice stern.

His nearly black eyes flashed surprise and he smiled. “No, I’m quite certain I would have remembered meeting you.”

Will looked in her direction again, his gaze cold. He'd begun paying more attention to Emma than her mother. She had to get rid of this guy before he ruined everything.

“Look, I know you think I owe you something because of what happened outside, but you’re wrong. I don’t.”

He laughed. “That’s harsh.”

“It's the truth. Besides, my complicated story is none of your business. So if you don’t mind…” She raised her eyebrows as her voice trailed off.

He rested his elbow on the table and leaned closer. “Okay, I can take a hint. I’ll leave on one condition.”

“What?” she asked, immediately regretting it. She should have just sent him away.

“Tell me your name.”

“I could waste my time and give you a name, but it wouldn't be my real one. So let’s just skip it.”

He appraised her, his eyes bright with appreciation. “All right. I’ll make a deal with you. If I ever save you again, you have to give me your name. Your real one.”

Will looked like he was about to come over any minute.

The man saw her frustration and laughed. “It's a safe bet. What are the chances I’ll ever save you again, let alone see you?”

He was right. She had a better chance of winning the lottery. “Okay.”

His hand reached across the table. “Shake on it.”

"Fine," she grumbled as she gave him her hand. His hand grasped hers, turned it over, and brought her knuckles to his lips, his mouth lingering. A shiver ran down her arm, like an electrical current, and her head swam.

"Until we meet again," he said in a serious tone before he released his grip.

Chills prickled up Emma's spine. The way he said it made her think it was a possibility.

He stood up and walked toward the front door without looking back.

Two encounters with the man were too much. Her mind reeled. Before she had time to dwell on it, her mother turned to see what had captured Will's attention, her eyes locking with Emma's. Dread and fear strangled the breath out of her. Her mother's mouth dropped open and she mouthed Emma's name. Her chest squeezed in anticipation.

Will shook his head as her mother got up and walked over to her table.

Her mother placed her hand on her hip and glared at Emma with contempt. "I should have known."

Emma studied her for the first time in almost six years. She looked older and harder. Years of cigarette smoking added more crow's feet around her eyes and lines around her mouth, which her mother tried to caulk with layers of makeup. Her blouse was low-cut, exposing her ample breasts. Her hair, dry and brittle from years of chemicals, was teased into a towering mess.

"You always did try to steal my men."

Emma shook her head, her eyes wide with denial. Her mother always had the ability to turn her into a pile of mush. "No…"

She snorted in disgust. "Bullshit. What are you doin' right now? I'm talking to this fine man and imagine my surprise to see he's not payin' attention to me anymore, he's busy lookin' at you."

People nearby began to stare, adding to Emma's humiliation.

"Brandy, why don't we sit down and discuss this." Will approached from behind, placing his hand on her mother's back.

"What are you doin' here, Emmanuella?" Her mother leaned over the table, her eyes narrowing with hatred.

Emma cringed at the use of her given name. Every time she heard that name, horror was usually close behind.

"Brandy." Will's voice was stern and direct.

Emma was surprised she actually obeyed. Will grabbed a chair and sat at the table, blocking her in.

Brandy gasped and turned to Will. "You in on this?"

Will leaned close to her, lowering his voice in a soothing tone. "How about another beer, Brandy?"

She didn't answer, which Will took as affirmation. He flagged down a waitress and ordered two bottles.

Brandy sneered at Emma. "You still too high and mighty to drink beer?"

Emma remained silent, her pulse pounding in her temple. She swore she'd never let her mother treat her like this again. And here she was reliving every childhood nightmare all over again.

"What are you doin' here Emma?" she asked again. "Going off the questions he's been askin' me, I take it your snooping' for information on your father."

"Why did you name me Emmanuella?"

Her mother looked puzzled. "Really? That's your question?"

The waitress showed up with the beers. Brandy grabbed the bottle and took a swig. "Your father insisted on it. That's why. The only thing he contributed, other than his monthly checks."

"He sent monthly checks?" She had always said her father abandoned them.

"Yeah, up until you came home and told me you were pregnant with my man's baby."

Will's eyebrows shot up.

"Mom, I was *not* pregnant with your boyfriend's baby. I never even came home after I started the fall semester and I told you at Christmas. How could he be the father?"

Her mother bristled and she took another swig. "I know how he looked at you. How all of them looked at you after you turned fourteen. Besides, tell me how your father knew you were pregnant if it wasn't with my man?"

A wave of dizziness hit her. "What do you mean, 'how did he know'?"

"Right before you came home for Christmas, your father called me and he *never* called me. He said you was pregnant and he wanted me to give you his name and phone number. He wanted you to call him."

"What? Why didn't you ever tell me?"

"Because, he stopped paying me and if I wasn't getting money, I sure wasn't giving him what he wanted."

"But what about me, Mom? What about what I wanted?"

Her mother shrugged and took another drink.

"We're going to need that name, Brandy," Will said, his voice hard.

She scrunched her face and laughed. "Why in the hell would I give you that?"

"Because it's the decent thing to do?" Will's eyebrows rose.

Brandy pointed a finger toward Emma. "Do you have any idea what that girl did to me? How she ruined my life? I woulda got rid of her a long time ago, but he wouldn't let me."

"He being her father?"

Brandy downed the rest of her beer and slammed the bottle on the table."Yep."

"Sounds like you were compensated pretty well for your trouble."

"Hmm…"

Will's face hardened for a brief moment, long enough for Emma to notice the throbbing vein on his forehead before the player's smile spread seductively. He leaned his mouth close to Brandy's ear. "What if I could get you more money?" His voice was silken with suggestion. "More compensation for your inconvenience."

She sat up straighter and turned to face him, the noses inches apart. Her eyes narrowed but Emma recognized the familiar gleam. Her mother thought she'd found her next mark. "What makes you think you can do that?"

"I'm sure he's still looking for her," Will tilted his head, his words soft and seductive. "I bet he'd give a nice finder's fee."

Her mother grabbed Will's beer and stared at the mouth of the bottle. "He kept callin', lookin' for her. I didn't know where she was so I couldn't tell him. He seemed pretty upset I didn't know."

"When was the last time he called?"

"Last month."

Emma gasped, and her mother's eyes raised and leveled on her.

"If I couldn't have him, you sure as hell weren't goin' to."

Finally, after all the miserable years she had a better understanding of why her mother hated her.

"Did you love him, Mom?"

Her mother's eyes softened and grew glassy before she picked up the bottle and took a swig. "What the hell does love have to do with anything. Love is for weak, short-sighted people. Love never got anyone anywhere but a mess of pain and heartache."

"Why do you think Emma's father wanted her, Brandy?" Will asked.

Brandy rolled her eyes. "God only knows. Never asked him."

"He paid you all those years. Do you think he has a lot of money?"

Her face lit up at the suggestion of money. "He was powerful."

"You mean wealthy?"

"Yeah, that too, but he was different. Like *real* power just oozed off him. I ain't never been with a man like him. Sometimes when he touched me it was like electricity shot through me."

Will shot Emma a knowing glance. They had stumbled upon something.

Her face darkened. "But he wasn't around long. Long enough to get me knocked up and then leave."

Covering Brandy's hand, Will softened his face and lowered his voice. "Brandy, why don't you let me help you? I can help you get the financial compensation you deserve. All you have to do is give me his name and number."

Her eyes narrowed as she turned from Will to Emma. "Why the sudden interest in your father, Emmanuella? Does this have anything to do with the men who've been comin' around lookin' for you?"

Will stiffened. "What men?"

Her mother glared at Emma. "The apple don't fall far from the tree, ain't that right, Emma? Like mother, like daughter. You always acted so high and mighty, like you was royalty. Like you was too good for me but look at ya now. You can't stick with one man, Emmanuella. It's not in your blood."

"Brandy, what men?" Will's voice lowered in menacing tone.

She raised her hands in mock surrender. "Don't be takin' it out on the messenger. I can't help it if Emma's whorin' around."

Will's face reddened.

Emma worried that Will was going to physically hurt her mother. Not that she didn't want to herself. "Mom, what men? What did they want?"

"They was lookin' for you. Wanted to know if I saw you. Asked me to call them if I saw you. Told me you was in some kind of trouble and they wanted to help you out. What kind of trouble did you get yourself into? You get yourself knocked up again?"

Emma felt the color drain from her face.

"You did, didn't you?" Her mother asked, grinning.

"Brandy, those men want to hurt Emma. Can you give me their number?"

A look of annoyance crossed her face. "I don't have their number. I threw it away. I never thought I'd see her again."

"What about her father's number?"

"I ain't got it either."

Will pulled a slip of paper out of his back pocket and set it on the table by her mother's hand. "If you happen across either of those numbers, I would appreciate it if you'd give me a call."

Brandy placed her hand over Will's as she took the note. "You know she won't stay with you. It ain't in her blood to stay with one man."

Will slid his hand away as though Brandy were a snake getting ready to strike. He stood up and pulled Emma out of the seat. "Emma, I think it's time to go."

"Don't be comin' back again, Emmanuella. You ain't welcome here."

Emma felt Will's indecision and spoke before he could. "Don't worry, Mom. I won't be bothering you again." She tugged on Will's arm and pulled him to the exit.

Will put his arm around her back and walked into the parking lot. "Oh God, Emma. I am so sorry. You said she was bad but I had no idea." He pulled her into a hug.

She stiffened, feeling defensive after her encounter with her mother. She broke his embrace, moving to the car. "It's okay. It wasn't anything I didn't expect."

"Why didn't you warn me?"

She stopped and looked into his face. He was upset. For her. She knew that for whatever reason, whether he really loved her as he claimed or because of the mark on his arm that mystically chained him to her, she knew he would do anything to protect her. While it sounded great in theory, and part of her relished turning over her struggles to someone else, she knew it made him dangerous. He would hide things from her. He would ignore challenges that needed to be faced to save her the pain. "Because we wouldn't have seen her. You would have changed your mind and we wouldn't have gotten the information we did."

"It wasn't enough. It wasn't worth it."

Her anger flared. "I'm not a china doll, Will. I've taken care of myself for nearly twenty-seven years. I don't need you to take care of me." He reached for her and she shoved off his hands. "It was worth it and you know it. We got information and sure, it's not much, but it's more than I've ever gotten in all the years I lived with her."

He ran a hand through his hair in frustration.

"This isn't going to work, Will."

Hurt then anger washed over his features as he lowered his arm. "What the fuck are you talking about, Emma?"

"Us, this isn't going to work."

His eyes narrowed. "What the hell do you propose? We go our separate ways? Like you suggested weeks ago in Kansas? It seems I've more than proved my loyalty to you."

"No. Yes." She heaved in annoyance. "But I can't trust you if you try to shield me from things you think will hurt me. I'm not a child and we have to make decisions together."

"My job is to protect you."

"How are you protecting me if you don't pursue leads because you worry they'll hurt me? You're thinking with your heart and not with your head. I need you to think with your head."

Will spun away from her, cursing under his breath as he walked to the car. "Let's go."

Emma followed and they sat in the car. He stared out the front window while she tried to sort through her emotions, unsure which one to trust.

Will jammed the key in the ignition. "Do you think she was lying? Do you think she still has the numbers?"

"No, I doubt it. She tends to live in the moment, never thinking about the long term. I'm sure she never thought she'd need them again."

He started the car. "She was wrong, you know. You're not like her."

She turned to him, caught by surprise. Was she? She'd never been with a man long enough to prove her mother right or wrong. Then again, maybe that fact alone was enough.

His voice softened. "You're *nothing* like her." He drove back to the hotel in silence.

Emma wanted to believe him, but her dream played on a looped tape in her head.

CHAPTER SIX

EMMA woke with a nightmare again, but refused to tell Will anything about it. Whatever it was left her shaken and her sullenness hung on into the morning.

They had returned to the motel and gone to bed, their disagreement unresolved. In the harsh light of day, Will realized she was right. He was trying to protect her at the risk of not doing a thorough job. The acknowledgment stuck in his craw. It was half-assed and he didn't do half-ass.

He wanted to ask her about the man who sat at her table, but he worried bringing it up would reinforce her mother's words. He hated to give them more weight than they already had.

While they had obtained some information about Emma's father, Will wished they had more to go on besides the fact that he oozed power and electricity shot through her. They didn't even know his name. One thing he knew, his suspicions that her father might be the source of Emma's unique traits were confirmed, but they had no idea who her father was. Or what he was. With all the freaky things going on, Will had to let his mind wander past the normal realm of reality, although he wasn't sure how long of a leash to let it have.

Will cast a glance at Emma, who lay on the motel bed watching the television, curled up with her cheek lying on a pillow. Her silence was suffocating. What she didn't tell him ate at his imagination, especially after she dropped the bombshell about them not working. Was she thinking about leaving him?

He lay down beside her, pressing his chest to her back, and whispered in her ear, "I'm sorry."

She turned her head to look at him, her eyes guarded. "I'm sorry, too. This is all new to me. Obviously I'm not very good at it."

He rolled her on her back and threaded his hands through the hair pooled on the pillow. "Neither am I, so we'll learn together, okay?"

Indecision clouded her eyes, before a small smile lifted the corner of her lips. "Okay."

He wished he could ask her what she was thinking, what made her hesitate, but he knew she'd never answer.

"I don't see any point in staying in Joplin. I want to go to Kansas City, but I don't want to go to my apartment until tonight, which means we have hours to kill."

She gave him a wry smile. "You're an excellent lover, but it won't take hours."

He laughed. "That's not what I was proposing. I'm open to suggestions, although now that you've mentioned it, that sounds like a great idea." He leaned down to kiss her to prove his point. "I think that should be first on the list. Make-up sex."

He expected her to protest. Instead, she wrapped her arms around his neck and pulled him closer. She clung to him, kissing him with an insistence and desperation that bothered him. But now that they had started, he was hungry for her.

He pulled back and caressed her cheek. "We don't have to do this."

Indecision flickered again before she said, "Shut up and kiss me, Will."

He obeyed, although his obedience had little to do with his bind to obey her commands. They made love in a frenzy of passion and desolation. Afterward, they lay sweaty and entwined. Emma stared at the ceiling as Will watched her face, trying to figure out how to give her what she needed.

Jake.

Jake was what she needed and he was doing everything he could to find him. Only it didn't seem like enough.

"Why are you looking at me like that?" she asked, still studying the ceiling overhead.

"Because I can't get enough of you."

She laughed. "You already have me, player. You don't have to throw me any lines."

In a quick jerk, he rolled on top of her, playfully pinning her arms over her head. "Do you want me to prove it to you?"

Her eyes widened in surprise. "Prove what?"

"How much I love you."

Her eyes sank closed with a soft shake of her head. "Will..."

"You can deny it all you want, but I love you anyway." He kissed her as his hand slid slowly down her arm until it found her breast. She inhaled at the contact.

"Please don't insult my attraction to you," he murmured against her lips.

He lifted his head and her eyelashes fluttered open. He studied her brown eyes, hoping they would give him insight to her thoughts. Instead, she grinned. "If I say I'm sorry does that mean we're going to have make-up sex again?"

"No, and although I'm tempted, I'm not your sex toy." He rolled to his side and pulled her into an embrace. "Let's get lunch, then do something before we go to my apartment. Got any ideas?"

She was silent for a moment then said, "We can stop and see my grandmother. She lives in Lamar. It'll be on the way."

"You have a grandmother?"

She snorted. "Of course, I have a grandmother. Contrary to the evidence in the bar last night, my mother isn't a fungus spore that spontaneously spawned."

"Why didn't you mention it before?"

"Because I rarely saw my grandmother growing up. She and my mother didn't get along and I suspect it might have had something to do with me or my father. Even though Mom moved to Joplin right after I was born, Grandma might have something to help us. At any rate, we should get a better reception from her."

"Then let's get lunch and go see her."

Emma looked at the clock. "It's almost eleven o'clock and it'll take less than an hour to get there. Grandma always loved to cook. I bet she'll want to fix us lunch."

Will's stomach growled at the thought of home-cooked food. He couldn't remember the last time he'd had a meal that didn't come from a restaurant kitchen.

****

They arrived in Lamar less than an hour later. Will drove through an older neighborhood. The canopies of massive trees loomed overhead as Emma studied the houses, trying to remember which one was her grandmother's. "I haven't visited her since I left for college and rarely before that," she apologized.

She was about to give up when she saw the small white house with the pink metal awning covering the porch. "There!" The house was smaller than she remembered, which threw her off, but she recognized the faded white-painted wishing well she'd thrown pennies in as a little girl. The giant snowball bush was still at the corner of the house, only now it was more overgrown and out of control.

Will parked the car at the curb. "Do you think she's home?"

Emma watched for a moment, looking for movement behind the frilly white curtains. "Probably. She retired my sophomore year of college and I remember she was always a homebody." Emma reached for the door handle when Will grabbed her arm. She turned back to face him.

He gave her a reassuring smile. "Anytime you want to leave, just say the word."

"Don't worry. Grandma is the complete opposite of my mother. You'll like her." She got out of the car and watched the house as she waited for Will.

They walked to the front door together, standing side by side on the porch as Emma rang the doorbell. A gray head peered around the curtains in the side window and Emma smiled. The door flew open and a small elderly woman clutched her chest, her eyebrows raised in shock.

"Emma?"

"Grandma!" she choked out as the woman threw her arms around her. To Emma's horror, her grandmother was crying. "Grandma? Are you okay?"

Her grandmother pulled back and dabbed her tears with a tissue she pulled from the pocket of her housedress. "These are tears of happiness! Come inside." She stopped and finally seemed to notice Will. "And who's this young man you've brought with you?"

"Grandma, this is—"

Will reached his hand toward her. "Will Davenport, ma'am. I apologize for our intrusion."

The respect he showed her grandmother caught Emma by surprise, but then again, Will was the master of charm. Except he seemed genuine, and she was suddenly proud that she could present this man to her grandma.

The older woman eyed him carefully as she took his hand, then pulled it free and patted his arm. "This is no intrusion! It's a cause for celebration!" She turned to Emma and took her hand, pulling her through the door. "Oh, how I've missed you, Emmanuella."

For some reason, her grandmother was the only person Emma felt comfortable using her given name. A wave of guilt surged through her. Emma's mother and grandmother might not get along, but that wasn't a reason to not visit. Then again, the last three years of her life had been on the run. Not exactly the right time to drop in on your grandmother for cookies and tea.

The house was exactly how she remembered it. Lace doilies covered the worn armrests of the 1960s sofa and armchair. Faded prints papered the walls. Threadbare lace curtains covered the windows. The ranch house was small, a typical midcentury tract house, but Emma always remembered it neat and clean. And more importantly, inviting. Coming to her grandmother's was like coming home.

"Have you kids had lunch?" her grandma asked.

"No."

She clasped her hands together, a broad smile filling her face. "Well then, let me fix you something."

Emma looked over her shoulder at Will and lifted an eyebrow in an I-told-you-so look.

Will grinned. "We don't want to put you to too much trouble, Mrs. Thompson."

She waved her hand with a *pft*. "It's no trouble at all. I rarely get to cook for anyone other than myself."

Emma sat in a vinyl upholstered chairs at the Formica-topped kitchen table. Nothing had changed since she was a small child. Will sat beside her, a smile on his face. She knew he'd like her. She shouldn't care whether he liked her or not, yet she found herself surprised that she did.

Her grandmother opened the refrigerator and began pulling out ingredients. "I hope you like fried chicken, Will. It used to be one of Emma's favorites when she was a little girl." She winked at Emma before she turned back to the counter. "I was going to make it for the church picnic tomorrow, but this seems like a better occasion."

Sitting at her grandmother's table brought a rush of familiarity and home. How had she forgotten this feeling?

"Emma, where's your boy? Your momma said you had a little boy a few years back."

To her dismay, her eyes filled with tears and before she could stop herself, sobs broke loose.

Her grandmother turned in surprise and pulled Emma's head against her stomach, patting her shoulder. "There, there, child," she soothed. "There, there."

****

Emma must have cried a good five minutes. Will watched in helplessness, a feeling that made him uncomfortable. If there was a problem, he acted. But in this case, he suspected Emma needed the older woman more than anything he could offer so he sat and waited.

When Emma settled down, her grandmother pulled a chair in front of Emma and took her hands into her own.

"What's his name?"

"Ja-ake," Emma hiccupped.

"Where is he?"

"They to-ok him."

"Who took him?" Her grandmother looked at Will.

When Emma had begun crying, he knew her grandmother would want answers and he wrestled with what to tell her. But she obviously loved Emma and they needed an ally. They might get more answers from her if she knew what they were up against.

Will looked her square in the eyes. "A group called the Cavallo. They've been after Emma and Jake for three years."

She clutched her hand to her chest in horror. "Why on *earth* would people be after them?"

"Because Jake has something they wanted."

"What could a small child possibly have that they would want?"

Will paused, still unsure if he should continue, but Emma needed her grandmother and he suspected her grandmother needed her too. "Power."

She turned to Emma. "What's he talking about, Emmanuella?"

"Jake can see the future. And now he can do even more since Will found us."

Her grandmother shook her head in confusion. "Maybe you should start at the beginning."

Between the two of them, they told her everything. They started with when Jake first saw things when he was two and when the Bad Men, as Jake called them, showed up to take him.

Will watched in amazement as Emma told her grandmother things she'd never told him. Such as when the Cavallo had first shown up at her door one night, asking to see Jake. She had called the police, who refused to take the threat seriously. And how they narrowly escaped that first time, and how, after that, she listened whenever Jake told her the Bad Men were coming.

She told her grandmother how they progressed farther and farther down the socioeconomic ladder as Emma resorted to low-end jobs that paid little, didn't ask for references and let her bring Jake to work. How their possessions dwindled from a house full of furniture, a minivan and a salaried job as an accountant to living in a pay-by-the-week motel, a suitcase and a beat-up Honda.

And as he listened, his need to take care of her grew until it became a mass of conviction burning in his chest. She'd gone through far more than anyone deserved and she'd done it alone. He'd be damned if she faced this alone again.

Emma explained how Will showed up a few weeks earlier when the Bad Men found them in Texas, and when Will offered to help Jake insisted she needed to trust him. She told her how Will protected them from the gunmen in a rest stop in Kansas, but that they'd taken Jake and made his truck explode in Colorado.

"How is it you happened to have a truck full of weapons, young man?" her grandmother asked in a stern voice.

Emma locked eyes with Will. He nodded, giving her permission to tell her everything, but her answer surprised him. "He was in the Marines."

Her grandmother looked confused. "But that doesn't—"

Emma paused and grabbed her hands, staring intently into her eyes. "Grandma, we can trust him. He's protected me and helped me escape from the other group—"

"*Escape?* What other group?"

"…and nursed me back to health after I was shot in the leg."

"*You were shot?*"

"Yes, and I almost died. But Will took care of me and protected me from both groups while I recovered."

"The other group is still after you even though they have Jake?"

Emma hesitated. "Yes, they're trying to kill me."

"Oh my stars." Her grandmother leaned back in her seat, both hands clutched at her chest.

"Has anyone been here asking for her?" Will asked. "Her mother said men had been there, telling her Emma was in trouble and needed their help."

She shook her head. "No, no one." Her thumb rubbed the tissue in her hand while she stared at the kitchen window. She turned back to Emma. "So why are you here now? You haven't been here since you were in high school? What do you need from me? Money?"

Emma hesitated and Will recognized her look of indecision.

"Not money," he said. "But we do need your help. We're hoping you might have information about Emma's father."

"Her *father*?"

"Yes, she knows nothing about him and we're hoping that what we find out will help enlighten us about her special abilities."

"Emma has special abilities?"

"Yes, and since Jake does too we wonder if they got them from her father."

The woman stood up. "I don't remember much about him and I'll be happy to tell you all I know, but first, I need to fix some fried chicken and mashed potatoes and gravy. Nothing like comfort food when you're in need of some comforting." She patted Emma's shoulder, then turned to the sink. "Emma, there's wash rags and towels in the bathroom if you want to wash your face."

Emma stood and hesitated, looking at Will. Her eyes were questioning. He could tell she wondered if they did the right thing, telling her grandmother as much as they had. He gave her a reassuring smile before she disappeared down the hall. After he heard the bathroom door click shut, her grandmother looked over her shoulder. "Thank you for bringing her to see me."

"It wasn't my idea, ma'am, it was all hers. In fact, after our encounter with her mother last night, I wasn't so sure it was a good idea. But she insisted you were different and I'm glad she was right."

"I wish she'd come to me when this all started, I would've helped her."

"Honestly, I'm not sure you could have. You would have only put yourself in danger, too."

"But she went through that all alone."

"She's not alone now. I'm with her."

She turned, a potato in one hand and peeler in the other and narrowed her eyes. "But for how long? She's had a hard life, Mr. Davenport. If you're gonna cut and run, do it now and save her the heartache later."

Will understood her concern. She didn't know anything about him and he'd only known Emma a few short weeks. "I can assure you, Mrs. Thompson, I'm not going anywhere. I love your granddaughter and I'll die before I let anything happen to her."

She studied him for several long painful moments before she nodded and turned back to the sink. "I believe you will."

They ate lunch in amicable silence, although Emma toyed with the food on her plate. Her grandmother admonished her to eat.

"I know you're missing your boy, but you won't do him any good wasting away."

Emma listened, to Will's relief. She'd lost weight since he met her and she didn't have a lot to spare to begin with.

Will was impatient to get information, but Emma's grandmother made it very clear she wouldn't discuss it until after lunch. And since her grandmother held all the cards at the moment, he didn't have a choice in the matter. He got a home-cooked meal and they weren't in a hurry. He saw no reason to complain.

Emma insisted on washing the dishes and Will helped while her grandmother sat on the ancient sofa and watched television.

"How is it you didn't spend much time with your grandmother? She's amazing."

Emma looked over her shoulder at the now-dozing woman. "I know. My mother didn't let me see her much when I was younger and then when I got old enough to see her on my own, it never occurred to me to do so."

"She really loves you."

"Yeah, I know." she smiled, a genuine smile that lit up her face. "It's so nice to do something so normal like washing dishes."

"Yeah, I could get used to normal."

She looked up at him with a grin. "I have a hard time picturing you with a house and a white picket fence."

He shrugged. "Maybe I like picket fences."

"I don't know, maybe it's the way I met you but assault rifles and picket fences seem juxtapositioned."

He stopped drying the dish in his hand and faced her. "Maybe I want more than assault rifles and car chases."

Her smile faded and her voice grew quiet. "I think assault rifles and car chases are a part of my life for some time to come."

"Not if I can help it. My goal is to not only get Jake but figure out a way to extract all three of us from this godforsaken mess."

She sighed. "I'm not sure how realistic that is."

"Hey, I've been in impossible situations before and gotten out, so I plan on accomplishing my goal. First, we need to get your grandmother to tell us everything she knows about your father."

When they finished in the kitchen, they moved into the living room and her grandmother roused.

Emma sat next to her grandmother on the sofa and Will in the chair, the springs sagging under his weight. He felt oversized and out of place in this room full of doilies and lace curtains.

Her grandmother folded her hands in her lap. "Now, what do you want to know?"

"Did you ever meet my father?"

"Once. Your mother was young when she met him, eighteen and just graduated from high school. She thought she had the world by the tail, that girl. She used to be pretty and popular, bet you find that hard to believe looking at her now, but she was. She met him over the summer and she fell fast and hard. He was older, but I didn't find that part out until later. I never got a straight answer as to where she met him, but she said he knew her, knew who she was without her even telling him. That it was destiny."

Will glanced over at Emma, her eyes widened in momentary fear before they deadened. But her hands fisted so tightly her knuckles turned white. He resisted the urge to take her hand in his and give her comfort. Her reaction wasn't a surprise. The same thing had happened to her when she met Alex, Jake's father.

"She was taken with his looks and his money. She was already planning her life with him, though to the best of my knowledge he never hinted at a future together. He came to the house once. He was tall and dark-haired, a fine looking man, probably the most handsome man I've ever seen. He was very polite but didn't speak much, yet he had this charisma. I could instantly see why Brandy liked him. She was the prettiest girl in town and she had big ambitions.

But I could see he was older and I thought maybe part of the reason Brandy liked him so much was because her daddy died when she was little." She nodded her head to Will. "I never remarried after my dear Harold passed on.

"In any case, she decided not to go to college, to stick around for him."

"What was his name, Grandma?"

"Aiden, but I don't remember a last name. Just Aiden."

Will watched Emma inhale and hold her breath. He couldn't imagine learning his father's name after twenty-seven years.

"Do you have any pictures of him?" Will asked.

"Heavens, no. Emma's momma didn't either. He told her he was camera-shy."

"Was he from around here?"

"I don't think so, never heard of him or his family. When he broke things off with your momma, he left town. Never seen nor heard from him again."

"Mom said he gave her money every month for me."

"Did he? Huh." She pinched her lips together, deep in thought. "She never mentioned it, but by then we weren't speaking much."

"Why not? What happened?"

"I warned your momma her relationship with Aiden wouldn't last, that it was obvious he wouldn't stick around here long. You could tell by looking at him that he was from money and power. But your momma thought he'd take her with him. So when she turned up pregnant, she was sure she'd just bought her ticket outta here, but he took off days later, not a word where he was going. She turned bitter after that, blamed everyone and everything for what happened. Blamed me because I warned her it would happen. Blamed you," she nodded at Emma. "because if she hadn't gotten pregnant she thought he woulda stuck around. Finally, she got angry with him and the anger turned to bitterness until she wouldn't listen to reason at all. After you were born, she got a job in Joplin and took you with her. I didn't see either of you much after that."

"Do you have any idea where he might be now? Like I said earlier, we think he might be the key to Jake's powers." Will said.

Her grandmother looked at Will with a furrowed brow, then back to Emma. "You said he could see the future. What else can he do?"

"After Will showed up, he could communicate with us telepathically. He also branded Will with the mark on his arm and Will saw him control fire."

"And why do you think this might have something to do with your father?"

"Because Emma has started exhibiting abilities as well. She and I could communicate with our minds. And she sensed when the Cavallo was nearby. Then there's her leg. She got shot in the leg and healed in remarkable time. No one normal would have healed that quickly. Has Brandy or anyone else in your family showed any signs of these abilities?"

"No."

Will leaned forward. "There's a mystery surrounding her father— who was he? Where is he? It's a lead we're following. Frankly at this point, I'd follow a hand-drawn treasure map if I thought it might give me any clues to where Jake is."

"Did Mom have anything of his, anything at all?"

Her grandmother nodded. "As a matter of fact, she did. I didn't even think about it until you asked. He gave it to her while they were dating. She used to wear it around her neck until after she had you and realized he wasn't coming back." She got up and disappeared into a back bedroom for a minute then came back and placed a necklace with a pendant in Emma's hand.

Emma paled, her eyes wide.

Will tensed. "Emma?"

She looked up, her face taut as she passed the necklace to Will. He held it in his palm, examining the oval pendant made of an iridescent black stone. In its center were swirls of orange and red in the unmistakable pattern of fire. In the shape of the mark on her back.

CHAPTER SEVEN

AFTER Emma passed the necklace to Will, the expression on his face confirmed he saw the resemblance as well. She stuffed her trembling hands under her legs. She didn't want to upset her grandmother and if Will saw, he'd baby her to death.

But the walls closed in and the air grew thick and stale. She resisted the urge to suck in a deep breath. So her father gave her mother a pendant of fire. That matched a mark that appeared on her back when she conceived her son. It didn't mean anything. Yet it meant everything. What if her father really did have special powers? What if he passed them on to her and Jake? What if there was more to her than she ever considered?

Emma bolted off the sofa, startling both Will and the older woman. "I forgot something in the car. I'll be right back." She stopped herself from sprinting the few steps to the door then walked to the side of the house, out of the front window's view. Hidden by the snowball bush, she braced her hands on the side of the house and she leaned over, sucking in deep breaths as she tried to curb her rising panic.

Why did she feel this way? This was what she and Will wanted. Answers. This is what she'd begged her mother for her entire life. So why was she so upset?

"If you want something out of the car, you're going to need the keys."

She turned to see Will next to the overgrown bush, dangling the car keys from his fingers. Dropping her head between her arms, she willed the burning in her eyes to go away.

"Are you okay?" Will asked.

"Do I *look* okay?" She regretted snapping the moment the words left her mouth. "I'm sorry. That necklace freaked me out."

Will moved closer. "Yeah, it freaked me out too. But it's good. We have a connection to your father now. We don't know what it means, but I think it confirms your father has something to do with who you and Jake are. Especially since he looked for you when he knew you were pregnant with Jake."

She turned around and leaned her back against the wall. "But *how* did he know? I hadn't told *anyone*. I was too embarrassed and ashamed."

"I don't know, maybe Alex?"

She shuddered. "What kind of sick twisted man would condone a man raping his daughter?"

"I'm not saying he did and even if he did know, you don't know that he condoned it. For all he knew, it was consensual."

"Still…"

"Emma, I'm not making excuses for the sperm donor who fathered you twenty-seven years ago. He left you with that bitch of a mother and never showed his face. I think the man's a piece of shit. I'm just saying you don't know what his motivation was."

She sighed, suddenly weary. "Finding out about my father was supposed to make me happy. I've wondered about him my whole life. Why am I so upset?"

Will slid next her, his back against the wall. "It's a lot to take in. That night in the cornfield you told me you'd always wished for a father when you were a little girl. I suspect you created a fantasy about who he was and why he couldn't be with you."

Her throat burned. How did he know her so well? She'd daydreamed that her mother stole her from him and he searched the earth looking for her. But her father never came. It was a stupid childhood dream.

Will laced his hand through hers. "Bottom line is he didn't live up to the fantasy. Of course you're torn finding out about him."

She closed her eyes and a tear fell down her cheek.

"But there's one positive thing."

Emma lifted her chin. "What?"

"Jake got his affinity for fire from you, not Alex."

She hadn't considered that aspect. He was right and it gave her comfort. She squeezed his hand and leaned her head into his arm. "We should probably go back inside. Grandma's going to wonder where we are."

"Oh, I suspect she knows, but you're right. Besides, we should probably leave for Kansas City soon. I'm concerned the Cavallo and Warren's men are close, watching for us. The sooner we get out of Missouri the better."

She nodded and Will pulled her into his arms and kissed her gently.

"What was that for?"

He brushed the hair off her cheek, staring in her eyes with a look of affection Emma couldn't deny. "I just want you to know I'm here."

She allowed herself this moment, hating herself for being weak enough to want more. Yet she couldn't commit to him, no matter how much part of her wanted to. Whatever Will felt for her wasn't real and she couldn't let herself forget it. If the mark were to disappear tomorrow, who was to say he'd still love her?

They told her grandmother goodbye and Will gave her his cell phone number in case anyone came looking for Emma. She watched the house as Will pulled away, doubting she'd ever see her grandma again. It was too risky to come back. She couldn't jeopardize her safety.

Once they were back on the highway, Will reached into his pocket and placed the necklace in her palm. "You should probably keep this."

She took the pendant, surprised that it felt so warm. "Did this feel hot when you held it?"

"No. If anything, it felt cold." He turned to her. "Why? Does it feel hot to you?" He took it from her and turned it in his fingers. "It's cool."

She took it back and held it in her fisted hand. Within moments it became unbearably hot, burning her skin. "Feel this." She grabbed his hand and placed his fingertips on the area on her palm.

His eyes widened. "Maybe you shouldn't hold that thing until we figure out what it is."

"My mother wore it for months and nothing happened to her."

"She got pregnant and became a bitch."

"Some might argue I got there without a heated medallion."

He looked straight ahead but his body stilled. "Are you telling me that you think you're pregnant?" His words were deceptively calm.

She sighed in frustration. When would she learn to censor her words? All the years she spent on the run, she never let anything slip but mere weeks with him and words just tumbled out. "No, I am not. I'm saying I already got pregnant out of wedlock and some people would call me a bitch."

"First of all, it's funny hearing you say something archaic like 'out of wedlock' and second anyone who calls you a bitch doesn't know you very well, which I suspect accounts for every person on the planet with the exception of Jake and myself."

His words were true, yet painfully so. A reinforcement of how screwed up her life really was.

"I'm just saying maybe you shouldn't wear it until we learn more about it."

She stuffed the necklace into the pocket of her skirt. Will was right. They already had enough trouble to deal with. "So what's our plan for tonight?"

"I want to sneak into my apartment once it gets dark. I live in Westport so there'll be crowds of people to get lost in on a Saturday night. But I'm still worried someone could be watching the building. I'm trying to decide whether to bring you inside with me or not."

"Of course I'm going with you. You think I'd miss an opportunity to see your man cave?"

"It might not be safe, not if we're ambushed."

"So you plan to just leave me somewhere while you run off to be ambushed?"

He scowled. "No. I don't know. I need to figure out what's safest for you."

"What *safest* for me is to stay with you."

He paused then cast a quick glance in her direction. "My gut says to keep you with me."

"Well, it's settled then. We stick together."

****

They parked in a lot on the edge of Westport and walked the streets, waiting for night to settle in. Will watched for anyone following them and while he didn't see anything, his instinct told him they weren't alone.

"How do you feel?" he asked Emma. "Any nausea?"

Her eyes narrowed and he suspected she was about to make a snarky reply, but she gave him a small smile. "No. I don't feel anything."

She'd been quiet since the visit to her grandmother's. He suspected what she needed was more time to process what they'd learned. Too bad time wasn't a luxury they could afford.

Once the sun had set they headed to Will's apartment. He still scanned the crowd, but it was Saturday night. People were everywhere.

A couple of blocks from his apartment building, he found a group of teenage boys and he offered them money to fake an argument outside the front entrance of the building. Once they created a disturbance, Emma would go in the door first and Will would follow a minute behind. It was a decent plan, but Will knew it wouldn't take much for it to fall apart.

The teens stopped several feet from the door and began shouting, while Will waited with Emma around the corner. He bent down and pulled his handgun out of the holster on his ankle, grateful the darkness helped hide it. Two more teens walked up, adding to the confusion.

"Time to go," Will whispered in her ear.

Emma turned back to him with a tight smile then walked toward the door.

Will watched her as she made it to the door and slipped inside, disappearing from his sight. He was tempted to go after her but told himself to calm down. She made it in without getting shot or chased. That was the hardest part.

The teens were beginning to draw a crowd. Will walked to the door, glancing over his shoulder one last time to make sure he wasn't being followed, and slipped inside.

****

Emma's throat tightened and her pulse pounded in her head as she stood in the lobby of the apartment building and listened to the arguing teens outside. What if something happened to Will?

Her senses were on alert, her nerve endings raw. The feeling that something was off niggled at the back of her brain although she didn't feel nauseous. She hadn't felt the sign since the day she was shot and she'd begun to wonder if it was a reliable barometer.

Will entered the lobby after what seemed like minutes later, but in reality was closer to thirty seconds. He looked behind him as he shut the door to the chaos on the sidewalk outside. When he saw her, his jaw relaxed. He pulled the gun from underneath his shirt and pushed the button at the elevator bank.

"Are you okay?" he asked, his eyes shifting around the room.

"I'm fine."

The elevator doors opened and they walked in the empty box. Will pushed four, the top floor. He lifted his gun when the doors closed. "Stay in the front corner until I know it's safe."

"Do you think someone will be waiting?"

"Do you feel sick?" It was a ridiculous question. They both knew if she felt sick she would have been heaving on the floor already.

Emma shook her head. "No."

"Humor me and hide in the corner anyway. Okay?"

The elevator stopped on the fourth floor. Emma backed into the corner by the control bank while Will hung to the wall on the opposite side. The doors opened and he poked his head out, looking around.

"It's safe."

Emma followed him out. The elevator opened in the middle of the hallway and Will turned left.

"I'm in 421. On the end."

"How are you going to get in? I know you don't have a key." She knew all he had were the Camaro keys.

"I have it covered." He stopped about ten feet from his door and pulled a Swiss army knife out of his pocket. Crouching down, he jammed the blade between the baseboard and pried up the carpet then pulled out a silver key.

"Impressive."

Will grinned and tilted his head. "I have a few skills that come in handy. If you're nice, I'll show you a couple of them later." He glanced up and down the hall. "Okay, let's go."

When they reached his door, Will placed Emma's back against the wall, on the side of his entrance. "Stay here until I know it's clear."

Her heart sped. "Will, be careful."

His shit-eating grin lit up his face and he winked before glancing down the hall again. After he unlocked the door, he swung it open. Greeted with silence, he turned to Emma and whispered. "Stay here, I'm going to check the inside."

She nodded, her sense of dread deepening.

Will came out several seconds later and pulled her in, shutting the door behind them.

She expected a bachelor pad, messy and with dorm-style furniture. What she found looked like a Pottery Barn catalogue. A tailored brown leather sofa, flat screen TV, pictures hanging on the wall, decorative lamps.

"Wow," she said, swiveling to take in the room.

"Don't be so surprised," he laughed. "My sister did it."

Emma's head jerked up in surprise. "You never told me you had a sister."

Will walked into the kitchen and opened the freezer door. "Yeah, well I do."

Irritation tugged at her frayed nerves. "Why didn't you tell me?"

Will shrugged. "It never came up."

She leaned against the kitchen counter while he pulled out a half gallon of chocolate ice cream.

"I always pictured you more of a vanilla guy."

"Shows what you know." He opened the lid and dumped the ice cream in the sink, a Ziploc bag of cash appearing at the bottom.

She was suddenly aware of how much she didn't know. "Any other siblings I don't know about?"

Will turned on the water and rinsed off the bag. "Nope, just my sister."

Given the fact that their lives were in danger, his not sharing he had a sister seemed like a minor issue. Yet it wasn't. If he expected her to share her previous life with him, he should be sharing his, too.

He brushed past her, through the living room and a door she suspected led to the bedroom. She followed, curiosity getting the better of her. She stood in the doorway, grasping the doorjamb in her hands as she watched him open a closet door. The bed had a low wooden headboard and was neatly made with an ivory duvet cover. The nightstand held only a lamp and a clock. A tall dresser across from the bed was clutterless. It looked totally unlived in.

"Do you have a maid?"

Will snorted. "God, no. I can't afford to have someone snooping around." He pulled a case out of the back of the closet and dropped it on the bed. He spun the code to the lock and opened it after it clicked.

"You're telling me you live this way? Impeccably clean?"

He looked up surprised. "Yeah, I was in the military, remember? Impeccably clean was beat into me at boot camp." He pulled several guns out of the case and laid them on the bed.

Emma wandered into the living room and opened the sliding door to the balcony, needing to clear her head. Seeing where he lived brought home the fact he had a life she knew nothing about and it overwhelmed her.

She stepped onto the balcony, feeling the wind in her hair. The evening air washed over her along with the sounds of music from the bars. She braced her hands on the railing and looked down at the people below then up to the stars. The moon rose in the sky, nearly full. It had nearly been a full moon when everything began less than a month ago.

"Emma, what the hell are you doing?" Will's angry voice came up behind her as he pulled her back into the apartment.

Emma stumbled backwards, stunned.

Will reached over and slammed the sliding door shut. "You could have gotten shot."

"There's no one out there. I would have felt sick and I don't."

"I don't want to take any chances."

Emma jerked out of his hold, pissed at him but also herself. She hadn't been thinking. When it came to Will, she found herself doing too many stupid things. And that was dangerous.

He shook his head in irritation then turned and headed for the bedroom. "Let's just get my things and get out of here." He came out with a duffle bag flung it over his shoulder, grabbed the bag of money off the counter, and stuffed into the bag. With a sigh, he took a look around the room.

"Okay, let's go."

Emma knew why he sighed, even if he didn't tell her. He'd never be back. He was saying goodbye to everything. Because of her.

CHAPTER EIGHT

THEY left the apartment and took the dark stairwell to the emergency exit, adding to the foreboding that already bombarded her. Something was about to happen. It hung heavy and oppressive in humid night air. Her thigh burned and she reached down and touched the pendant, still in her pocket. It was hotter than before.

Will stuffed the gun down into his waistband, and grabbed Emma's hand, pulling her into the parking lot.

They walked in silence, the knot in Emma's throat making it difficult to breathe. After traveling a block, they came upon a homeless man on the street corner. His long salt-and-pepper hair hung in greasy strands around his face, his gnarled hand holding out a paper cup for donations. A folded piece of cardboard was propped next to him, *The End is Near* written out in squiggly capital letters with black marker. They stopped at the corner, waiting for a red light, and Emma turned her gaze in his direction and tensed. Will glanced down at her and slipped his arm around her waist.

The homeless man swung his head toward Emma, his eyes vacant as his hair fell into his face and his body began to twitch. "Woe to you, daughter of Jezebel. Woe to you, betrayer of the truth."

Emma eyes widened as she looked up at Will. His jaw tensed and he pulled her to his side, his body a shield between her and the beggar.

The light changed and Will pulled her into the street. "Ignore him, Emma."

She turned back to look again, unable to stop herself. The man convulsed and began to shout. "The fate of mankind is in your hands!"

She froze in the middle of the street, her heart racing. An electrical charge ran from the pendant up her leg.

He pointed a crooked finger, his hand shaking violently "You will be the downfall of the world."

"Emma, let's go." Will tried to pull her, but her feet were rooted to the asphalt.

The current coursed through her body and her vision faded. She stood by a roaring fire, electricity tickling her skin. *The choice is yours.* A voice said. *But you must choose.* Then the image changed and she stood on top of a hill overlooking a valley. Tendrils of smoke dotted the scorched landscape below. *You have caused this destruction. The death of the world is in your hands.* A gust of wind swept dirt and debris around, obscuring her vision. When it cleared, swirling columns of fire surrounded her, the flames shooting into the clouds overhead. Thick smoke filled her lungs. Screams echoed in the darkness and she heard Jake's voice calling out "Mommy!" Panic gripped her as power shot from her hands into the air, covering the world around her in a sea of flames.

"Emma!" Will jerked her arm, pulling her back to the present.

She gasped for air, afraid she would pass out.

"You will end us all!" the man screamed.

People on the sidewalks stopped to stare. The light had turned and a car's horn honked. Emma stood dazed in the street, blocking traffic.

Will pulled her to the corner and she stumbled to keep up. "What the hell were you doing?" he asked through gritted teeth. "He's a crazy old man. *Ignore him.*"

The images still played in her head, hazy and fading. She wanted to tell him what she saw, but the words caught in her throat, making her unsure where to even begin. They continued two more blocks, Will dragging her by the hand. The shadows seemed dark and menacing.

"Shouldn't there be more people here?" Emma asked. It seemed odd there was no one around considering the swarms of people they had pushed through only a few blocks earlier.

Will's grip tightened as he looked around. "Yeah."

They crossed the street at a corner, cutting over to the parking lot on the other side. The car was parked several rows away, A street light overhead blinked twice then faded out with the sound of an electric zap.

The hairs on Emma's arms stood on end. A cool breeze blew out of nowhere, whipping her hair and the hem of her skirt. "Will…"

A man walked out from behind a car. His dark eyes glittered as one side of his mouth lifted into a grin. "Going somewhere?" Another man stepped out of the shadows and joined him.

Will pushed Emma behind him. He held up a hand, the shiny glint of the metal keys dangling from his fingers. "We don't have anything you gentlemen would be interested in. Just let us go on our way and we'll forget this ever happened."

The first man laughed, a guttural sneer. "We want *her*. Just hand her over and we'll be more than happy to let you go about your business."

"Then you have a problem because the lady isn't going anywhere with you."

A third man appeared carrying a long metal pipe. He smacked it into the palm of his hand. The dull thud filled the quiet night. The sounds of music down the street faded to a faint roar. "Funny, I don't see a dilemma."

Emma's chest constricted. Heat from the pendant burned the side of her leg.

Will let the duffle bag slip off his arm and fall to the ground. The first two men rushed him before he could reach for his gun.

Emma jumped into the street as a fourth man appeared.

Will hit the first man, with his keys in his fist. The man staggered back, yelping as streaks of blood ran down his face. The other man charged and Will staggered before punching the man in the stomach. The man with the pipe slapped it into his palm in a steady rhythm as an evil grin spread across his face. The first man got up, bloody stripes down his cheek.

Will tossed the keys into the street behind him. The metal clanged on the asphalt as they skidded close to

Emma's feet. She reached down and picked them up with trembling fingers.

"Emma! Run!" Will shouted as he reached to pull the gun from his waistband. Both men attacked at once and the gun fell to the pavement. One of the men kicked him in the stomach and Will doubled over.

The man with the pipe stepped forward and picked up the gun with an evil grin. Again, that horrible grin. He tossed the gun behind him, between two cars.

Emma couldn't leave him, but she didn't know how to help.

"Get her," the man with the pipe said. One of the men rushed past Will.

"Goddamn it, Emma! RUN!" Will lunged for the man's legs and they hit the pavement.

She bolted down the street toward the crowd of people, two of the men in pursuit. Struggling to keep her sandals on her feet, she kicked them off. The warm asphalt was rough on her bare soles as she sprinted toward the crowd. The move had slowed her down, but she hoped to make up for it with the speed she gained.

The street ahead had been blocked off. A rock band played at one end. Emma ran past a barricade and into the throng, pushing her way past people dancing in the street. She collided with a woman who held a cup above her head. The drink spilled over both of them.

"Hey!" the young woman shouted.

"Sorry," Emma mumbled, looking over her shoulder. The men were gaining on her.

She pushed on, her lungs burning and her nearly healed leg aching. She ran to the sidewalk, the crush of bodies slowing her down, fueling her rising hysteria. She looked back to see one of the men collide with a woman. The woman's date came to her defense, but Emma's pursuer shoved him easily to the side. The encounter bought her about thirty additional feet. The second man had disappeared.

Emma turned left onto a cross street, running blindly. *Think, Emma. Think.* An alley opened to her left. She cast a glance over her shoulder. Neither man was behind her, so she ran into darkness, sprinting for a trash dumpster halfway down. She ducked behind it and turned to see a man standing in the middle of the alley entrance.

She pressed her back against the brick wall, the stench of rotten food and urine making her gag. Her breath came in shallow pants as she heard the dull thud of his shoes move closer.

Her options were to hide here or run, and neither was good. There was a chance he hadn't seen her. The alley was dark and she'd rounded the corner of the dumpster when she saw him. But if he had seen her, she was sure she couldn't outrun him. Sucking in her breath, she tried to squeeze behind the metal dumpster. If she could get behind it, he might not find her and even if he did, she might be able to get out the other side and run.

"Emma," the man called. "Olly, olly oxen free."

She choked on her terror and shoved her hip into the opening between the wall and the metal bin. The space was too narrow and her side lodged in the tight space.

"I'm not going to hurt you," he sing-songed. "Come out like a good girl."

She stuffed down the rising hysteria and tried to break free from the crack.

A body stood at the corner of the bin, shrouded in darkness. "There you are." His voice was deceptively sweet.

The pendant in her pocket burned, shooting an electrical current throughout her body.

His hand gripped her arm, jerking her free. Emma remembered Will using the keys as a weapon. She gripped them in her fist and swung toward his face, grinding the ends into his cheek and dragging down with all her strength. Instead of letting go, his grip tightened and he swung at her face with his free hand. The impact caught her on the cheek, swamping her head with an invading blackness. Fury built in her chest, replacing her fear. She'd be damned if she passed out and just let this bastard take her.

The burning in her leg became unbearable as she shot a knee to his groin, with more power than she knew she had. His hold loosened as he fell to the ground, curling into a ball with a moan.

Emma tore down the alley to the street and turned the corner, not stopping to see if he was after her. The fact that she was running farther away from Will ate her resolve.

An outdoor cafe lay ahead with people dancing on the sidewalk. She raced for it, hoping to get lost in the crowd. Almost there, she stepped on a rock, sending a shooting pain through her bare foot. She stumbled in pain, tears burning her eyes. She couldn't afford to stop now.

Turning to look over her shoulder, she saw the man stop at the street corner, searching for her. A crowd of people stood in front of the cafe. If she could get inside, she might lose him, but she doubted that she'd make it before he caught up.

"In trouble again, already?" she heard a man ask. "That didn't take long."

Emma looked down at the table next to her, shocked to see the man from the bar the night before in Joplin. He sat alone, with a half-empty plate of food in front of him.

She froze. Her pursuer was headed in her direction.

The man at the table glanced down the street and stood. "Is he after you?"

She nodded.

He grabbed her hand and pulled her into the dancers, standing at the edge in the shadows. "Play along." He swung her around into his arms, drawing her body flush against his. Emma, too surprised and scared to protest, let him. Her brain turned fuzzy. He turned his head slightly to check on the man's progress. He was shorter than Will, his face almost even with hers. His dark eyes pierced hers as he said, "Sorry for this."

He put his hand behind her head and pulled her mouth to his. It was for show, she instinctively knew this as his body swayed to the music, pressing her close with the arm he wrapped around her back. His attention remained on the man chasing her. She saw the man pause and search the crowd. The man who held her turned her slightly, moving his back to her pursuer. He deepened the kiss, his tongue gliding over her lips, searching for hers. She wrapped her arms around his back, clinging to him as her body responded, heat rising from her core and melting her from the inside out.

He pulled back and turned slightly, making sure the man had moved on. He held her close, still swaying to the music, his desire for her evident. The knowledge sent her head reeling. "I believe you now owe me your name." His voice was seductive in her ear, his breath sending shivers down her back.

"Emma."

"Emma," he murmured, her name sounding lyrical on his tongue. He held her tight, his face hovering next hers, his breath fanning her cheek. Her body screamed in anticipation, as though she had no will of her own. His eyes locked onto hers, mesmerizing her. "Whatever happened to that boyfriend of yours?"

Oh, my God. Will.

Emma's breath sucked in and she stumbled backward, out of his embrace. She tripped on something and he grabbed her elbow to keep her from falling.

"I won't tell him what just happened, that is, if he exists," he said, righting her. "But I'm guessing from your reaction that he does."

"I have to get back to him. He was fighting off the men who attacked us." She heard the panic in her voice even though her body seemed slow to catch up.

He led her to his table, pulled out his wallet, and threw some cash by his plate. "Which way?"

She blinked in surprise.

"I didn't just save you to let you get into trouble again. Where is he?"

Emma hesitated. Leading this man to Will seemed like a very bad idea.

"You're wasting time. I'm going with you, like it or not."

She started walking. "This way."

They hurried down the street in silence. Emma wrestled with her response to the man next to her. *What the hell had just happened?* It was like her body had a will of its own.

"Where are your shoes?" he asked.

"None of your business." She worried about Will's reaction when he saw him.

"You never asked my name."

"*What?*"

"Raphael, my name is Raphael."

She ignored him and kept walking.

"You didn't do anything wrong, you know. You were only hiding from that man. It was only an act."

Emma knew what she experienced more than just an act. The fact the she was so easily turned on by this man scared the shit out of her.

A wave of pain swept through her side and she wobbled, confused. She realized it was Will. When she was held captive in the Vinco Potentia compound, she and Will had shared a psychic link. But they had tried it since and it never worked so this caught her by surprise. She stood still, concentrating. *Will*, she called out to him.

"Are you okay?" Raphael asked.

"Shh!" She scrunched her eyes shut. *Will?* He didn't respond, but she knew he was in tremendous agony. She took off running, Raphael behind her.

"What happened?"

"He's hurt. I have to get to him."

"How do you know this?"

"I just do."

They reached the end of the block and peered around the corner. Emma's car was close to the corner of the building. Will was a row over, his face covered in blood. He stood hunched over in front of the leader. Shadows edged the perimeter.

Emma gasped. "Will."

"Do you have a plan?" Raphael asked, standing out in the open.

"No."

He found a three-foot length of wood against the building. "You go get your car. I'll take care of the guy attacking your boyfriend. When it's safe, we'll load him into the front seat."

"What about you?"

"Don't worry. I can take care of myself. Stay behind me and wait for my signal."

Emma was thankful she still held the keys in her hand, opening her fist to reveal gashes where she'd gripped them so tightly. She followed Raphael as he walked into the parking lot. He sauntered toward the men, carrying the board, arrogance in his stride.

Emma stopped at the car and watched, terrified. Will took jagged breaths and struggled to stand upright.

"Can I join in?" Raphael asked.

The leader was now weaponless. He was battered and bloody but in better shape than Will. The other man lay motionless on the ground.

Will saw Raphael approach and tried to straighten.

Raphael held up a flattened palm toward Will. "I am here to help you."

Will fell back to his knees.

The attacker turned to Raphael and smiled as he moved to pick up his pipe off the ground. Raphael circled, holding his board out at his side. The other man lunged, raising the pipe and swinging down toward Raphael's head. He raised the board and blocked the blow. The crack of splintering wood filled the air. Raphael reached up with his other hand and grabbed the pipe then twisted his body around, bringing the weapon with him.

The leader hesitated for a half second, long enough for Raphael to kick him in the chest. He fell back, landing on the hood of a car. Raphael twirled the pipe expertly in his hand slamming it down on the hood inches from the man's head. He tried to get up, but Raphael kicked him again, knocking him back into the hood. Raphael brought the pipe down on the hood on the other side. His eyes looked murderous.

"Emma, bring the car now," Raphael said, his gaze never leaving the man.

Will grabbed his side and tried to stand, spitting blood onto the ground.

Emma inserted the keys into the ignition, her hands shaking so badly it took several attempts. She pulled forward through a gap between two cars in the row ahead. Raphael continued striking the hood, keeping the leader contained. She got out and started toward Will.

"Emma, stay where you are." Raphael said, still facing the man.

Will staggered and fell to his knees.

Emma knew that Will, even as injured as he was, worried more about her than himself.

"Did you plan to hurt the lady?" Raphael asked with a growl.

The man on the hood looked up, his eyes wild. "No, man, we were just supposed to scare her."

Raphael swung the pipe into the man's legs. "Wrong answer."

The leader screamed in pain, his legs buckling. "Dude, I swear!"

Raphael paused and studied him before he hissed. "*Transi per umbras.*" He swung the pipe like a baseball bat against the man's head. Emma twisted her face away as the sound of a splitting melon filled the air. She gagged, almost vomiting.

"Emma, you may get your boyfriend now."

Emma sucked in a breath through her mouth as she ran to Will, holding back her sobs and her fear. Neither would help right now. He looked up at her, blinking the blood out of his eyes. One eye was already swelling shut. His lip was split. He had a gash on his forehead.

"Will." She reached for his arm and tried to lift him off his knees.

He moaned with the movement. Raphael reached down and slung Will's arm over his shoulder. "Emma, open the car door and I'll help you get him into the car."

Will glared at Raphael. "Who the fuck are you?"

"Will, he's a friend. He helped me hide. We can trust him." *It's me you can't trust.*

Raphael lifted Will's body as Will cried out with the movement.

"I'm sorry, my friend," Raphael said as he lowered Will onto the seat and closed the door. Raphael picked up Will's bag out of the street and carried it to the car.

Emma opened the trunk and Raphael tossed it in. As he slammed the lid shut, she turned to get in the car.

"Emma, wait." Raphael touched her shoulder. She spun to face him.

"Emma, when you leave here, drive and don't stop." His voice was low and insistent. "I know you want to get help for your boyfriend, but there are men searching for you. You must get far away from here."

Her eyes widened in alarm. "How do you know?"

"Trust me, I know." He lowered his voice. "You need to know that your boyfriend has significant injuries."

Her tears fell and Raphael wiped one off her cheek. "Don't worry, he'll recover. But listen to me." His eyes pierced hers and she felt herself becoming lost, forgetting all sense of where she was. "Emma, you can help him. You have power that you don't even realize. Find your power and you can heal him. Use the pendant. Now go." He led her to the driver's door. His eyes held hers, dark and captivating. To her dismay, the familiar heat spread throughout her body. Raphael leaned into her ear, brushing her cheek against his lips. "Not yet, my love. But, soon. Soon I will come for you."

He turned and walked down the street, into the darkness.

CHAPTER NINE

EMMA'S hands trembled as she pulled out of the parking lot, her thoughts spinning in a vortex as she tried to figure out what just happened with Raphael. How could she react to him that way?

"Who the hell was that?" Will slurred, his head slumped toward her.

Her face burned with shame, making her grateful for the darkness. "He was someone who helped me. Helped *us*." She turned down the street and she tried to remember where the highway was.

"What did he say to you just now?" His words rushed out in a gasp of pain.

"Will, you shouldn't talk. You're hurt."

"Emma, *what did he say*?" He coughed from the exertion, then tensed with a moan.

"Will, *please*. He didn't say anything. He told me to take you far from here. He said he thought you were really hurt." *Where was the highway?* She parked at a stop sign, her fingers numb from gripping the steering wheel so tight.

"*Did he touch you*?" He coughed again, then doubled over in pain.

"Will, *stop*!" She turned to look at him, fear constricting her chest as she watched him spit blood onto his lap. "I need to take you to a hospital." Her voice shook.

"No. He was right," he said in a defeated tone. "You have to get far away from here." His body sagged in the seat.

Emma held back her sobs, tears streaming down her face. *Where was the highway?*

"I saw him get too close to you."

"Will, stop. Just stop. Nothing happened." So, she now was a slut *and* a liar. She not only made out with Raphael while Will got the shit beaten out of him, she also would have done it with Will watching in the car. *What the hell is wrong with me?* Hysteria bubbled below the surface.

She drove several blocks, lost. "*Where is the fucking highway*?" She had to get Will out of here before they got caught. Sobs erupted, despite her intentions to hold them in.

"Emma."

She braked at another stop sign, searching for any signs for the interstate.

"*Emma*."

She turned to look at him, gasping at the sight of his battered body. She did that to him. She didn't beat him up herself, but she might as well have. He had the shit beat out of him because people wanted her. And she repaid him by jumping the first guy that came along. Her sobs intensified.

"Emma. It's okay. I'm okay. Shh... stop crying."

****

Will lay in the seat, pain deluging his body with every movement. He was sure he had broken ribs from that goddamned metal pipe. He was lucky that was all that was broken, other than his ego.

He'd seen the way that man had talked to Emma. The way he said her name with such familiarity. The way he leaned close to her before she got into the car.

The way Emma didn't push him away.

The fact that if Will had tried to get that close to her when they first met she would have slapped him wasn't lost on him.

Emma was beside herself with agony, sobbing so uncontrollably that Will worried she would have an accident. He knew she was upset over him, but he suspected there was more, something else she wasn't telling him. He groaned in frustration and a sharp pain shot through his chest.

When Emma heard his gasp, she cried harder.

Maybe he was reading too much into it. "Emma, it's okay. Turn left up here." The entrance ramp to the highway came into view.

"Which… way?" She fought for breath through her hiccups.

Which way? He couldn't protect her in this condition. He didn't even protect her just now, some other guy did. His gut burned in fury. He was lucky she wasn't hurt or dead. He still had to find Jake and get answers about what all this fucking shit meant. He couldn't do that while worrying about her. She needed protection. He couldn't get the answers and protect her at the same time. He needed help.

"Go north."

Her mouth dropped open in surprise. "North? But Jake was in Arizona and the Vinco Potentia is north."

"My friend James lives in Minnesota," he gasped for breath as pain stabbed his side. "He'll help us."

Her eyes widened. "Can we trust him?"

"He's been my best friend since second grade." He hung his head, holding his breath. "If I can't trust James, I don't know who I can trust." He realized too late bitterness had slipped into his words. Emma shot him a look of shock, mixed with fear. *What the fuck had happened?*

"Will, I have to take you to a hospital." She swiped the back of her hand across her cheeks, a look of determination in her face.

"No." He laid his head back, wishing he had some type of narcotics. But he wouldn't have taken them anyway. He needed to be alert in case they were attacked again.

"But Will…"

"No. You know we can't. They'll find us."

She sucked in her breath, her eyes welling with tears again. Will felt pain in his arm, where his mark was.

Fear seized his chest. "Emma, are you hurt?"

"No, don't talk, Will. Just rest and tell me what to do." Her sobs became uncontrollable again. "Tell me…what to...do."

His mark burned, the pain worse than his side.

****

Emma drove through the night. Will wanted her to stop, worried that she would get tired since she was always tired these days, but her guilt kept her awake. Every so often she noticed Will rub the mark on his arm.

He dozed off and on. The pain in his side bothered him more than he admitted. She could feel it inside her own body when it got intense. She offered to stop and buy him alcohol to help ease his discomfort, like he had when she was shot, but he refused. Raphael told her she could use the pendant to heal Will, but she didn't trust him. Raphael addled her brain and made her lose sense of everything. She'd be better off ignoring anything he told her.

Images of Raphael invaded her thoughts. She couldn't figure out what had happened. She had never reacted to a man the way she did with him. Not even Will. She was confused, embarrassed, and horrified. And scared.

Raphael told her he would come for her.

Not if she had anything to do about it.

The sun rose as she continued north, exhaustion overtaking her after she drove around the edge of Minneapolis. Will suggested that she stop, but the early morning light made his injuries more evident and she was even more anxious to get him help.

"Will, you're really hurt. I need to take you to a doctor. It might be safe here. They have no idea we came to Minnesota."

"No," he moaned, his breath raspy. "James will be able to help. Just get to James."

So she ignored Will's insistence that she stop to rest and prayed that James really could help.

She turned onto a two-lane highway. They were out in the middle of nowhere. Raphael would never find her here. She realized how ridiculous it was to be more afraid of a single man than two groups of powerful gunmen. But she had the feeling he was more dangerous than all of them put together.

"How close are we?" she asked. They'd been on the unpopulated road for a half an hour.

"Close," he croaked. His face was pale and sweat beaded his forehead.

The street grew blurry through her tears.

Will told her to turn down a single lane dirt road. She drove for a quarter of a mile until a cabin came into view nestled in the trees, about a hundred feet from a lakeshore.

"What if he's not home?"

"We can go in." He paused to catch his breath. "James won't care."

Emma pulled in front of the cabin, the gravel under the tires crunching. She ran to the front porch and pounded on the door.

A muffled voice called out, "All right. I'm coming. Keep your pants on." The door swung open, a man wearing jeans and tugging down a t-shirt stood in the entrance. He ran a hand through his short, cropped hair and eyed her with appreciation. "Or in your case, *don't* keep your pants on."

"Are you James?"

He grinned. "At your service."

Emma shook her head. "God, no wonder your Will's best friend. You're exactly alike."

He looked surprised. "Will?"

She started toward the car. "He's in the front seat." When she opened the door, Will's labored breathing scared her. It had gotten even worse. "He's hurt. He said you could help."

James sucked in his breath. "Fuck. What happened to him?" He leaned down and unbuckled Will's seat belt. "Dude, you look like shit."

Will's swollen mouth formed a pathetic grin. "Yeah, you don't look so great yourself." The words came out in raspy gasps.

James looked at Emma, his face stricken. "What happened?" His teasing tone was gone.

"Three men beat him up," her voice broke and tears filled her eyes again. "One of them had a metal pipe." The memory of Raphael hitting the man with the pipe made her gag.

James turned back to Will. "You let three men beat the shit out of you? You're losing your touch. We gotta get you out of there. This is going to hurt like hell."

James pulled Will out of the front seat. Will stifled a cry of pain as he leaned into him.

"Open the door so I can get him in." James directed her.

Emma ran and held it open as James and Will shuffled into the cabin. James led Will to the kitchen and sat him down in a chair.

"In the bathroom is a stack of washrags and towels. Bring them here," James said. She ran down the small hall and grabbed an armful of linens, carrying them to the kitchen. When she returned, James was cutting Will's shirt off.

"Son of a bitch, Will. What the hell happened?"

"I had a little encounter with a metal pipe."

"Looks like more than just *a little*."

Emma gasped when she saw the red and purple mottling that covered Will's left side. James glanced over his shoulder. "Bring those over here."

Emma put them on the table and stepped back, worried that she'd get in the way.

"Candy, Barbie, whatever the hell your name is, get some ice out of the freezer and put it in a bag."

Will's hand jerked up and grabbed a fistful of James' shirt, his eyes narrowing. "Her name is Emma and you will treat her with respect or I will fucking beat the shit out of you."

"Will, it's okay," Emma said. Her racing heart strangled her words. James was their only hope at this point.

"The hell it is," Will snarled.

James held up his hands in protest. "Sorry, honest mistake, Will. Seriously, when was the last time you had anything to do with a decent woman?"

Emma turned her back to James and opened the freezer door, her face burning with embarrassment and anger.

"Shut the fuck up, James."

She scooped ice into a bag as James knelt down in front of Will, pressing his fingers into Will's side.

Will winced and started to cry out but stopped.

James turned and glared at her. "Emma," he said her name slowly emphasizing the syllables. "Do you think you could wait outside? I don't care if you're in here, but apparently, your boyfriend thinks it's unmanly to show his pain in front of you."

She hadn't even considered that. "Of course," she said as she started to leave the kitchen.

"Emma," Will gasped.

She stopped in front of him, the sight of his beaten face and bruised side bringing a fresh wave of tears.

"I don't want you alone out there. Stay here."

"It's okay, Will. I'll go get a gun out of the bag and stand watch."

"If you see *anything*…" he said through gritted teeth.

"I promise if I see anything, I will come straight back here and let you know."

He stared at her through the slit of his half-swollen eye. The other was completely swollen shut. "All right."

Emma leaned down and kissed the top of his head and walked out the front door, into the morning sunshine. She opened the trunk and pulled out the duffle bag, surprised at how heavy it was.

After dragging the bag to the front porch, she unzipped the opening. The bag of money lay on the top, with Will's clothes underneath, and several shotguns and handguns at the bottom. Although she was more familiar with handguns, she knew a shotgun would be a better choice. Will had taught her how to shoot one a few weeks ago and about twenty minutes after that, she killed a man with the same gun.

She sat on the wooden porch swing hanging in the corner, the gun across her lap, and looked out at the lake. A dock extended from the shore with a fishing boat tied to one side, bobbing in the water.

Birds chirped and soft sunlight filtered through the canopy overhead. As she looked out onto the water, Jake came to mind. She sighed in disappointment. With Will hurt, she was even farther from finding him than before. She closed her eyes and searched for him in her mind, reaching out and calling his name. Just like all the other times except the first time she tried, she could feel him on the other side, but he refused to answer. She opened her eyes, shelving her hurt feelings and telling herself he had to have a reason. Surely he still loved her. But maybe he didn't. She'd failed him, too. She left him alone in the truck, allowing the Cavallo to kidnap him.

Leaning her head against the swing chain, exhaustion overwhelmed her. She closed her eyes and the image of Will, bloodied and battered in the parking lot, flooded her vision. He could have been killed. Because of her.

The front door opened moments later. She opened her eyes and saw James in the doorway, watching her, his emotions guarded.

His lack of expression sent her fear racing. "Is he okay?"

"For now." James walked to the swing and sat beside her, looking out into the lake.

Emma chewed on her lower lip. "He needs to go to the hospital, doesn't he?"

"I think he should, but he refuses. What do you know about that, Emma?"

In her peripheral vision she saw him turn to her, waiting for her response. "What did he tell you?"

"Not a fucking thing. That's why I'm asking you."

She fingered the gun in her lap.

"Why do I think this has everything to do with you?"

Emma turned to face James, his eyes full of hatred. Inwardly, she reeled but held his gaze with a defiant expression. "You'll have to ask Will."

"What kind of mess have you gotten him into?"

Anger surged at his question, but she couldn't deny it. James was right. It was her fault.

"It's up to Will to tell you what he wants you to know," she said.

James stood and leaned against the railing, looking out into the water. "He wants you. I tried to give him something for the pain, but he refused to take it until he talks to you."

Emma headed for the door, but James got there first, blocking her path with his arm. She waited, her face expressionless.

His eyes narrowed as he lowered his voice. "I don't know what you're mixed up in, but I sure as hell know I'm not letting Will dig himself into some goddamn mess for a piece of ass, got it?"

She tilted her head. "Loud and clear. Now let me through."

James lifted his arm and Emma brushed past him, eager to see Will.

CHAPTER TEN

WILL lay on the bed waiting for Emma, still amazed at the physical discomfort he felt when she was out of his sight and protection. His left side screamed with pain, eating at the edges of his consciousness, but he tried to focus on the muffled voices outside the front window. James had a burr up his ass and was outside with Emma. Alone. He had no doubt she could take care of herself, but he worried nevertheless. He knew how difficult James could be, but then again, so could Emma.

A few moments later, she stood in the doorway with a shotgun in her hand. To anyone else, she'd look hard and dangerous, but he saw the tremor in her hand. Her face was so drawn and pale that Will worried she'd collapse in the doorway. But he released a sigh of relief at the sight of her, which only sent a fresh round of pain.

"Will." She rushed to bed and knelt beside him. "What did James say?"

He gave her a lopsided grin. "That I should be at a hospital."

"He's right. I told you that already. So what are we waiting for? Let's go."

"You're both wrong. The only thing I need is you." He lifted his right arm out to her, motioning for her to lie next to him.

Emma shook her head, her eyes widening in horror. "No, I'll hurt you."

"No, I'm not hurt on this side. You're exhausted, Emma, and this is the only bed you can sleep in unless you sleep in James' bed." He knew it shouldn't, but the disgust in her eyes pleased him. "Come here. I promise to be a gentleman."

"No, James would kill me."

James appeared in the doorway. "Damn straight I will. Are you fucking insane, Will? Did you incur some brain damage I didn't figure out in that expert medical exam I just performed at my kitchen table with some wash rags and an ice pack?"

Emma stood up and Will grabbed her hand, tugging her toward him. "James has always been overprotective. Ignore him."

Emma hesitated, glancing over her shoulder.

He snorted and walked out of the room. "Do whatever the fuck you want, you always do anyway. At least take your damn pain pill."

She stood still, watching the empty threshold.

"Shut the door, Emma."

She studied him, the pain on her face so palatable it burrowed in his chest and became his own. "Will, I can just sleep on the floor or out in the car. I only need a nap."

But he could see it in her eyes, the need to be with him, and victory and validation replaced his fear and uncertainty. "Emma, don't you get it? I need you. *Need you.* Please. When I'm worried about your safety, it kills me." He held out her hand to her. "Please."

Emotion vacillated in her eyes as she bit her lip.

"Shut the door," he whispered.

She walked to the opening and stopped, her hand gripping the jamb. For one heart-stopping moment, he thought she was leaving. Walking away from him. Then she shut the door, her hand still holding the knob as she leaned her forehead in the wood. With a heave of her shoulders, she spun around she walked the short distance and took his fingertips into her hand.

"I don't want to hurt you." Her eyes filled with tears.

"It will hurt me more if you're not here."

She eased onto the edge of the bed and it creaked with the movement. She watched his face, her lips pressed tight.

He smiled up at her. "See? So far so good, now lay beside me."

"Take your pain pill first." She let go of his hand and handed him the pill on the nightstand along with a glass of water.

He swallowed the narcotic and pulled on her hand. "Now lay beside me."

Emma set the glass on the table and lay on her side, facing him. He lifted his hand and she laced her fingers in his, the touch sending ripples of solace to his soul. He listened to the sound of her even breaths, a contrast to his ragged ones. Deep in his gut, he knew the sound was a bad sign, but he was at a loss of how to handle it. A hospital was out of the question.

"Will, I'm so sorry." Emma whispered. Tears slid through the cracks of her closed eyes, falling onto the pillow.

He knew she meant something more than just his injuries. Something happened to her, something she wouldn't tell him yet. He couldn't imagine what occurred after she ran off that tormented her. His heart ached that he didn't prevent it. He had failed her. He lifted her hand to his lips and softly kissed her fingertips.

Her lips trembled as she fought to control her tears.

"I love you, Emma. Everything's going to be okay."

Her gentle cries shook the bed, sending sharp pains shooting through his side, but the burn in his mark was ten times worse.

****

Emma woke to the sound of Will wheezing.

She pushed herself up, her heart pounding. Pale moonlight filled the room from the window, but she could see a gray pallor covered his face and sweat beaded his forehead.

"Will?"

His eyes were wide and he gasped thick woofs of air. "I think I need to sit up."

She reached an arm around his back and tried to lift him, but he cried out and fell back on the pillow.

"James!" Emma screamed, getting up on her knees. "JAMES!"

Will panted, gasping as James appeared in the doorway, throwing on the light. She blinked as her eyes adjusted.

"What happened?"

"I don't know… I was asleep... he woke me up gasping…" she babbled, fear lapping at her reasoning. "I tried to help him sit up…"

James moved to the end of the bed. "Will, enough of this bullshit. You need a doctor, fuck that, you need a hospital. I wouldn't be surprised if you have a collapsed lung."

Will shook his head, a slight movement that tightened his jaw. "No…"

"Why? Because of *her*? Well, lucky for me you're really not in much shape to argue. I'm taking you anyway."

"No..." Will panted, his eyes wide and pleading.

"Will, please." Emma begged through her tears. *"Please."*

"Fuck this, I'm getting my car." James stormed out of the room.

Will's hand gripped her arm, his fingers digging deep and his eye desperate. "Emma. *No."*

Panic bombarded her limited control. She forced herself to take a breath. "Will, you're going to die. I need you. You can't die on me."

His body shook with his uneven breaths and his face looked more gray than before.

"I found a couple of fake IDs in the bottom of the bag. James can check you in under one of those names." Her voice shook, revealing her hysteria.

He closed his eyes. "I... can't… leave you," he said through gritted teeth.

"Don't be stupid, Will. If you stay here, you'll leave me anyway because you'll be *dead*." Her words were harsh, but the reality was harsh. *Will dead.* She lost Jake. She couldn't lose Will too. Her shoulders shook with suppressed sobs.

Other than Jake, he was the only good thing she had in her miserable existence. She might not deserve him, but she refused to lose him this way. The pendant in her skirt pocket burned fiery hot against her leg and she pulled it out, amazed to see it glowing in her hand. Raphael's words came back to her.

Emma, you can help him. You have power that you don't even realize. Find your power and you can heal him. Use the pendant.

Raphael had told her she could save Will. Was it possible? What if it was a trick?

The pendant glowed a brilliant red in her hand, brighter and hotter yet not burning her palm. She had nothing to lose by trying, but she didn't know how what to do. She gripped the stone tight in her fist.

Heal him.

Will's breath gurgled and his hand on her arm grew limp.

Hysteria swept through her mind, stripping away all reason. Then anger replaced it, searing with an intensity that rivaled the stone in her hand. *I can't lose him.* A blaze filled her chest, electricity rushing behind it. She gasped in surprise.

Will turned his head toward her, eyes wide.

The fire and electricity built into a raging inferno until she felt herself burning on the inside. The power was going to kill her. She reached out her free hand to Will's side, his abdomen jerking as he fought for breath.

She concentrated on his breathing. "Heal him."

Electricity burst from its dam and raced through her arms and legs, through her left hand into Will's side. His body jerked in response and his wheezing stopped.

She snatched back her hand, leaving a red mark on his chest. *Oh my God, I killed him.* The room spun and blackness closed in around her.

****

"Emma," someone said her name softly. "Emma." It grew louder and more insistent.

It was Will's voice, but it sounded so far away. She stirred, her eyes fluttering open in her confusion. Will leaned over her, his grim expression relaxing as he studied her face.

"Thank God. You scared the hell out of me."

"Are we dead?" she whispered.

He cupped her cheek. "No, far from it. You healed me, but you nearly killed yourself in the process."

She remembered the electricity coursing through her body. Into him. "I thought I killed you."

His face softened and his eyes filled with love. "No, Princess. You saved me."

She sat up and pain ricocheted throughout her head. "Oh."

Will wrapped an arm around her back. "Are you okay?"

"I just need a minute. I feel like I have a massive hangover." Her tongue lay thick in her mouth and her head throbbed.

"Emma." He gently lifted her chin, searching her eyes. "What did you do?"

She stared at him in confusion.

"Do you remember what happened?"

"I thought it was a dream," she whispered.

"It wasn't a dream. What do you remember?"

She closed her eyes. "My head... just give me a moment."

Will handed her the water from the nightstand.

She took a sip and handed it back. "Seriously, Will. What are you doing out of bed? James is going to kill me. Where is he, anyway? He was supposed to be getting the car to take you to the hospital."

"James walked in and saw what you did. Once he realized I was okay, he left. What you did completely freaked him out. What *did* you do?"

She told him what happened, and shook her head in disbelief. "I was sure it was a dream but it seemed so real. Like my other one." Her body tensed at her mistake.

"What other one?"

She ignored his question. "It really happened? You don't have any pain?"

"Yes, it really happened. You healed me." Will looked down at her trembling hands. "Emma when was the last time you ate?"

"I don't know… dinner before you got attacked?"

"That was over twenty-four hours ago."

"You haven't eaten either."

"Yeah, but I was unconscious a good portion of it. I'm going to get you something to eat. I'll be right back."

Emma watched Will leave, the room spinning. Did she really heal him? That was impossible. *Impossible.* Yet, so many crazy things had happened over the last month, it was conceivable. And undeniable.

But why now? The obvious answer was the pendant. Jake said Will made everything change and while he started it all, the pendant continued the evolution. The Vinco Potentia thought her only purpose was to have the baby, but Will always insisted there had to be more. Even Raphael said she had powers.

Raphael. Just thinking of him made her stomach twist with dread, but if she was honest with herself, something else happened inside her too, adding to her growing anxiety.

Will handed her a sandwich. "Emma, eat this."

"I should be taking care of you, not the other way around," she said, taking a bite.

"I'm telling you, other than feeling exhausted, I'm better. My broken ribs are gone."

She looked up him and shook her head. "How can that be possible?"

"I don't know, but it's true."

They ate in silence until Will said, "Emma, what other dream? You said it happened in another dream."

Stuffing the sandwich in her mouth, she chewed slowly, stalling. There was no way she could tell him, especially after her encounter with Raphael. She could try to change the subject again, but Will was smart; he'd figure out what she was doing, which would only make it worse. Maybe she could tell him part of it.

"I dreamed I had electricity flowing over my skin, just like I felt when I touched you."

"And?"

"I was outside, in the woods. In front of a fire."

"And?"

"I told you, I dreamed I had electricity covering my skin."

"That's it? What were you doing when this was happening?"

"I don't know, Will, it was a friggin' dream. Everything's all weird and crazy in dreams."

His eyes narrowed, but he didn't say anything.

"I'm sorry, I didn't mean to snap at you. My head hurts and it's making me cranky." She reached out her hand and laid it on his arm. "I still can't believe you're okay."

She scrutinized his face, noticing the cuts and swelling was better as well, his face covered with only mild bruising. Her fingers gently caressed his cheek as she searched his eyes. He sucked in his breath, covering her hand with his.

"How do you do that?" he whispered.

"What?" she asked, lost in his steady gaze.

"How do you drive me crazy with just a single touch?" Leaning down, Will brushed his lips on hers as he wrapped an arm around her. He pulled her tighter, deepening the kiss.

Emma braced her hands on his bare chest and pushed away. "Will, we can't do this."

"I'm sorry. I forgot about your headache."

"No, it's gone." she said, surprised it was true. The pain in her head faded when she touched his cheek."But you..."

Will kissed her again, more insistent and she sank into him, needing his reassurance. That he was here and she hadn't lost him. "I'm fine so I don't see a problem here." He pulled off her t-shirt and tossed it to the floor as he gently pushed her down.

Would she ever get used to the way he looked at her, a mixture of adoration and hunger? "James will—"

"I don't give a shit about James." He growled, lowering his mouth to her breast.

She gasped and arched her back, her stomach tightening.

"You're what I need, when will you realize that?" His eyes narrowed as they pierced hers. "You're mine," he said with a guttural sound.

Emma's stomach dropped. Did he know about Raphael? Did he suspect? But his mouth and his hands assured her that she was his. She belonged with Will. He entered her possessively and she answered with a possessiveness of her own. She needed him, needed his claim to drive away her demons.

They lay together when they were done, Will's arm tight around her waist, holding her close. She breathed in the scent of him, pushing away the memory of someone else.

****

Will held Emma's naked body flush against his, marveling that she was his. Had he imagined the flicker of fear in her eyes when he told her that she belonged to him? He wondered again about the man who helped them and Emma's reaction to him. He looked down at the profile of her face, lying against his chest. He pulled her closer, telling himself Emma was here with him.

He was being paranoid.

****

Jake lay on his bed with his eyes closed, but he wasn't sleepy. His days were boring.

Even though Alex told him that he was going to find his mommy, he didn't trust him. The man in his dreams had told him to trust no one. So he didn't. But he was tired of waiting.

Mommy had called to him again in that afternoon. She felt so sad and hopeless that he almost talked to her. But he stopped in time. He didn't want Alex to find her.

Jake buried his face into the dog that he had renamed Rusty and cried. He missed her so much that his stomach had a constant ache, like part of him was missing.

He fell asleep, his cheek pressed into the damp stuffed animal. Once the darkness enveloped his mind, he dreamed of her. But it wasn't a real dream, it was like the dreams *he* showed Jake after Will showed up.

Mommy ran down a crowded street at night, wearing a blue skirt with tiny white flowers he'd never seen before. She never wore skirts unless they were part of her waitress uniform. She was so pretty and her hair was down, not in her usual ponytail. She stopped on the street corner next to him, looking over her shoulder. Her eyes were hard, the way she looked when the Bad Men showed up. She was so close he could hear her panting, close enough to touch. He wanted to hug her and tell her he loved her and how pretty she looked, but he knew she couldn't hear him. His chest burned. He was this close yet not close enough.

She ran again and another man pulled her into the shadows and kissed her. Jake was confused. Where was Will? But Mommy held onto the man until she fell backward and the man held her arm.

The scene changed. Mommy stood in the woods. A fire lit her face, but something else shone in her eyes. Her face glowed, a golden light shining around her body. Her hands reached toward the fire. She was pretty in a white nightgown that fluttered in the wind, and her hair blew around her. A man appeared from the darkness in the trees. He crept behind her and kissed her neck. Someone else stood on the opposite side of the fire, watching. The shadows covered their face but the figure's hands clenched at its sides.

Everything faded to black and Jake heard *his* voice. Finally. After all these weeks, *He* had come back.

"Jake, I'm so proud of you. You have been so patient, but you must be patient for a bit longer. Soon we will all be together."

"Alex said that, too."

"Yes, Alex wants your mommy to be his, but he is a bad, bad man. You saw that when you touched him, didn't you?"

"Yes," Jake whispered.

"You must not help him. Do you understand?"

"Yes, but I want my mommy." Tears stung Jake's eyes and burned his throat. "She keeps calling to me. Can I talk to her?"

"No, your mommy isn't ready yet. First she has work to do and then you can see her. But I will give you a gift for being such a good boy."

The darkness gave way to a bedroom he had never seen. Mommy wore a t-shirt and slept next to a man, curled up into his side. Jake released his breath, happy to see it was Will.

"Would you like to stay with your mommy tonight?" the voice asked.

Jake nodded, in awe that he stood next to her. He climbed onto the bed, pressing his tummy to her back. He breathed in the flowery scent of her shampoo as the warmth of her body seeped into his. Tears ran down his face and wet the sheet. This was only a dream, but it felt so real.

"Thank you," he whispered, wrapping his arm around her stomach. He touched her belly, knowing a baby grew inside her. Would she love the baby more since he was gone? Would she love the baby more since Will was its daddy?

Even in her sleep, she sensed his arm and reached down, grabbing his hand in hers. He closed his eyes grateful that he could be with her, even if it was while she slept. Even if it was just a dream.

Jake fell asleep, wishing the morning would never come.

CHAPTER ELEVEN

WILL woke up with Emma curled against his side. Her slow, steady breath warmed his skin filling him with a foreign sentiment he struggled to name. Contentment. He marveled at this place of belonging as he studied her face, the tension smoothed away while she slept. Her hand draped over her abdomen, her fingers curled as if she held onto something. Leaning his face into her hair, he breathed in her scent, committing it to memory as his lips brushed her forehead. The desperation to cling to this moment only reinforced his conviction of what he had to do. As tempted as he was to stay, he needed to go before she woke. And he needed to talk to James.

He eased himself off the bed and pulled a shirt over his head. The pendant lay on the nightstand, reminding him of the events the night before. It should provide him with a sense of victory, that the stone was more than just a necklace. That it was an incredible source of power. But the fact they knew so little about it gave him more hesitation than relief. Everything came with a price. What was the cost of the stone?

He grabbed a cup of coffee and stood on the front porch. The sun still hung low in the eastern sky making the peaks on the water glisten with gold. James sat on the dock in a camping chair, a fishing pole in hand. An empty chair sat to James' left with a rod beside it on the deck. The old ritual soothed the edges of Will's anxiety.

James ignored him as he approached. Will sat down, sipping his coffee as he watched the dragonflies dance on the water's surface. "No clients today?" Will already knew the answer. James was a fishing guide and if he'd had a client, he'd be gone already.

James's gaze stayed out on the lake. "Lucky for you, my clients have been a little thin lately. Damn economy." He paused for a moment. "I see you're all better."

"Yeah."

James reeled in his line and recast. "Who the hell is she? Or maybe the more appropriate question is *what* is she?"

"Her name is Emma. And she's a person, just like you and me."

James shook his head, slow and deliberate, his mouth set in a grim line. "She is *not* like you and me." His face reddened then he erupted with a slew of questions. "Where did you meet her, Will? A crappy bar? On the side of the road? Was she a job?" He paused and sucked in his breath. "Shit, she was a job, wasn't she?" James's eyes widened and he turned to look at him. "Oh. My. God. She was your *big* job. The job you said you'd retire on. You didn't finish it, did you? The people who beat the shit out of you are the people who hired you. Shit, Will. You fucked up big-time on this one."

Will took a deep breath and shook his head. "No. For once I got it right."

James's eyes filled with hatred. "Who is she? Who wanted her? What did she do?"

"She didn't *do* anything. They wanted her for her *potential.*" He spat the last word with disgust.

"What the fuck does that mean?"

"You wouldn't believe me if I told you."

"News flash. I saw your girlfriend glowing in the bedroom. Try me."

Will understood his anger and his confusion. If it were the other way around, Will suspected he would react the same way. "I'm telling you, James, it all sounds crazy. You just have to trust me."

"That's just it, Will. I *don't* trust you. Before you showed up with that woman, I would have trusted you, but this isn't you. This isn't the Will I know, cussing me out in my own kitchen over a woman. It's always been you and me, dude. You and me. We agreed to never let women get between us and look at you." James sneered in disgust. "How long have you known her?"

"Almost a month."

"Almost a *month*? You're throwing your life away over a woman you've only known for a month?"

"Yeah, but I'm not throwing it away."

James doubled over with laughter.

"What's so funny?"

"You. You're a fucking idiot." James reeled in his line. "I never thought I'd see the day Will Davenport got snared by a woman."

He understood James's reaction and he considered arguing that Emma saved him, but he knew it would be a waste of breath. James needed time to see how important

Emma was to him. Will took a sip of coffee, averting his gaze. "James, I need your help."

"I'm already giving you my help."

"I need more."

James groaned. "Of course you do."

"Is there any chance you can do a little investigating for me?"

"What kind of investigating?"

"Just computer sleuthing. My laptop burned up when my truck exploded and I haven't had time to replace all of my contacts."

"Your truck exploded?"

"Yeah, old news. But I need you—"

"Old news for you maybe, but not me. Let me guess, this had to do with Emma."

Will tempered his growing irritation. "James, I told you, she hasn't done anything wrong. A group of powerful people want her because of the things they think she's capable of. She was completely clueless to any of it until the Vinco Potentia tried to hire me to work for them as part of their security team. I was the one who told her."

"Who?"

"The Vinco Potentia. They're a secret organization of politicians and influential businessmen. And from the members I'm aware of and the money backing them, they're powerful. I want to figure out who else is in their group. That's where you come in."

"And they're the people that hired you? They hired you to take Emma to them?"

"Yes, but there's another organization after her, too. They're the ones who caused my truck to explode." Will decided it was best to leave Jake out of it at this point. He could only imagine James's reaction to that. No need to overwhelm him any more than necessary.

"*Two* organizations?" James shook his head. "Shit, Will."

"Yes, but the second group wants to kill her. At least the Vinco Potentia wants her alive."

"What the fuck does this girl do?"

"It's what they *think* she can do." He paused. "The head of the Vinco Potentia is none other than Phillip Warren."

James' mouth dropped. "*Senator* Phillip Warren? The guy running for president?"

Will pinched his lips. Part of him wished he'd killed Warren when he had the chance. "Yeah, pleasant fellow," he said, but his tone implied otherwise. "His right-hand man at the South Dakota compound was Scott Kramer. He's the guy who actually hired me. Also, Warren's son, Alex Warren. He's part of them too. There was another guy named John, middle-aged guy. Dark hair with a bit of gray. I don't know his last name."

"Gee, middle-aged guy named John, that narrows it down to a couple hundred thousand guys."

"Look, James, I wouldn't ask your help if I didn't need it. You and I both know you're a hell of a lot better at finding info on people than I am."

"I don't know, Will. I've never heard of the Vinco Potentia and I heard about a lot of political groups when I was in communications in the service."

"They were all Brown graduates. That should narrow it down. Also, I have Warren's cell phone. Maybe his list of contacts will help."

"Do I *want* to know how you got Senator Warren's cell phone?"

Will grinned. "I can assure you he handed it to me himself."

James raised his eyebrows in a challenge.

"I tried to sort through the list, but I spent most of my time taking care of Emma. She was in really bad shape when we escaped." Will's voice faded as he thought about how scared he was that first week.

"And do I want to know what was wrong with her?" James shook his head. "Scratch that. I don't. Did you get the cell phone before or after you escaped?" Sarcasm dripped from his words.

"Do you really want to know?"

"Hell, no."

Will paused, then held James's gaze. "I have another favor to ask, even bigger than that." His voice softened.

James' eyes narrowed with suspicion. "What?"

Will strengthened his resolve. He had to do this even if the mark on his arm protested otherwise. "I have to go back to South Dakota. There's a book at the Vinco Potentia compound. A book that has answers. I need that book."

"You're going to invade a compound owned by a powerful, secret society on your own and steal a book?"

"No, I'm only going to do surveillance and try to figure out the best way in."

"And then what?"

"And then you and I are going to go back and steal it."

James let loose a long string of curse words. "How did I get roped into this? Is that your favor?"

"No, excitement and adventure with me is a given."

James scowled. "So what's the favor?"

"I need to leave Emma here. She won't be safe with me."

"Are you fucking serious?"

Will hated to ask, hated to leave her even more. He could see James didn't like her, but she was safer with James than she would be traipsing around so close to the Warren territory. "It's only for a few days."

"What? Am I supposed to take her out on the lake with my clients? Be her babysitter?"

"No, I'm hoping she'll be safe out here in the middle of nowhere. And if something happens, you'll be here to protect her. I'll be back in a few days."

"And if someone shows up?"

Will's chest tightened at the thought. "I doubt anyone will, but if they do..." His eyes hardened. "I have no doubt that you're capable of protecting her."

James shook his head in disgust. "Goddamit. I can't believe I'm fucking agreeing to this. You know she's not going to like it. What makes you so sure she'll stay?"

"Because I'm not telling her that I'm leaving and she won't have any way to take off."

"What the hell do I get out of all of this?"

"My undying gratitude?"

James snorted. "Yeah, just what I was looking for."

"I'm going to leave now, before she wakes up. Can you look up some of the info before I get back in a couple of days?"

"Sure." James scoffed. "Maybe I can cook you a turkey dinner, too."

Will grinned. "Well, now that you mention it, that sounds—"

"In your dreams, asshole."

****

Emma woke up in an empty bed. Her fingers trailed over sheets where Will had lain. Had saving him been a dream? But if it had, wouldn't he still be here?

The memory of Jake's hand gripping hers rushed into her mind, taking her breath away. Even though she could almost feel his body pressed into her back, there was no denying it had been a dream. Her eyes sank closed with grief. It had felt so real.

She sat up, irritated that it was after ten o'clock. Why had Will let her sleep so long? Lying in bed all day didn't get her closer to finding Jake and she'd wasted enough time in bed, delirious with a fever, the weeks before. She got up and wandered through the empty house then moved to the front porch, her mouth dropping open. The Camaro was gone.

James walked up to the house carrying an armload of firewood, keeping his eyes down. "Will left."

Her breath hung in her throat. "Left? Left where?"

He dumped the wood in a pile close to the porch then stared at her, a blank expression on his face. "South Dakota."

The blood rushed from her head as the heat of anger replaced it. "South *Dakota*?"

James put a foot on the porch and leaned an arm on it. "Yeah, something about a book. And *you*." His eyes held hers in a challenge.

She tried to control her breathing as her temper boiled.

"He hired me to be your babysitter for the next few days."

"*Days*?"

"Yeah, that was pretty much my reaction, too." James turned around and walked toward the dock. "He left you a note on the kitchen table."

Emma stormed inside to find a folded paper with her name written on the outside. She'd overlooked it before.

Emma,

I'm sorry I left like this. I thought it would be easier this way. I need to do some reconnaissance in South Dakota and I didn't want to risk taking you. You'll be safer here with James. I'll be back in a few days.

Love,

Will

James walked in the side door, stomping his dirty boots on a rug. "You can earn your keep by catching up my laundry and cooking. You look like you've worked in a restaurant or two. I'd like a roast and potatoes for dinner." He brushed past her down the hall.

She crumbled the note in her hand. "Excuse me, but I was an accountant."

"Yeah, sure you were, honey." His voice was muffled as he shut the door to the bathroom. The sound of the shower followed.

Emma clenched her fists, her nails digging into her palms. Who the hell did he think he was? And what in the hell was Will thinking leaving her here? He expected her to stick around for days just waiting for him?

She felt lost and alone without Will and that pissed her off. She'd spent her entire life alone, so when did she start needing him? And look where needing him got her. Farther away from Jake than ever before and stranded with the dickhead singing in the shower.

Will made his choice and she made hers. He expected her to sit here barefoot and possibly pregnant while he ran off and did manly things.

To hell with that.

She dug in the bag he left behind and found his stash of money. She wouldn't take much, just enough to get a new pair of shoes, some food and a bus ticket to Arizona. She'd walk to the nearest town and catch a bus to Tucson. Hopefully, they had a bus station out in the middle of Timbuktu.

She found an old backpack in the bedroom closet. Stealing it from James almost made her feel bad, but the fact he was an ass negated any guilt. She stuffed the few clothing items and toiletries she had into the pack. As an afterthought, she grabbed a handgun and bullets. Unfortunately, she'd probably need to use it. She pushed away the fear that blossomed at the thought and placed them in the front pocket of the backpack. A purse would have been better and given her faster access to the gun, but she didn't have one anymore. Hers burned up in Will's truck, which reminded her that she'd need to get a fake ID soon. With a huff of anger, she strode for the door when the pendant on the nightstand caught her eye.

She couldn't believe she almost left it.

The stone warmed her fingers when she picked it up. She unfastened the clasp and hung the chain around her neck, the weight heavy on her chest. She wasn't used to wearing jewelry, but it gave her comfort. Right now, she could use all the comfort she could get.

The water was still running in the bathroom as Emma slipped out the front door. The gravel in the lane dug into her bare feet, but she hurried anyway, moving to the grass along the side of the road and cursing when the occasional rock or thorn stabbed the tender flesh of her sole.

By the time she made it to the main road, she felt a sense of victory. She doubted James would actually come looking for her this far. He made no secret of his dislike of her, and was probably glad to be rid of her.

After she'd traveled a mile or so, she wished she'd grabbed some food before she left. She chastised herself for being in such a hurry that it never occurred to her make better preparations. If Jake were with her, that mistake could have been disastrous.

If Jake were here.

The fact that Jake wasn't there burned, mixing with her anger and Will's betrayal. What gave Will the right to leave her without consulting her first? He should be out looking for Jake, not on some snipe hunt in South Dakota. Yet she knew that wasn't fair. He'd been trying to find Jake. In fact, he probably hoped to get clues from the book at the Vinco Potentia compound. Just as she began to question whether leaving James's house was a good idea after all, a car pulled beside her and slowed.

She was pissed anew that she had been so lost in thought that she missed its approach. Goddamn, she was getting sloppy.

"Need a lift?" a familiar voice asked.

Emma turned in anticipation and dread, her suspicion confirmed.

Raphael had found her.

His arm draped over the steering wheel and he leaned over, looking out the open passenger window, wearing an amused smile.

She looked straight ahead, ignoring the yearning in her gut. "No, thank you."

The car rolled along side of her. "Where are you going?"

She kept walking. Talking would only encourage him.

"Emma, are you seriously going to walk to town *barefoot*?"

She stopped and turned to him, screwing on her fiercest look. "How did you find me?"

He smiled. "I stay in a cabin at this lake every summer. How is it that you keep showing up in my path?"

"You really expect me to believe that?" She put her hand on her hip. "You're seriously trying to tell me you're not following me? Un*fucking*believable." She started walking again.

The car stopped behind her and she hoped he had given up, although the primal part of her hoped he didn't. She shoved that part way down and stomped on it.

Footsteps approached from behind her. "Emma, wait."

"Why the *hell* would I do that?" she shouted.

"Do you really think I would follow you to a lake in Minnesota? Do I look like a stalker to you?"

At this point, if the pope himself was following her, she'd consider him a stalker. "Yes."

He laughed, a rich, deep, melodious laugh. It rumbled through her, teasing the instinctual reaction she still fought to suppress.

"Where's your boyfriend? I'm surprised to see you out here walking shoeless on a country road instead of nursing him back to health." He was beside her now, less than a foot away.

Emma shook her head in irritation. "He's better. He's fine."

"You mean he's recovering just fine?"

"No, I mean he's completely healed."

He stopped and to her annoyance she halted and turned to face him. A look of pride crossed his face before it was replaced by polite congeniality. "Wow, that's quite a miracle."

She studied him closely. "Yes, it is. What do you know about it?"

His eyes widened in surprise. "Me? How would I know anything about it?"

"You told me I could heal him. You told me I had the power to do it."

"I meant figuratively, not literally, Em. I meant that your beauty and sweet presence would surely make him better."

"That's a crock of bullshit and you know it. How do you keep showing up where I am?"

"Perhaps it's fate."

"No way. You're following me. Why?"

"Are you telling me you don't believe in fate or destiny?"

That's a good question. She honestly wasn't sure. Everything with Will, Jake and her was all supposed to be chalked up to destiny, but destiny at this point pointed to one cosmic train wreck.

"Where is that boyfriend of yours?"

She started walking again.

"Emma, where are you going?"

"Away from you. For all I know you're a psycho serial killer."

Raphael's laugh echoed behind her. "Emma, if I was going to murder you, don't you think I would have done it by now?"

"I have no idea how serial killers work, but I don't intend to stay and find out."

"I concede." Raphael called behind her. "It's not a coincidence."

She stopped and turned back to him, brushing the hair out of her face.

"If you get in the car with me, I'll drive you into town and answer some of your questions."

"No, I want answers right now."

He shook his head. "No, I can't answer them all right here. It would take too long. If you come with me, I'll tell you what I know."

"Like what?"

"How did you heal your boyfriend?"

"Will?"

"Yes, Will," he said his name as though it left a bad taste in his mouth.

She knew she should run. But he said he knew things. He might be able to provide answers to her questions, which in turn, might help her find Jake. "How do you know I healed him?"

Raphael took a couple of steps toward her. He stopped when he saw her alarm. "Emma, you and I both know he was far too injured to be just fine. How did you do it?"

"How do you know about me?"

Raphael took another step toward her. "For now, you answer my questions and I promise to give you information… as I think you need it."

"That hardly seems fair."

Raphael's mouth lifted into a sad smile. "Emma, you of all people know that life is far from fair. But I'm presuming no one else around you has answers to the questions racing through your mind. What are the marks on your back? What powers do you possess? How did you heal

Will?" He paused and his eyes narrowed, making them look black in the shade. "Who your father really is?"

Her eyes widened in alarm. "How do you know those things?"

"I just do. Spend the afternoon with me and I promise to give you information."

"How can I trust you?"

He lifted the corner of his mouth into a sardonic grin. "Can you afford not to?"

She eyed him with wariness. He was right. She only hoped the price wasn't more than she was willing to pay.

CHAPTER TWELVE

"ALL right." She relented, then her cheeks flushed remembering their kiss. "But you can't touch me."

"Fair enough. You have a *boyfriend,* after all. Any other conditions?"

She looked into his dark eyes. "You're not going to hurt me, are you?" It was a ridiculous thing to ask. It wasn't as if he would tell her that he would.

Raphael started to reach for her arm, then stopped, lifting his hands in mock surrender. "Emma, haven't I saved you twice already? Three times if you've seen horror movies and count my picking you up off this deserted road. If I wanted to harm you, why would I have intervened? I only want to help you."

She didn't want to trust him. It pissed her off that once again she was at some man's mercy, yet she wanted answers more than anything. "All right."

"Good. I'll take you into town and buy you lunch. Then we can talk."

She nodded and walked beside him toward his car, making sure several feet separated them.

"Do you have some aversion to shoes? I keep finding you without shoes."

"Shut up."

He laughed, a rich, rumbling sound.

"The pair I kicked off running were my only shoes. I've been a bit busy to worry about shopping."

A half an hour later, after buying a pair of tennis shoes at the Dollar General, Emma and Raphael sat in silence at a table in an old cafe overlooking the lake. Emma ate her sandwich while Raphael studied her. He claimed he wasn't hungry but refused to answer any questions until she finished. Emma looked out onto the water, trying to avoid eye contact with him, but she noticed he watched her every move.

"Didn't your mother ever teach you it was rude to stare?"

He laughed and glanced away. "I'm sorry. I'm not used to being so close to you. I see you're wearing the pendant."

Emma sat up straighter. "How did you know about the pendant and what do you mean so close to me? So you *have* been stalking me."

"I have seen you before, but no, I haven't stalked you." Raphael grimaced. "This is harder than I expected."

"Yeah, it's not so easy for me either, except I'm totally clueless. You know a hell of a lot more than I do."

"Aww, now *there's* that spirit I've missed. How did you get so broken?" His voice softened.

Emma stood, frightened. "How the hell do you know anything about me?" she asked, her voice nearly a whisper.

"Emma, sit down. You're making a scene. I told you I'm not going to hurt you." His voice was soft and soothing, but firm in its command.

Emma felt her body relaxing, in spite of her anxiety.

"There you go, my love. Sit down. Let me explain."

"I am not *your love*, so stop calling me that." Emma sat on the edge of her chair. "Have you been watching me?"

"There's not an easy way to answer that."

"Actually, it's quite easy. It's a yes or no question. Have you been watching me?"

"Yes."

She knew she shouldn't be surprised, yet the confirmation frightened her. "Did the Vinco Potentia hire you?"

His eyes widened in surprise before he curled his lip. "No, I haven't been *hired* by anyone."

"Then why?"

"Let's just say I have a special interest in making sure you're safe. I've been like a… guardian angel at times." He smirked and leaned over the table, resting his weight on his elbow. Dark, curly hair hung close to his head and his eyes were so dark they looked black against his dark complexion.

"Ha. You don't look like any guardian angel I've ever seen."

He lifted a corner of his mouth. "And exactly how many guardian angels have you met?"

Why was she always getting mixed up with arrogant assholes? "I don't need a guardian so I suggest you stop stalking me or I'll make sure you wished you had. Besides, Will has the protection job covered." But the thought of Will stoked her irritation. First, she had taken care of herself for so long, she didn't want to think she actually needed someone to protect her. And second, she wasn't so sure Raphael should know that piece of information.

Raphael's eyes darkened and his face contorted with rage. His eyes bore into hers. "He's incompetent. Where is he now if he's supposed to protect you? Will is too dense to grasp your worth. If he did, he would have an army protecting you." He paused leaning closer. "If I were your protector, I would never leave your side," he said seductively, his eyes holding hers.

Emma felt her stomach tighten and flip-flop with his words. She turned toward the lake, breaking eye contact. Self-loathing rolled through her. Why did she react to him this way? She turned back with a glare. "Will is doing the best he can. If he had an army at his disposal, I wouldn't put it past him to use it. He's only one man."

Raphael raised his palms in surrender and sat back in his chair. "I apologize if I spoke out of turn."

"Why are you following me?"

He crossed his arms with an amused smile. "You seem to be asking all the questions and that's not our arrangement. I'll give you some answers, but I need to ask some questions of my own first. How did you heal Will?"

She found his question irritating. He said he was going to help her. Shouldn't he know the answer? She lifted her chin in defiance. "I have no idea."

He raised his eyebrows, obviously questioning her honesty.

"I'm not lying. I really don't know."

"Tell me what happened."

After she told him, Raphael watched her for a moment. "You were lucky you didn't kill him… or yourself. What were your thoughts when you touched him? Did you say any words?"

"I think I said *heal him.*"

"In English?"

"What? Does it work better in Spanish?" Her sarcasm was biting.

He chuckled.

"So what happened? How did I heal him?"

"I don't know."

She stood and glowered over him. "You said you *did* know. You said you had answers. You fucking liar. I'm done." She walked out of the restaurant into the parking lot.

"Emma."

She ignored him, walking toward the bus stop.

"Emmanuella." He stood behind her, practically breathing in her ear.

Her heart raced when he used her name. She whirled around to face him. He was so close she nearly bumped into him. "You lied to me!"

"No, Emma. I swear, I didn't lie. You didn't let me finish. Calm down and let me finish."

She tried to catch her breath as she took a step back. "Finish what? You said you didn't know!"

He reached out and grasped her hand. "I can't tell you, Emma. You have to figure this out for yourself. That's the way it works."

His touch sent waves of desire rippling up her arm, spreading throughout her body. She jerked her arm out of his grasp. "I told you not to touch me," she spit through gritted teeth.

He lifted his hands and took a step back. "I'm sorry."

She inhaled a shaky breath and ran her fingers through her hair, trying to focus. "So there's a process for learning this? You know what it is and won't help me?"

He shook his head. "No, I can't and you have no idea how quickly I want you to learn but every moment I spend with you inhibits your progress." His voice lowered into a soothing tone. "Come back so we can discuss this. I'll tell you what I can." His hand reached for her neck, stroking lightly.

Her head swam. "You're touching me," she murmured. "You promised not to touch me." But she didn't pull away, mesmerized by his dark eyes.

"I said I wouldn't. I'm not foolish enough to promise." He stepped closer, his chest touching hers as his hand slid up and caressed her cheek. His fingertips left tingles in their wake, igniting a fire in her stomach.

"Why do you feel so familiar?" Emma whispered, her face inches from his.

"You'll figure it out when you're ready."

This is wrong.

She stepped back and his hand dropped, breaking the magnetic pull. "Stay the fuck away from me. I don't know what you're doing but stop it right now." How could she feel simultaneously drawn to him, yet revolted by the thought? She shook her head, trying to clear out the last webs of attraction. "You said no one could help me with my process. Why not?"

"Let's just say you are special and extraordinary, and no one near you is capable of giving you what you need."

"And let's just say that sounds like a load of bullshit."

He laughed. "Come inside and we'll discuss this more."

"No way. I'm not going anywhere with you."

"You want to discuss the secrets of your power in the parking lot of the Griddlecakes Cafe?"

She threw her hands into the air. "Sure. Why the fuck not? It's not like anything else in my life has come with tea and crumpets."

Pity replaced the arrogance in his eyes."And you have no idea how sorry I am about that." He looked over her shoulder down the street. "Okay, we won't go back inside. But there's a bench half a block down. We can sit there and try to add a little dignity to the mysteries of your life."

She nodded and they walked to the bench in silence. She sat at the edge of one end and Raphael, taking her cue, sat on the opposite end.

"Back to your power," he said. "What else can you do?"

"Occasionally Will and I can sense each other in our minds."

"You said occasionally, not all the time?"

"No, usually we just feel the other person. Once we could actually talk."

"And why was that situation different?"

"Will had left me with the Vinco Potentia and Jake's father, who I hadn't seen since..." She shook her head. "He walked in my room. I was shocked and upset and without even thinking about it, I reached out to Will in my mind.

We could hear each other's thoughts. It was the only time it happened."

The veins on Raphael's neck bulged. "Will left you there with *him*?"

"You're not being fair. He was trying to protect me and Will didn't know that Alex was there. *Wait.* You know about Alex?"

Raphael's eyes darkened. Emma could almost swear his pupils were tinged with red. "Yes, I know Alex Warren. He is a very dangerous man." He turned away from her and took several deep breaths. "Have you discovered any other talents?"

"Can you call sudden and debilitating nausea a talent? When the Cavallo would get close, I got severely ill."

"When did you start noticing any of this?

"After Will showed up. That's when Jake started changing too."

"And the next talent, sensing each other, when did it show up?"

"Around the time I was shot."

"And did you ever get sick again after that?"

"No…but it could just be because I wasn't around the Cavallo anymore."

"But you were around the other group, also your enemies, and you weren't sick? Yet you could communicate with Will telepathically?"

"Yes."

"Then you received another gift? You healed Will."

"Yes."

"The nausea confuses me. But nausea is a primal reaction and it served as a warning system, but it's rudimentary. It could be that as your powers mature, you could lose the primitive ones."

She only hoped it was true. "And I'll have other powers?"

"Most assuredly, yes."

"What will they be?"

"That's for you to determine."

She groaned in frustration. "That's not very helpful."

"I'm sorry."

She scowled. "You said it was for me to figure out my abilities. How do I find them?"

"Practice. Play with it and discover what you can do. Don't let your conceptual mind limit the possibilities. Let your imagination have free reign." Raphael paused. "So, the baby. It's true?"

Emma's face burned. "Yes, I think so." Why could she admit this to him but not Will?

"And how do you feel about it?"

"Scared, sad, angry that people want me because of a poor defenseless baby. The Vinco Potentia doesn't realize that I have powers. Not yet, anyway. Will says they think my only purpose is to have this baby. He doesn't want them to find out."

"That is one thing we both agree upon." His voice softened. "Emma, I bring this up only to point out the obvious. You haven't told me what you think about the baby so this might offend you and I apologize in advance."

He stopped and she turned to look at him. His eyes locked on hers, his hypnotic pull returning. "You are hunted by men because of the potential of the baby. They don't know of your powers. I can assure you of that." He paused again. "You need Will because of the baby. If there's no baby, you don't need Will forever. Do you understand what I'm saying? You don't have to have this baby."

Emma's heart sputtered.

"You *do* need Will to continue the development of your powers, as much as it pains me to tell you that. But once your powers are developed, if there's no baby, you can free him."

The blood rushed from her head. She didn't need Will? Wasn't that what she wanted, to not need him? She had thought so, but contemplating a life without Will seemed empty. And what about the baby? She bit her lip as she struggled with her war of emotions.

"What do you think about what I told you?" he asked, his voice soft in her ear.

"The baby part, I have no idea. It wasn't like I planned to get pregnant, but I'm not so callous that I can casually think about ending a pregnancy." She paused and took a deep breath. "But Will…" Her heart ached at the mere thought of losing him.

Raphael's gaze changed, his desire evident, and all breath squeezed from her lungs.

"Emma, I assure you, you would not be lonely."

She jumped up from the bench. "I have to go." She whirled away and started down the street.

"You can't go," he called after her. "You still need Will."

She stopped, her back to him.

"I hate to say this, but you still need him to gain your powers."

Her heart twisted in confusion. How could she want Will, yet be so eager to run away from him too? She spun to face Raphael. "I refuse to go back to James's house."

"I agree with you. I don't want you there either. By tonight I'm sure James will have called Will and told him you're missing. I suspect he'll return by tomorrow morning. You can stay here in town and I can drop you off at James's tomorrow."

"Why? Why would you do that?"

"Emma, I already admitted I have a vested interest in your well-being," he said, raising his hand as she prepared to speak. "However, I can't tell you why. You'll find out soon enough."

She put her hand on her hip, weighing her options.

"I'm staying at a lodge next to the lake. Why don't you get a room there for tonight and I promise to take you back first thing in the morning,"

"I'm *not* spending the night with you."

"And I'm not proposing that. You'll have your own room. As much as I would love to spend the rest of the afternoon and night with you, I can't. I've spent too much time in contact with you as it is." He smiled, a cross between a seductive grin and a patronizing gaze.

She sighed in frustration. When had she sunk so low that she let men dictate her actions? But there was no valid reason to refuse his suggestion other than obstinacy.

God, if this didn't smack of when I first met Will….

"Fine," she huffed, shaking her head.

They got in his car and drove the short distance to the lodge. Raphael waited outside while she went inside and signed in under an alias she had picked up somewhere along the way. Raphael walked her to her room, insisting on carrying her backpack.

"This is it." She waved to the door. "Can I have my bag now?"

He handed her the pack, but grabbed her free hand, bringing it to his lips. His face raised, shining with a playful grin. His tongue darted out and licked lightly as a fire ignited in her abdomen. "Until tomorrow."

She jerked her hand away and shut the door behind her, wondering if she'd just made a pact with the devil.

****

Will had watched the compound through binoculars for several hours. A nine-hour drive brought him there in the early evening. Most business was probably done for the day, not that he expected much to happen. Kramer himself had said members of their group didn't visit very often.

Will hoped to make note of delivery schedules and use that to his advantage. Later, in the dead of morning, he planned to check out the private airstrip where the helicopter they flew in a few weeks ago had landed.

He twisted the cap off a bottle of water and took a swig as the phone in his pocket vibrated. *Emma.* It surprised him that she hadn't called sooner to cuss him out. He dug out the phone and checked the screen, confirming James' number. His shoulders tensed, preparing for the verbal onslaught. "Hello."

"Will."

James' tense voice on the other end stuck Will's breath in his chest and he choked on his words. "Oh, God, Emma."

"I'm sure she's fine, Will. She got pissed at me and took off. I figured she took a walk down by the lake, but when she didn't come back by dinner, I started looking for her. I have no idea where she is."

"How long has she been gone?"

James hesitated. "Since late morning."

Will's heart jumped into overdrive. "And you're just now calling me? Anything could have happened to her in the last twelve hours." Will threw his items in his bag and tossed them in the car, thrusting his keys in the ignition. "I gave you a simple job. How could you possibly *fucking lose her*?"

"I didn't ask for this job, you shithead. Now calm your ass down. Freaking out isn't going to do any good."

Will took several deep breaths as he tried to regain control. James was right. He needed to calm down and think this through. Where would she have gone? What would Emma do? He remembered when he first met her. She had planned to take a bus after her car got a flat tire.

"Is there a bus station in town?"

"Not a station, just a stop she could have gotten on. But I already checked and no one matching her description got on a bus today. I would have started calling the local motels asking if she's checked in, but I don't even know her last name."

Will looked down at his speedometer, realizing he was driving twenty miles over the speed limit. He eased off the gas. He couldn't afford to be pulled over. "Thompson, Emma Thompson. But I guarantee she won't be using her real name. She's too smart for that." It never occurred to him to ask her what alias she might have used in the past. He slammed his hand down on the steering wheel. Goddamn it, he never should have left her. "*Fuck!*"

"Okay, calm down. She couldn't have gotten very far. I'll make some calls and I'll call you back when I know anything. I presume you're coming back."

"I'm already on my fucking way."

James hung up and Will hoped he was right, that she hadn't gotten very far. He remembered how he had sensed her before, when he worried about her safety. But they had only been about fifty feet away, not six hundred miles. He cursed himself again, and decided he had nothing to lose by trying. Besides, Emma had done it with Jake and there had likely been more distance between them.

He concentrated on the mark, picturing her in bed this morning, the pain of the memory sucking his breath away. He felt a twinge of her presence. Forcing himself to remain calm, he thought of her again, reaching out and calling to her. The presence of her slammed into him with a force he hadn't expected, consolation washing over him in waves. He tried calling to her again but only heard silence. He had the impression that he could have talked to her if she were conscious. Terror stabbed his chest at the thought and he glanced at the clock on the dash. Eleven-thirty. She was most likely asleep, as tired as she had been lately. He concentrated and felt her slow even breathing. His shoulders shook with relief. She was sleeping. He had no idea where she was, but it had to be enough for now.

He drove to Minnesota, swearing to never let her out of his sight again.

CHAPTER THIRTEEN

DREAMS plagued Emma's sleep. She had spent most of the afternoon hiking around the lake in an attempt to avoid Raphael. After picking up dinner at the lodge's restaurant, she returned to her room, where she fell asleep by nine o'clock.

But she was restless, hovering on the edge of the dream world and reality. She dreamed of her grandmother and fried chicken. She was a little girl again swinging on the old tire swing in her grandmother's backyard. The dream shifted and Jake was in the swing, swinging higher and higher until he flew away, going farther and farther until he was just a speck in the sky. She dreamed of Will, calling her name, insistent, worry in his voice. She tried to answer, but she was too tired and when she found the energy, he was gone.

She dreamed of Raphael. On the country road and in the diner. The dream shifted once more. She stood in the woods. The light of the full moon pierced through the canopy overhead. The fire called out to her as her body felt alive with electricity. Excitement filled every molecule. Raphael was behind her, his breath warming her neck, the fire inside her rivaling the heat of the fire before her.

"You are not bound to destiny." His warm, husky voice filled her ear as he kissed her neck below her earlobe.

Waves of pleasure washed through her. She wanted more of what he offered. She wanted him.

"You're so close," he said, his very breath pushing her closer and closer to ecstasy. "So very close."

"Emma." She heard Raphael's voice, but it was harsher, insistent.

She moaned.

"Emma! Wake up!"

She sat up in a panic when she realized it was dark and Raphael was in her room.

He tossed a dress toward her. "You have to hurry. You have to get out of here."

"What are you talking about? How the hell did you get in here?"

He stopped and turned to her. "You have to hurry. They're coming."

They're coming.

His words were like icy pinpricks. Jake used to say that when the Bad Men were coming.

"How do you know?" she asked, jumping out of bed and grabbing the dress. She ran into the bathroom, shouting over her shoulder. "*How do you know?*"

"I just do."

Jake told her that too. In the beginning.

She scrambled to get dressed, her fingers fumbling with the buttons.

"Emma, you have to hurry. They're almost here."

His voice was frantic. She never considered that the Raphael who calmly smashed in a man's head as if he was playing baseball could become frantic.

And it terrified her.

She threw open the bathroom door, the top part of her dress not fully buttoned.

He was waiting for her, grabbing her nightgown out of her hand and handing her the gun. He ushered her out the door as he stuffed the nightgown into the pack. "You're going to have to take my car."

She stopped in confusion. "What about you?"

"I'm not going." He grabbed her arm and dragged her, electricity shooting through her arm and a languid warmth crept in, flowing up her arm into her body, slowing her down even more. Raphael dropped his hand, irritation sweeping across his face.

"Gods be damned for choosing that man," he muttered under his breath. "Emma, snap out of it."

She shook her head and blinked. *What the hell had just happened?*

"You have to hurry. You'll be lucky to get away at this point. I'll stall them as best I can, but I'm not allowed to interfere."

He stopped next to his black Lexus and opened the door, tossing her backpack onto the passenger seat. He put the keys in the ignition and started the engine.

"Who are you?" she asked, her eyes wide with fear.

"The more appropriate question would be *what* am I. But we'll save that for another day. Get in the car and go!"

"Where?" She slid into the front seat, her heart hammering into her chest.

"Anywhere but Minnesota. *Now go*!" He slammed the car door shut and turned as three cars tore into the parking lot, sending gravel flying in all directions. Raphael walked forward, toward the cars. Shadows licked at his feet.

Emma stomped on the gas pedal, heading for the parking lot exit when one of the cars swerved toward her. She backed off the gas, spun the wheel to a hard right, fishtailing and sending gravel into the cars parked in the lot. The other car swerved to miss her. She jerked the wheel to straighten the car and floored the pedal, aiming for the exit.

Gunshots rang out behind her and she ducked out of instinct. The bullets popped against the glass but it held.

Raphael had given her a bulletproof car.

An explosion rocked the air behind her as she turned, fishtailing the car onto the two-lane highway. Forest surrounded the road, with only a narrow gravel shoulder on both sides. Up ahead she saw a curve. She reprimanded herself for not paying closer attention to the roads, another slip of habit. She always knew the escape routes. Being with Will made her careless.

A mistake she'd never make again.

The rearview mirror reflected the headlights of a car turning onto the road, the taillights of another as it spun around. Two of them.

Easy.

She flipped the lights on high, glancing at the clock on the dashboard. Three-fifteen. That was good, fewer cars on the road, more room to maneuver. She gunned the gas, shooting for the outside edge of the curve ahead, praying that no one approached from the opposite direction. The car whipped around the curve .

So this was how the rich drove.

The two other cars were close behind, but Emma knew she could keep ahead of them with the Lexus. More gunshots echoed behind her as she led the cars toward town and a two-way stop, the flashing red lights a beacon. The high beams showed an empty intersection and straight road ahead for another quarter mile. An eighteen-wheeler approached on the cross highway from the left, barreling toward the crossroads. She punched the gas. If she could cross the intersection first—

She laid on the horn, her foot literally touching the floor, the two cars close behind. The speedometer inched close to one hundred. The rush of adrenaline combined with her fear was intoxicating.

She cast a glance toward the eighteen-wheeler, which didn't show signs of slowing down. She gauged the distance between her and the truck. It was going to be close.

The eighteen-wheeler's brake lights glowed in the darkness as the flashing red lights grew closer. The cars behind her still followed.

The town was less than a half-mile away. Tearing through with a high-speed chase was a sure way to get the police hot on her ass.

Goddamn, she wished she paid attention. She should have gone the other way.

She shot through the intersection. Straddling the center lane, the truck's brakes screeching in the summer night and missing her car by a good thirty feet. One of the cars hit its brakes and skidded off the road. The other car made it through, hanging on her bumper.

Emma swerved to the right and took her foot off the gas, tapping the brakes. She wasn't stupid enough to come to a complete stop. Pure physics foretold that impossibility, but she could use the bulletproof windows to her advantage, to turn the car around and head away from the town. She thought she'd seen a road sign pointing to Minneapolis.

The car behind her pulled up to the side and tried to shove her off the road. The Lexus had slowed, closer to sixty now. She hit the brakes, tires screaming. The car continued in front of her for several seconds. Emma used it to her advantage, turning the wheel hard when she thought she was slow enough, then hitting the emergency brake and swinging the car around in a 180-degree turn. She released the brake and stomped the gas heading for the highway to Minneapolis. It didn't take long for the headlights of the other car to appear in her mirror.

****

Will's phone vibrated in his shirt pocket. A quick glance told him it was James.

"We've got trouble."

"What?" His heart lodged in his throat.

"My police scanner is screaming with an explosion at the Oak Tree Lodge and multiple gunshots."

"Fuck!"

"Now there's reports of a high-speed chase near the town."

"She got a car."

"What?"

"She got a car. She can drive like a bat out hell. Somehow she got a car. At least she has a fighting chance now."

"Not if the police catch her first."

"You've never seen her drive."

****

Emma couldn't believe the police hadn't made an appearance yet. But now that she was on a state highway, the highway patrol couldn't be far behind. She had to lose the other car and hide.

Think, Emma. Think.

She was on a four-lane divided highway, but she knew there were smaller roads opening onto the highway. A side road not too close to town seemed like a good plan.

Her high beams revealed an intersection ahead. The crossroad to the right was lined with houses. The left disappeared into woods. But it meant crossing to the other side of the highway and the car behind her was trying to pass her to the left.

Emma straddled the center line, swerving back and forth to keep the car behind her. At the last possible moment, she turned, shooting for the intersection at an angle rather than a curve, praying she didn't flip the car. The other car slammed into her back bumper, adding to her momentum. She held the steering wheel as the car swerved sideways.

"Shit!" Her car barreled off the road into the ditch. Her head pitched to the side, smacking the side window, filling her vision with a white light.

She shook her head to clear it. "Oh, fuck no." Clinging to the steering wheel, she gave the car enough gas to climb out of the ditch. She whipped her head around, pain shooting through her temple as she looked for the other vehicle. It lay flipped on its side in the median, leaving part of a street sign in its path.

Sirens blared in the distance.

Where could she hide?

The houses on the other side.

She spun around and crossed the lanes to the other side of the road, forcing herself to drive the speed limit. Houses lined the street for a half-mile until she saw a car repair shop on the right. She cut the headlights and slipped between two cars parked in the lot. The sirens in distance grew louder. Emma saw flashing red lights heading down the road in her direction.

She killed the engine and ducked onto the front seat, ignoring the instinct to run, but she knew she had little chance of escaping the police, especially the highway patrol. Her best hope now was to hide and wait them out. It was three-forty-five. At least she had a few hours before the mechanics showed up and found her.

****

Will answered his phone on the first ring.

"Three crashed cars but no woman. Just six men. They know there was another car involved from skid marks and ruts on the side of the highway, but they don't know what kind of car nor where it is."

"She got away."

"For now."

"Where the hell is she?"

****

To her irritation, she dozed off. She'd tried to stay awake, but her pounding head and perpetual exhaustion won out.

There was no use denying the source of the exhaustion anymore.

She watched the sun as it rose over the horizon, wondering where to go. Out of Minnesota, Raphael had said. Only one thing held her back.

Will.

But she had no idea where Will was. She didn't even have his fucking phone number. Maybe Raphael was right. Maybe she didn't need him. But that wasn't exactly true, either. Raphael said she needed Will to gain her powers, whatever the hell those were. She only needed him until they developed.

If she didn't have the baby.

If she didn't have the baby, an option she never even considered when she was pregnant with Jake, a child conceived in the most vile of circumstances. How could she consider terminating this baby conceived with Will?

Will. How the hell did she feel about him, anyway? There was no denying her draw to him, the deep connection she felt when she admitted it. But it scared the hell out of her, completely trusting and committing to someone. That had never worked out for her before. And if she were honest with herself, the physical pull to Raphael was stronger.

I'm just like my mother.

But she had to wonder about the source of her attraction to Raphael. There had to be more to it than just physical attraction. It was as if he held some power over her.

Out of nowhere, nausea and fear overwhelmed her. She fumbled with the door handle, barely getting the door open before she vomited onto the parking lot.

They're back. Son of a fucking bitch.

She had three options. One, sit here and see if they showed up. Not happening. Two, drive out of here, possibly getting into another car chase. Not the best the idea with the likelihood of police still looking for her. Three, get out and run.

Goddamn. And I just got a bulletproof car.

Maybe she could come back and get it. The thought cheered her up as she checked to make sure her gun was loaded. Climbing out of the car, she dropped the car keys in her backpack and slung it over her shoulder. She crept along the side of the building looking for signs of trouble. She wondered if she had overreacted, if maybe her nausea had been morning sickness. But then she doubled over again, heaving the remaining contents of her stomach onto the dewy grass.

They were coming.

She knew it was going to be ugly. The number of men and cars increased after each failed attempt. They sent three cars hours ago. God only knew what they'd send this time. As long as she was still heaving, she knew they weren't there yet.

She wasn't sure which to wish for.

Raphael's damned theory was wrong.

She was pissed, irrationally angry, but she welcomed the anger like a long-lost friend. She'd rather be angry than scared. Emma Thompson was done being scared and she was done being the pawn of men. She racked the slide of the gun.

"Bring it, you fucking assholes."

Emma sprinted to the woods, knowing they would find her. But at least she'd have the element of surprise on her side.

****

Will had driven back to Minnesota for the pure reason of not knowing where else to go, speeding on the flat stretches of North Dakota. He hoped he could find Emma's trail and follow her to wherever she ended up. He realized on the long drive back that she didn't even have his cell phone number. He had never considered that she might need it.

What a fucking idiot.

As he drove up to the edge of the town, evidence of the early morning's activities lined the highway. Emma sure knew how to make an entrance. Or an exit.

He was exhausted but adrenaline and fear spurred him on. His arm tingled as he prepared to turn onto the two-way highway leading to James's cabin.

Emma.

He concentrated on her, locating her easier than last time. Was it because he had more practice or because she was closer? Excitement filled him at the thought of the latter. But if his arm tingled, it meant she was in danger.

How in the hell was he going to find her?

****

Emma ran deeper into the woods, surprised and disappointed she hadn't yet ended up in someone's back yard. The trees had grown more dense. She fought to push her way through the thick brush that slowed her down. She was leaving them a blazing trail to her location, but she saw no other option. If she had her bearings right, the highway should be straight ahead of her. Once she found it, she could make a run for it.

She stopped to vomit again, a violent episode that brought dry heaves. At least she knew they weren't close enough to kill her yet.

There was a cheerful thought.

Goddamn you, Will! You're supposed to be here! She screamed in her head, pushing the thoughts toward him without even thinking. A sob of fear rose in the back of her throat and she forced her anger to rise and override it. She'd be damned if she cried because of them.

Emma? Will's voice in her head caught her off guard.

He'd heard her. Like in South Dakota with Alex. Will heard her. *Where the fuck are you? You're supposed to be here and now I'm in the woods alone preparing to fight off a bunch of fucking gunmen.*

She felt his fear and guilt. *I'm outside of town. Where are you?* If he tried to hide his own panic from her, he did a piss-poor job.

I'd send you my GPS coordinates if I'd remembered to bring one with me. She knew she was being a bitch, but it was all she had to cling to. If she let down her wall of anger, she'd be overcome with terror. But she felt a crack in the barrier anyway.

Jake. Think of Jake. She told herself. Jake needed her to be strong and get out of this.

Yes, think of Jake. Yell and scream at me, just keep talking. I can feel you getting closer.

Will was coming. She should have been reassured but the wall cracked more, fear spilling in a steady stream now.

The brush snapped behind her. *Oh, God.*

No! Don't be scared! You're strong! You can do this Emma. If they're catching up to you, find somewhere to hide, but don't give up. I'm coming.

Emma hid, pressing her back behind a thick tree trunk. Sucking deep breathes in through her mouth, she leaned her head back, bark digging into her scalp. She looked up through the swaying leaves, the filtered light dancing before her eyes. The crackling grew closer.

Emma. What's going on? The panic in his voice was far from reassuring.

Shut up! I'm trying to listen. She closed her eyes and concentrated, trying to determine the direction of the sound. Birds flew screaming into the air and crunching grew louder. To her left, to her right. She was surrounded except for the woods in front of her, and if she gauged right, and the highway somewhere off in the distance. But from here, with gunmen approaching, it seemed too far, out of reach. Her breath came in short pants and she willed herself to calm down. *I have a gun.* The metal handle in her palm gave her momentary comfort until she realized how hopelessly outnumbered she probably was. She didn't have enough bullets.

She peered her head around the trunk just enough to get a glimpse of advancing figures.

Hold on, Emma! Stay hidden. I'm coming!

She shook her head. They would be upon her in seconds. Will wouldn't reach her in time. Her hands trembled and the gun in her hand shook. *If I don't get control I won't be able to shoot even one of them.* Where the hell was her anger? These men took her son and were now intent on killing her to keep them apart. The pendant on her neck grew hot on her skin.

Emma?

She heard the confusion in his voice, but she was past the point of answering. She stepped from behind the tree, the gun still in her hand, yet she knew that she didn't need it. It fell to the ground with a thud.

Emma!

Her chest burned and electricity rose until she thought she would pass out from the pain and pressure. When she saw the first man raise his gun, she held out her hands and released all the power she had. A glowing ball of energy shot forward, exploding in the trees twenty feet ahead. The force threw her onto the ground. She slammed hard on her side, her face pressed against pine needles. Blackness hovered at the edge of consciousness.

No! Emma! You can't pass out! I'm almost there. Get up. Run!

She didn't think she had the strength.

Emma, don't you dare give up on Jake. He needs you. Get the fuck up, Emma!

She crawled to her knees, her lungs burning from the black smoke that filled them. The forest was on fire, the canopy over head glowing with flames.

Yes! Get up! You can do it!

She gagged, her head hanging between her arms. *I'm too tired.*

She felt his fear and then his anger. *Don't be such a goddamned baby, Emma! Get up! Do I always have to do everything for you? God, you're a grown woman. When are you going to learn to take care of yourself?*

She had a vague memory of him saying something similar after she thought Jake died. His words stoked her anger. Who the hell did he think he was? She stood and staggered toward the direction of the highway, away from the fire. *I never asked you to take care of me, you fucking asshole! Who the hell do you think you are deciding to just leave me with that prick?*

Who knew you'd need an army to babysit you? What in the hell were you thinking, running off?

She walked another twenty feet before she stopped, grabbing a tree to hold herself up. The fire had become unbearably hot, burning her exposed flesh. It was gaining on her. *Did it ever cross your mind to tell me before you left?* She hung her head over, coughing out the smoke that invaded her lungs.

Why are you stopping? You expect me to come in there and save you again? Do I always have to save you from everything?

Dizziness caused her to stumble. She pulled the front of her dress up over her mouth and nose, hoping to block out some the fumes, but her vision grew fuzzy.

Sunlight burst through the trees ahead. She was so close. *Save me? SAVE ME? Here's a newsflash for you, Will. I'm fucking saving myself!* She continued forward another fifteen feet, the edge still so far, before she tripped and collapsed onto the ground.

It couldn't end this way.

Strong arms scooped her off the ground. For one horrifying moment, she was scared to see who had her. She looked up into Will's blackened face and released a cry of relief.

"You did, Princess. You saved yourself."

She slumped against his chest as she gave into the darkness.

CHAPTER FOURTEEN

WILL picked Emma off the forest floor, barely recognizing her soot-covered face, her eyes wide until she looked up at him. She collapsed into his chest, her body growing limp. He carried her to his car parked on the highway shoulder and shoved the car door open. Placing her in the front seat, he stripped off the backpack that still hung over her shoulder, tossing it into the backseat. When she didn't stir from the movement, he gripped her wrist, taking a deep breath before he checked for a pulse. Her vein thrummed faintly into his thumb, her breathing shallow. He grabbed a bottle of water and poured it onto a t-shirt from his bag, trying to wash the black soot off her face. His hands shook as he swiped, only smearing it and making it worse.

He cast a glance to the inferno racing to the forest edge, still in disbelief that she'd created it. Good God, what had she done? She was lucky she made it out alive.

What if I hadn't reached her in time?

Sirens shrieked in the distance and he knew he needed to get away, yet unsure where to go. If these people, whichever group they were, could find her here, James's house wasn't safe. And neither was James.

He started the car, heading to the cabin as he called James. "I found her."

"Amazing. Where?"

"You'll never believe me. I'm almost to your house. If they found her here, you're not safe. You need to come with us."

"You're only saying that because you need me."

"That, too."

James swore. "I've got a life, you know. Clients. I'm supposed to just walk away from that over a—"

"Only for a few days, maybe a week. Just until they've realized she moved on."

James sighed. "Fine, I'll start throwing things together."

"Thanks, man. I owe you."

"You have no idea."

Highway patrol cars flew past Will from the opposite direction. He stopped on the shoulder and watched them zoom toward the town he'd left behind. Casting a quick glance to Emma, he pulled back onto the road. Her head slumped to the side, her breathing still shallow. She hadn't come to and it scared the shit out of him. If it was smoke inhalation, she needed a hospital, but if it was from whatever happened in the forest…

He wasn't sure what she'd done, but the energy that saturated his mind through their mental connection had almost fried his brain. If he hadn't pulled back in time, they'd probably both be dead.

When she healed him, she had glowed, a bright yellow light emitting from her body like an aura. Energy had burst from her hand into his body. It had to take a massive amount of power to create the firestorm in the woods. And it came from inside her. No wonder she'd been too tired to walk. She probably had nothing left.

She needed food and he wondered when she'd eaten last. He'd know if he hadn't left her. Brushing a blackened strand of hair off her forehead, his fingers trailed down her cheek.

She stirred as his hand left her face.

After Emma healed him, she told him her headache went away with his touch. Had she said that to make him feel better or had it really happened?

He turned down James's gravel road and slammed to halt in front of the house. Unbuckling their seat belts, he pulled her over onto his lap. Her head leaned against his chest, her legs draped over the center console. He tilted back her head and cupped her cheek.

"Emma, you're safe. I need you to wake up."

She moaned as her eyelids twitched.

It was working.

"Come on, darlin'. I need you to wake up. I need you." He pressed his lips into her forehead, tasting smoke and perspiration. His eyes sank closed and he pulled her closer, his hand trailing down to her neck and resting on her chest. He needed her more than he'd ever needed anything in his life.

"There you go again, always trying to feel me up," she murmured, her voice raspy.

He lifted his head to look into her eyes. "Thank God," he exhaled.

"About time you showed up," she said before she coughed, leaning forward to catch her breath.

"Well, you know, better late than never."

He held her against his chest, his arms wrapped tight around her, needing to feel her warmth an affirmation that she was alive.

Her body wracked with coughing. He pushed the door open and carried her out of the car to get fresh air into her lungs.

"Will, put me down. I can walk."

He considered protesting but dropped her legs. Her body slid down the front of his until her feet touched the ground, yet he couldn't bring himself to let go of her.

"This scene might be a bit more touching if you two didn't look like you'd been rolling around in charcoal." James said from the porch. "What the fuck happened?"

"There was a fire."

"No shit. The police scanner is lit up with it. I suppose you had something to do with it."

"Trust me," Will said, leading Emma to the porch. "You don't want to know."

James raised his eyebrows.

"Why are we here?" Emma stopped at the bottom of the steps before breaking out into another round of coughing. "I'm not staying here with him."

Will tightened his arm around her waist. "Emma, we're not staying here. We're going to take a shower and leave."

She conceded, allowing him to usher her into the house, past James. Will shot him a glare, warning him to keep his mouth shut. James shook his head and chuckled.

Will took her into the bathroom and had her sit on the side of the bathtub. The short walk zapped what little strength she had and her body swayed until she leaned her head against the tile wall.

"Emma?"

"I'm so tired," she mumbled.

She needed food. He ran into the kitchen and made a sandwich and returned to the bathroom to find her slumped against the wall.

"Emma, I brought you a sandwich. You need to eat, okay? Just a little bit," he said, raising it to her mouth.

To his relief, she grabbed it and took several bites and seemed to regain some strength.

"You eat the rest while I go pack our stuff, okay?" He stood and watched her, waiting for her reaction.

She gave him a small smile. "Go. I'm fine. You're just across the hall."

He gave her a long look before he walked out and shut the door.

****

Emma still couldn't believe Will had found her. How had he done it? As much as she hated to admit it, she'd be dead if he hadn't shown up when he did.

Thinking about what she'd done turned the lumps of sandwich in her stomach to stones. Had she killed those men? She had no choice, not that she even understood what she'd done. Where had that come from?

The pendant.

She stood up and stared in the mirror, hardly recognizing herself. Her face was almost completely black, spots smeared where Will had rubbed against her. Her clothes were covered in soot. She smelled like a bonfire. But the pendant glowed a fiery reddish-orange against her chest. She wondered how Will had recognized her in the forest, but she suspected there weren't many women running for their lives in the woods. Her heart lurched. Maybe there were. What if she'd hurt other people by what she had done?

Raphael had told her she'd gain other powers. Who knew it would include throwing massive fireballs? That wasn't true, either. A glowing orb came out of her, not flames. She looked down at her hands, turning her palms over in amazement. How could her hands cause so much destruction? She turned on the faucet, wringing them in the water. Raising her gaze to the mirror, she stared into the face of a woman she didn't recognize. Evidence of her crime covered her body, the river of tears streaming down her cheeks a poor penance for her deeds.

Her power was a harbinger of death.

The room closed in and the smell of smoke and grime made her gag. She turned on the water and stripped off her clothes, tossing them into the trash can. Stepping under the scalding water, she sobbed as the water washed away the soot but not her guilt. Then Will's arms were around her, holding her naked body to his, his lips finding her face, chasing away the demons that haunted her.

How could she have considered leaving him?

Her hands reached for his cheeks, pulling his mouth to hers, desperate. Why was she always so desperate for him? Shouldn't that tell her how much she needed him?

He responded to her demands, with an urgency of his own. She knew he'd been terrified of losing her. She felt it through their connection in the woods. She'd just never realized how strongly he felt.

It eased her conscience as her body persuaded his to give her what she needed. She selfishly needed him, reassuring her of his love even when she couldn't give it to him in return. This had to be enough. It was all she was capable of giving.

Her fingers entwined in his hair and he lifted her up. She wrapped her legs around his waist, her back against the cold tile wall. She didn't care; she couldn't wait. She needed him now.

She opened her eyes to see his piercing her own as he entered her, fierce and possessive.

"Will." She dug her fingers into his back as she held on.

Her cry caused his own guttural response, bruising her shoulder blades against the wall from the assault. She clung to him until they came together in a knot of limbs and tongues. As she spiraled down to reality, she found herself holding onto him by his hair.

She watched for his reaction.

Tenderness.

He grabbed her face in his hands and kissed her lightly, a sharp contradiction to the frenzy they just experienced. He pulled back, looking into her eyes, the love so evident it drenched her. He pulled her head to his chest, his arms wrapped tightly around her back as the water pelted their bodies.

"Don't ever scare me like that again," he said.

She tilted her head to look up at him and smiled. "I'll try not to."

They finished in the shower and dressed. Will grabbed their bag and carried it outside where James waited in the swing, his foot resting on the porch rail.

"I would've loaded the car, but you never said which one we were going to take, yours or my truck."

"*We*?" Emma asked.

Will's brow furrowed. "James isn't safe here right now. If they know we're this close, they might make the connection and find him. Besides, he can help."

He was right but she refused to acknowledge it so she fumed in silence.

"We still didn't answer the 'yours or mine' question," James said.

"Neither," Emma said. "I have a car we can use."

Both men turned to her, eyes wide.

"Trust me, we want it. It's a bulletproof Lexus. We just have to get it."

James turned to Will, his mouth sagging. "Do I *want* to know where she got a bulletproof Lexus?"

"She's always been resourceful." Will mumbled as he walked down the steps.

She could see he was curious himself but refrained from asking. She'd have to tell him at some point, but she'd put it off as long as possible.

"Come on, we'll take the Camaro and ditch it where the Lexus is parked, if we can recover it."

Emma gave him directions to the repair shop and the three rode in silence. When they passed the still-burning forest, James's eyes fixed on the scene, casting a quick glance at Emma before turning back. But Emma had seen the emotion behind his eyes and her blood slowed in her veins.

Fear.

She tried to avert her gaze from the flashing red lights of the emergency vehicles lining the highway. The pendant warmed her chest while her horror chilled her blood.

She had caused this.

The Lexus was still in the lot, undisturbed. Will decided that the least suspicious move would be to go inside and tell them that the Camaro needed work. He also hoped to get information about the fire.

James and Emma got out of the car as Will started for the door. He stopped and grabbed Emma's arm. "Maybe you should come inside with me." His jaw locked as his eyes darted around the lot.

She reached up on tiptoes and kissed him lightly. "I'm okay. Just hurry up and let's get out of here."

He nodded and disappeared inside.

Emma smoldered as she watched James heft a bag out of the trunk. Just the thought of being around him indefinitely turned her stomach.

James saw her glare and lifted his mouth into a snide grin. "I'm not any more excited about this than you are." He turned his gaze to the road. "You're a helluva lot of trouble and I'm not even getting laid for the effort."

"*Excuse me?*"

His eyes pierced hers, full of hatred. "You're fucking up his life and I intend to do everything to get him out of your train wreck."

Will walked out of the building and she bit back the response on her tongue.

Will looked around again. "We're set. Let's go."

Emma climbed into the backseat and Will stood outside, confused. "What are you doing? James can sit in the back."

"I'm tired, so I'll sit back here and nap. You and James can sit in front." She cringed at the thought of James behind her, sharpening the blade he planned to stab into her back.

Will tossed the keys to James. "You drive, I'll sit in the back with Emma." He climbed into the back and wrapped his arm around Emma's back, pulling her head to his chest.

James shook his head and pulled onto the highway, past the billowing smoke that rolled from the trees. "We're going to South Dakota, I presume."

"Yep." Will looked into the forest. "The mechanic said they haven't figured out the source of the fire. They think it was some kind of explosion, but they don't have any clue what caused it. He said they'd already found the bodies of six armed men, although the fire's still burning so I suspect they'll probably find more. The dead bodies aren't public information yet. He got it from a friend of a friend."

Breath stuck in Emma's throat. She'd killed six men and probably more. *That planned to kill you.* She reminded herself but it didn't make her feel any better. How many men had she killed? Was she so callous she'd lost count?

"They must be getting desperate to send men in broad daylight so close to town." Will said under his breath. "They're sure it's connected to the gunshots and high-speed chase early this morning."

"Shit." James murmured, shaking his head. "What the fuck has this girl done?"

"It's more like what she's capable of doing. I have a feeling they now know she's more than they expected."

"Hey, I'm right here!" Emma protested, but she trembled with the thought that Warren or the Cavallo knew about her now. They'd hunt her down even more aggressively.

Will tightened his grip around her waist and kissed the top of her head. "It's okay. You're safe."

For now was unspoken, yet understood. The movement of the car was already lulling Emma to sleep when Will whispered in her ear. "We have a few things to talk about. First is how you made that explosion."

She nodded against his chest, not surprised. Unfortunately, Raphael would be part of the discussion.

CHAPTER FIFTEEN

WILL dozed off for a few hours and woke with Emma's head against his side, her hair plastered to her forehead. He shifted slightly and glanced out the window, a North Dakota road sign catching his eye. Now they just had to get to the other side of the state, then down to South Dakota.

James looked over his shoulder. "You should sleep more. You didn't sleep at all last night and let's not forget the minor fact you had busted ribs and a collapsed lung less than forty-eight hours ago."

"I'm healed from the injuries and you and I both know I used to get a lot less sleep on a regular basis. You were there."

"Well, we're not getting any younger, buddy."

"Yeah…" Will shifted his leg at the thought, careful not to disturb Emma.

James cleared his throat. "Will, how long have we been friends now? Twenty-five years? Remember when Johnny Morehead stole your lunch money in the second grade and I came to your rescue?"

Will grinned. "I seem to remember it the other way around."

"What does it matter who defended whom? The point is we've had each other's backs since we were kids. Hell, your dad even pulled strings to get us in the same unit in Iraq."

Will shifted his weight again. He could already see he wouldn't like where this conversation was headed. "Your point?"

"My point is, I've always stood by you. I've had your back even after that fucking mess with the Iraqi school and your court-martial. I backed you up, dude. All the way. But I don't know about this one."

Will's chest burned. "What are you saying, Buckner? You want out? Just say the word and all we have to do is drop you off at the nearest town. You can run back to your hideaway, because we both know what that little fishing spot really is. Your attempt to hide from the world."

"Will..." James tone softened. "It's not a matter of me being in or out. I'm saying, how long have you known this woman? What do you really know about her? If someone like Senator Warren wants her, maybe you should think about turning her over."

Will saw black spots. "Stop the car."

"Will...."

"Stop the fucking car," he growled.

"No. I'm not stopping the car. We're having this discussion whether you like it or not. In fact, unless you want your girlfriend to be part of it, I suggest you calm down or you're going to wake her up. Now answer the question. How well do you really know her?"

"I know her well enough to know I love her."

"That's not an answer."

"What the fuck do you want me to say?"

"What's her favorite color? What's her favorite movie? What kind of books does she read? Does she like anchovies on her pizza?"

Will inhaled, trying to gain control of his temper. He didn't know the answer to any of those and he knew what James' reaction would be.

"See?" James said. "You're throwing your life away for a woman you know nothing about. What about our plan, Will?"

Will shook his head in frustration. "It was your plan, James, never mine, so let's not kid each other, okay? Maybe I don't consider it throwing my life away."

"What *do* you know about her?"

"I know she grew up in Joplin, with a drunk, no-good mother who blamed all her problems on Emma. Her father disappeared while her mother was pregnant and Emma didn't even know his name until a couple of days ago. I know her grandmother is awesome and seeing her gave me a little bit of insight to who Emma will be in fifty years."

His voice softened. "I know she's a loving mother who got pregnant after she was raped then threw her life and her dreams away to keep him safe when he was two and people started chasing her. I know she's strong and resilient and she doesn't trust easily. Hell, who could blame her? Everyone's always treated her like shit. But when she does trust, she'll be loyal to the end."

James cleared his throat. "She has a kid?"

Will ground his teeth. "You heard that entire list and that's what you latch onto?"

"You want to be saddled with a kid? Seriously? Where is he now?"

"He was kidnapped. By the men who were after Emma last night, at least I'm guessing it's them. They seemed to be able to find her anywhere, even in a deserted cabin in the Colorado mountains. Or it could have been Warren's men who spurred the car chase. At least they want her alive. When she wakes up I'll ask her if they seemed intent on capturing or killing her."

"Kidnapped? You believe that?"

"Damn it, James. I saw it happen. I was there."

"Let me guess, she's convinced you to help her find her kid."

"She didn't have to convince me of anything. I volunteered."

James burst out laughing. Emma stirred, but her breath remained slow and steady. Will placed a hand on her leg.

"That's rich, Will. Rich. Although I'm not surprised. You always had a thing for underdogs."

"What the fuck are you saying?"

"I'm saying you find this woman whose son has been kidnapped. She's got two groups of men after her and she needs help. You can't resist. Your hero complex makes you want to save the innocent and downtrodden. *Of course*, you want to help her."

Will released a derisive laugh. "You sure as hell haven't known me the last three years. That's not me at all. Not anymore."

"Maybe I would if you'd come around. Or let me come see you. You shut everyone and everything out since your court-martial. Yeah, forty kids died in the fire and you were held responsible, but you caught a high-level terrorist. Doesn't that count for something? Haven't you beaten yourself up enough?"

No amount of atoning would make up for the deaths of those children. It pissed him off to think about it. He'd thought about it more the last few weeks than he had in the three years since the trial. "Again, what's your point?"

"So you've been an ass for the last three years, you're entitled, but don't pick this woman to suddenly turn your life around. She's trouble, Will. I'm telling you. I feel it in my gut."

Will turned and looked out the window. He couldn't tell James about the mark on his arm or the fact the mark made it impossible for him to not do what she asked. And there was no way he could tell him about the baby. He'd just try to convince Will that it was a scheme to trap him.

Will had known she was trouble from the moment he climbed in her car. It wasn't hard to figure out when she drove like a crazed woman in her beat-up Honda, outmaneuvering the SUV chasing her. But when she told him she learned to drive on a racetrack then smiled, he fell. He could admit it now, even if he couldn't before. The truth was he was attracted to her before Jake burned the mark on his arm. He admired her devotion to her son before the first time he felt the nearly irrational urge to protect her. James could mock him all he wanted, but he knew where his destiny lay—it was here sleeping next to him.

****

Emma forced her breathing to remain steady. She didn't want Will to know she was eavesdropping after she woke up and heard them talking about Jake. She felt vile deceiving him, but she needed to know how James really felt.

How Will really felt.

Will has a thing for underdogs. She supposed that was her, an underdog. You couldn't get much more underdog than her situation. Even she couldn't see a way out, yet Will remained obstinate.

The mark. Sometimes she cursed Jake for branding that mark on Will's arm. It bound him to her; he had no choice but to protect her. Was that the source for his love for her? Was nothing in her life real?

She sat up with a jerk, the car too confined, her life too confined. Her chest tightened and she found it difficult to breathe.

"Emma?" Will asked, startled.

"I need to get out."

"What?"

"I need to get out of the car! James! Stop! Pull over!"

Will's eyes widened in alarm. "Are you sick? Are they coming?"

"*Are they coming?*" James yelled over his shoulder as he hit the brakes. "What the hell are you talking about?"

"No." Her breath came in short bursts as she struggled to gain control. "I just have to get out."

The car stopped on the shoulder. She jumped out the door and stood next to the grass, gulping deep breaths of air. Her eyes stung with tears. She was done with crying, yet her eyes protested otherwise. The pendant on her neck grew warmer.

"Emma, what happened? What's going on?" Will had gotten out of the car and stood beside her. He tried to grab her arm, but she jerked away. His eyes widened in surprise.

"I heard you!"

His face paled. "Heard what?"

"I heard you and James. Talking about me. Is that what I am to you, Will? A way to ease your conscience? A way to appease your need to help the underdog?"

Will grabbed his head and looked up into the nearly cloudless sky. "Son of a fucking bitch!" He lowered his face, which now seethed with rage. "I'm going to beat the shit out of James. NO! That is not why! What did you hear?"

"What happened with a school and forty kids?"

His face lost all expression. "It happened years ago. It's not important."

"It's obviously important if you still feel like you have to make up for it."

"James doesn't' know what the fuck he's talking about! *Goddamn it*!"

She pointed to his arm. "It's that mark! It's the mark on your arm!" She shook her head, sobbing in anguish. "I thought you really loved me, but it's the mark."

"No, Emma." He took her in his arms. "My love for you isn't from the mark."

She tried to shrug him off, but he held her tight in his arms. "I thought you loved me. I believed you."

"Oh God, Emma. I do. I swear to God I do. The mark makes me want to protect you, not make me love you."

"How do you know? How can I believe you?" she shouted.

He lifted her chin to look up at him. "Because I started falling in love with you before Jake ever burned me and said I was the Chosen One. Remember the night in the cornfield?"

She nodded, watching his face through blurry eyes.

He cupped her cheek. "God, you were so beautiful in the moonlight with your hair hanging down. You always had it pulled back, but that night it was down, blowing in the breeze. You'd just driven like a stunt car driver getting us off that highway and crashing the SUV. But when you cleaned my forehead, the way you looked at me. You were so open, so unguarded. It made me want you. It was more than lust. I knew it and it scared the shit out of me. I had to sit on my hands to keep from touching you."

She bit her lip. Was he lying?

"Remember the next morning when you were crying? I almost kissed you."

"You laughed at me and called me predictable."

"I knew if I kissed you I'd be lost forever. I was scared and stupid. Emma, I'm trying to prove that I love you in spite of the mark."

James leaned his head out the passenger window. "This is touching and all, but can we get out of here already?"

Dropping his arm from Emma's waist, Will lunged for the door handle.

"Will, no!" Emma shouted.

He grabbed James' shirt and jerked him out of the car, onto the shoulder. James landed on his ass, his eyes wide in shock.

"Will!" Emma lunged for him.

He pulled James up, reaching back his fist.

Emma grabbed his arm with both hands. "Will, I order you to stop."

His arm froze, then he lowered it and shoved James against the car.

James stumbled. "What the fuck are you doing, Will?"

"I was planning to beat the shit out of you." Will spit through gritted teeth.

Emma forced her body between them. "Stop! Both of you stop! If you get into a fistfight on the side of the highway, you're both going to get arrested. Then what's going to happen? Let's just get back in the car and figure this out."

The men glared at each other and remained where they stood.

"He's not going with us," Will grunted.

"Do you need him?"

He turned away from James and walked toward the front of the car.

"*Do you need him*? You said you needed him. Tell me the truth."

"Yes," he snarled.

"James, get your ass in the car."

James mouth dropped open and he turned to her in disbelief. "*What*?"

"I said get your ass in the car. Will, you too. Let's go. I'm driving."

Unbelievably, they both got in—Will in the front seat and James in the back.

She slid in the driver's seat and took a deep breath. This was going to be a long drive.

It was her fault. The entire situation was her fault. She should have kept a check on her emotions, but after the car chase, and the gunmen and the fire… then in the shower with Will. For the first time she had believed there could really be a *them*, believed his feelings for her were real. She *felt* them when they were connected in the woods. But the conversation she overheard suggested otherwise and she'd lost control.

Stupid. Stupid. Stupid.

There was no love lost with James, but he'd been Will's friend for years. She couldn't get in the way of their friendship. She'd tolerate him even if it killed her.

Without warning, longing for Jake washed through her, taking her breath with it. Will's speech dredged up her last memories of him and she tried to remember the smell of Jake's head the morning after Will almost kissed her. Baby shampoo and sweat. But it was fading into the fuzzy corners of her memories. She'd already lost him. She couldn't lose those, too.

She called out to him, reaching out in her despair. She felt him, as always, could sense his presence. She briefly wondered if it was like that for Will when he reached out to her.

It was enough to feel him and know he was there, even if he didn't talk to her. She basked in his essence, imagining that she held him in her lap, stroking his hair. Two nights ago, she had dreamed he slept with her, cradling her from behind. Now, she could almost feel him taking hold of her hand.

She forced herself to concentrate on the road, still maintaining the hold on Jake's hand. She cast a quick glance to Will, who glared out the side window, still too angry to talk to her or James.

****

Jake stood in the backyard next to a playground. Mountains grew out of the ground in the distance like giants. Sometime he imagined them ripping themselves from the ground and coming to save him. But they never did. They only stood like stiff old men.

Alex had told the men that Jake was a little boy and needed to play outside, but Jake wasn't interested in playing on the jungle gym right now.

His mommy was there.

Jake climbed to the top of the slide, and sat in the shade at the top, his back against the warm plastic. He liked to play in here, so the men watching wouldn't think anything of him sitting up here awhile.

The men were still scared of him.

The truth was he could kill them all in seconds. He knew this from Hernandez, but *he* insisted Jake stay. So he did. But he was tired of waiting. Tired of following the rules. He'd followed the rules for days and days and days and where had it got him?

He wanted his mother.

Now she reached out to him, more insistent this time. *Touching him.* He sat in the shade, feeling her body next to his, sitting on her lap, feeling her hand on his head as her fingers brushed his curls. He closed his eyes, the tears flowing down his cheeks. He missed her so much.

He worried she would forget him, love the baby more. But she was here now. *Holding his hand.* He laced his fingers in hers and squeezed. She squeezed him back.

She had given up talking to him long ago, but now she spoke, her words a whisper in his ear, his hair tickling his neck from her breath.

I love you, Jake. I love you so much. I'm coming for you. Will is coming for you. Don't give up on me. Please. But I need to know that you hear me. That you still love me.

He had said Jake couldn't talk to her, couldn't communicate in any way. If he knew Jake held her hand right now, he would be angry. But he wouldn't know. Jake wouldn't tell him.

In an act of defiance and love, Jake picked up his mother's hand in his mind and with his real finger, he traced the sign they used to use when he was little. He traced a heart in the palm of her hand. He kissed it, then broke contact before he burst into tears.

CHAPTER SIXTEEN

WILL fumed in the seat next to Emma. He'd suspected he had to take her orders—the prophecy told him so—but on the side of the highway he knew it with all certainty. When she ordered him to stop, his body followed her will, not his own.

And if that didn't chap his ass, he didn't know what did.

If anything, it amazed him that James followed her orders to get in the car. If he hadn't been so pissed, the look on James' face would have been hilarious.

Emma drove in silence, wiping tears off her cheeks with the back of her hand. Who could blame her for crying? She'd been through hell in the last twenty-four hours. He needed to know what that hell was.

He reached over and picked up her hand resting on the console between them, encouraged when she let him lace her fingers through his.

"Emma, I'm sorry." He murmured quietly.

She kept her eyes on the road. Pressing her lips together, she gave him a small nod.

So far, so good. "We need to talk about what happened last night and this morning. Why you left James."

Her fingers tensed and his grip tightened in case she tried to pull away.

She looked over her shoulder and shook her head.

Will looked back at James, who raised his eyebrows with a cocky smile. "Don't mind me. I'm curious myself."

"We could always put him in the trunk," Will said with a smirk.

"Don't tempt me."

"I believe that falls outside the terms of Treatment of Prisoners of War in the Geneva Convention." James crossed his arms across his chest and leaned back. "Comfy seats, by the way. Why don't you start with telling us how you stumbled upon a bulletproof luxury sedan."

Will's mark tingled, which meant she was frightened or in pain. What was she frightened of?

"How about we start at the beginning," Will suggested. It might be better to ease her into it. But that didn't help either. The tingling continued.

"I don't have to tell that asshole anything." Emma narrowed her eyes and refused to look at Will. "He's the reason I left in the first place, not that I wasn't good and pissed finding out you dumped me there." She shot him a furious look. "What the hell were you thinking, leaving without telling me?"

Will almost regretted starting the conversation. He didn't want to get his ass chewed in front of James. "I thought it would be easier for both of us. I knew you'd want to come and it wouldn't be safe. But I couldn't bear to tell you no, so I left while you were sleeping. It was stupid."

"Damn right it was! Don't you ever do that again."

Fuck, that was an order. He felt it to his marrow. "Now I can't. You just *ordered* me not to."

"You mean you won't."

"I mean I *can't.*"

She turned to him, wide-eyed.

He decided to change the subject before she thought of other things to order him to do. "So what did James do to piss you off enough to make you leave?"

"He insulted my intelligence and ordered me to cook him dinner."

James laughed. "I'm sure chefs worldwide are offended that you found my comment insulting."

"Really? I don't recall you ordering coq au vin."

Will shook his head. "So you left?"

"I had no idea how long you were going to be gone and I was pissed. There was no way I was going to spend days with *him.*" She tilted her head toward the back seat.

"Where were you going?"

She looked contrite, her eyes darting to him before looking back at the road. "The bus stop."

His hand stiffened, but she didn't pull away. Had she really planned to leave him? "Where were you going?" *South Dakota. Please say South Dakota.*

She scrunched her mouth on one side. "I hadn't figured it out yet, I planned to go find Jake. But..." she turned to look at him. "I was mad and wasn't thinking straight. In the end, I couldn't leave you. So I decided to go back, especially after Raphael was certain you'd be home by morning." She stopped and cringed.

"Raphael? Who is *Raphael?*" His tone was quiet but direct, and there was no denying that she noticed.

She shook her head, looking annoyed. "He's no one. He helped me. When *you weren't there,* I might add."

"He helped you? I'm sure he did everything in his power to *help* you," he said through gritted teeth.

"Are you serious?" she shouted. "You abandoned me with that dickhead in the backseat and then have the audacity to insinuate the man who helped me did so for ulterior motives?"

The strength of her protest screamed a warning at him. He wondered if she convinced herself as little as she'd convinced him.

"Let me break it to you, sweetheart," Will drawled, his playboy attitude slipping out from years of use. "Men don't help beautiful women for altruistic motives. He hoped to get laid." Just the thought of another man even thinking about touching her drove him insane.

She seethed with anger, rolling off of her in ripples and filling the car. "Perhaps he was, Will. Maybe he hoped to score big-time with *pretty-little-ole-me.*" She used the fake southern accent she had used on him the night they met. "But he was too busy warning me to *get the fuck out of there* before I got my head shot off."

"What?"

"Yeah, while you were off in South Dakota playing Military Commando Guy, Raphael woke me and said they were coming and I had to leave. He gave me his car."

"How did he know they were coming?"

"I don't know! I asked him and he told me he just knew."

"How could he just know? That doesn't make sense." He sucked in his breath. "What if he was one of them?"

Emma shook her head, scowling. "Why would he be one of them and help me? What motive could he have?"

Will lowered his voice as he fought to control his anger and think rationally. "Emma, you're forgetting how we met."

Her body stilled.

"Oh, that sounds like a good story." James chortled. "How *did* you two meet?"

"Fuck off, James." Will lowered his voice and turned to Emma. "Tell me everything that happened. How did you first meet him?"

He saw the emotions vacillate across her face, the way her grip on the steering wheel twisted slightly. *She doesn't want to tell me.* Why wouldn't she want to tell him? Her eyes shifted to Will then back to the road.

Her teeth caught her lower lip and she pulled her hand from Will's to grip the steering wheel with both hands. She took a deep breath. "No matter what I tell you, Will, you're not going to like it. So how about we just skip the story and look at the facts."

Anger mixed with a healthy dose of fear. "Perhaps we *could* look at the facts, Emma, if I had some to actually study." His words were cold and clipped, with carefully enunciated syllables.

Still, she held her tongue and his heart began to stammer.

"He knew me," she said, her voice barely audible. "He knew my name, knew you. He knew about this pendant and my powers." She stopped, to test his reaction, leaving her eyes on the road.

Questions pummeled Will's brain, but she had opened up and if he were too aggressive she'd shut down. He forced his voice to remain calm. "Did he say how he knew you?"

"No, but he said he had watched me. That he had a vested interest in my well-being."

"Sounds like a stalker." James snorted.

Will took a deep breath before he lost it on James. He was beginning to regret bringing him. But James's comment added a fire back into Emma's spirit. She sat up straighter, a hard glint in her eyes.

"I accused him of that. He, of course, denied it. But he helped me escape and didn't come with me." She shot a glare at Will. "Seems to me if he wanted to get laid the best way to make sure that happened would be to come with me. Worked for you." Her knuckles whitened from her grip on the wheel, but her quick inhale and exhale told him she was holding something back.

She was right. On both counts, but damned if it didn't sting for her to put it that way. If this Raphael guy had just been trying to get lucky, he would have gone with her. But he wanted something more than to get her into bed if he had been watching her, finally made contact then let her go. Or had he just made contact?

"Emma, had you ever seen him before yesterday?"

It was a simple yes or no question, yet she hesitated and his blood ran cold. "When was the first time you saw him?" he asked through clenched teeth, unsuccessfully shoving his jealousy to the side.

He needed the answer for their safety, to work out where this man fell into the chaos of their world. He knew she needed his assurance that he wouldn't lose his temper, yet the words of comfort stuck in his throat.

But he also needed the answer as a man, her partner, to reassure him she still wanted him. His hold on her was tenuous at best.

"In Joplin, at the bar. That night with my mother."

The memory rushed in. The dark-haired man sitting with Emma across the room, the way he leaned in, too familiar. Yet she brushed him off, her eyes on Will.

He tensed, his shoulders twitching. "Then again, in Kansas City," Will said. "In the parking lot." His words were straightforward, but the accusation implied.

She gave two small nods, her eyes ahead.

Will would gladly relive the beating he received in that parking lot to the pummeling his heart was taking now. Not only had the man known her name, but she listened to him and let him tell her what to do. When she stood next to the car, he'd gotten close, far too close. She hadn't pushed him away. He closed his eyes.

She placed her hand on top of his and squeezed. He turned and she gave him a grim smile, her eyes set in determination before she turned back to the road.

"In the parking lot, he told me that I could heal you, to use the pendant. I didn't think about it at the time. I was too scared. But then when you woke up and couldn't breathe, I was terrified. The pendant got so hot in my pocket that I took it out and saw it glowing. I remembered what he said. I couldn't believe it worked."

He turned his palm up and squeezed her hand.

"When I saw him yesterday, he asked about you, if I healed you. When I told him I had, he said I would get other powers. That I had to practice." She stopped and glanced at him, her eyes locking with his. "He said I needed you."

The significance of her words crashed into him and he released the breath he hadn't known he held.

"And the explosion in the forest? How did that happen?" he asked.

"I was scared and pissed at being scared that I was at their mercy. It made me angrier and the pendant got hotter the madder I got. The heat and pressure began to build."

"I felt it," he said. "I felt your fear turn to anger. I felt the energy."

"It took over. I had no control and it built until it became unbearable and I knew what to do. So I released it through my hands and there was an explosion."

"And you almost died."

"But I didn't, you found me."

"No, not just the fire. You almost died doing whatever you did. It took too much out of you. I felt it through our connection."

"Let me get this straight," James leaned forward between the seats. "Not only is your girlfriend hunted by gunmen but she's got freaky powers too." He shook his head. "You sure know how to pick them."

"I'd watch it if I were you, James." Emma lifted an eyebrow and glanced over her shoulder. "Make me angry and I could turn you into a roasted marshmallow at any moment."

James's eyes widened before he slid back in his seat.

Will shot James a glare. "He said he had an interest in your well-being. Did he say why? Do you think he's working with Warren?"

She shook her head. "No, when I realized he knew so much about me, I asked him if they hired him. He acted offended and said *no one* hired him."

Will inhaled slowly. "Shit, I almost wish they had. Now he's one more unknown variable in this whole fucking mess."

"He did say he needed me to develop my powers. He didn't say why, but he said I needed you to be able to do it."

The dread returned. "So he does want you. Just not yet."

Her face paled. "One more thing," she said quietly. "When he woke me and then gave me his car, I asked him who he was. He told me it was the wrong question." She turned to look at Will. "He said I should ask *what* he was."

"What the fuck does *that* mean?" James asked.

Will rubbed his chin and sighed. "I don't know, but I'm thinking a whole lot differently than I did a month ago, so anything is possible."

****

They checked into a rundown motel off the highway about thirty miles from the compound. Emma was thankful that Will got two separate rooms. She'd already had enough togetherness with James to last a lifetime.

James had napped in the car after their conversation so he excused himself to start digging up information on the Vinco Potentia and the Cavallo. He claimed that he'd spent so much time looking for Emma he hadn't had a chance to research, although she doubted that.

Will had gotten a map of the area and marked the location of the compound as well as possible local sources for deliveries. His plan was to go back first thing in the morning and begin surveillance while James continued to look for information and sift through the contacts on Senator Warren's cell phone.

"And what about me?" Emma asked. "You're planning on taking me with you, right?"

"Emma…" He sat down on the bed next to her and kissed her head. "You'll be safer here with James than with me that close to Warren's compound. I have a hard enough time with you being thirty miles away from them, let alone a few miles. Think about it, if they realized you were in their own backyard, they'd stop at nothing to get you." He put a finger under her chin and tilted her head up to look at her. "I can't afford for something to happen to you."

"You can't seriously consider leaving me here with him. Let's say we can even get along … what if they show up again? Do you think he'll protect me like you would?"

Indecision flickered over his face.

"Isn't this what got us into the latest mess? You leaving me behind?"

"No, what got you into this latest mess was your temper."

She scowled and changed tactics. "Think about it. You're watching the compound. What if they figure out we're here? What if they find the motel? Find me? I'd be dead before you ever got here."

His face hardened.

She lightly cupped his face. "Will," she searched his eyes. "I'd rather face fifty men with you than one with James. I'm safer with *you*."

When he closed his eyes and groaned, she knew she'd convinced him. If all else failed, she'd order him to take her but only as a last resort. She saw how hard it was earlier for him to accept her ability to do so. She needed to remember to be careful with her wording.

He pulled her into his arms and growled in her ear. "You fight dirty. This will cost you."

"What did you have in mind?" She kissed his neck, finding his pulse point.

"I think you figured it out."

She pushed him back on the bed and straddled his waist.

With a grin, he pulled her down. "I think maybe I did."

Later they lay in bed, Will's arm wrapped around her waist. "Emma?" he murmured, tightening his grip.

"Hmm?"

"I need to know."

She knew what he wanted, she just wasn't sure how much to tell him. She hated telling him about Raphael. She was tired of hurting him. He deserved so much better. It was bad enough he continued telling her *I love you* without her reciprocating. She decided to tell him as little as possible without lying. Rolling over, she looked up into his worried eyes.

"All right. What do you want to know?"

"Did you sleep with him?"

"Of course not. How could you ask me that, Will?" she asked softly, but without recrimination.

"You said he woke you. You were at a motel."

She caressed his face with her fingertips and kissed him with tenderness. "He didn't sleep in my room. I had my own room. I just woke up and he was there standing over my bed."

"God, Emma, he could have hurt you while you slept. How did he get in?"

"I swear, I have no idea. I even had the chain latched, but the door wasn't busted open. Besides, it all happened so fast. He woke me up and told me I had to hurry. I got dressed and he took me to his Lexus and told me to leave Minnesota. They showed up as I got in the car."

"Why didn't you tell me after you saw him in Kansas City? Isn't that odd, seeing him again? Quite a coincidence," he said bitterly.

"I'm sorry. I was more worried about you dying in the car."

"What did he say?"

"I already told you, Will."

His eyes narrowed. "But not everything. I can see that. What did he say?"

She wanted to cry. How could she tell him? She steeled herself. "He said he would come for me."

His jaw clenched. "Over my dead body."

She believed he meant it. "I doubt there's anything to worry about. He sent me away."

"He said you weren't ready yet. That's why he sent you away, Emma." He sat up, pushing up his knees and resting his elbows on his thighs. He sat for several long seconds. "Do you want him to come for you?"

The memory of her body's reaction to Raphael made her feel like a traitor, but she wrapped her hand around his arm. "Will, I'm with you right now, aren't I?"

"That didn't really answer the question, now did it, Emma?"

She bit her lip. "No. I don't want him to come."

He turned to look at her. "Why won't you tell me you love me?"

Tears burned her eyes and shook her head. "Will, I wish to God I could, but I can't. Not yet. I want to, please believe me when I say I want to, but I refuse to lie to you. You deserve better than that. Just give me some time, okay? We've only been together about three weeks and it's all happening so fast."

He looked away and nodded.

She kissed his shoulder. "No man has ever made me feel more safe or loved."

"But it's not enough."

"Will, you of all people know my history. Just give me time."

You can free him Raphael had said. Was she selfish to keep him with her? Should she consider it? But she couldn't. Selfish or not, she needed him and not just to protect her.

He pulled her down and she laid her head on his chest, the beat of his heart reassuring her that he was there. He smoothed the hair off her face. "I'm sorry. I shouldn't pressure you."

"I want to, Will. Really I do."

"I know." He kissed her head. "It's okay."

She fell asleep in his arms, praying that Raphael would stay out of her dreams.

And knowing that everything was far from okay.

CHAPTER SEVENTEEN

WILL watched the compound for three days while Emma grew impatient. He did his best to convince her that it was rash to rush in. He needed to figure out the routine of the compound and find their weaknesses, yet there was no denying it—not much was going on.

"This is stupid." She sat on the ground in the shade of the car, leaning against the door. The stifling August heat, coupled with a non-existent breeze, made her cranky. The fact that Jake refused to acknowledge her presence since the day he traced the heart in her hand didn't help. "Nothing is happening down there, Will."

"This is the way it works, Princess. It's the dirty little secret of surveillance. Ninety-nine percent of the time it's boring."

She swatted at fly that buzzed around her head. "What has James been doing for three days? We leave him back there to work and he's got nothing to show for it. I suspect he's renting pay-per-view movies and jacking off."

Will laughed. "I wouldn't put it past him, but we both know that wouldn't take all day. Besides, he is making progress. It's just slow. The Vinco Potentia isn't a secret group for nothing. But the contact list is helping and he's slowly building a dossier."

"What about the Cavallo? I'm more interested in them."

"They're even more difficult. At least he has a contact list for Warren's group. He's got nothing besides Alex and we don't even know if he's really one of them."

She released an exasperated breath and blew a strand of hair out of her face. "This is pointless. I could at least be practicing with my power." She'd had three long, boring days to consider it. While she didn't want to use her power to blast a forest, there was no denying it had saved her life. And if she learned to control it, perhaps she could use it without hurting people.

"No."

"Will!"

"It's too dangerous."

"But Raphael said—"

"Fuck Raphael," he growled.

She got up and stood next to the tree he was perched in. "Will, I have power and I need to learn how to use it."

He looked down at her, his mouth pinched in anger. "No, you're going to kill yourself. You need to get that goddamned thing off your neck."

She grabbed the pendant, warming her fingertips. "Take it off? It's what saved me before. Will, you're obviously not thinking straight. Look what I did in the woods."

"Exactly, look what happened in the woods, Emma. You caused a raging inferno and nearly died. Do we really want that to happen again?"

She grabbed his arm and leaned into his face. "If I am in that situation again, I will do it again." As difficult as it was to live with, she'd do it again if it meant keeping her alive to find Jake. "Do we want me knowing how to handle it or just throwing it out there?"

He groaned, rubbing his hands over his eyes. "How many marshmallows should I get for you to roast?" he said as he hopped off the branch.

She threw her arm around his neck and kissed him. "A couple of bags. Maybe some hot dogs, too."

"The first time I think you're in danger, you have to stop."

She twisted her mouth into a smile. "We'll start off small and work our way up."

"We'll have to go somewhere more inconspicuous. My work's done here anyway. I think I've figured out our way into the compound, but we won't be able to use it for a day or two. That'll give you time to practice."

"So what's your plan to get inside?"

"I'm still working on it. I'll let you know when I work out the details."

She raised an eyebrow as she frowned. "That's a bullshit answer."

"For once, just trust me." He gave her a quick kiss. "You'll be the first to know, now let's go."

It was so little to ask. *Just trust me.* Part of her protested with a vengeance. He shouldn't keep secrets, but who was she to point fingers, with secrets of her own? She forced herself to concede. She gave him so little. She could give him this. "Okay. I trust you."

His eyebrows lifted in surprise and his face lit up with happiness, making Emma feel guilty that she didn't give him what he asked more often.

They stopped at a Wal-Mart and bought a couple of fire extinguishers, some fruit, and a six-pack of beer.

"Got a craving for watermelon?" she asked.

"You gotta have some kind of targets. Tin cans don't seem appropriate in this instance."

She could see the logic in his answer. Exploding cans could get dangerous. "What about the beer then?"

"It's hot out there and I might need it to deal with what you're about to do."

Will drove into the middle of a recently cut, deserted field. "I'd prefer to take you to the desert," he said as they got out. "I'm worried you're going to set the southwest corner of South Dakota on fire."

Emma scowled. "Very funny."

"Who said I was joking?"

They leaned against the trunk of the car while Will popped open a beer and handed Emma a bottle of water.

"So tell me how this works," he said. "How did you do it before?"

"I'm not really sure. When I healed you I thought about healing you. But in the woods, I just thought about how I wasn't going to let them take me."

"Okay." He got out a watermelon and set it on the ground twenty feet in front of them. "Can you do something to it?"

"'Do something?' You mean, like make a watermelon slushy? We should have stopped at Sonic for that."

"Ha. Ha. Very funny. What do you think you can do to it? Blow it up?"

"I haven't got a fucking clue, Will. That's why we're here, right?"

He raised his hands in surrender. "Okay, do your thing, Princess."

She stared at the melon on the ground. What *was* she going to do to it? Set it on fire? Was that possible? Blow it up? That seemed like a good start.

She focused, narrowing her vision, imaging the watermelon exploding. After a half minute, Will swallowed a gulp of beer. "You going to start anytime soon?"

"Shut up, Will."

"Oh, I guess you've started. It's not working?" he stood up. "So that's it then, we'll call it a day. That didn't take long."

"Sit your ass back down. I'm not done yet."

He leaned against the trunk and picked up the fire extinguisher that lay at his feet. "I'm ready."

"Shut up."

He chuckled as she grabbed the pendant in her fingers. It must have something to do with the pendant. Holding the warm stone in her fingertips, she focused on the fruit.

After several minutes, she stamped her foot and spun around in frustration.

"Damn it!"

Will grabbed her arms and pulled her to him. She tried to tear herself away. She wasn't in the mood to hear him gloat.

But he tilted up her chin and stared into her face with patient eyes. "It's okay. You can do this."

"Obviously, I can't."

"You just started. Give it a chance."

She nodded. He was right and, surprisingly, encouraging, but it frustrated her. Before she hadn't even tried to do anything and it worked. It just happened in both instances.

Closing her eyes, she took a deep breath and cleared her mind. She thought about the watermelon and making it blow into thousands of pieces.

Nothing.

Her anger began to rise. *What the hell? Why I can't do this?*

The pendant on her chest grew warmer.

Just like when she healed Will.

Just like in the forest.

She focused on the heat and it began to cool. Okay, so that wasn't it. What had caused it to heat up?

Her anger.

She thought about how pissed she was that the stupid melon hadn't blown to smithereens yet. She thought about Jake and Alex and whoever else kept her and Jake apart. The pendant on her chest grew warmer and warmer.

"Emma…"

She ignored him, focusing on the watermelon and imaging that it somehow had wronged her. It had to be disposed of.

"*Emma…*"

She narrowed her eyes at the green oval on the ground and suddenly fragments of pulp and rind flew in all directions.

She smiled to herself, giddy with excitement.

"Oh, fuck. You did it." Will tipped the can up and drained it. Then he turned to her, a worried expression on his face. "Are you okay? Are you tired?"

She shrugged. "Maybe a little, but not too much. Did you see that?"

Will brushed a piece of rind off his arm. "Uh, yeah. Hard to miss when it's raining melons. How did you do it?"

"I got angry."

"What? You were pissed at the watermelon?"

"Yes. No. I was mad because it seemed so simple compared to healing you and the forest fire. But more angry about Jake and the pendant got hot."

"That's what I was trying to tell you. It was glowing."

"When I healed you, it glowed in my hand."

"So the power must come from that stone. That's good to know. What do you want to do now?"

"Try it again. What else do we have?"

"What about something smaller? Like a peach?" He grabbed one out of the bag sitting the trunk behind them and handed it to her.

She took it and sank her teeth into it. "That's a waste of a good piece of fruit. What else do you have?"

He chuckled and pulled out an apple. "You opposed to making applesauce?"

"Nope." She took another bite, the juice running down her chin. Will's eyes followed the trickle and she recognized the look on his face. "Down boy, we've got work to do."

A wicked glint flickered in his eye and he wrapped his arm around her back, pulling her closer. "Maybe we need to take a little break," he murmured.

She pushed his chest playfully. "Nope, we haven't been working long enough to take a break. Now go put that apple somewhere."

He loosened his grip and started to let go before he leaned down and sucked the peach juice off her chin and lower lip.

She tingled down to her toes. "You fight dirty," she said, relaxing against his chest.

"If that's not the pot calling the kettle black." His arms dropped and backed away, grinning. "Just wanted you to see what you turned down. Maybe you'll think twice next time."

She snorted. "Whatever. You'll just offer it again ten minutes later."

He laughed as he walked over to set the apple a few feet from where the watermelon had been. He looked over his shoulder. "Did you see there's a small pit in the ground where the watermelon was?"

"No."

He backed away from the apple. "Let me get away before you start blowing things up, okay? I don't want a hook for a hand."

She laughed. "Don't worry, you're too precious to blow up. Yet." She winked at his upturned eyebrows and threw her peach pit in the bag.

When he stood beside her, she concentrated on the apple, focusing on her anger at the people after them and how she wished for a normal life. The pendant became warm within seconds and the apple flew into the air, pieces flying in all directions.

"You did it again. Damn. What did you feel?"

"Anger."

"Again? Are you always this angry?" He shook his head. "Sorry, that was a stupid question."

Her eyes widened, stricken. "Am I really that angry?" She was. Anger had been her constant companion for so long she'd grown accustomed to it.

He saw the pain in her face and lowered his voice. "If you weren't angry, I would think there was something wrong with you. Your entire life has been one fuckup after another."

She rolled her eyes. "Wow, thanks. That makes me feel better."

"You know what I mean. Your mother is a piece of work. You've raised Jake alone. You gave up the secure life you wanted for him because of other people's selfish greed." He paused and she looked up into his eyes. "I realize how important security is to you."

It surprised her how much he saw in her. What else did he see that he didn't mention? "But it seems wrong to get power from anger."

He brushed away the hair that blew in her face. "Maybe you can use something other than anger. Maybe you just need a strong emotion. Why don't you try a different one?"

"Like what?"

"Like love." He saw the guilty look on her face and grimaced. "I was trying for something more pleasant. Obviously, that wasn't it. Try fear, or pain, or a whole host of other negative emotions. See if one of those works."

She bit her lip and nodded.

Will put another apple on the ground near where the other one had been placed. When he came back he shook his head. "There's another pit in the ground. You're not just blowing these things up but creating some kind of force. Are you getting tired? Do you need to eat something?" His eyebrows furrowed with concern.

"No, I ate that peach. I'm a little tired, but nothing I can't handle."

"I think when you do this you use energy, which makes sense. It's simple physics. You can't create energy, it has to transfer from one form to another."

"What do you mean?"

"You're blowing things up, or in my case, healing me. Blowing up fruit probably doesn't take much energy. They're relatively small. But healing someone or creating a huge explosion would take large amounts of energy, which had to transfer from you into whatever you caused. That's why you passed out after you healed me and almost passed out after the explosion. The only reason you didn't then was because I was in your mind, verbally berating you to get up."

He lowered his head so his eyes were level with hers. "But if you attempt something too big, that sucks too much energy, it could kill you. It could completely deplete all the energy in your body."

One side of her mouth lifted into a grin. "I thought you were a history major."

He laughed and shrugged. "While you were taking accounting and advanced race car driving, I took biology and physics."

"Very funny, but there might be something to your theory."

"Yeah, it occurred to me after the fire, which is why I made you eat something. But I think maybe I can transfer energy to you too. When I touched you after you healed me, you said your headache went away."

"Yeah, it did."

"And when you passed out in the woods, I touched you. You stirred and then woke up. We should probably practice with that, too. But first I think you should try another emotion. Let's use another apple since we know that you could blow one up."

She sighed. "Okay, but anger's so easy."

"Try fear. You're likely to be afraid if you need to use this to defend yourself."

"What? Am I supposed to be afraid of an apple?"

Will shook his head with a grin. "Were you really that pissed at the poor innocent watermelon? What did it ever do to you?"

"Point taken."

She closed her eyes and remembered being in the woods alone with the men chasing her. Slick fear slid down her spine, catching her breath at the memory. She felt Will tense beside her. Trying to ignore him, she remembered being hunted through the woods, outnumbered by men with guns. The helpless feeling returned, sending her heart racing.

The stone around her neck remained lukewarm.

After a few more minutes, she opened her eyes and groaned. "That didn't work."

"Maybe you need something that doesn't make you feel powerless. Fear's a strong emotion but not empowering like anger."

"You could be right. I was completely freaked out in the woods, but it wasn't until I got angry that the pendant warmed up."

Will wrapped his arm around her back and they leaned against the car watching storm clouds blow in.

"I think we should head back before the storm hits. We can try again tomorrow."

"But I hardly did anything today. I made no progress."

"That's not true. We learned you can make applesauce and you need to be angry to make it work."

"But that's not much."

"Emma, the first time you hurt yourself I'm putting a stop to it, so if you want to keep doing this you need to take it slow."

She knew he was right, but who knew how long they had until the next group of gunmen found them? Especially this close to the compound. She wanted to be prepared.

"Emma..." Will hesitated, taking her hand. "I want to talk about something else."

Her back stiffened in apprehension. "You're not wanting to leave me again, are you?"

His grip around her waist tightened. "No, that's not it." He paused and her heartbeat quickened, wondering what could make him so nervous. "I want to talk about the baby."

Her mouth went dry. "And...?"

"First of all, is this a discussion we need to have? *Is* there a baby?"

Guilt ate at the edges of her conscious. How could she have discussed this with Raphael before Will? And why did she still not want to discuss it? But she owed it to him. "Yes, it's a discussion we need to have."

"Does that mean...?"

She turned to look at him and nodded.

He pulled her close and kissed her, like he was a happy expectant father and this was fantastic news. It only added to her guilt.

"How can you be happy about this, Will? This is terrible."

"Why? Because Warren wants the baby? He'd want you anyway, baby or not."

"Is that supposed to make me feel better? Because it doesn't."

"Emma, we can't let other people rule our lives."

Her derisive laugh filled the air. "Are you kidding me? Have you *seen* our lives? That's exactly how we're living. How are we supposed to run with a baby?"

"We've got at least eight months before we have to worry about that. Maybe this will all be over by then."

She didn't see how that was possible. Too many people were after them. It all seemed so hopeless if it weren't for Jake she'd consider giving up. But to do it with a baby?

You need Will because of the baby. If there's no baby, you don't need Will forever. I'm saying you don't have to have this baby.

Was it true? Did she really not need the baby? But not needing Will, was that something she really wanted? She looked into his loving eyes. Selfishly, she didn't want to give him up. "I don't want to tell James. He hates me and he'll hate me even more if he knows I'm pregnant. He'd probably accuse me of lying about you being the father."

Will pinched his lips and nodded. "In this case, you're probably right. We'll keep it between you and me for now."

"Thanks."

"Let's get out of here," he said. "James is bound to wonder where we are. I'll call him on the way back and fill him in on your progress." Grabbing her arm, he gently led her to the car door.

She jerked her arm out of his grasp. “Oh, my God. You’re treating me like an invalid. I’m pregnant, not sick.”

“Emma—”

She glared at him. “If you treat me like anything other than a normal healthy person, you will regret it.”

He opened the car door. “Okay, sorry. I’ve never dealt with a pregnant woman before.”

“Yeah, that’s what I’m worried about.”

CHAPTER EIGHTEEN

EMMA stood in the forest, a raging bonfire before her, her nightgown blowing in the breeze. An electrical current danced along her skin, tickling her with expectation and promise of fulfillment. A longing grew within her, a need to that begged to be satisfied.

"You are not bound to destiny." Raphael breathed into her ear, adding to her yearning.

Emma sucked in a breath of surprise. He offered her completeness.

"You're so close. So very close."

She gasped, the tingling jumping from one follicle of hair to the next.

He circled in front of her, slowly, seductively. A patient lover claiming his long-awaited prize. His eyes darkened to nearly black pools of desire, piercing her own and captivating her. "I've waited for you for so long, Emmanuella, and you for me. Our wait is nearly over."

He leaned down slowly, as though a sudden movement would startle her. His lips sought hers, the lightest of pressure, testing her response. Her breath sucked in. His tongue skimmed her lower lip, a low growl purring in his throat. Her lips parted and he pressed his chest to hers, holding her at the waist. Electrical sparks lit the night from contact, but she didn't feel pain, only pleasure. He nipped her lip, drawing blood. His tongue licked the drops away.

"It's time."

Emma sat up in bed, panting with fear and excitement. Will instantly woke and wrapped an arm around her back.

"Emma?"

Guilt coursed through her veins. She had wanted Raphael and everything he promised. She couldn't deny it. She shrugged Will off with a grunt. "I'm fine."

He rubbed her arm. "You had another dream."

Swinging her legs off the side of the bed, she stood up and wrapped her arms around herself. Her heart raced as she gasped for air. "I'm fine. It was just a dream."

Will watched her, worry in his eyes. "It might help to talk about it."

She ran a shaking hand through her hair. Had it been this cold in the room when they went to sleep? "I don't remember. It was just a stupid dream, Will. I'm going to the bathroom."

She stormed into the restroom and shut the door, turning on the water.

Oh God, what was she dreaming? Was this really going to happen? How could she prevent it?

She cupped her hands beneath the cold water and splashed her face several times. Standing up, she patted her face with a towel and stared at her reflection. She had washed away the flush from her skin but her eyes burned with desire, the cut on her lower lip evidence of her betrayal.

Did she really want to prevent it?

She sat on the toilet seat, head between her hands, staving off the rising panic. She had to get a grip. Sucking in deep breaths, she thought of Jake. *Jake.* Jake needed her. Everything else was secondary. Will was secondary. Raphael was secondary.

Just the thought of his name made her stomach tumble in excitement and her skin warm. *What is wrong with me?*

"Emma. Open the door."

She took several gulps of air. "Just a minute. I'm going to the bathroom."

"Why did you lock the door?"

She stood up and flushed the toilet to cover her lie. Oh, God, she was lying to him. "Habit."

She turned the water on again, splashing her face and drying it before opening the door.

Will's face was pale and tight. "You need to tell me what's going on."

"I had to go to the bathroom. Haven't you heard that pregnant women have to go to the bathroom a lot?"

He shook his head. "I thought that was later in pregnancy. When the baby is sitting on top of the bladder."

She pushed him out of the doorway and shoved past him. "Goddamn it, Will. Do you fucking know everything?"

He turned to watch her. "Apparently, not everything."

She wanted to cry. She wanted to scream. But she couldn't do either under his watchful eyes. The walls were closing in around her. She needed fresh air. She had worn a tank top and panties to bed. She snatched her skirt off a chair and stepped into it.

"What are you doing?"

"I need some air. I'm going for a walk." She sat on the edge of the bed and shoved her feet into her shoes.

"Okay," Will picked up his jeans. "Give me a second."

"I don't need a fucking babysitter! I can go outside by myself!" she shouted.

His eyes widened in alarm. "Okay. Calm down before you wake people up. If you want to go out, I'll go with you. It's the middle of the night. It's not safe."

Emma pulled her gun out of the duffle bag and pulled back the slide. "I'm safe now. Don't follow me." She opened the door and walked into the still night, the air so humid she could slice it like a stick of butter. She waited outside the door, expecting Will to follow her anyway but a full minute later she was still alone. Either he respected her request or took it as an order.

She'd take either one.

The motel sat off a divided four-lane highway that didn't see much traffic at two in the morning. One of the many perks of their location. Emma had chosen many a motel like this herself while on the run with Jake.

Jake.

Her eyes welled with scalding tears. Three fucking weeks and nothing. She swiped her cheek with the back of her left hand as she walked behind the motel toward an empty, cracked concrete pool on the back edge of the parking lot. Dilapidated pool furniture scattered along the edge. Long shadows covered the asphalt, reaching to the edge of the fence. She had no destination in mind but walking along the highway seemed foolish even in her state.

"Taking a midnight stroll?"

Raphael sat in a rusted pool chair, leaning an arm on the flimsy frame. He wore gray dress pants and a long-sleeved button-down shirt, open at the collar. His black hair was slightly ruffled, adding to his mysterious, exotic look.

She thrust out her arm, pointing the gun at him with her shaking hand. "How did you find me?" she hissed.

He held up his hands in mock surrender. "Calm down, Emma," he chuckled. "No need to shoot. You have nothing to fear from me. I helped you escape, remember?"

She shook her head, still muddled from her dream. He might have helped her, but there was no denying he stalked her.

Raphael settled back in the chair with a Cheshire grin and crossed his arms over his chest. "Really, you weren't that difficult to find. I expected a little more originality out of you or your boyfriend."

She glared, still aiming the gun at his chest.

"What happened to set you on edge? You and your boyfriend have a lover's quarrel?"

"Will. His name is *Will.* Please stop belittling him." She kept the weapon trained on him as she approached, glancing at the padlocked chain-link gate. "How'd you get in there?"

He shrugged. "We have more important things to discuss."

His eyes locked with hers as she stopped next to the six-foot barrier. Her resolution had begun to dissolve.

"Why are you so nervous?" His words were like wine, rich and warm, melting her insides.

Her gun had lowered. She jerked it up higher. "Why *wouldn't* I be nervous?"

"Where is *Will*?"

"None of your business."

His eyes narrowed. "Now that's where you're wrong." His face relaxed and he smiled. "How's your training going?"

"What training?"

"Now, Emma. Don't be coy. We both know you've been practicing."

He was too presumptuous. She stood straighter and thrust out her chin. "Will thinks it's too dangerous. He's concerned it will kill me and doesn't want me to try it." It was all entirely true.

Raphael rose from the chair and stood next to the chained fence quicker than Emma thought humanly possible. His hand threaded the link, his eyes piercing hers. "You haven't been practicing?" he asked in a guttural voice.

What did he care if she learned her powers? What did he possibly have to gain from it? Her dream rushed into her head and she pushed it to the background.

Raphael's eyes lit up.

"You've dreamed of me?" he asked in a whisper.

Her eyes widened. She shook her head, backing up. "No…"

"Emma." His words were like a prayer of reverence.

Her body reacted, relaxing. The gun lowered.

His eyes stayed locked on hers and she felt hypnotized, sucked into those dark pools. "Emma, my love, you need to practice. You need to learn to defend yourself like you did in the woods. That was good. Very good."

She walked toward him, drawn to him against all reason.

His fingers lifted, reaching for her. Without thinking, she lifted her hand to the fence and he laced his fingers with hers, the metal cold against her palm. Her hand tingled with the contact, drawing her breath.

"You feel it too, don't you? You're close." His eyes glittered with excitement. "But you need to practice. You're in grave danger and you must learn to defend yourself. You can't count on him to protect you."

The need to please him washed through her and she nodded.

"Good," he murmured, staring into her eyes. "You must go back to him now. He's looking for you." Raphael released her hand.

Disappointment filled her when he dropped contact.

"Emma!" Will called in a hushed tone across the parking lot.

His voice brought back her guilt, which was the reason she had rushed from the room in the first place. She turned in his direction, considering what to say, how to explain Raphael's presence. She turned back to warn Raphael to keep quiet, but he was gone.

Her heart pounded. Had she imagined him being there? Hallucinated it? She raised a hand to her head. Maybe she was losing touch with reality.

"Emma." Will's voice was louder and more insistent and she knew she had to answer him. If nothing else it was unfair to worry him. He hadn't done anything wrong, only loved her and tried to take care of her and how did she repay him?

He deserved better.

"I'm here," she called out softly, her voice carrying across the quiet parking lot. She walked in his direction, hoping to intercept him.

He rounded the corner, a shotgun in his hand and relief on his face. "Thank God. You scared me."

She pointed her gun at the ground as she walked toward him, hoping he didn't see her hand shake. "I'm sorry. I just needed some air."

When he reached her, he pulled her into a hug. "Are you okay? Really?"

She leaned into his chest. "Yes, I'm sorry. I'm not used to someone babying me. I just felt a bit smothered. It was stupid to walk out and I'm sorry."

"It's okay, let's just go back inside. I've got a really bad feeling out here."

Emma looked back to the unoccupied pool area. Will was more perceptive than she gave him credit for.

****

Will worried about Emma even after she finally fell asleep. He knew pregnant women needed a lot of sleep and he seriously doubted Emma got enough, especially with the nightmares. He had tried again to coax her into telling him the dream, but she refused, saying she didn't remember.

He didn't believe her. She was lying, which in itself killed him. What could she possibly be dreaming that she couldn't tell him?

Will wasn't sure he wanted to know.

He slept restlessly, his responsibilities weighing heavily on his shoulders. He woke up weary, a feeling of hopelessness settling over him. He had to finish working out his plan to get into the compound and steal the book, not to mention what to do with Emma when he did it. James was making agonizingly slow progress, and while he'd defended his friend to Emma the night before, he'd also wondered what James had really been up to. He planned to find out this morning.

He sat up and looked down at Emma's face, her hair covering her cheek. Leaning over, he brushed the strands away, his fingertips lingering on her soft skin while he released a deep sigh. He was going to be a father and the harsh reality of the situation added to his hopelessness. At this point, everything hinged on that stupid book and the secrets it contained. God help them if it didn't tell him what they needed to know.

He wondered if he should have a backup plan in case the book didn't pan out, but he couldn't even attempt to let his mind wander in that direction. For now, he'd focus on the book.

He reviewed his notes: deliveries, guard shift changes, the traffic at the private airstrip. He was tempted to try to use a delivery truck to get in, but that meant either stealing or hijacking one, either of which could draw unwarranted attention. The tall chain-link fence surrounding the property wasn't electrified nor were many cameras watching the fence, just the entrances to the buildings. James should be able to disable those, although it would get noticed. He hoped to create a diversion to take attention away from the brief seconds it took to get inside.

Emma stirred in the bed. He looked over his shoulder to see her watching him.

"Feeling better?"

She sat up and rubbed her eyes. "Yeah. What are you up to?"

"Nailing down the details of my plan."

"Want to share?"

"I want to have James with us first."

She groaned.

Will ignored and dialed James's cell phone. He picked up on the fourth ring.

"What the fuck time is it?"

"Time for you to get up. We've got some work to do."

"I've been working."

Will lowered his voice and kept his back to Emma as she walked in to the bathroom. "Yeah, I can see from all the progress I've seen."

"You don't like the progress I'm making, you feel free to take over, *William*. I never asked to join this expedition."

Will cringed at his use of his full name, reminding Will of his asshole authoritarian father. James knew which buttons to push. "Do you have anything for me or not?"

"Some."

"Then I'm coming over to see."

"No," James said. "I'll bring it over to you."

"Fine, you come here but give me five minutes so Emma has time to get dressed first."

James grunted and hung up.

Emma stood in the bathroom door. "So James is going to let us see his precious research?"

"He says he has something. We'll see what it is."

Emma grabbed a dress from their bag and headed back to the bathroom. "I hate to complain, and I know I have dresses and skirts because it was easier with my leg, but I feel more comfortable in jeans instead of worrying about the wind kicking up my skirt while I'm running for my life."

She sounded annoyed but she grinned and winked.

"Yeah, I can see how that might be an issue. We can get you some today."

"Thanks."

She shut the door, something she did a lot lately. He tried not to let it bother him, telling himself she shut the door so James wouldn't see her. Not because she had something to hide from him.

James knocked on the door a minute later, walking in with an armload of papers.

"We could have come to your room, James."

He laid the stack on the desk next to Will's papers. "Seemed easier to come here than clean up my room."

Emma opened the bathroom door and James turned to look at her. "Emma."

She gave him a tight smile. "James. So we finally get to see what you've been up to for several days?"

"Oh you know, this and that. Trying to save your ass. The usual. I hear you've been busy learning how to blow up fruit. Should prove useful if there's a killer tomato invasion."

She gave him a haughty look.

Will groaned. The two of them were worse than bickering children. "James, what do you have?"

He leaned over and spread the top papers out. "I've been going through Warren's cell phone contact list, which is quite extensive, I might add. It's taken awhile to figure out who the numbers belong to and then cross-reference and see who attended Brown University. I came up with a list of a handful of people, some of whom attended around the time Warren did. Most did not."

"I don't think it matters if they were in school at the same time," Will said, reviewing the list. "The group's been in existence for over fifty years. As far as I know, they might still be recruiting."

"Among the list are Scott Kramer, who graduated a year ahead of Warren." James handed Will a piece of paper.

Will scanned the paper. "Ah, yes. Mr. Kramer."

"Isn't he the guy who came into my room?" Emma asked, sitting on the edge of the bed.

"That's him. He's the guy who hired me and was my only contact until I got to the compound. He ran the debriefing meeting after I turned you over."

James leaned against the edge of the desk. "Kramer and Warren go way back, even roomed together in college. Kramer was always the behind-the-scenes guy while Warren was the charismatic charmer."

"I can attest to that. I might have actually fallen for his charm under different circumstances, I can see why he's so popular."

"He's definitely popular with the people. Polls show Warren a full ten percent ahead of Dixon in the presidential race. It may only be August but most people are already declaring him the winner. It would take a miracle to throw him off his throne."

"Then we'll hope for a miracle because I can't think of a bigger disaster than him being the president of the United States." Will shuddered.

"You said the other guy in your debriefing was John, but no last name. Middle-aged guy. This him?" James handed Will a photo.

Will sat on the bed next to Emma. "Yep, that's him alright."

"John Monroe, CEO of Monroe Industries, also a fellow Brown graduate. The three were thick as thieves in their younger days. Monroe Industries has their hands in all kinds of pies but most notably is their leading role in technology and technological research. They're not out front like some bigger companies, but they're quietly raking in money while their influence is everywhere. It would be easy for a company like them to gather information on anyone. They probably own it."

"That's comforting." Emma said.

"That's the facts. John Monroe and many of his business associates are contributors to Warren's campaign and to his political party, including multiple fundraising dinners."

Will didn't find that surprising.

"Monroe Industries has a lot to gain with Warren in the White House, chief among them projects funded by the American people. Monroe Industries has stalled with the current administration, but with the change on the horizon along with the possible changing of the guard in the House and the Senate, let's just say a lot of those people owe something to Monroe."

Will sighed. "Next."

"Alexander Warren, Phillip Warren's only child." He handed Will a photo of Alex. Emma tensed.

"Ah, Alex." Will said, clenching his teeth. "Alex and I are already acquainted."

"Charmer like his father. An attorney, working for his father's firm although I could find very few cases the man has actually worked on. He was a political science major at Brown and also got his law degree there. He spends a lot of time in Washington with his father. He's popular with the women in California."

Emma snorted. "They obviously don't know him."

James shrugged. "He was a big part of his father's campaign before the party convention this summer, but he's been MIA the last few weeks. Although some news media has picked up on that, no one's making a big deal about it. Yet."

Emma turned to Will. "Could he be with Jake?"

"It's possible. It looked like his daddy had no idea about his involvement with the Cavallo or his knowledge of Jake. Daddy may have kicked his ass to the curb or he could have cut his losses and ran to take advantage of the

Jake situation." Will looked up. "Tell me, James. Can you track him down?"

James' mouth twisted. "*Anything* is possible. Some things are more difficult." He shrugged. "One thing to our advantage is he's in the media. They help keep tabs on him. But if he's in hiding, that won't help. I can try to track down credit card numbers and usage but that will take more time and digging."

"Can you work on it?"

"You need to prioritize here, Will. I'm only one guy and you've got me working on a half a dozen things as it is."

"Did you find out anything about the Vinco Potentia?"

"No, only rumors here and there. Mentions on the blogs and websites of wackos and lunatics."

"So they are on the radar."

"A small, miniscule blip."

"What about the other group? The Cavallo?"

"Absolutely nothing. I question their existence."

Will questioned everything at this point. "Well, someone took Jake, whatever the fuck their name is. But we might not even need it if we can find Alex. Make him your top priority. Any idea where Warren is the next few days?"

"No, but that should be an easy find. It's public information."

"Good, find out and make sure he's not coming to South Dakota soon. I want to break into the compound tonight."

James eyes widened. "Tonight?"

"Yeah, got a problem with that?"

"No, I just thought you'd give me more notice. What do you need me to do to prep?"

"Not much, most of what I need from you will be tonight. This looks like a simple breaking and entering."

"On an armed compound?" James's voice raised in disbelief. "Have you lost your mind?"

"No, sometimes simpler is better. Besides, security is lax at best and tonight there's a company scheduled to polish the floors. That should provide some distraction so we can move around."

"We're posing as floor polishers?"

"Nope, I said breaking and entering, remember? We're crawling under the fence and sneaking in the back door. There's no security guards in the back. The fence isn't electrified and you can scramble the cameras on the door so we can get in."

"It's insane, but it will probably work. When do you want to do it?"

"Just after dark."

"What about me?" Emma asked. "Where do I fit in all of this?"

"I haven't worked that part out yet."

James crossed his arms across his chest and gave Emma a cold stare. "I think she should come with us."

"You *do*?" Emma asked.

Will stood up. "Have you fucking lost your mind?"

"Think about it, Will. If we leave her somewhere, you'll be so worried about her you'll do a piss-ass job and get yourself caught. And if I'm with you, I'll get caught too.

No thanks. This way, she'll be with you and you can focus on what needs to be done. Weren't you the one who said it was an easy job?"

"I didn't use those words exactly."

"It was implied. She goes."

CHAPTER NINETEEN

EMMA couldn't believe James wanted her to go, and while thankful, she was also suspicious. She didn't trust him.

Will planned to load the car and stake out the compound until nightfall. James gathered his papers and returned to his room. As Emma and Will packed their belongings, Emma asked, "Why does James want me to go?"

"I was surprised too, but his reasoning makes sense."

She rested her hand on his arm and looked up into his face. "Will, I don't trust him."

He closed his eyes and when he looked at her again she saw the worry on his face. "Look, I know you two don't get along and you have no idea how much that bothers me, but I've known James since we were kids. I trusted him with my life in Iraq, which is not an exaggeration by any stretch of the imagination. James has my back."

She raised her eyebrows. "But does he have mine?"

He brushed off her hand and resumed packing. "That's a crazy question."

"No, it's not, Will. He hates me. Why would he protect or help me?"

"Because you and I are a package deal."

"Yeah, but does James know that?"

He turned and glared. "It's a given, Emma. I need him. I can't do this alone."

"Okay, okay," she mumbled. "But I just wanted to make my opinion known."

Will stewed the rest of the morning, snapping at her over little things. Not that she blamed him. He was caught in the middle between his best friend and his girlfriend. And his pregnant girlfriend was keeping secrets from him and running off in the middle of the night.

James noticed the tension and a satisfied smile curved his lips, adding to Emma's irritation. The sooner they got rid of James, the better.

They spent the rest of the day going over the plan and circling the compound in the car and on foot. The entire scheme made her nervous as hell. She couldn't imagine the book wouldn't be under armed guard, but Will assured her Warren had said that the book was a duplicate. The original was somewhere in Washington D.C.

She wished she'd practiced using her power more. It was all still a large unknown. If needed, she could use it, but it was dicey at best. She'd like to have a better handle on it before she began blowing things up.

As the sun began to set, they drove to a country road that ran parallel to the compound and strapped on their backpacks. A wheat field lay a half-mile between the two.

"This is where we hike," Will said as they got out.

Will took the lead, with Emma and James following behind. Emma was glad Will had made good on his promise to get her a pair of jeans. Her legs would have been scratched up in minutes otherwise.

They moved in silence as the sun set. A half moon rose in the horizon, hanging over the tops of the stalks and promising the offer of light in the cloudless sky. They had flashlights, but a beam from one would be a dead giveaway.

"Now, tell me again what the plan is if we get caught. We're supposed to sprint the half-mile back to the car?" Emma asked.

"Yep, or improvise if necessary," Will said.

"It's the improvising that worries me."

"I can think of a few times I enjoyed your improvising."

James groaned. "Stop. Please. That's disgusting."

They hiked the rest of the way in silence, crouching at the edge of the field when they reached the chain link fence that surrounded the back of the compound. Emma was surprised how close the buildings actually were to the fence.

"Why would they do that?" she whispered.

"Arrogance," Will answered. "They think they're untouchable here."

"Even after we escaped?"

"Apparently. I haven't seen any increased security. Of course, no one's really here to guard at this point. Warren probably never thought we'd try to break *in*."

"Okay," James said. "Let's get this show on the road."

Will had already located all the security cameras a couple of days before. He pointed them out so James knew what to target.

James pulled a small case out of his pack. "I suggest you be ready to get under the fence and sprint to the door. The longer we jam the camera signals, the more suspicious it'll look. If you can pick that lock and get in within twenty seconds, they'll probably attribute it to sunspot interference."

Will nodded and pulled out a pair of wire cutters and a small case. "Once you're ready, let me know. We're in the shadows here so I'm going to cut the fence then have you start jamming."

"I'm ready when you are."

Will cut the links a foot and a half tall and bent back a flap, glancing at James. "Ready."

James flipped a switch in the case. "Let's go."

Will crawled under first, followed by Emma and James. They ran the fifty feet to the back of the building, plastering their bodies to the side. James looked as his watch as Will used small tools on the lock on the door.

"Ten seconds, Will."

"Got it." He cracked the door and peered inside. "It's clear."

They followed him into the hallway. The sound of a floor polisher hummed in the distance. Next to the exit was the door to the stairwell. Will opened it and slipped inside, the other two behind him. James turned off the jamming device while Will pointed two fingers toward the stairs and took the lead.

They climbed the stairs silently. Emma's heart pounded and she forced herself to take even breaths. They stopped on the fourth floor and Will looked into her eyes, a grave expression on his face. For all his bravado, he was as nervous as she was.

Will opened the door and looked around. He motioned for Emma and James to stay in the stairwell.

Emma watched out the small window of the door and saw him go several feet down the hall, stopping in front of an ornate wood door. He pulled his lock case out of the back of his jeans and quickly opened the door with his tools. He disappeared inside, then motioned for them to follow.

Emma and James were in the apartment within seconds.

She gasped in awe of the ornate decor. Marble floors, antique furniture. No expense had been spared. Will had told her how pompous it was, but she still found herself shocked that people could actually live this way, especially when they were hardly ever here. Will walked over to the intricately carved bookcases and started scanning the shelves while James nosed around the room. Emma hung back, waiting, unsure what else to do. She was thankful they had gotten this far.

Will pulled a leather-bound book off the shelf and waved it in the air with a smile. She breathed a sigh of relief as he slid it into his pack. He moved to the desk in the corner, rifling through the drawers and thumbing through its contents, then disappeared through a door behind the desk.

Emma hesitated, unsure whether to stay or follow him. James had gone into another room, leaving her alone in the living room. She stared out the windows facing the Black Hills, making sure she was far enough back to go unnoticed from outside. The knob on the front door jiggled. She turned in horror. Someone was coming in.

A closet on the opposite side of the room taunted her, but she'd never make it in time. The door pushed open and she ducked down behind the wet bar. Hopefully, she could remain hidden until she figured a way out.

Cowering in the dark corner, she heard an odd noise, then a telephone ringing. Whoever came in was making a video call.

"Scott, what is it?" She heard Senator Phillip Warren's voice, but it didn't come from the room. She peeked around the corner and saw Scott Kramer sitting in front of the monitor on his desk.

"Philip, this entire situation is out of control. You have to get a handle on your son."

"What the hell do you think I've been trying to do? How did Emmanuella slip through our grasp in Minnesota?" Warren asked, annoyed.

"Our source was correct, but somehow she was alerted. She was leaving the parking lot as our operatives arrived."

"What the hell happened in the woods?"

"That wasn't us. It had to be the Cavallo. But my source said she had some kind of power."

"Is it true?"

Kramer paused. "We can't be certain since none of the men in the forest survived, but the last report we had was that she had a gun, nothing else. Besides, it would have taken powerful explosives to cause the damage they found out there. Davenport could have set it up but our source says he was out of the area." He paused again and lowered his voice. "It killed fifteen men, Phillip, and they weren't all packed together. They were spread out over fifty feet."

Emma struggled to catch her breath. She'd killed fifteen men.

"But how could she do it? She's only supposed to carry the child. She wasn't supposed to have any power."

"Obviously, we underestimated her."

She heard Warren's dry laugh. "Obviously, we underestimated many things."

"Phillip, you couldn't have known about Alex."

"Couldn't I? He's my son. How could I not realize he was working both sides?"

"He fooled us all. I knew he wasn't happy with our philosophy, but I never considered that he was feeding them information about us. They almost killed Emmanuella."

"It's not like she's a lot of good to us at this point, and now Alex is obsessed with her."

"She's still of great use to us. She still carries the child, even if the Chosen One isn't one of our group. That's a bitter disappointment, but the child has always been our main objective. We'll just wait for our source to inform us of her whereabouts again. We *will* capture her."

"And what about Davenport?"

"He's an issue. I would love nothing more than to kill him. He's a huge pain in the ass. Nevertheless, I think we should capture him as well. If she has powers we didn't suspect, he might have some himself."

"Do we know where they are now?"

Emma held her breath even though Kramer appeared clueless that she was less than twenty feet away. She fingered the trigger on her gun. Could she really shoot Kramer if he found her?

"No."

"You said Davenport wasn't with her when she caused the explosion. We need to find out if they're together now. If he has powers, they might be more powerful together. We should try to capture them separately. See if the contact can arrange that."

"Agreed."

"How do we know we can trust your source?"

"Because he's the only one providing us any information at this point."

A door creaked. "Mr. Kramer," a male voice interrupted.

"What is it?" Kramer replied, annoyed. "I told you I wasn't to be disturbed."

"Mr. Kramer, there's been an irregularity with the security cameras."

"And?"

"We lost reception to two security cameras at the back of this building for eighteen seconds. It could be a simple electronic glitch, but you said you wanted to be notified of anything unusual."

"Thank you. Send a security team to investigate."

"Already done."

Emma heard footsteps leave the room and a door close before the men resumed talking.

"What do you make of this, Scott?" Warren asked.

"It's probably nothing, but it's wise to treat it seriously."

"Have we gotten any information about Alex's whereabouts?"

"We suspect Montana."

"*Montana?*"

"We think he has the boy there."

Emma sucked in her breath. They had information about Jake.

"Send some men after him, and the boy too. Maybe we should just capture them all and bring them here to sort this out."

"On it."

Emma heard a blip as they disconnected. Kramer walked to the windows overlooking the compound and pulled his cell phone out of his pocket.

"Kramer, here. Send a team of men after Alex Warren. We want him alive and unharmed, and the boy too. Report back to me when they've been located and before you move in."

She needed to find out where Jake was. She knew what Will would say—let James take care of it—but she had doubts the son of a bitch would help her. Maybe it was time to take matters into her own hands.

Kramer moved toward the bar when a knock on the door interrupted him.

"Mr. Kramer?"

"What did you find?"

"The fence at the rear of the compound has been cut but no sign of intruders."

"Lock down the compound. No one gets in or out without my knowledge."

"Yes, sir."

Shit. So much for a clean getaway.

A shadow fell over her and Emma stared up into the surprised face of Scott Kramer. She bolted to her feet, pointing her gun at him, her heart hammering in her ears

"Emmanuella, I'd say what a surprise, but that would be an understatement. You're the last person I expected to find hiding behind my bar."

"Why don't we have a little chat." She waved the gun toward Kramer.

He grabbed a decanter off the counter and poured into a glass. "I'd offer you a drink, but in light of your condition…"

"Let's cut the small talk. Get your ass in a chair before I blow it off."

He sat down, an amused expression on his face. "Here we've been searching everywhere for you and you found us instead. To what do I owe your visit?"

"I want my son."

He twisted his lips and shrugged. "Sorry, we don't have him, but then you know that already."

She slid back the chamber on the gun and pointed it at his chest. "Don't play games with me. I know Alex has him and you know where Alex is."

"That's not entirely true. We last spotted Alex in northwest Montana, but we aren't sure exactly where he is. I know you were eavesdropping so surely you heard me tell them to contact me when Alex was located."

She had, to her disappointment.

"Is that the real reason you're here?" Kramer asked, shifting his eyes. "Where's your babysitter?"

"Babysitter?" She raised her eyebrows.

"I'm surprised Davenport let you out of his sight, although we knew he wasn't with you in Minnesota."

Her anger rose while the pendant on her neck grew warmer.

"You knew we didn't have your son. Why are you really here?"

"I want answers."

Kramer laughed. "You didn't have to break in to ask them. You could have simply shown up at the front gate."

"The difference is I plan to *leave* when I'm done."

"Well, therein lies the problem. You know I can't let you leave, Emmanuella. But for the time being, let's pretend you can. I'm curious what you wanted to know badly enough to come back here."

She couldn't tell him they were there for the book. "Why did Alex find me six years ago? What was he looking for? I'd never seen him before in my life."

He sighed. "Alex wished to take matters into his own hands. None of us were aware of what he did until we found out from you. We would never have condoned it."

"So you condone kidnapping but not rape."

"Kidnapping is such an ugly word. I prefer detained."

"Why me?"

"We've suspected for years you were the woman of the prophecy. We've simply watched you since we saw no reason to make contact yet. Then the other group began trying to kidnap your son, and we lost you both. We found you just in time to bring you here for the deadline in the prophesy. Of course, that didn't go as planned. Davenport was supposed to bring you here and we would have explained the situation to you, hoping for your cooperation. We never expected to have so many *issues*."

"And if I didn't cooperate?"

Kramer shrugged. "We hoped for the best. We can be very persuasive."

"For the sake of argument, let's say I'm really stuck here. What are your plans for me?"

"Until we learned of your special talents, we simply planned to offer shelter and aid."

Emma rolled her eyes. "How generous of you."

"There's no denying that men wish to harm you. We offer you protection."

"And after the baby is born?"

"After learning of your special talents, you're even more valuable to us now." He leaned his arm on the back of his chair in a casual stance. "Tell me, Emma, what *are* you capable of?"

The situation was so crazy she wanted to laugh, but his nonchalance grated on her nerves. "I could fry you where you sit. Are you afraid?"

"No. Intrigued. Fascinated." The way his eyes lit up told her it was true, to her aggravation.

"You caused an explosion in the woods. How did you do that?"

"You and Warren said Alex was obsessed with me now. Why?"

Kramer laughed. "Don't wish to share your secrets? Fine. For now. Besides, I'm interested in your thoughts on this. After you escaped, Alex had some type of breakdown. He seemed determined to not only find you but *claim you.*"

"What the fuck does that mean?"

"Like I said, he had some sort of mental breakdown. He mumbled on and on that he realized who he really was and some nonsense about his destiny. Phillip tried to reason with him and tell him that Davenport had the mark, that it was too late, but he insisted it wasn't. He said something about not being bound to destiny."

Raphael's words echoed in her head.

"Alex said we were thinking too small, too immediate, that this didn't concern us at all. He said this was a game that had been played for centuries, always ending before a winner was declared, only to be rebooted decades later. But this time was different." Kramer sipped his drink, then narrowed his eyes. "He said this time *you* were different."

Her heart raced. "What does *that* mean?"

"We don't know. I had hoped you could tell me."

"I have no idea. I didn't know about any of this until you dragged me into it."

"That's not true. Your son has a gift. Surely you were aware of your specialness."

"I only have a son because of Alex. And I assure you, there's nothing special about me."

"Oh, you are so wrong. Even we were unaware how special you are."

"Great, I'm special, but I am not your property. I just want my son and to be left alone."

"I know how you can get your son back."

"How?" Why would he tell her? Then she remembered they wanted Jake now. He hoped to use her.

"There's no denying Alex's obsession with you. If you really want to find your son, I know how to do it." He paused. "*You* could lure Alex out. You find Alex, then you find Jake."

"Why would I do that?"

"For your son, of course."

"Do you think I'm stupid enough to trust you?"

"Of course not. I'm just pointing out your options. We could help you."

"No, thanks." She shook her head. "I still don't know why you're telling me this. What's in it for you?"

"Alex. He's a loose cannon with Phillip's presidential campaign. He's unstable and needs to be neutralized."

"*You would kill Warren's son?*"

"No, of course not," he scoffed. "Merely contain him."

"Like you contained me."

He shrugged. "You wouldn't need to be contained if you would only cooperate."

"Okay, I've heard enough. I'm out of here."

"I'm afraid I can't allow that."

"In case you haven't figured this out, I have a gun." She waved the weapon to emphasis her point.

"Emma, be reasonable. I have armed men outside my door. How will you get past them?"

Will stepped out from behind the bedroom door. "She won't be doing it alone."

CHAPTER TWENTY

KRAMER laughed and folded his hands under his chin. "I wondered when you'd show up. If she's here, I knew you couldn't be far away. This just keeps getting better and better. Phillip thought you would come back, but I didn't peg you for being that stupid."

Will winked and flashed his grin, pointing his gun toward Kramer. "Just goes to show that sometimes you never really know a person."

"This isn't like last time, Will. You just can't waltz out of here with a hostage. They'll be prepared for that. I have armed men all over the compound. You'll never get away."

Kramer sat in his chair so smug and sure of himself that anger overrode Emma's fear. What gave him the right to order her around? Destroy her life? He smiled at her as he reached toward his pocket.

Will raised his gun. "I wouldn't do that if I were you."

"Now, Will. Are you going to shoot me and have all those men out in the hall rush in here and possibly kill Emma? I've given them orders to shoot to kill when they see her."

"I don't believe you. She's too valuable."

"Are you really willing to bet her life on that?" Kramer asked. "Our men shot at her in Minnesota."

Emma reluctantly nodded. "It's true. They did."

"So why didn't you send men with guns in Kansas City?" Will asked. "Why just some thugs with a pipe?"

Kramer shook his head with a frown. "That wasn't us." He tilted his head to Emma. "See? I told you we are more than eager to help protect you."

"While you threaten to kill me? Yeah, that makes me feel all warm and fuzzy." The pendant on her neck lay under her shirt, warming against her chest.

"It's obvious we're at an impasse," Kramer said. "Who's going to make the first move?" He locked eyes with Will and slowly slipped his hand into his pants pocket.

Will's demeanor screamed cold and calculated, but Emma saw the vein pulsing on his neck. He was hesitating. Because of her. Anger burned in her chest and the pendant scorched her skin.

Kramer slowly slipped out a phone with a smile of victory raising the corners of his mouth. "Excuse me while I make a call." He began to push buttons.

Emma held her breath. *Oh, my God. We're trapped.* They'd be locked up and watched like caged animals possibly for the rest of her life and she'd never get Jake. Rage over his smugness and intimidation blistered her throat and she recognized the ball of power and electricity building in her core. She couldn't let him get away with this.

"Stop." She growled, electricity tingling on her arms.

Kramer paused, his finger hovering over his phone. His arm jerked and shook. He looked up his eyes wide and his mouth gaping.

She couldn't believe he did what she said. In her peripheral vision, she saw Will turn to her in shock.

"Who are you calling?" she asked.

His mouth twisted in a grimace. He appeared to be struggling against himself. "Security," He muttered through clenched teeth.

"Put the phone down on the table."

Kramer's hand shook as he reached for the table, phone in his hand. His face paled and his voice rose in panic. "What are you *doing to me*?" The phone dropped onto the table with a clank.

"Ensuring our getaway." She turned to Will, unsure what to do next. "Where's James?"

"Taken care of. I only need to worry about you."

She raised her eyebrow in mock surprise. "Funny, I thought it was the other way around."

Will walked to the door and put his ear next to it.

"What should we do with him?" she asked, fear creeping in to replace her anger. How had she controlled him? Kramer's mouth twisted in agony, his eyes wide with terror.

"Can you make him tell them to remove the security guards outside the door?"

"I don't know." She turned to Kramer, but the stone around her neck had already began to cool. She thought about what he planned to do to her and the rage returned, along with the power.

Will moved toward her and she lowered her voice. "I have no idea how much I can control him. What if he's on the phone and he tells them we're here?"

"I'm willing to take the chance. If we walk out of here with them still out there we'll get the same results. At least this way we have a shot."

She nodded. "Okay." She focused on the power and then on Kramer and making him do what she wanted.

Kramer grabbed his head. "Stop," he groaned.

"Emma…" Will said.

"I'm trying."

"I think you're trying too hard. Scale it back."

Kramer seemed to be in even more pain than before. What if she killed him? "I've never done this, Will. I don't know what I'm doing." Her voice rose with her panic.

"It's okay, take a deep breath. You're doing great. Maybe not so intense."

The power in her chest felt like it was about to explode. Kramer laid his head on the arm of the chair, rolling in agony. She knew she had to release some of it or the result would be disastrous. Instinctively, she lowered the gate to the power, letting it travel down her arms and through her fingertips, The room filled with electricity.

Kramer stopped moaning.

"Emma, what the hell was *that*?" Will asked.

"It's okay." She took a deep breath. She felt more in control and centered herself on the power tumbling inside. Somehow she knew she could do this. "Kramer, pick up your phone."

He sat up and retrieved the phone off the table.

"Look at me," she said.

He looked toward her, the fear on his face dissolving into blankness.

"Scott," she said in a soothing voice. "I need you to do something for me. Will you help me?"

He nodded.

"That's good, very good." Her voice was soft and sweet, like a mother to a child. "I need you to tell the security guards in front of the apartment that you don't need them and to leave. Will you do that for me?"

"Yes," he mumbled softly.

"Thank you. You can call them now." She moved so that she could keep an eye on him and on the door.

He punched numbers on the phone and Emma tightened the grip on her gun, the slick of sweat on her palm making the handle slippery.

Kramer raised the phone to his ear.

Will lifted his gun.

Kramer stared at the wall with a dead look in his eyes. "This is Kramer. Call off the security guards in front of my apartment." His voice sounded tired.

"You can hang up."

Kramer pressed a button on the phone.

"Thank you, Scott." She turned to Will. "Now what?"

"We'll wait for the guards to disperse, then we'll leave."

"What about him?"

"We'll leave him here. We should have enough time to get away."

Remnants of power still coursed through her body. She took a deep breath and shook her arms.

"Are you okay?"

"Yeah."

Will leaned toward her. "Look at him. He's still under your control."

"Is there anything we want to get out of him?"

"Of course, where to start is the question."

Emma knelt down in front of Kramer. "Scott, why did your group think I was the woman in the prophecy?"

His vacant eyes stared at her. "Walker told us. He read the papers and did the research and translations. He said you were the one."

"But how did he know? How did you know where to find me?"

"Walker insisted it was you. Alex said Walker gave him your location six years ago."

Emma shot a glance to Will.

His mouth pressed into a tight line.

"So why not capture me sooner? Why wait?"

"Walker insisted that you not be brought to us until it was time. He said we weren't allowed to interfere."

The hairs on Emma's neck stood on end. Raphael had said the same thing. That he wasn't allowed to interfere.

Will knelt beside her. "I thought Warren was in charge. Why is Walker calling the shots?"

"No one questions Walker."

"Why not?" Emma asked.

Kramer didn't answer.

"Why not?" Will asked, lowering his voice.

"I don't know." Kramer said.

Emma's eyes widened as she turned to Will.

An explosion rattled the windows and shouts erupted behind the building. Will stood and dimmed the light, checking out the back window. "They've found James' trap. That's our diversion. We need to go."

Emma rose. "But—"

"You already got more out of him than I ever hoped to. Let's not take any chances. The guards are focused on James in the back. We'll go out the front. Keep an eye on Kramer." Will moved to the door to the bedroom and stopped in the opening. "If you feel threatened, go ahead and shoot him."

She held her gun on Kramer, but he seemed more a zombie than the man she talked to ten minutes earlier. His eyes were vacant and his mouth now drooped on one side. What if she'd damaged his brain?

Will returned with several neckties. "Have him move to the office chair."

Emma gave him the order and he rose and sat in the seat she pointed to.

Will tied his arms and legs to the dining room chair then gagged him with a tie.

"Should I try to release him?" Emma whispered. As much as she wanted him in his zombie state, she needed to know she hadn't permanently injured him.

Will sensed her apprehension. He lifted her chin with his fingers, searching her eyes. "If it were up to me, I'd have you scramble his brains, but I know what that would do to you. So, if you need to release him, go ahead."

She nodded, her lips pressed tight, then knelt in front of Kramer. "Scott, look at me," she whispered.

His expressionless eyes stared into hers.

"You are no longer under my control. I free you." To her surprise, she felt the bond disconnect.

His eyes widened as he realized he was bound. He began to rock in his chair as he struggled to free himself.

Her shoulders tensed and her voice tightened. "I'm feeling generous today. I might not be so lenient next time." She stood up and turned to Will. "Let's go."

****

Will looked through the peephole. "There's still one guard in the hall."

"What are we going to do?" He heard the anxiety in her voice.

He never should have brought her along. Goddamn that James. Now he had to worry about keeping Ema safe, although he had to admit she had gotten information from Kramer. The way she controlled him...when had she learned that? Shivers crawled down his spine. What was Emma capable of?

"I'll take care of the guard," he said.

"Don't kill him."

He looked down at her, shaking his head. "You know he wouldn't hesitate to shoot us."

"That doesn't mean we need to sink to their level."

He took a deep breath. "Okay, stand over there." He pointed to a corner in the entryway then cracked the door open after she'd moved.

After a few seconds, the guard shoved a shoulder through the crack. "Mr. Kramer?"

Will smashed the shotgun butt onto the man's head and he crumpled to the floor. Will dragged him out of the opening while Emma shut the door behind him.

Kramer rocked the chair in the other room, the gag muffling his shouts.

Will took off the guard's belt and tied his hands behind his back, looping it around a table leg in the process. Reaching into his pants pocket, he pulled out a set of keys. He figured the guy had to have a car on the grounds. The only problem would be finding it. He walked over to the window and saw a parking lot scattered with cars at the other side of the complex.

"That will detain him for awhile, but not long," Will said. "We need to get moving." He glanced out the peephole again and mumbled, "It's clear." Opening the door, he peered into the hall before he grabbed her arm and pulled her out the door and into the stairwell.

"Where's James?" she whispered as they sprinted down the stairs.

"I sent him to the car. I told him I'd call him after we got away."

"Aren't you worried? You said they found him."

"No, they found the diversion he created. He should have been long gone by the time they found it. I sent him off when Kramer came into the apartment. He snuck out the window."

"He *jumped* four floors?"

"No, he rappelled."

"Of course he repelled." Sarcasm dripped from her words.

Will couldn't help his smile. They reached the first floor and Will continued descending.

"Where are we going?"

"The basement." It amazed him that she didn't ask why and just followed his lead.

He'd prefer to go out the back door and slink along the back of the buildings, working their way to the parking lot full of cars. But the guards would be out there after finding James' pipe bomb. The front was more inconspicuous, but he doubted Emma would be inconspicuous. She was a woman in a compound filled mostly with men. She'd draw the attention of the guards.

Which meant he had to hide her.

They stopped at the basement landing of the stairwell. After checking for activity, they entered a large room with concrete walls filled with discarded furniture.

"What are you looking for?" she asked.

"This." He walked over to a rolling trash cart, half full of trash bags. He took her hand and led her to it.

"Oh. No."

"Oh, yes. But not yet." He opened a closet door and rummaged around until he found a work shirt, shrugging his arms into the sleeves.

"Carl?" she asked, reading the name on the shirt. "I knew a Carl once."

Lifting an eyebrow. "Did you, now?" He put his hands on her waist. "Time to take a ride."

She didn't argue as he lifted her up and swung her over the cart edge. He released her as her feet touched the bottom and she began shoving bags out of the way.

"This is disgusting."

"Exactly, that's why it's the perfect place to hide."

"Are you sure I can't push you?"

"No way. When I was a little boy I wanted to be a trash man. It's the fulfillment of a lifelong dream."

She squatted down and looked up at him, surrounded by bags. "Far be it for me to keep you from fulfilling your fantasy."

"Princess, I've had plenty of fantasies about you and none have ever involved trash." He handed her his gun and backpack. "I hope this works, but in case we get into trouble, don't hesitate to use this."

"What about you?"

He tucked his handgun into a holster under his shirt. "I've got this, but hopefully I won't need it." She nodded.

"Sorry, time to for you to hide now," he said as he moved some to the bags to cover her head.

"You get us out of this and maybe we can work on one of your non-trash-related fantasies," she said, her voice muffled by the bags.

"Now there's an incentive." He pushed the cart toward the elevator. "No talking from here on out."

The doors opened to an empty box. Will released a sigh of relief as he wheeled the cart inside and pushed the button for the first floor. He tried to act lackadaisical for the camera in the corner. It would be a miracle if they got out of this without gunfire, but he still hoped for the best.

The first-floor lobby was empty with the exception of a security guard at the front desk, the hum of the floor polishers noticeably absent. The guard looked up at Will with narrowed eyes and stood up from his chair. Will pushed the cart toward the front doors, ignoring the man.

"Where's Mitch?" the guard asked.

"Uh, I think he's off tonight." Will kept his head down.

The guard walked around the desk. "What's your name? I need to check your credentials."

"Stan McEntire."

"How come you're wearing Carl's shirt?" His hand gripped the handle of his gun on his belt.

Will shrugged, trying to look bored. "I'm a temp. Got called in the last minute and had to use his shirt."

The guard studied him, dropping his hand from the handle of his gun. "I wasn't notified that you were filling in. After the incident a few weeks ago, they always notify me of personnel changes." He walked behind the desk.

"Incident?" Will asked in a anxious voice. "I never heard anything about an 'incident.'" He looked around. "I dunno if this job's gonna work out if you're having incidents."

"Relax," the guard said picking up the phone. "It's not as bad as it sounds."

Will walked up to the chest high counter and pulled his gun out from under his shirt, keeping it below the ledge. "I better go. I was told to take this trash bin down to the medical building on the end and I don't want to get in trouble." His thumb pointed to the bin behind him.

"This will only take a minute." The guard held the phone to his ear as he punched the numbers.

Will glanced over his shoulder toward the cart. He wished he could ask Emma to stop this guy with her mind control trick but even if he did, he doubted there was time for her to do it before he got someone on the other line.

Shit.

"That call isn't necessary." Will lowered his voice.

The guard looked up in surprise.

Will raised his gun over the counter, pointing it at the man. "If you could be so kind to just get up and step away from the phone."

Anger flashing in his eyes, the guard took a step back and reached for his gun. Will squeezed the trigger before the man got the weapon out of the holster. He fell backwards, blood splattering the wall behind him. Will moved behind the counter and shoved him under the desk. The now-familiar burning in his mark returned. Of course, Emma had no idea who got shot.

Since his mark burned, he knew he had a connection to her and decided to use it.

Emma. I'm okay.

Thank God.

I didn't want to shoot him. He reached for his gun. He found it odd that he felt the need to explain himself to her for doing what he was trained to do.

I know. It's okay.

But it wasn't okay, he thought, trying to keep it from Emma as he pushed the bin through the front door into the warm, humid night. He hadn't wanted to shoot the guy. For one thing, there was a good chance it was caught on a security camera. For another, the sound alone was bound to alert someone. Either scenario meant that they needed to move before the other guards figured out what happened.

The vibrations of the rolling cart along the concrete sidewalk rumbled through the night, calling more attention to Will than he would have liked. He ambled down the sidewalk from the farthest building on the west side to the farthest building on the east, having to pass two buildings in between. Jagged shadows filled his path. His goal was to look like a janitor avoiding doing any more work than necessary instead of a man desperate to escape. But it was all about perception. You could make people believe you were whom you wanted them to believe just by playing the part well. And Will was an expert. He'd fooled everyone for so long he'd even fooled himself the last few years. But until the last few weeks, he'd never had so much at risk.

Halfway down the sidewalk, he heard a commotion from behind. He glanced over his shoulder. Men ran from the building he'd just passed toward the entrance of the one he just left.

Fuck. He pushed the cart faster but tried to look like a confused temp worker caught in the middle of chaos.

He'd almost made it to the medical structure when five armed men ran out and moved toward him. He tensed but realized they were focused on the scene behind him, barely giving him a second glance. One of the men stopped in front of the cart, forcing Will to stop.

"Hey buddy, you seen anyone suspicious tonight?"

"Yeah," Will grimaced. "I saw two guys dressed all in black run off that way to that building." He pointed behind him. "They almost knocked my bin over halfway here."

The guard rested his hand on the edge of the cart and looked Will up and down. Will gave him an annoyed glare, like he was tired of people interfering with his work.

"All right then," the guard said, standing upright and shifting his weight to his side. "You might want to stay inside until all of this is over."

Will nodded and pushed the cart to the doors, releasing a sigh and some of his tension with it. He opened the double doors maneuvering the cart halfway through.

"Wait a minute," the guard called, his voice sharp.

Will leaned over the cart and grabbed the barrel of the shotgun. Rising, he kept the gun behind him, still inside the trash bin. "Yeah?"

"Why do you look so familiar?"

Will shrugged. "Dunno, got one of those faces, I guess. I hear that all the time."

They locked eyes and Will kept his face expressionless.

"Yeah," the guard scowled. "I guess so." He turned and took a few steps as Will moved the cart inside the lobby.

"Stop!" The guard shouted as he spun, gun in his hand.

Will shoved the cart into the building as he swung his shotgun out and fired, hitting the guard in the chest.

"Emma! Let's go!"

She threw bags out off of her and stood in the cart, starting to climb over the edge. Will wrapped an arm around her waist and pulled her out in one movement, carrying her several steps before her feet touched the ground. He raced for the back door.

"This is going to get hairy," he said pulling the keys out of his pocket. "I'm gonna need your help."

"Okay."

He hoped the security guard had a halfway decent car. Then again, anything would be better than the beat-up Honda that Emma drove the night he met her. He shoved Emma against the wall next to the back door before he opened it, expecting to find half a dozen men or more shooting at him. But the lot was empty. He realized they had all rushed to the other end. He definitely planned to use that to his advantage.

He pushed the lock button on the keys. The brake lights of a sedan flashed and he wrapped his hand around Emma's wrist and pulled her out the door.

His heart hammered in his chest. He was used to the adrenaline rush and even fear. It was the guys who were no longer afraid when in battle who were dangerous, but he wasn't used to the building terror. They were hopelessly outnumbered, locked inside a chain-link fence. Even if they got out, they still had to outrun who knew how many cars. As he reached the sedan and shoved Emma in the driver's seat, he realized that the car wasn't fast enough to out run them all.

Shit.

But at the moment, he had the advantage and he planned to buy all the time he could.

CHAPTER TWENTY-ONE

EMMA jammed the gear into drive. "How fast do you want me to drive?"

"Like there's a rabid dog on your ass."

She pressed on the gas, tires squealing. "You realize this will get all kinds of attention?"

"Princess, no matter what we do, we're going to get attention. Let's do it with style."

"Alrighty then." She forced a grin and headed toward the circular one-way road that looped around the compound, going the wrong direction. Throwing a glance at Will, she tore down the asphalt. "This is the shortest distance to the front gate. I thought it best not to drive past all those men with guns."

"Good thinking. Where've you been all my life?"

"Waiting for you," she snorted.

They neared the guard station at the front entrance. Headlights glowed on the road behind them.

"We have two choices," she said. "We drive right on through or we stop and try to talk our way out the gate, although I doubt even your smooth talking will get us through."

Will released a tight laugh. "I don't feel like talking."

"Okay, you might want to bend down in case something flies through the windshield."

"I was thinking about ducking to avoid bullets, but I guess it's dual-purpose." He braced his hand on the dashboard and looked out the back window. "When you get to the road, turn right."

She floored the gas pedal and ducked down as they flew past the guard station. Bullets shattered the side windows, but she held onto the wheel, hoping she stayed on course. She rose in time to see the wooden gate arm as the car crashed through. The board ripped apart, flying over the roof. The tires screeched as she reached the road and turned right, trying to keep the car from skidding off the road.

"Are you all right?" Will asked.

"I'm still driving, aren't I?" She looked in the rearview mirror and saw headlights closer than before. "They're coming."

He looked over his shoulder. "Shit, just as I suspected. There's a fleet back there."

"What are we going to do? They're gaining on us."

Will ran his hand through his hair. "We need to go to the airport. Once we get there, do you think you can take care of them?"

"Take care of them?" she asked, raising her eyebrows. "You mean like feed them and tuck them into bed?"

Will let out an exasperated sigh. "You know what I mean. With your…"

"Power?"

Will grunted.

She could see he hated asking her to use it. She also knew it wasn't because it stung his male pride. The fact he always had her drive in situations like this assured her of that. He worried that it would hurt her, yet she'd warned him that she needed practice. What happened with Kramer proved just how little she knew about what she could do. "Have anything in mind? Blow them up?"

"Yeah."

"So is the plan to lure them to the airport, blow them all up and then leave?"

"Kind of."

"Kind of how?"

"We're not driving out."

"Then how are… *we're flying*?"

"Yep."

"I guess now's a bad time to mention I'm afraid of flying." She groaned. "Are you planning on kidnapping a pilot?"

"Nope. I'll fly it."

"*You know how to fly*?"

"No, but I figured, how hard could it be?" He turned to see her shocked expression. "Of course I know how to fly a plane."

"*Of course, James repelled down a forty-foot wall. Of course, I know how to fly a plane.* No, Will, these are not *of course* situations for me."

Will reloaded his gun. "But after everything we've been through…"

She checked the rearview mirror and saw the headlights getting closer. "You forget that I'd never been in a gunfight until I met you. Outrun them with my car? Sure.

But never with guns. So forgive me if I seem a little *slow*." Her voice rose along with her panic.

Will put his hand over hers on the steering wheel. "Emma, it's okay. I'm gonna get us out of this." He squeezed her fingers and she gave him a quick glance before turning back to the road. "We're *both* going to get us out of this. Okay?"

She nodded.

"We're almost there." Will pointed to the tower in the distance. The spinning red and green light called like a beacon. "Can you crash through a chain-link gate?"

"Yeah, I guess so. But I remember the gate being fairly close to the road. I'll have to turn and I'm worried I won't have enough speed."

"You'll have about fifty feet after the turn. You okay with that?"

"Do I have a choice?"

"No."

She gripped the wheel and took a slow steady breath. If she didn't angle it right, they could end up in the ditch and flip over. The headlights in the mirror reminded her of the alternative. She focused on the turn first, thankful that the side road was paved. Twisting the wheel left, she let off the gas then swung the wheel right, the back end of the car sliding to the side. Once the nose faced the side road, she punched the gas pedal, shooting down the road.

"God, I love you."

"We're not there yet." The wheel was slick in her hands.

Her heart raced as she aimed for the padlocked opening, wondering if this was suicide. But it was too late to back out now. The car hit the gate and flung it open as they flew through. The car bounced on the uneven pavement and Emma fought for control.

Will let out a breath of relief. "Drive up to that metal hangar ahead. Stop before you get to the double doors and stay in the car until I tell you to get out."

As she skidded to a halt in front of fifty-foot-wide building, Will threw the car door open and jumped out, running to the padlocked door with his lock picking kit in hand. Headlights from the pursuing cars filled the paved runway.

The lock fell to the pavement. "Can you blow those things up before they get close enough to shoot us?"

"I don't know." She ran to the hangar. "I'll try."

Will pushed a metal door open enough for both of them to slide through. Industrial fluorescent lights flicked on overhead as they entered the metal building, which housed two planes and a jet.

"Stay behind the door while I figure out which one we can use." He ran to the middle plane and ducked under the overhead wings.

Her irritation over the situation already heated the stone on her neck and pushed aside her fear. She let her anger build. Soon the churning mass of energy burned in her chest.

"This one will work." Will shouted around the plane door. "I'm going to start the engine so it's going to get loud. When I wave to you, slide the doors open and run and get in the plane. Now would be a good time to take care of some of those cars."

Her back to the metal door, the electricity in her body was to near capacity now. She turned and stood in the opening of the doors as three cars screeched to a halt in front of the building. Car doors flew open and men scrambled out, pointing guns toward her.

Energy gathered in her palms. Sweat trickled down her neck, every nerve ending raw. Could she do this?

"Emma, what the fuck are you doing?" Will screamed behind her.

The men hesitated as she watched them, her hands her only weapon.

"Just come on out, Ms. Thompson. We don't want to hurt you."

Her entire body burned, shocks jumping from one hair to the next. She raised her palms as a glow surrounded her.

Bullets whizzed over her head.

Without thinking, she released the energy and pushed it to the closest car. The vehicle exploded into flames, metal pieces raining down on the asphalt. She swallowed the vomit that rose in her throat, flooded with self-disgust. How easy it was to kill.

The plane engine roared to life behind her. The wind whipped her hair around her face while the energy grew and replaced what she'd used. The power removed all fear and she faced her attackers as they regrouped.

The men shouted, but their words were lost on in storm of wind and energy. When she heard the shots, she blasted the other two cars, the force of the explosions pushing against her. She held her ground. If she killed these men, the least she could do was witness it. She looked out into the street for signs of other cars. Headlights shone off in the distance, approaching their direction.

What has she become, that she could so callously kill? The glow from the stone began to fade.

She turned to look at Will, who sat in the cockpit wearing headphones, his head bent over the control panel. Gas fumes filled the air and she breathed in through her open mouth to keep from gagging. The flaps on the wings moved in rapid succession, as well at the tail. The plane rolled forward a few feet and the engine revved louder. Emma's hair blew in all directions and she reached up and tried to control it as she looked out the crack in the door. The headlights in the distance were closer and the three fires burned fifty feet from the building like funeral pyres.

Will glanced up and waved. She leaned into the metal door and pushed. The heavy doors slid open, the scrapping of the metal wheels barely audible over the roar of the engine. She looked out to the road and saw the headlights turning onto the side road.

They were close. *Shit.* She ran for the plane, giving a wide berth to the propeller. Grabbing the handle of the side door, she scrambled in as the wind forced the door shut behind her.

Will handed her a pair of headphones. "Here. Put these on," he shouted over the roar of the engine.

She slipped them over her ears as Will rolled the plane to the entrance, easing through the opening. Once out, he made a sharp turn, barely missing the side of the building in an effort to stay clear from the burning cars.

Headlights entered the airfield.

"Can you do anything to them while you're inside the plane?" Will asked through the microphone on his headphones.

"I don't know!" she shouted. "I have no idea if I can do something through glass. I suspect I can't."

Once around the burning cars, Will revved the engine as they turned, heading for the runway. He cast her a quick glance. "The window will tilt open, although not very far. You'd have to be careful with the wings overhead. They're filled with gasoline."

Emma looked in the backseat and saw the shotgun. "Fuck that." She grabbed the gun and opened the window, sticking the tip out the opening at the bottom.

The cars spread out, two barreling toward them on the outer strip and two coming down the runway.

"Shit, I don't have enough room to take off." Will slowed the plane.

"What are you *doing*?"

"You're going to have to lose a few of them, otherwise we'll never get off the ground."

"Great."

The two cars on the outer road drove past, heading away from the plane. Emma shot several rounds at the nearest car. The back tire blew and the car swerved to the side before it crashed into the hangar. The two cars on the runway split up and drove on either side, driving to the end of the runway but not firing any shots.

"I don't suppose I can open the window in the back?" she asked, looking over her shoulder.

"No."

The two cars behind were now approaching on either side. Emma tried to aim at the car on her side, but the window didn't open far enough. She considered trying to blow up the cars by opening the door, but a glance up at the wing full of a highly flammable substance stopped her.

"Grab my shirt and make sure I don't fall out." Jerking off her headphones, she grabbed the handle on the door.

"*What?*" He watched her push the door open. "Emma!"

She ignored him, turning sideways in the seat, she lay backward so her head and shoulders were outside the plane. Will grabbed her shirt as she rotated her shoulders to face them, gun in hand. The wind from the propeller slammed the door into the shotgun butt and her body jerked as she tried to hold onto it.

Gunshots from the car hit the back of the plane.

"Emma!" Will's grip stretched the fabric of her shirt. "Get back inside!"

Ignoring her racing heart, she steadied herself and aimed for the windshield. She squeezed the trigger twice, thankful that one of the shots actually hit the target in spite of the bouncing plane.

Will tried to pull her in and she braced her feet against the seat. "I haven't taken care of them yet," she tried to yell over the roar of the engine. She doubted he even heard her.

"*Emma!*"

She aimed again, both shots connecting with the windshield, but more shots echoed from the cars. The plane bounced violently and the door slammed into her scalp. She saw black spots and shook her head, sharp pain accompanying the movement.

"Emma, get your goddamned ass in the plane! I have to turn the corner and I can't do it holding onto you."

She reached in and grabbed the seat belt and pulled herself up. "Then turn."

He scowled as he let go, putting both hands on the yoke.

They neared the end of the runway and she was about to lose her opportunity. She looped her arm around the shoulder belt and leaned back again.

"Goddamn it, Emma! What the fuck are you doing?"

She was prepared for the banging door this time so she braced herself as it slammed. Tensing her back muscles to hold herself up, she aimed and released multiple shots into the windshield over the driver's seat. The car swerved out of control before it jerked away and rolled off into the grass. She lost sight of it as the plane turned the corner and she pulled herself in.

Will turned onto the runway and faced the car headed toward them. "Son of a fucking bitch." He shot her angry look. "You try to go out the door again and I'll drag your ass back in by your hair."

"Yeah, you're welcome," she sneered as she put her headphones back on. But she knew she'd scared him.

Will jerked the plane to the right, off the runway, and onto the grass. The car drove past and Will turned back onto the asphalt. The aircraft barreled ahead, nearing the end of the runway.

"Aren't you going to take off?"

"I can't. I have to turn around."

"Then we'll be back in the same situation, facing the fucking car."

"I need the headwind to take off." He turned onto the taxi lane.

One car followed behind. The other turned onto the outer road and drove toward them

"Hang on, we're going to take off from the outer road." Will revved the engine then the plane hurtled down the pavement. The car from behind moved to Will's side. Will ducked down and popped the latch on his window. "Give me the gun."

She passed it over and he grabbed it with one hand.

"Grab the yoke and hold it while I shoot."

"I don't know how to do that!" she shouted.

More shots rang out, one flying through the window.

"It's like holding a steering wheel. Just hold tight but don't pull back."

She gripped the handles, the vibrations shaking her hands and arms.

Will picked up the shotgun and jammed the tip through the window, firing at the car on their side. The car swerved back and forth but steadied itself.

Will sat up and looked over the dashboard as more shots hit the plane. "Fuck!"

Emma raised her head to see the car in front heading toward them. The bullets whizzed through the back window and into the roof. She ducked down.

Will shot at the car again. "Emma, pull back on the yoke!"

"*What?*"

"*Pull back on the yoke!*"

Her breath came in short bursts as she pulled the handles, only to meet resistance. She pulled harder and the nose of the plane lifted up. "Oh, God." She looked out the window to see the wheel on her side inches off the ground.

The bullets came in a more rapid succession. "You have to pull back more!" Will shouted.

She yanked harder and the plane lifted off the ground.

The yoke jerked toward her in a sharp movement. She panicked before realizing Will had grabbed his handles and pulled back. The plane lifted higher and flew over the car in front, barely missing the roof.

They flew higher, over the trees at on the other side of the road, leaving the cars behind.

CHAPTER TWENTY-TWO

WILL flew east and lifted the landing gear as they continued to climb. The motor whirred until the wheels stopped in the belly of the plane with a thud.

Emma jumped in her seat. "What the hell was that?"

"It's just the landing gear. Relax, it's normal. Are you really afraid to fly?"

Her knuckles turned white from her fingers digging into the seat cushion. "Yeah," Emma took a deep breath, but her back remained stiff. She reached a hand to the back of her head and pulled it down. In the light of the control panel, Will saw dark red pools on her fingertips.

His stomach dropped. "Are you hurt?" He looked her up and down. *Please God, don't let her have gotten shot again.*

"I'm okay. I just banged my head on the door when I was hanging outside."

"You scared the shit out of me."

"It had to be done."

He reached over and checked her shirt and pants for signs of a gunshot wound. He lifted her hair from the nape of her neck. Blood trickled down her neck. He grabbed his backpack from the backseat, setting it on Emma's lap. "We'll discuss that stunt later. There's a first aid box in there. Get out some gauze to stop the bleeding."

She opened the pack and pulled out a gauze square, pulling her hair over her shoulder to access her wound. He worried about the amount of blood on her neck but reminded himself it was a head wound.

She winced as she dabbed the pad on her head and tilted her head to look out the window. “Shouldn’t we be flying higher?”

“Yeah, but we're not out of the woods yet. They could send someone after us so I’m trying to hide.”

“What do you mean *hide*?”

“If we fly low enough we can stay off the radar, great in theory but terrible with this terrain which is about to get pretty rough. It’s even worse that it’s night.” He nodded his head to her lap. “There’s a small flashlight in the backpack. Can you get it out and look around and see if you can find a map?”

“Like a road map?”

“Kind of. A topography map. It’ll show us anything tall like the hills or towers. Any obstacles we might encounter.”

She pulled out the flashlight and turned it on, looking all around the plane. “Nothing.”

“I thought that would be too easy,” he sighed. “I need you to help me keep an eye out for anything we could fly into.”

“Shit.”

“Exactly.”

She sat straighter, looking out the window. The glow of the instrument panel on the windows reflected the anxiousness on her face.

Will decided he'd gone far enough east. Since they were flying over a field, it would be a good time to change direction. He banked the plane in a hard right, turning southwest.

Emma pressed her back into the seat, bracing her feet against the floor. "Oh, God. We're going to crash," she choked out.

"No, we're just turning."

"In the future," she said through gritted teeth. "could you please tell me before you do something like that again?"

"I'll try."

The field gave way to gently rolling hills, but he knew they were about to get bigger. His current direction was south toward Nebraska, skirting the Black Hills but heading toward the Badlands. Not exactly ideal conditions for flying illegally low. The brewing clouds to the west didn't help matters.

Emma eased her grip on the seat, although she still held on. She looked out the window, scanning the horizon. "Where are we going?"

"South then west into Wyoming. The more distance I can put between us and them the better. We're definitely not flying straight to Montana. That's the first place they'll look for us. "

"But—"

"We're still going to Montana, just not flying. It's a lot easier to track a plane than a car."

She nodded, biting her lip.

He knew it had to be hard being this close to finding Jake and yet still be so far. He reached over, wrapping his fingers around her hand that gripped the seat edge. "We're going to get him, Emma. I promise."

She turned to look at him over her shoulder. Tears brimmed her eyes as she nodded.

He turned his attention back to the view outside the windshield, thankful he still had moonlight to illuminate the hills rising in the distance. Under normal circumstances, he would fly over ten thousand feet, clearing them without a problem, but if he hoped to evade radar detection he needed to fly no more than a thousand feet off the ground. With some of the hills in front of them rising two thousand feet, that could be a problem.

The clouds in the distance billowed, glowing with lightning bursts. Will estimated the storm to be about fifty miles away. When they turned they'd be flying toward it, but not into it. He might take chances, but he wasn't stupid.

When they hit the Badlands ten minutes later, he sighed. "This is going to be like a fucking roller coaster ride," he said, increasing the throttle.

"I hate roller coasters more than I hate flying."

"Then your night's about to totally suck."

****

The first hill loomed ahead and Will pulled back on the yoke. The nose of the plane lifted, soaring over the top to the slope, only to dive down on the other side.

Her fingers grew numb from gripping the seat.

"One down, a few hundred to go," he said as the plane dipped into a valley, skimming several hundred feet over the grassland.

"Are you fucking serious?"

"Maybe a few less."

She caught her breath, preparing for the next hill but dismayed to see a forest of jagged monoliths projecting from the ground.

"Are we going to dive down into those?" she asked, her throat constricting in fear.

"No, we'll try to skim the top of them. The problem will be if a peak sticks out higher than the others. I'm going to need you to help me keep watch."

"Okay."

They approached the next batch, an endless parade of pinnacles, and she thought of Jake. Had she come this close to finding him, only to crash into a fiery ball?

She looked over at Will. He wore the intense gaze she had seen when he was in a difficult situation, his fingers wrapped around the handles in front of him.

"I never asked if you were a good pilot."

His mouth lifted into a small grin. "A little late to be asking that now."

Her stomach dropped when she realized it was true.

"Relax, Princess. I'm an excellent pilot. I got us off the ground, didn't I?"

"Seems like I had something to do with that too."

"So you did." He pulled back the yoke. "Hang on, this is about to get rougher."

They rose again and her guts churned in anticipation. The plane leveled out, sailing over the peaks below. Emma scanned the horizon.

"There's something ahead."

Will rose in his seat to look over the panel. "Where?"

She pointed to her right. "There."

"That's at one o'clock. It's like we're a clock and the nose is pointed at twelve. If you see something, tell me where it is in relation to time on a clock."

"Okay."

The wind picked up and a gust hit the plane, rocking the aircraft. "This could get a little hairy. We've got a gusty crosswind, which means the plane's going to get pitched sideways a bit." The wind blew to demonstrate his statement. He gripped the yoke and adjusted a knob. "It wouldn't be as big a problem if we were higher off the ground. Worst-case scenario, we turn into the wind and deal with rising and falling, not tilting sideways."

"Why is that bad?"

"Because we'll be flying straight into the Black Hills."

She turned to her right. The dark forested mountains taunted her.

"We could always land, right?"

"Sure, but someone's going to notice a plane landing and Kramer's sure to be listening for unusual plane activity. We're still close enough that we run the risk of being caught.

She pointed out the window. "Three o'clock."

He swung the plane to put ample space between them and the ridge. Another valley appeared and Will angled the plane into the wind and dove.

"Are you sure we can't fly higher?"

He didn't answer. Looking at the gauges, then out the windshield, tension crinkled his eyes.

"What's wrong?" she asked.

He sighed. "The storm to the west is worrying me. It's approaching faster than I expected."

She looked above to see dark gray clouds choking out the stars, rolling toward them.

"We can't fly in clouds?"

"Without radar contact, no. We'd want a control tower to help us." He raised an eyebrow. "Obviously, we don't want that. Another option would be to try to climb and fly over the clouds but I have no idea where they top out. We run the risk of flying into something by flying blind like that. But right now, that's not an issue. We're flying below the clouds. What I'm more concerned with is thunderstorms. They can produce wind shears that could rip our wings off."

"*What?*"

"I'm not flying into a thunderstorm. Not if I can help it." He tapped a screen low on the instrument panel. "See this? It's a storm scope. It's radar for lightning strikes. Right now the lightning is about thirty miles west of us, so we're still good. We want to avoid the lightning."

"Oh, God..."

The patter of rain hit the windshield. "This just keeps getting better and better." Will grumbled. "Hang on, more hills ahead."

He lifted the nose and they rose. She looked out the window dismayed to see her visibility had diminished.

"I can't see anything."

"That's the better and better part."

The onslaught of rain flooded the windshield. The flashing lights on the wings lit the streams of water that hit the plane, filling Emma with a sense of dread. Water dripped into the cabin from the bullet holes in the roof. "Can't we just land?"

"No."

"Are you sure?"

"Emma, where are we going to land? On top of one of those hills? Keep a look out."

The plane swung to the right, avoiding a tall ridge on Will's side. She tried to focus on the darkness outside the window, but the flashing lights on the wing obscured her view, adding to the throbbing in the back of her head. She turned to look behind and swung back to the front. A large point rose up to the right of the plane, closer than she would have liked.

"Oh, God! One o'clock!" She shouted, pointing.

"Son of a bitch," Will groaned as he saw the obstacle. The plane lifted and banked a hard left, turning the plane sideways. After he swung around it, he struggled with the yoke as he straightened it. "Try to let me know sooner."

"I didn't see it!" Emma's breath came in short bursts of panic.

"Emma," Will growled. "I need you. You can freak out later."

"I'm trying."

"Not hard enough."

The plane banked again to the right and jolted with a gust of wind, throwing her in to the door. Her head banged into the window. She caught the sight of a peak directly in front of the sideways plane.

"Twelve o'clock!"

"Son of a fucking bitch." The plane turned left and to the right again. A flattened peak passed by Emma's window, slightly below the plane.

"I'm gonna have to climb," Will said as the nose lifted and the pitch of the engine roared higher.

They flew for half a minute before the plane lowered slightly. Will released a measured breath. "I think we're about done with this set."

"There's more?"

"I don't know."

She wasn't sure how much more she could take. The plane dove. It was so sudden that it caught her by surprise and a gasp escaped before she could hold it back.

"It's okay. Another valley."

The way he said it implied what she already knew. "There's more."

"Yeah."

When the plane lifted, she was prepared. The rain had increased, coming down in sheets but she used the flashing lights to aid her this time, pointing out numerous obstacles before they descended again.

"I think that might have been the last one." Will sighed, relaxing in his seat. "I wish visibility was better, but according to the GPS we're almost to the Nebraska border. This is where I planned to turn into Wyoming. We're good here, pretty much grasslands with hills now, nothing like what we just went through."

"And then where?"

"We'll just keep going for now."

****

When grasslands appeared on the horizon, Will let out a sigh of relief. He needed to start thinking about where they were going to land.

He pulled out his cell phone. He still hadn't checked in with James.

"Who are you *calling*?" Emma asked in disbelief.

"James."

She scowled and shifted her gaze out the window.

James answered on the first ring. "Where the fuck are you?"

"Somewhere over Wyoming."

"*Excuse me*?"

"We borrowed a plane."

"Borrowed?"

"It's a relative term. Where are you?"

"Driving around aimlessly in South Dakota. Did you know they have a palace here made entirely of corn?"

"No kidding?"

"Where do you want to meet up?"

"We need to go to Montana."

"Oh, hell no. I signed up for a week in South Dakota. I did my part. I got you information and I helped you break into the compound. Now I'm done."

"Just one more job. Even you can't say no to this one."

James was silent for a moment. "What is it?"

Will heard the defeat in his voice and grinned. "We're going to rescue a kid."

Emma turned to him, her eyes hopeful.

"Oh, God… how did I know?" James groaned.

"How can you say no to saving a kid?"

"Fuck."

Will knew he'd won. "Just start driving Interstate 90 and we'll meet somewhere in Wyoming. I'll call you when I know where somewhere is."

"You're going to owe me so much."

"Tell me about it."

Will stuffed his phone in his pocket, looking out the window again. The storm was moving northwest and they were moving west, just at its base. The rain had stopped for the moment, although he wasn't sure how long the break would last. Emma seemed more relaxed, her hands merely resting on the edge of the seat rather than trying to claw the cushion out with her nails.

Will glanced down at the instrument panel and noticed the oil temperature gauge pointed to high. He tapped the plastic and the needle didn't move.

"Emma, where's that flashlight?"

She pulled it out of the backpack. "Here."

"Keep an eye out and let me know if there's anything ahead I need to worry about." He turned sideways, shining the flashlight out the window and up to the wing overhead. "Shit."

"Goddamn it, Will. One word I don't want to hear while flying is *shit*."

"We've got a gas tank leak. See?" The beam of light shone on a string of droplets trailing behind them.

"What does that mean?" He heard the panic in her voice.

"It means we're running out of fuel." The fuel gauges read half full. He tapped them and both fell to empty. He shook his head, swearing under his breath "But that's not our biggest problem."

"What could be worse than that?"

"I think there's a hole in the oil tank. The oil temperature is high."

"What does that mean?"

"That we're going to have to land soon."

****

"Are we going to crash?" They couldn't die now. Not after everything they'd been through. What would happen to Jake?

"Not if I can help it." Will said, pulling back on the yoke. The plane rose several hundred feet. He looked over the dash.

"What are you looking for?"

"Someplace to land before the engine seizes up and forces us to."

"Why are we higher?"

"In case something happens and we need more time to find a place."

"But won't they see us?"

"I don't think so, Emma," he snapped, then ran a hand through his hair and sighed. "Sorry. No, they shouldn't see us since we're still pretty low. But the higher we are, the more space there is between us and the ground, which is a good thing in this situation. The problem is, although the land here is relatively flat, there's too many trees."

He banked right, flying north toward the storm.

"Why are we flying this way? What about the storm?"

"Trust me. We'll be on the ground before we reach the storm. I know there's grassland up here, pretty remote, too. I used to camp here with my dad when I was a kid."

The engine sputtered.

Emma gripped the seat and her heart pounded. "What can I do to help?"

"Look for a road or a field with no trees. We're not going to last much longer." Will lifted the plane higher. "Buying us more time," he answered before she asked.

Off in the distance, she saw a field. "There!" She pointed.

Will leaned over in his seat to look out her window. "Yep, that'll work." He turned the aircraft in the direction of the grassland.

Within a few seconds the engine sputtered again, then stalled. "Here we go." Will gripped the yoke.

Emma took several deep breaths, forcing her constricted airway to expand. They glided toward the field, but she wasn't sure they would reach it. A huge patch of trees lay between them and their intended destination. "Will, in case we don't…"

"We're going to land this fucking plane. Got it?" he growled through gritted teeth, his eyebrows furrowed.

"Yes."

Emma took off her headphones, the interior eerily quiet without the roar of the engine as the aircraft glided to the field.

The plane lowered and the branches beneath them barely cleared the bottom of the plane, the field agonizingly out of reach. The moonlight cast deep, menacing shadows in the trees, increasing her rising anxiety. Emma gripped the seat and held her breath. Will's taut face told her all she needed to know.

They cleared the trees, leaves brushing the tail as they floated to the ground. She wasn't prepared for the jolt when the back of the plane touched down. The ground tossed them around as she clung to the seat and tried to look out the window, the view obscured by their shaking.

"*Son of a bitch,*" Will said through gritted teeth as the nose lowered, the vibration increasing. "Bend over and cover your head!"

She obeyed him as the plane bounced off the ground, landing with an impact that rattled her head.

"Come on. Come on," Will mumbled. His knuckles whitened from his grip on the yoke.

The plane slowed and the vibrating lessened. She began to think they might make it out alive when the nose pitched forward and to the side. The collision threw Emma into the door, her head smashing into the metal frame of the window. A sharp pain shot through her skull. Then nothingness.

CHAPTER TWENTY-THREE

WILL hung from his seatbelt for several seconds before he realized they had come to a halt. The plane leaned forward and to the right, nose tilted down. Emma slumped against the door. Her arms dangled and her hair hung over her face. "Emma."

His chest constricted when she didn't respond. He reached for her shoulder. "Emma!"

She groaned and shifted her weight.

He released his breath. "Are you hurt?"

"No," Her hand reached to her head. "I just have a headache. Did we stop?"

"Yeah, but we need to get out of here. I'm going to get my pack, then we're going to try to go out your door, okay?"

She nodded, pressing harder on her temple.

Will unbuckled his seatbelt and braced his feet against the floor. The plane creaked and groaned as he reached into the back. He grasped blindly on the floor until he found a nylon strap and pulled the backpack onto his lap. "Can you open the door?"

She fumbled with the latch, her movements sluggish.

His heart beat faster. He had to get her out of the plane and figure out if she was really hurt or not. He reached his arm around her waist and held onto her as the door popped open. Her body sagged and his grip tightened. "I don't want you to fall out. Can you see how far down the ground is?"

She paused. "It's close, but I don't think the door will open all the way," she mumbled.

"We only need to open it far enough to climb out. I'll undo your seatbelt and you step down."

She nodded again and his thumb pressed the metallic button. After a moment of hesitation, she stepped down and ducked through the opening, standing next to the plane.

Bracing his arms on the dashboard and the chair back, he swung his legs down through the door. He bent down, clearing the door and the wing overhead.

Moonlight found a break in the clouds and lit the field. The plane had ended in a shallow ditch, nose forward. Will searched the vast grassland that lay in all directions for any signs of life then looked at Emma. Blood covered the right side of her face and drenched her shirt. Swiping it with her hand, she rubbed the blood on her jeans.

"Got another piece of gauze?" She tried to grin, but her lips turned into a pucker and her non-bloodied cheek appeared pale in the moonlight.

Trying to keep calm, he picked her up in his arms and moved away from the plane.

"Will, I can walk."

But he noticed that she didn't protest with her usual vehemence.

The fuel tanks were empty, so he doubted he needed to be concerned about an explosion. But he didn't care to press his luck. When he thought they were a safe distance away, he dropped her legs. "Emma, sit down and let me look at your head."

She sank to the ground, facing the plane. "Thanks for keeping us alive."

He reached into his backpack as he knelt beside her. "I told you I'd land the plane."

"So you did."

Will pulled out the first aid kit and removed several gauze squares, wishing for a bottle of water to wash off the blood. His fingers cradled her chin as he gently lifted, her eyes searching his. He turned his gaze to her cheek, dabbing the smeared blood.

"Why am I always cleaning you up?" he asked, his finger carefully lifting the hair matted to her face.

The encroaching clouds obscured the moonlight so he pulled out the flashlight. Her pupils were even and reactive—no concussion—but he found an inch-long gash close to her hairline. A scar ran close to it, healed but slightly pink in the harsh light. Had it only been a month ago that he had tended to her nearly the same way?

Will cleaned and patched the wound as best as he could with what he had. When he finished, he lifted her chin again, inspecting his patch job. "You scared the shit out of me too many times to count tonight," he whispered.

She smiled. "You scared the shit out of me too, so we're even. Let's go. What's your plan?"

Pride filled him that she trusted him to have a plan. "I glanced at the GPS going down. There's a small town to the northeast. I'll call James and tell him to meet us there."

"How far?" she asked.

"Hard to say. At least five, maybe ten miles."

Determination hardened her face. "Then let's get going. We've got a long walk ahead of us."

Will reached down a hand to help her up. He called James, the call broken by the spotty cell phone coverage, but good enough to get the message through.

Following Will's compass, they headed northeast. The grass was only knee high, but the trek was rough going in the dark. Emma stumbled several times, Will there to grab her arm and keep her upright. Clouds rolled in and the wind gusted. They had reached a good stride when the rain began, a light pitter-patter that turned into a downpour. Emma trudged on, but he could tell she was tiring. He was surprised she lasted this long.

Lightning streaked the western horizon. An outcrop of rocky hills rose to the east and Will steered her in that direction. Thunder rolled across the valley as they neared the hills and Will hoped that they could find shelter in time. They risked getting struck by lightning out here.

He found a hollowed area, deep enough for them to climb into and get out of the rain. Emma crawled in first and Will followed behind as thunder shook the ground. The space was just large enough for them to sit with their legs tucked in. He wished they had dry clothes to change into or wood to start a fire, but he had neither. Not even a blanket.

"Emma, take off your shirt." He reached the bottom edge of her t-shirt, tugging upward.

"I know I rarely say this, Will, but I'm really not in the mood," she said but lifted her arms.

Her banter eased his mind a little as he pulled the shirt over her head and tossed it aside. "Aw, just when I found the perfect getaway spot." His soon joined hers and he leaned back against the rocky wall, pulling her to his chest. "This isn't much, but it will help warm you up."

"I'm warmer already," she murmured into his chest, her breath soaking into his skin and settling into his soul. "Should we look at the book?"

"Not now, we can look at it tomorrow." He kissed the damp hair above her forehead, careful to avoid her gash. "Go to sleep. You need to rest."

Her body melded into his as her muscles relaxed. "Will?" she asked, her voice nearly lost in the storm now raging outside their enclosure.

"Yes?" He murmured into her head.

"Thank you."

His arms tightened around her. "You don't have to thank me, Emma."

"Maybe so, but I can still say thanks."

He smiled in the dark as he closed his eyes. Only after he knew she drifted off did the tension in his shoulders slip away, and he fell into a troubled sleep.

****

She was first aware of the birds tweeting outside the enclosure, followed by the pounding in her head. She groaned as she shifted, a rock poking into her thigh. The backpack lay behind her head as a pillow, with Will nowhere in sight. She felt a momentary panic but quickly calmed herself. He had to be close by. Will would never leave her there alone.

She groped around the dirt floor for her shirt, finding only gravel. She crawled out more stiff and sore than she expected, the gash on her forehead throbbing. The cool morning air hit her nearly naked upper half and damp jeans. Wrapping her arms across her front, she scanned the empty field then looked up on top of the bluff. The sun peeked around the edge of the thirty-foot rock formation, forcing her to shield her eyes. Will stood on top, his feet spread apart and a pair of binoculars held to his eyes. She watched him and an unfamiliar feeling swept over her, catching her by surprise. What was it? Pride? Respect? Possession?

He lowered the field glasses and lowered his gaze to her, a slow grin spreading across his face. "Good morning."

"You're up early."

"Just enjoying the view." But he stared down at her.

"I see you have your shirt on. Care to tell me where mine is?"

"And spoil the view?" He laughed. "Around the corner of the rocks, in the sun."

She trudged around the bluff and found it hanging from a rock ledge. The t-shirt was still damp but she pulled it over her head anyway as Will climbed down.

"How are you feeling?" he asked.

"Other than a killer headache, a throbbing forehead, and a variety of aches and pains, never better."

"At least you still have a sense of humor." He wrapped an arm around her waist as they walked back to their shelter. "I talked to James and he's in Wyoming and headed to the nearest town to pick us up."

"How far is it?"

"Probably three miles."

"Then let's get going."

Will grabbed his pack and they hiked through the grass. Will reached over and laced Emma's hand with his. She looked up at him in surprise but didn't pull away. Curling her fingers around his, he smiled and pulled her closer to kiss the top of her head as they walked.

By the time they got to the edge of town, Emma was more worn out than she cared to admit and her stomach grumbled in protest. Will called James to coordinate their whereabouts and they met him on a deserted two-lane road. He parked the car on the shoulder and stood next to the open door with his arms crossed, smirking. "Need a ride?"

Emma ignored him and crawled into the backseat. She leaned her head against the back, closing her eyes as Will sat next to James.

"What the hell happened?" James asked, pulling back onto the road.

Will filled him in. "Did you have any trouble getting away?" Will asked.

James shook his head. "Nah, it was almost too easy. I set the pipe bomb to go off and crawled under the fence. Halfway back to the car I heard the explosion. No one ever followed me, not that I know of anyway. I drove around until I got your phone call an hour later."

"And no one followed you after that?"

"Not unless you count the raccoons that darted in front of my path a few times."

Will grabbed the road map from the seat. "Kramer said Alex had Jake in Montana. I say we head up 90."

"I hate to be a party killer here, but *where* in Montana? If you take a look at the map, it's a hell of a big state."

Will ran his fingers through his hair. "I don't know yet."

"Again, I hate—"

Will looked over his shoulder at her. "Can you try to talk to Jake? Maybe he can help us."

Emma sighed. "I don't know. He's never answered me since Colorado. But the other day…" Her voice trailed off as she remembered him tracing the heart in her hand. "He might talk to me if I tell him how close we are."

"Um..." James's hands twisted on the steering wheel. "If you can call him, why can't we figure out where he is? I'll just trace the number."

"She's not going to *call* him," Will answered.

James was silent for a moment. "Oh, fuck. Mumbo jumbo shit."

Emma glared at the back of his head before she closed her eyes. "Can we get some food soon?"

"We can get something in town before we head to the highway."

She nodded then delved deeper into her mind, focusing on Jake. She could feel him out there. If only she could get him to answer.

****

Jake played with the scrambled eggs on his plate, twirling the spoon in his hand. He hadn't been given a fork for days, not since he sent the last one flying through the air, narrowly missing Duncan's head. Jake smirked. Didn't they know he was only playing with them? If he wanted to kill Duncan, he wouldn't have missed.

His interest perked up when he heard the commotion in the hall. He'd grown used to their reactions and this one meant Alex was on his way in. Jake slouched over the card table they'd set up in the bedroom in which they'd locked him, plastering on a bored expression. The door opened and Alex strutted in, reminding Jake of the peacocks he'd seen at the Fort Worth zoo before they moved again. The memory of holding Mommy's hand brought tears to his eyes. He missed her so much. His resolve weakened, sadness slamming him with an unexpected force. Then he reminded himself these people were the ones who took him from her and resentment bubbled in his chest.

He hadn't talked to Jake in days, not since Jake slept beside Mommy in his dreams. Jake could escape anytime he wanted and his patience had worn thin.

Alex sat in a chair, leaning both forearms on the table. His head lowered to Jake's eye level. A smug grin lifted the corners of his mouth. "Hello, Jake."

Jake glared, not bothering to disguise his contempt. "I want to go home. I want my mom."

"Jake, you know I want nothing more than to reunite you with your mother. You've seen this. But she's proving hard to locate since we lost her in Minnesota. I'm beginning to think she doesn't want to find you."

Jake slammed his fist on the table, sending eggs flying into the air. "That's not true."

Alex tilted his head, his face remaining expressionless. "Has she tried to locate you?"

Jake's expression wavered.

A grin spread across Alex's face. "She has."

"No!" Jake's chest burned.

"Jake, if I tell you where we are, you can tell her and she can come and get you."

"You're lying." Electricity shot down his arms.

Alex studied him, yet didn't look frightened. "If you don't believe me, look into my mind. You'll see it's true."

Jake reached out into Alex's consciousness. It was different than before, puzzling Jake, but he pushed deeper, looking for his answer. His eyes widened in surprise. It was true. Alex intended to let him go with Emma. As he made the discovery, Jake realized Alex had pushed back, into Jake's mind, scanning and searching before Jake panicked and shut down his thoughts. He shrank back in his chair, frightened.

"You're right," Alex said, his face blank. "I'm different. I can read your mind and do other things, too." He bowed his head slightly. "Thank you. Your thoughts were *most* helpful. The next time your mother reaches out to you, tell her you're in Montana. White Horse, Montana. Tell her Alex said to come and get you."

He stood and turned to leave. Jake's fear turned to rage and before he could stop himself, he shot a ball of energy toward Alex, but it stopped at his back, dissipating in the air. Alex turned and winked, his mouth lifting into an evil grin. "That was one of the other things." Then he walked out of the room.

Jake jumped on his bed and crawled under the covers, clutching Rusty to his chest. Tears welled in his eyes. He struggled to hold them in, finally releasing them in gulping sobs into the pillow. As he calmed, his mother called out to him, her words a warm comfort to his fears. He pretended that he sat in her lap, her arms wrapped tight around him. Her voice became frantic.

"Jake, please," she begged. "Talk to me."

He hiccupped, torn in indecision. He wanted his mommy so much. He had never wanted anything more. Yet, he knew Alex was bad. Even *he* had said so. What if Alex hurt her?

He'd let his guard down and she picked up on his thoughts. "Jake, Will is with me. Alex can't hurt me. Tell me where you are."

"He's different. He *can* hurt you." His tears fell again. He didn't mean to answer.

Her relief washed over him. "It's okay. I'm different, too. I can take care of Alex and so can Will. Will even has his friend James with us to help. We can protect you, you just have to tell me where you are."

Jake didn't know how Mommy could take care of Alex. Not this new Alex. But Will had guns. Maybe guns could take care of Alex, though something deep inside told him bullets weren't enough. Could he take the chance?

She sensed his indecision and her tone became desperate. "Jake, baby, *please*. Tell me where you are. Are you in Montana? We think you're in Montana."

A fat lump lodged in his throat and he struggled to swallow his fear. "Yes," he whispered into the darkness.

Warmth and love covered him with her presence. He realized that the more he let her in, the more he could feel her. "That's good, Jake. Do you know where in Montana?"

He buried his face into his pillow, sobbing anew. He couldn't tell her. He couldn't risk it. But his guard was down and she rushed into his mind and she knew, without his even saying it. He clamped down, completely shutting her out, and she was gone.

****

Emma sat up in the backseat with a jerk. "Oh, God. I know where he is."

Will turned to face her, wide eyed. James stared at her in the rearview mirror.

"He's afraid." Her voice broke and her eyes burned. "He's in White Horse, Montana. Alex is with him." She paused, the full impact of what she saw hitting her. "He told Jake to tell me to come and get him."

Will's face turned red as his jaw tightened. "That son of a bitch has nothing to worry about. I'm coming to get him, all right."

CHAPTER TWENTY-FOUR

WILL took a deep breath and told himself to calm down and focus. He had to come up with a plan and the first was to get to White Horse. He and James plotted a route to the northwest corner of Montana. The drive was simple enough, just long. They'd be in the car all day. Which gave him plenty of time to scour the book.

He pulled it out of his backpack and studied the leather binding. *The Complete Essays of Lorenzo de Luca* emblazoned the front in gold letters. Opening the cover, he found the title page and behind it the first page of text. It didn't have a copyright page to tell him the book's age, but it had obviously been printed for the Vinco Potentia.

Will scanned the pages one by one, carefully separating the pages that stuck together at the edges from the rain. The book contained the papers of the 18th-century Italian philosopher. Senator Warren had told him that most of the papers were rubbish and he was right, until the last quarter. The previous pages contained the English translation of de Luca's work, but the last several pages of the book were written in a language Will didn't recognize. Will found Warren's version of the prophecy in English printed below the undecipherable text.

Will found the drawing of the mark on his arm, the preordained mark of The Chosen One. The final proof to

Warren that the prophecy was true, but the irony was the Vinco Potentia had it wrong. Their version of the prophecy was different than the one Jake gave him.

He looked over his shoulder to Emma. "I'm not sure..."

She slumped in the seat, staring out the side window. Dark circles underscored her eyes and the bruise from her injury spread across her forehead in dark purples. Her head turned at the sound of his voice, her eyes welling with tears and her words came out in a raspy whisper. "He's scared."

Will's heart lurched. He turned in his seat and took her hand in his. "We're going to find him, Emma. I swear it."

She nodded, a tear sliding down her cheek.

He turned back to the book with a renewed purpose. Even when they got Jake, this whole nightmare wouldn't be over. He needed the information in book to help dig them out of it.

But, after an hour of reading, he knew they needed more. Other than the vague list of foretold events, there was little new information. Will couldn't believe the Vinco Potentia had so much hinged on so little. He couldn't even figure out how they tied Emma to all of this.

****

James drove for several hours while Will napped, then Will took over. Emma tried to sleep but every time she closed her eyes, the memory of Jake's fear rushed in and stole her breath.

They reached White Horse before nightfall, but Will continued driving to the next town, Spruce. Emma protested, demanding they stay in White Horse but both men agreed that it was too dangerous. If Alex was waiting for her, it was bound to involve a trap. As they drove through, Emma pressed her hand to the window, calling out to Jake in her mind, telling him they were close. When she felt his wall, she steeled herself and refused to cry. She was too close to him now to break down.

They found a secluded campground with a cabin available. It was farther from White Horse than she liked, but Will insisted on the distance. The location reminded her too much of staying in the lodge with Raphael. But she couldn't voice her opinion without dredging up a host of feelings and reactions she couldn't handle.

They rented the last one-bedroom cabin, which was set back at the edge of the forest with a view of the lake. The campsite lay closer to the water's edge. Will and Emma carried their bags into the cabin while James shopped for dinner at the small campground store.

Will dropped their bag in the only bedroom. "We're taking this room and James gets the sofa. If you want to go lie down for a little bit and rest, I'll let you know when dinner is ready."

Emma shook her head. "No, I'm too jumpy to sleep. Maybe I can after I eat."

"How's your head?" he asked, lifting her hair off of her forehead.

"It still hurts, but it's better."

"You sure you don't want to take some Tylenol?" Worry lines crinkled around his eyes.

"No." She glanced toward the door to make sure James hadn't returned, then lowered her voice. "I don't want to take anything because of the baby."

His hand lingered on her cheek as he searched her eyes. He lowered his head and kissed her gently. "I'm just worried about you."

She smiled and wrapped her arms around him. "I know. Thank you."

The front door swung open and James groaned. "God, get a room," He carried a bag full of groceries and he kicked the door closed behind him.

Will sighed into her hair. "Hey, Einstein. We did get a room."

James grumbled as he unpacked the bag. "Hope you like spaghetti because that's what you're getting."

"No complaints," Will said.

Emma didn't answer, sure there was no right answer as far as James was concerned.

Will took a jar of sauce from James. "I'll take over cooking dinner. You go find out everything you can about White Horse."

James camped out at the kitchen table while Emma sat on a barstool at the kitchen counter, watching Will work in the kitchen.

They ate dinner in silence, the room thick with tension. James resumed his work while Emma helped Will clean up the kitchen. They fell into a comfortable rhythm and she let her imagination wander to the daydream of a normal life, with a husband and a family. She and Will, with Jake and the baby. A cute little house with a picket fence. She watched Will dry a plate and her heart strained with the possibility of it all. In front of her was the chance at everything she'd ever wanted. She handed Will a plate and he caught her wrist in his hand, wrapping his fingers around her. She looked into his face in surprise.

"I'm going to get him back, Emma. I promise you."

She bit her lip as she struggled with her emotions. They were so unsettled around Will, she was no longer sure of anything. "I trust you, Will. I know."

He leaned down and kissed her and her hope blossomed.

They finished washing the dishes in silence and as Will put the last plate away, James called out. "I think I have something here."

James looked over at Will. "I doubt they're going to hold a kidnap victim at a permanent residence. They might be cocky, but I doubt they're stupid. So I suspect they're renting. I drew up a list of all the rentals listed right around the time of the kidnapping and then sectioned off all the rentals that no longer show up as available. The list is still fairly lengthy, about thirty houses." He handed a print out to Will. "But at least it's a place to start. I'll do some cross referencing and see if I can link Alex to any of these locations."

Will took the list and looked it over. "But this is just the rentals that were listed. They could have rented from someone who knew someone. Or just broke into an abandoned house."

"True, but I doubt they'd go the second route. Too risky. You've got nothing to lose by searching the recently rented houses. You just might get lucky."

Will sighed. "Yeah, it's worth a shot. I'll get started on it first thing in the morning."

"No!" Emma shouted.

Both men turned to look at her in surprise.

"He's scared and alone. I'm not leaving him with that bastard Alex a minute longer than I have to. Let's go now."

"Emma..." Will's eyes were full of love. And pity.

She burst into tears. "I can't leave him there. I can't."

Will put his hand on her arm. "Emma, you're exhausted. You had a head injury and you've hardly slept in the last two days. You won't be any good to Jake if something happens to you."

"As much as I hate to admit it," James crossed his arms across his chest with a frown. "She might be right. It might be best to scope some houses out at night. You'll be less obvious that way. If you like, I'll play babysitter while you do some surveillance, see if you can knock some of those off the list. Emma can stay here and rest."

"No. No way." Emma protested. "I'm going. He's my son."

Will looked torn with indecision.

"Will, surely you can see the sense in this. I'll stay behind and do more research while you get some legwork done. Emma can stay here and get some rest."

"I'm going!"

Will closed his eyes. "I don't want to leave her."

"Emma," James said, his voice softening. "I promise to be on my best behavior. It doesn't take a genius to see that you're exhausted and I'm sure you have a raging headache guessing from the bruise on your forehead. I'll keep guard while Will is gone and he'll be back before you wake up in the morning, isn't that right, Will?"

Will studied her for a moment before he nodded, his jaw tensing. "I'd feel better if you stayed here and got some rest. I'll be back before you notice I'm gone."

"But he's *my* son. I should be there when you find him."

Will cupped her face. "Even if I find Jake, I'm not trying anything until I know what we're getting into, especially since Alex is hoping to lure you there."

"But—"

His eyes plead with hers. "Emma, I want him back too, but I'm not going to risk his life trying to rescue him. We need to go into it with a plan."

Her chin quivered and he pulled her head to his chest.

"I promised you that I'd get him. Just let me get him back my way, okay?"

Emma nodded. She had no doubt Will meant it when he said he wouldn't try to save Jake unprepared. And if Will found him tonight, she doubted she could sit in the car and not rush in and try to rescue him. "Okay."

Will's body relaxed. "You stay here and get some rest and with any luck at all, we'll have him soon."

She looked up into his face. "Tomorrow I'm going with you."

He smiled. "I have to admit you come in pretty handy." He released her and restocked his bag as he and James discussed the most promising houses on the list. Emma sank into a kitchen chair watching him, dread rolling in like a morning fog.

Will sensed her hesitation and knelt in front of her. "Are you okay with this?"

"Something just doesn't feel right," she said. "But it's stupid. I can't see any reason for you not to go, yet something is off."

"Do you feel sick?"

"No."

"I can stay if you like and we can start tomorrow."

Emma inhaled deeply and smiled. She wasn't about to let her paranoia get in the way of finding Jake. "No, I'm just being weird. I'll go to bed and tomorrow I'll go with you and we'll get Jake back."

He pulled her up from the chair and into his arms. His hand threaded in her hair as he pulled her mouth to his. She clung to him, a deep sense of foreboding overwhelming her. But she pulled back and smiled. "Promise me you'll be careful."

"Always."

She stared into his warm, brown eyes searching for something she couldn't fathom, sure she'd find it in him.

He kissed her softly. "I love you."

The words were there, on the tip of her tongue, three little words that would mean so much to him. She thought she loved him, but how could she be sure?

One side of his mouth lifted into a lopsided grin that didn't reach his eyes. With a sigh, his arms dropped. "I'll be here in the morning when you wake up."

Her vision blurred as she watched him pick up his bag and head out the door. She ran to the bathroom, choking back a sob. Why couldn't she give him what he wanted? After everything he did for her, after he proved his trustworthiness time and time again. She considered running after him, but what would she say? She still couldn't tell him what he wanted to hear.

Panic struck her out of nowhere and she splashed cold water and her face, chastising herself for her unease. She was not a clingy woman. She was capable of being on her own and taking care of herself, but the thought of something happening to Will sent paralyzing fear coursing through her blood. Was she worried something would happen to Will or was she worried he'd give up on her before she finally told him? She didn't want to think about living without him.

Maybe that was her answer.

She took several deep breaths before she left the bathroom, not wanting James to see her anxiety.

"Aw, there you are. I wondered if you were going to lock yourself in the bathroom all night to stay away from me." James poured water into two mugs and looked up at her. "I'm having some tea. Would you like some?"

She stopped, caught off guard by his change in attitude. Her eyes narrowed. "You made me tea?"

He held a spoon over a mug and raised his eyebrows. "Sugar?"

She nodded, still cautious.

"For heaven sakes, Emma. I'm not going to bite. We got off on the wrong foot and it's obvious Will is crazy about you. Even a fool can see you're not going anywhere so I thought I'd make more of an effort to get along."

Her shoulders relaxed as she perched on a barstool. James handed her a mug.

"Thanks," she murmured taking a sip. "I know you and Will have a long history and I don't want to get between you two. Let's start over." She held out her hand to him. "Hi, I'm Emma Thompson."

He took her hand in his. "James Buckner. Pleased to meet you." He smiled, but his eyes were dead as he released his grip. Her apprehension returned.

James leaned over the counter, sipping his tea. "Is it too soon to ask what your intentions are regarding my friend?" He tried to sound teasing, but the tone fell flat.

She started to rise. "I don't think—"

He held his hands up in surrender. "Sorry, that was out of line. Let's keep it more neutral."

She lowered onto the stool, ready to bolt if needed. Her nerves were already tangled enough without having to spar with James.

"What's your little boy's name?"

Her eyes widened in surprise. "Jake."

"How old is he?"

"Five." She cradled the cup in her hands, trying to hide her shaking hands.

James noticed her tremor. "Maybe we should start a fire. You want to light it?" He laughed.

She knew what he meant and her stomach twisted.

"So is it true? You get your power from that stone hanging around your neck?"

She raised her chin in a challenge. "I don't know." Her voice was hard and unyielding.

His cold eyes held hers. "Will thinks you do."

She broke contact first. She should have gone with Will. Or made him stay. She was stupid to think James could be trusted.

"You should drink your tea. It will warm you up."

She took several sips just to avoid talking to James and shifted her gaze around the room. A folder stuffed with papers set on the end table next to James's laptop. Could that be what James had worked on?

He set his mug down, the thud filling her ears with uncharacteristic loudness. Was it her imagination that the room suddenly seemed bigger?

"I'm going outside for a minute. I'll be back right back."

After he slipped out the door, she jumped off her stool, heading for the file. Dizziness swamped her head and she lost her balance, grabbing hold of a chair to keep from falling. *I must be more tired than I thought. Focus.* She might not get this chance again. Shaking her head to clear the persistent fuzziness, she rifled through the pile of papers. He'd been researching for days with few results and she suspected he was holding back. She found a printout with a photo and a bio. Andrew Garcia, lawyer and congressman from Texas. The initials VP were hand written in the top corner. Her breath stuck in her chest. Thumbing through the stack, she found others— politicians, influential businessmen. James told them he hadn't found any other members of the Vinco Potentia, yet here was a stack of twenty men, all with VP scrawled across the top.

The name on the last page caught her breath in her throat. Aiden Walker. Entrepreneur. No photo. Kramer said Walker knew she was the woman in the prophecy. Walker sent Alex to see her six years ago. Walker's first name was *Aiden.*

Her father's name was Aiden. It couldn't be...

A creak on the porch outside alerted her to his return. She slid to the stool, wobbling as she took her seat. She rubbed her head, wondering if she should go to bed.

"You feeling okay?" James shut the door behind him. "You don't look so good."

"Yeah, I'm fine." She glanced over her shoulder and lost her balance, falling of the stool.

James ran up behind and caught her before she hit the floor. "You must really be tired."

"I guess." She blinked several times, trying to ground herself.

James led her to the bedroom. "A woman in your condition needs to take better care of herself. You wouldn't want anything to happen to the baby."

She sat on the edge of the bed.

"You go to sleep and I'll take care of everything."

She sank back into the pillows, closing her eyes. James covered her with a blanket then leaned down to whisper in her ear, "Sweet dreams."

Before she drifted off, she jerked with awareness. James knew she was pregnant.

****

Will drove into White Horse, the list on the seat next to him. He rubbed his face, trying to wipe away his fatigue. Maybe he should have stayed with Emma. She hadn't been herself when he left. The need to hear her voice overwhelmed him. He'd call her and make sure she was okay. If she sounded the least bit worried, he'd go back and work on this tomorrow.

He reached into his pocket for his cell phone, pressing the speed dial for James.

"What's up?" James answered, sounding surprised. "Where are you?"

"I'm in White Horse, but I'm worried about Emma. Let me talk to her."

"She's fine. She's sleeping."

"Really?"

"Yeah, she was exhausted and went to bed right after you left. She's been asleep for about twenty minutes."

Will paused. Something didn't feel right. "I'm thinking about heading back. I'm beat and I doubt I'll get much information tonight. Hopefully, Emma can contact Jake tomorrow and we'll be able to pinpoint his location."

"Will," James chided. "You're already there. What would it hurt to check a few houses? I say you give it an hour or so, then head back."

"It's a good forty-five minute drive, James."

"Get a cup of coffee, you'll be fine. We've pulled all-nighters before. What, are you getting old, Davenport?" James's teased, but he seemed tense.

"No, I'm just worried about Emma. She seemed upset when I left."

"Of course she's upset. She wants her son back so why don't you stick it out a bit longer and see what you can find?" Will heard a door close. "Look, I know Emma and I have had our differences, but I know how important she is to you and I don't want to risk our friendship over this. I'll protect her if something happens."

"Maybe you're right..."

"Of course, I am." James sounded rushed. "I have to go."

Will listened to the dead silence in his ear for several seconds after James hung up, deciphering what James had said. While he was glad for James's attitude change, something wasn't right.

He parked at a stop sign, leaning over the steering wheel and staring out into the vacant street. The moonlight cast long shadows from the streetlights adding to Will's foreboding. This fishing expedition could wait. He needed to get back to Emma.

A rap on the window caught him by surprise. He jumped and found a police officer outside his car. *Son of a bitch.* Will rolled down the window, steeling himself for a performance. If the policeman checked his license and registration this would get ugly.

The officer leaned over, peering into the car. "Is everything all right?"

Will released a lighthearted laugh. "Oh yeah, everything's fine. I'm just a little lost." He pointed his thumb behind him. "My wife's back at the campground in Spruce and is dying for a Starbucks frappuccino. Made me go find one."

The officer stood, shaking his head. "We don't have a Starbucks here, son. The closest one's a couple hundred miles away. If you're camping, you drink campfire coffee, not that fancy stuff."

"That's what I told her, but you know women..." his voice trailed off.

"Boy, do I. Got one just like her at home." He shuffled his feet. "You head on back and tell her if she wants to drink five-dollar coffee on vacation, she should head to Seattle next time."

Will laughed. "Sure will, officer. You have a good night."

He watched the policeman climb back into his car before he breathed a sigh of relief. He turned on his blinker and drove around the block before heading back to the cabin.

****

Emma woke to the sound of muffled male voices. She tried to open her eyes, but her eyelids felt weighted. The scratchy wool blanket irritated her arms but she lacked the energy or will to move. The voices rose, louder and protesting. She cracked open one eye, enough to see that the door was closed.

"That's not the deal we had," James said in the other room.

Who was he talking to? Had Will come back? She tried to sit up but couldn't move. *Oh my God. I'm paralyzed.*

"Take it or leave it, Buckner. Unfortunately, at this stage of the transaction, you don't have much room to negotiate." The man's voice was familiar, Emma's mind still too fuddled to determine whom it belonged to.

"You promised to leave Will out of this. That's the only reason I agreed to this in the first place."

"Again, it's too late to negotiate. Now where's Davenport?"

"Gone. I told you, he took off and left her here with me."

"You're lying. He would never voluntarily leave her. He's incapable of it."

"You don't see him here, do you? Look around if you like."

The man swore. "You're right. If he were here he would have met us with a shower of bullets. Where is she?"

"The bedroom."

The door creaked open and Emma tried desperately to open her eyes. She needed to protect herself yet her body refused.

"Emmanuella." He uttered her name in awe. Then she recognized it. Kramer. Fear and disgust slithered in her belly. "She's drugged?"

"Yes, and I removed her pendant."

"May I have it, please?"

"Not until you agree to leave Will out of this."

The warmth of the pendant was gone from her chest. Panic spread as she realized James had betrayed them. *Will.*

Would they hurt him? Did James realize what these people would do to them? He must since he was so adamant that they leave Will alone. Fear sent her heart racing and she forced herself to remain calm. James told them Will wasn't here. He had gone to White Horse. Will could still find Jake.

A piece of furniture banged into the wall, vibrating the bed. "You're making me have second thoughts about our arrangement, Mr. Buckner. I thought you were smarter than this." Kramer's voice was deceptively calm. "I will get the pendant with or without your help. I suggest you cooperate."

She kept her eyes closed, not a difficult task considering her eyelids refused to budge. Better to let them think she was still unconscious. After her momentary panic, she slowed her breathing. She'd just wait until she gained back control over her body, then get away. Even though the likelihood of success of escaping was slim, she chose to ignore the fact. One thing she was sure of— they'd have to kill her before she let them lock her away.

James cursed under his breath.

"Aww, very nice. I knew you'd see things my way. I wonder if the power is specific to the owner or if anyone can use it?" Kramer asked. He drifted to her side and leaned over, his warm breath fanning her face.

She forced her rising terror into submission. *Not yet. You can freak out later, but not yet.*

"The last time we were together you treated me as though I were a puppet, Emmanuella. I think it's only fair if I repay the favor soon. Take her to the van while I finish up in here."

Hands grabbed her legs and under her armpits, hoisting her off the bed. Her butt sagged as they moved. She felt awkward and vulnerable as she swayed with their out-of-sync gaits. Her hip hit the doorframe as they passed through and she stifled a cry.

"Careful," Kramer droned. "We don't want to damage her. Yet."

She swallowed hard despite her nausea. Will would show up. Will would save her.

Will was an hour away.

The cool night air hit her arms and goosebumps erupted. The wind gusted, whipping her hair around her face. One of the men stumbled, nearly dropping her as they descended the steps. Despite her best efforts, she began to tremble. Fear that they would figure out she was conscious gnawed at her control.

The man carrying her top half shifted, her back pressing against his chest. She heard the creak of a metallic door as her body swung, then landed on a hard metal floor with a thud. She landed on her side and her head. The contact forced the air from her lungs.

The doors slammed shut and she cracked her eyes, taking a few seconds to adjust to the darkness. She was in an empty cargo van, alone. She needed a plan. What the hell was she going to do? She needed to get away now rather than later, if for no other reason than the van wasn't moving. She really didn't have any desire to jump out of a moving vehicle.

Her arms and legs now responded to her simple commands of movement, but were still sluggish. There was no way she could outrun men in her condition.

Unless she hid in the woods.

She crept to the front seat and peered out the windows. Two men stood next to the van, watching the cabin, Kramer nowhere in sight. If she was going to do this, it had to happen now.

Searching the dashboard, she found the switch to kill the interior lights. With her head bent low and eyes on the men, she found the door handle on the passenger side and eased it open, listening for creaks. The door was halfway open before she heard the soft whine of the hinge. She stopped and glanced over her shoulder at the men. Deep in conversation, they hadn't noticed.

She pushed again, opening the door enough to squeeze through. Turning sideways, she slid out the door, slowly closing the door with a soft click.

Emma crouched down, her blood rushing in her ears. The woods were behind the cabin, but it meant going past the men to reach them. She considered walking up to a tent or camper and begging the owners to hide her. She could tell them her boyfriend was angry or drunk, but she dismissed the idea. For one thing, they would probably insist she call the police, something she was unwilling to do. And for another thing, she could put them in danger if Kramer found her.

The woods it was. First she had to get there.

Their cabin perched atop an incline. She waited for a strong gust of wind to hide any sounds she made and walked over to the edge of the hill, thankful for the darkness. Sliding down the embankment, she steered with her hands, ignoring the stings of cuts and scrapes. She could deal with those later.

When she made it to the bottom, she stayed along the edge, blending in with the shadows. She ran toward the tents, separated from the cabins. It was late enough that most families were zipped inside, but a few stragglers sat by campfires, casting perplexed looks in her direction. She ignored them. Glad that the drugs James had given her were wearing off, she gained strength with each passing moment.

The edge of the campground came into view and she allowed herself a moment of victory until she heard crashing behind her. She looked over her shoulder to see the two men running after her, throwing things out of their way.

Emma's heart leapt in her chest. They were gaining on her quickly. The trees were just ahead, taunting her with their nearness. She wasn't sure she would make it and even when she did, they could still catch her. But it still seemed her best option, offering more places to hide. She reached for her pendant, terrified that it was gone. The stone was her only weapon and now she was defenseless.

Her feet pounded the rough earth, sending shock waves into her already throbbing head. She reached the edge of the forest and pushed through the dense undergrowth. The wind howled, masking the crunch and crackles made by her feet as she plunged deeper into the trees. Rain began to fall, dripping through the canopy and down to the forest floor, making the leaf-covered ground slick as she ran. She slipped and fell to her knees, bracing herself with her outstretched arms. Swiping the mud off her hands onto her jeans, she pushed on until she found a rocky outcropping. She found a crevice to duck behind while she caught her breath and watched for her pursuers.

****

Even before Will felt the tingle in his arm, before it began as a twitch and worked its way up to the full blown pins-and-needles sensation, he knew something was wrong. He drove back to the cabin, keeping to the speed limit after his run in with the police and assuring himself everything was okay. Emma was all right. Yet, he knew.

She wasn't.

His panic spread, but he had to wait until the sensation in his arm reached its peak before he could reach out to her, to find out what terror she faced now, without him. Again.

And when he knew she could hear him he called out, his words laced with his own agony. *Emma.*

Will!

Where are you? What's happened?

James… There's two men following me with guns. Kramer. Kramer's here.

Kramer? How?

James. He drugged me and Kramer showed up. But I got away and I'm running in the woods.

Will's chest squeezed, threatening to crush his heart. James had betrayed him. *Use your stone, Emma. I know you're worried about starting a fire, but you have better control now.*

I can't. James took it.

Will's pain turned to murderous rage. She was completely defenseless. *Do they know where you are?*

No, there's a storm. I think I lost them.

I don't need the stone to find you. I'm already halfway there. I will *find you.*

****

Jake lay on his bed and held Rusty close. Outside, the wind whistled and rain slapped the windows. On nights like tonight, he used to curl up in bed with Mommy. He fit in the curve of her tummy, cocooned by her body, her arm wrapped around him holding him close.

But tonight he was alone.

He couldn't sleep, thinking of her. Thinking about Alex and how he could hurt her. Thinking about *him.* Jake hadn't heard from him for days. Maybe *he* wasn't coming back.

Maybe Jake didn't want him to come back.

Jake could sense Mommy was close. She had reached out to him earlier, so close it was if he could reach out and touch her. But he ignored her calls, shutting her out. He couldn't risk Alex knowing anything about her, no matter how much Jake needed her.

He began to consider escaping. It wouldn't be hard. The guards were only for show. He'd played with their fears enough to know they were scared. He might not even have to hurt any of them. But he would if they tried to keep him from his mommy.

He could walk out of the house, but then what? He could call out to her and she would come and get him. If one of the men tried to hurt her, Jake would hurt them first.

Knowing what they planned to do before they did it was useful.

Alex was the one to worry about, but he didn't stay here and only dropped in every couple of days. And he had been there in the morning.

He began to work out a plan so simple he didn't know why he hadn't considered it before. He'd walk out the bedroom door, through the front door, and start walking down the street.

Before he could plan the rest, an inhuman howl blew through the house, creating a whirlwind of chaos in his mind and the minds of the men in the house. Jake gripped his head between his palms as a presence grew closer and closer.

He was here.

Jake sat up on the bed clutching Rusty to his chest.

The house shook, the walls and floor vibrating manically. Jake struggled to stay on the bed. The guards outside the door began to panic and scream, their swirling thoughts silencing into shattered bits.

There was nothing. No thoughts. No emotions. Blissful peace washed over him. The door creaked open and a man tilted his head through the crack.

"Hello, Jake."

Jake blinked in disbelief. He was really here. "Hello."

The man pushed the door open farther, stepping into the crack, and extended his hand. "Ready to go?"

Jake stood and took a step toward him. "Where?"

The man smiled. "To get your mother, of course."

CHAPTER TWENTY-FIVE

EMMA broke her telepathic link with Will. Talking to him took concentration and she didn't want to wander the woods without focus. One thing was certain—she couldn't go back to the cabin, but she was unfamiliar with the layout of the land and had no idea where the nearest road could be. She had no choice. She had to go deeper in the woods.

Grabbing onto the tree trunks, she pulled herself up the gradually increasing incline. The rain continued to fall, soaking her hair and clothes. She was sick to death of rain and woods.

The man tackled her out of nowhere, slamming her face-first into the ground. She gasped from surprise and pain. His knee ground into her thigh and his hands pushed her arms into the decaying leaves. She bucked and twisted, but he pressed harder.

"Where do you think you're going?" He snarled into her ear and flipped her over on her back. He glared, his lip curling in a sneer. His fingers dug into her upper arm as he pulled her off the ground and tugged her down the incline. Emma fought against his grip, but he was stronger and outweighed her by a hundred pounds. His fingers dug deeper, his nails cutting into the soft flesh of her inner arm.

Her mind ran rampant with panic. She couldn't get back in the van or her life would be over. If her life was going to end, she wanted to be the one in control. She planned to put up one hell of a fight.

She planted a hard kick to the back of his thigh with her heel while she twisted her body out of his hold. He grunted and stumbled forward from the force. He turned, his teeth bared and eyes slitted in rage. Charging forward, he lunged with both hands. Emma aimed a kick to his groin, relieved when it connected and he doubled over, moaning.

She turned and ran sideways on the hill, her feet slipping on the rain-slick leaves. He recovered and followed. "I'm going to kill you, bitch."

Adrenaline surged through her body, fueling her leg muscles to push harder. His hand snagged her shoulder, spinning her around, his fist smashing into her cheek before she could think to duck.

Rage filled her. Why wouldn't these people leave her alone? Her cheek throbbed as she bent over in pain. He stood in front of her, grabbing her arm to pull her up. Emma raised a knee to hit him in the groin again, but he was prepared and stepped back, kicking her in the chest. She fell backward, into a tree and slid down, the rough bark scratching her back as she struggled to recover. As she hit the ground, she fell on her side and began to crawl.

"Not so tough now." He sneered as he followed, stalking.

"Kramer's going to be pissed if you bring me back damaged."

"Kramer said to use any means necessary. I can't help it you put up a fight."

She tried to sit up, but he kicked her again. His foot aimed for her shoulder but she twisted as she tried to roll away and it connected with her abdomen. Falling on her side, she released an agonized sob.

"You going to mind me?" He reached for her arm.

Not ready to give up, she kicked the back of his ankle and he stumbled. She pushed up on her hands and knees, gasping for breath.

He growled and pushed her over, pressing her shoulders in to the ground as he stomped on her back. She pushed against him but he pressed harder, squeezing the air out of her lungs.

Emma twisted sideways, catching him off guard, and rolling onto her back. Her hands reached out blindly for anything to grab onto. The fingertips of her right hand brushed against a rock.

He stood over her. "You just don't learn, do you?"

She rolled to her hands and knees, the rock in her grasp when he stepped on her back, pressing her to the ground again. Groping blindly, her fingers grasped for it before slipping off. She jerked forward, ignoring the pain, her hand curling around the stone.

He grabbed her shoulder and she let him flip her over. Grabbing her shirt, he pulled her head and shoulders several inches off the ground. "You wanna play? I can play."

Her arm lay on the ground, the rock fisted in her hand. She swung upward, using all the force she had, and smashed the stone into his temple.

His eyes widened. She smashed again, blood streaming down his face. He fell forward, covering her body with his. The rock still in her hand, she pushed him off of her and jumped to her feet. Her breath came in short bursts as she stared down at his motionless body.

Oh, my God. Oh, my God. I killed him.

Killed who?

She heard the panic in Will's voice.

Emma! What happened?

They found me.

She took off running blindly through the trees, ignoring Will's voice in her head. Drowning in her terror.

Emma ran until she gasped for air and couldn't go any farther. She bent over at her waist, sucking in deep breaths. A cramp seized her abdomen and she cried out, bending over in surprise as she clung to a tree, the bark digging into her raw palms. Her entire body ached but she had to keep going. She couldn't stop now.

Stumbling through the dark, she came across a small house in a small clearing. She hid at the edge of the forest, watching. Soft light glowed from the windows. Between her wet clothes and the cool night air, she was freezing, but she had no idea if she could trust the people inside.

The front door opened and a stout figure stood on the threshold. "Who's out there?" an elderly woman called, her voice shaking.

Emma held onto the tree as another pain shot through her gut. She moaned, trying to ignore what it might mean.

"I know you're out there and I have a gun. Show me who you are!"

The pain eased. Emma straightened and took a few steps toward the house. "I'm sorry to disturb you, ma'am. I was wondering if I could I use your phone?"

The woman flipped on the porch light. Emma's eyes squinted in the glare.

"Oh my stars! What happened to you?" she asked, walking onto the porch.

"I got lost in the woods."

"How on earth did that happen? Come in. Come in." The woman waved toward the front door. "I'm out in the middle of nowhere. You're lucky you found me."

Emma limped toward her, the aches and pains of her body increasing with the drop in adrenaline. "I don't know. I was at the campground to the west and...I got lost." Emma climbed the stairs to the porch.

The woman's gaze lingered on Emma. "Looks like you been through more than getting lost. What happened to your face?"

"I fell."

The woman watched her with narrowed eyes for a moment, clearly not believing her. Just when Emma was sure she was going to send her away, the woman shooed her through the door. "You're soaking wet! You got caught in that sudden rainstorm? It just appeared out of nowhere and cleared off already."

Emma turned to look over her shoulder at the sky, the moon visible in the clearing. Rainstorms seemed to follow her around lately. She could do without so much rain.

The woman muttered under her breath, "You've been traveling a ways. That campground is a mile and a half from here."

The living room was rustic but warm. A plaid sofa and worn recliner faced the television, a basket of yarn with knitting needles sat on a table by the recliner. A couple of lamps and the glow of a television screen lit the room.

"I'm really sorry to intrude." Emma made her way to the vinyl floor in the kitchen, not wanting to drip on the carpet. "I'll just call my friend and have him come get me." She turned around and the woman gasped.

"Oh my stars in heaven! Your face is worse than I thought. What really happened to you out there?"

Emma gave her a cold stare. "Nothing. I got lost."

The old woman lowered her voice. "You and I both know you didn't just get lost. You need to call the police." She pointed to a kitchen chair. "You sit here and let me have a look at you."

"No. No police."

She squinted and tilted her head. "Why won't you tell me?"

Emma shook her head, irritated when her eyes filled with tears. "It's complicated. If I could just make that phone call, then I'll leave and meet him out on the road."

"What's your name?"

She hesitated. "Emma."

"I'm Sophia." She stared into Emma's eyes then patted her hand. "We all got reasons for doing things that don't seem normal. If you say you can't call the police, I believe you. But I'm not letting you walk out in the dark and meet your friend on the road. Not after you've just been attacked. You can wait in here."

"I'd like to make that call now."

Sophia stepped backward, scrutinizing Emma as she reached for the phone. The older woman held it toward her without releasing it. "I'll let you make your call but afterward, I'll give you something dry to put on and then you wait for your friend inside. Otherwise, you can't use it."

Emma knew she could easily wrestle the phone out of Sophia's hands, but she'd walk out before she ever tried such a thing. She gave a sharp nod, sending pain shooting through her head. "Okay."

Sophia handed her the phone and she punched in Will's number, thankful Will had given it to her in South Dakota.

"Yeah," Will grunted.

She realized he didn't recognize the number. "Will, it's me."

"Emma. Oh, God...when you didn't answer me... " The relief in his voice was palpable. "Where are you?"

"I'm safe. I'm at the home of a kind woman. She's letting me to use her phone, but I don't want to impose on her hospitality any longer than I need to." She heavily accentuated the phrase, hoping he understood.

"Are you safe, Emma?" She heard his fear.

"For now, but I'll feel better when you get here."

"Tell me where you are."

The woman handed her a paper with the directions. Emma relayed them to Will.

He groaned. "I'm traveling back to the cabin, but where you are is off another road, I'll have to backtrack. I should be there in thirty minutes. Sit tight."

"Okay." She resisted the urge to tell him to hurry. She knew he would anyway.

"Emma, call me if anything happens and do what you need to do to be safe."

"I will."

"I love you."

She hesitated. "I'll see you in a little bit."

Emma handed the phone back. "He'll be here in thirty minutes. Could I use your bathroom?"

"It's down the hall. I'll get you something to change into."

"That's not necessary."

Sophia blocked her path. "You walked in here soaked to the bone, shivering and your face all beat up. Giving you something to wear is the least I can do."

Emma didn't answer and the woman moved down the hall.

"You wait outside the bathroom door. I'll be out in a second."

Emma looked at the dark paneled walls in the hallway covered with family pictures. She moved from photo to photo of children and families.

"Those are my children and their children," Sophia said and Emma jumped, startled. She rested her hand on Emma's shoulder. "Relax, you're safe here."

Emma turned around. "Your family is beautiful. You're so lucky."

"Yes, I'm a very rich woman. Not by the world's standards." She waved to her living room. "But where it really counts, I'm richer than most. Do you have a family? Children?"

Emma's throat burned. "I have a son. He's five." She paused, suddenly feeling an urgency to share her pregnancy. "And a baby." She put her hand on her stomach and smiled in spite of her sadness choking her heart.

The woman glanced at Emma's finger. "And the father?"

"He's the one coming to get me."

The woman took Emma's hands in her own. "Does he love you?"

Emma nodded, tears falling. "Yes, very much so."

"You hold on to that. Love is more powerful than all the money in the world."

Emma pushed open the bathroom door, worried she couldn't keep her emotions in check much longer. Sophia handed her a small white bundle. Emma glanced down and back to the woman in confusion.

"You're a wee thing, not much I own will fit you. This is all I have that will work."

Emma shook out the cloth to find a white nightgown in her hands. Her eyes grew round as her heart seized. "Oh, no… I can't…" She handed the gown to the woman.

The woman waved her off. "It's an old gown. I never wear it anymore. Just the other day I considered cutting it up for rags. You put it on to get warm and dry."

Emma couldn't figure out a logical reason to refuse. She told herself to calm down. It was just a nightgown. Just because she wore one in her dream with Raphael didn't mean anything. "Okay," she said as she shut the door and pressed her back into it. She looked up at the ceiling, willing her tears away then turned to the mirror, surprised by her reflection. Her left cheek was swollen and cut, her right side fuller than usual. Her arms were covered with cuts and scratches. Leaves and small twigs had embedded in her hair.

She stripped off her wet, muddy jeans and t-shirt and folded them into a pile on the side of the tub. She wet a washcloth and scrubbed the dirt and grime from her arms and face, being careful around her abrasions. She waited until the very last moment to slip the nightgown over her head. The woman was several sizes larger than Emma, and the gown swam on her. She told herself it was only until Will got there. He'd get her something else to wear.

Opening the door with her clothes sandwiched in her hands, she peered into the hall, half expecting someone to jump out at her. When she returned to the kitchen, Sophia held a kettle in her hand, pouring water into a cup.

"I was making myself some tea. Would you like some?"

The thought of drinking tea made her want to hurl. "Uh, no thank you. Maybe a glass of water."

Emma sat on the edge of a chair, scanning the room. The woman tilted her head. "You can trust me, you know. You can tell me what happened to you."

"It's better if you don't know." She paused. "Did you say you have a gun?"

"Why?" Sophia's words were crisp as she straightened, more alert.

"Just in case someone shows up looking for me."

"No, I made that up."

Emma's shoulders sank. She was weaponless.

"Who's after you? Do you think they'll come looking for you?"

"I don't know. I hope not, but I should probably just go. I can start walking to the road and Will can meet me out there."

"Will, is that your friend?" She nodded. "Will can pick you up right here. If you think someone's out there looking for you all the more reason to *not* be out there."

"But…"

"Sweetheart, I didn't get to be eighty-six years old by being stupid. Now I may not be very fast on my feet, but I can stand up to the best of them. I've got a cast-iron frying pan or two at my disposal."

The corners of Emma's mouth lifted. "I don't think a cast-iron skillet will hold off men with guns."

She winked. "They haven't met *my* cast-iron skillets."

"Why are you helping me? You know you're putting yourself in danger, yet you let me stay. Why?"

Sophia put a glass of water on the table and patted Emma's hand as she sat next to her. "Because I'm a good judge of character. You're a good person."

Emma pressed her lips together and slowly shook her head. "I don't know about that. I don't know about anything anymore."

"You *are* a good person. I can see it in you. I can see your spirit. Most people just think I'm crazy when I say that, but I've always been able to see the goodness or the evil in a person. They have a glow and I can see yours clear as day."

Emma's heart leapt at the thought. She'd believed differently for far too long. "Are you sure?"

"Yes."

"And my baby? Can you see if he's a good person?" If only she had confirmation that this baby wouldn't be born to destroy everything and everyone she loved.

"No, child. I can't see unborn babies."

Emma tried to contain her disappointment.

"Why would you think you're bad?"

She looked down at her lap, twisting the gown fabric between her fingers. "It's complicated."

"You keep saying that, but things often aren't as complicated as they seem."

Emma lifted her head and gave her a twisted smile. "Men." It seemed pretty stupid in light of everything else going on.

Sophia laughed and patted her hand. "There's plenty of man trouble to make the world go round. This have anything to do with your friend who's coming to get you?"

She sighed. "Yeah. And someone else."

"Ahh..." Sophia took a sip from her mug. "You have to make a decision?"

Did she? Was it really so difficult? The only thing Raphael had ever done for her was give her a car. But how did she explain the feelings he evoked? That had to mean something.

"Emma," Sophia paused and Emma looked up into her warm eyes. "At the end of the day, you have to figure out who makes you happy. Who loves you for you and is good for your soul."

Emma shook her head. "I've hurt him."

"If he loves you and you're meant to be, he'll forgive you. You need to trust him."

Emma's lip trembled. "I haven't trusted anyone or anything for so long, I don't even know where to start."

Sophia's hand squeezed Emma's "Start by trusting your heart."

If only her heart wasn't such a mess.

Emma's eyes widened when a gunshot rang out in the woods. "Do you hear gunshots out here very often?"

Sophia gripped her mug tighter. "No."

Emma jumped out of her seat, banging her leg into the table. Water sloshed out of its glass. "I've got to go."

"You can't leave. If there are men with guns out there looking for you, you'd be foolish to go out there."

She jammed her feet into her shoes. "No. They'll come here looking for me. They'll hurt you. I can't let that happen." Emma dropped her clothes on the chair. "Hide these somewhere so they can't find them, just in case they look. If they know you helped me…." Emma moved to the back door.

"Emma, don't go out there. Stay here and let me help you."

She shook her head and pushed open the door. "You helped me enough. No one can help me now."

CHAPTER TWENTY-SIX

GOOSEBUMPS erupted on Emma's arms from chill and fright. The wind picked up, swirling around her, her gown flapping around her legs. Thousands of stars twinkled over her head in the narrow gap between the trees. A feeling of dread crept over her.

She kept moving down the gravel road, the woods on either side of her silent. With any luck at all, she had imagined the noises before. She hoped that Will was closer than he thought.

Did she love him? Sophia told her that she would know. She could never ask for a better man than Will Davenport and he loved her unconditionally. Yet there was no denying the unstoppable pull to Raphael. It was as though he had cast her in a magic spell.

Emma nearly scoffed at the thought, then stopped. After every other crazy thing that had happened to her in the last month, it didn't seem so crazy after all. The pull to him was almost magnetic. She found herself unable to resist, especially if he touched her. And every time she saw him, it grew stronger and stronger.

She didn't even know what Raphael wanted from her, but she was sure he wanted something. Why would he keep showing up out of nowhere? If only she had the stone, maybe she could use its power to defend herself from him.

Goddamn James. He'd drugged her, handed her over to Kramer and stolen her pendant. The one tie to who she really was and what she was capable of. Her anger grew, mushrooming into a near explosive level. Then she felt it. The burn in her chest.

Her eyes widened at the possibility.

A noise in the trees startled her. Emma stopped turning her head to the sound. The wind died down and a voice floated on the remnants.

"Emma." It was only one word, but it was laden with warmth and promise. And beckoning.

She froze, grabbing onto a tree for support as a cramp griped her lower abdomen. She shook her head, sure she had imagined the voice. Her pain eased and she straightened, her worry for the baby growing stronger. The man had kicked her in the stomach and she was sore. That was all.

She continued toward the main road, shadows creeping along the edges, moving with the breeze as though they beckoned. The wind lifted the hem of her nightgown, as though it played with her, taunting her. Her chest tightened. Her imagination had gone into overdrive.

"Emma." The wind called again, warm and inviting. It pulled her into the trees.

She gripped the nearest trunk, clinging as her will fought against the pull that drew her. It was too strong, her curiosity too piqued to deny the call. Step by agonizing slow step, she walked toward the force that drew her, a roaring bonfire in a clearing in the forest. She stopped far enough away to feel its warmth without getting burned.

The cool, damp air clung to her skin contrasting with the heat of the blaze that warmed the front of her. Her breath came in shallow pants, her chest rising and falling while her heart beat savagely against her chest. An undercurrent of electricity flowed along the surface of her skin, causing a tingle that rippled across her body. She wasn't frightened. She was more alive than she had ever been and she felt power, unimaginable power. Her excitement mingled with the electrical current, causing an unexpected pleasurable sensation to spread through her. She gasped in surprise and delight.

The fire called to her. Every part of her being shivered with anticipation. Emma felt a presence approach from behind. It lifted the hair off the side of her neck. A soft breeze blew and the leaves of the trees rustled, whispering in the night. Stray hairs tickled her face, leaving tiny electrical jolts in their wake. Warm, soft lips moved to her neck, kissing lightly and moving up to her ear. Warm breath fanned her damp skin and a slow burn began to ignite in her stomach. Emma tilted her head, looking up into the leaves of the trees above her before closing her eyes.

"You are not bound to destiny." A warm, husky voice filled her ear as the lips that spoke the words kissed her neck below her ear lobe. Waves of pleasure washed through her. Every part of her yearned for more. She wanted what he offered. She wanted him. Only it wasn't Will.

"We're so close," he said, his very breath pushing her closer and closer to ecstasy. "So very close."

Her body agreed, straining for more. He circled in front of her and she knew who it was even before she saw him. Raphael.

His eyes glowed, feral and hungry. Raphael reached up, touching her cheek. The firelight danced on his face. "What have they done to you, my love?" His finger traced her cheekbone, electricity following in its wake. "Again, he hasn't protected you." His fingertip slid along her lower lip, hesitating at the fullest part. She inhaled and he smiled.

His hand slid down to her neck, his thumb tracing along her pulse point. Raphael's face inched closer to hers until his breath mingled with her own. His mouth hovered over hers, so close that her lips ached with need.

His mouth touched hers, a whisper of a kiss, taunting her. She moaned and he smiled against her lower lip. "You want this too." He nipped and she cried out again. His tongue licked her upper lip, then darted in finding her tongue. She froze as his tongue teased hers.

"Do you remember the words?" he murmured against her mouth.

She was lost. Lost in feelings and sensations, smoldering in the fire that swept her body. "No."

He wrapped an arm around her back, pulling until her chest molded into his. His hand skimmed her shoulder with agonizing slowness up to her neck, his thumb tracing a line up to her ear. "You always liked this. Do you really not remember?"

His mouthed claimed hers with ferociousness, as though he could breathe the words into her. She clung to him overwhelmed by the onslaught of sensations. His mouth moved to her ear as she panted for breath. "We're so close now. Closer than we've ever been, my love. How can you not know the words?"

"Because it's not her." A man's voice called out.

Raphael's arm tightened around her waist and he hissed. "Alex."

Emma's eyes widened and she looked over her shoulder to see Alex standing on the other side of the fire. Passion swept away with the wind, leaving anger in its wake. She clenched her fists and pushed against Raphael's chest, but his grip tightened.

"You're a little late to the party, Alex. Emmanuella was about to choose me."

The light of the bonfire accentuated the glint in his eyes. "It's not her."

Raphael jerked the nightgown down to reveal her shoulder blade and the marks embedded there. "This proves that it is." He caressed her cheek seductively, and she found herself lost in him again. Raphael smiled in triumph. "And this proves it as well. She has never been able to resist me."

"Maybe so, but it's not your Emmanuella. She's different."

Raphael gripped Emma's cheeks in his hand, looking into her eyes. "What makes you say that? She's the same as always."

"No, look deeper, Raphael. She's similar but not the same. She fights harder. She resists us both more."

Raphael laughed bitterly. "Of course, she does. That's how she got this far this time. She's a fighter."

"No, Raphael. She's different. When did you ever see her fall in love with the man sent to protect her?"

Raphael's eyes narrowed. "She doesn't love him. She cares for him, but love him?"

"She carries his child."

"She carried your child too, you son of a bitch. That didn't change anything, did it? Did you really think it would?"

"I hadn't remembered at that point, but you and I both know we're still drawn to her even before we remember."

"You're goddamned lucky that didn't restart the whole thing."

"Exactly. Why didn't it?"

Raphael stood in stunned silence. Emma's mind found a tiny foothold on sanity and pulled out of Raphael's grip. "What the hell are you talking about?"

Raphael's head whipped around to face her. "Do you really not remember?"

"Remember *what*?"

Raphael turned to Alex. "How can she not remember?"

"I keep telling you it's not her."

Emma backed up several steps. "*What the hell are you talking about?*"

Alex walked around the fire, keeping his gaze on her.

Raphael reached for her. "If you kill her this time, Alex. I will rip you apart with my bare hands. I haven't gotten this close to lose her now."

"No!" She held her hands up in front of her. "Stay away from me. I don't know how you do that to me, but stay the hell away so I can think."

"Emmanuella…" Raphael cooed, his hands reaching toward her, coaxing.

Alex moved toward her and she backed up another step. "Stay back, the both of you."

"See?" Alex asked, turning an eye to Raphael. "Our Emmanuella is meeker. This one is a warrior. When I first met her, before I remembered who she was and who I was, she was like our Emmanuella, but she changed. When I met her a month ago and the memories returned, I knew it wasn't her."

Raphael looked crestfallen as he searched her face. "What does it mean?"

The air stilled before a voice broke the silence. "That everything has changed."

They all turned to see a man standing on the other side of the fire.

"Aiden." Both men spoke at the same time.

Emma's heart skipped a beat. "My father?"

But the man before her couldn't be her father. Tall, with a solid physique. Wavy brown hair covered his head. His face looked like a Renaissance painting, regal and cold. He looked far too young to be her father.

"Hello, Emmanuella. You've done well."

Dizziness washed through her and she stumbled a step before catching herself. "Where the hell have you been for twenty-seven years?"

"Waiting for the right time."

"Right time? Right fucking time for *what*?"

"What the hell is going on, Aiden?" Alex snarled. "She doesn't remember anything. It's not her, yet she has the marks. She has the power. Are you changing the rules of the game now? After all these centuries?"

Aiden shrugged and turned out his hands. "I'm bored. You all do almost exactly the same thing, time after time after time. She wants Raphael. You get angry and kill her before she can pick him. That is if you two even get that far. It was time to shake things up a bit. It's time to end this."

"About fucking damn time," Alex said.

Aiden lifted an eyebrow, a bored look in his eyes. "I tried to help you out this time, Alex. I gave you an unfair advantage and sent you to her before you even knew who she really was. You had a chance to woo her and make her love you before her protector showed up. You could have won over Raphael this time but what did you do? In your human shortsightedness, you raped her and made her hate you even more."

Raphael took a step toward Aiden, his hands clenched in fists at this side. "Why doesn't she remember?" Torment and rage mixed in his words.

"Alex is correct. She isn't the Emmanuella you know."

A slow mournful wail filled the night air. "Why?" His torment carried on the wind, swirling around and filling her ears.

"Because time is running out for us. She loved you as much as you loved her. Alex never had a chance."

Emma had had enough. "*What the hell is going on here*?"

Aiden looked at her and smiled, full of pride and arrogance. "You are my greatest creation yet."

Raphael lifted his head to face Aiden. "Where is my Emmanuella?"

"Gone." His tone was detached and cold.

Raphael fell to the ground, weeping. Emma's chest filled with icy fear. Whatever was going on, she wanted no part of. She took a several steps backward, toward the trees.

"Not yet, Emma." Aiden called to her. "We're not finished."

"You all are crazy." She stood at the edge of the tree line.

"Not all of us, although Raphael seems to have temporarily lost control."

"You haven't told me what's going on. What do I have to do with any of this?"

"You have everything to do with all of this. You are the *prize*."

She looked from man to man, her eyes wide with fear and horror. "Prize?"

"The man you choose wins."

"Have you lost your fucking mind? You can't do that. It's the twenty-first century, for God's sake."

Aiden laughed. "Oh, this started long, long ago before women had liberties and rights. Besides, you have all the power. You choose who wins or loses."

"Wins or loses what?"

"Control, power. The world."

"Do you work for Kramer and Senator Warren?"

Aiden laughed. "Now that is funny. No." His face hardened. "They're stupid humans. They're minor players. My pawns."

"They didn't seem so minor when they tried to kidnap me and beat the crap out of me a short bit ago."

Aiden shrugged. "They're for my amusement. To add another dimension to the game."

"It amuses you to see your daughter physically abused? And raped? And chased with guns? I gave up my entire life because of your little game." she asked, incredulous. "You told the Vinco Potentia about me. You set all of that into motion. How can you live with yourself?"

Alex laughed, but it was cold. "You find it surprising because you equate him with a human father who would love and protect his child." He put his hands on his hips and turned to her. "You need to think of him more as an ancient god who has little affection or concern for his progeny."

Emma's eyes widened. "Wait, are you saying…?"

Alex's eyes hardened and narrowed. "Yes."

She shook her head. "No… no… this is too crazy…"

"Is it really so hard to believe after everything else that has happened?" Alex asked.

"Yes! Yes it is!"

"Emma, you're not that simpleminded." Aiden said. "Look at me."

She turned to stare at him, taking in his incredibly sculptured face. The beauty and perfection hinted at his godliness. Her head whipped to Alex. He was perfect too. She'd noticed it the first time she had seen him, wondering why a man as beautiful as him could be interested in her. And Raphael, he too was perfect.

But she was not. How did that figure in?

Her stomach cramped again and she gasped in surprise, bending over in pain for a moment before standing again. "Who are Alex and Raphael? Who am I?"

"Centuries and centuries ago, Alex, Raphael and I were equals. There were others, but they lost their power and turned to whispers and howls in wind. They live in the shadows and creep in the night. We oversaw the creatures that lurk in the darkness. We each had a realm. Air, land and fire. We governed the creatures. And the elements." Alex said.

"But Aiden was bored." Raphael's head lifted and turned to Emma. "So he challenged us to a game."

"It was a simple game, a dice game and the stakes were low. But Raphael and I were winning."

"So Aiden suggested we up the stakes. Winner after the next game would take all, literally. Winner would take the others' power over their realms for a limited time. We figured what did we have to lose? Limited time. What we didn't know was that Aiden would create an eternal game that looped on and on, neither of us ever winning."

"Not to mention that we lost our immortality."

Aiden snorted. "You both are such overreactors. Neither one of you lost your immortality."

"No, it was just transferred to reincarnation."Alex said. "Forced to live as humans, a human lifetime and then reincarnated after death. All the while searching for the prize. Aiden's daughter."

Emma looked from man to man to see if they were serious. "How long has this been going on?"

Alex took a step toward her. "Centuries. Some lifetimes you were there, or rather your predecessor was. Others, you weren't. None of us were aware at birth. At some point, usually in our twenties, although centuries ago we found out in our teens. After the Chosen One found you, we would all awaken to our true identity and we would search for you. He was your guardian and protector until we could find you."

"But there were rules." Raphael growled. "Aiden and his fucking rules. We couldn't tell you who you were if you hadn't remembered yet. And you couldn't choose until you had come into your full powers."

Alex stood several feet from her now. "But the more contact we had with you, the slower your powers developed. Ours overpowered yours. And we weren't supposed to interfere."

"What do you mean interfere?" Emma asked.

"Your father threw that stupid prophecy out for men to stumble upon. To search you out and try to use you for their own purposes."

Emma shook her head. "That's crazy."

"Just another obstacle in our course."

"So how were they supposed to win?" Emma cast a glance at the man who was supposed to be her father. She'd rather go back to being fatherless.

"You were to claim one and join their power with yours. Then they could win back their realm. But the choice was yours," Aiden answered.

"What happens to the one not picked?"

"His realm is shared by the other two and he joins the ancients to live in the shadows."

"So why don't you just keep their power for eternity?" Emma asked Aiden.

Alex laughed. "Because he forgot he needed balance. Good needs evil. Light needs dark. Aiden needs an opposite. Without it, the power he stole from us—"

"Willingly gave..." Aiden said with a bored sigh.

"—has begun to fade. And so has ours. He needs this to be over so he can regain his lost power."

"So, let me get this straight. I'm supposed to choose? What if I didn't agree?"

"It never got that far," Alex said.

Raphael stood. "Often you were killed by men. Or we got too close and your powers never fully developed so you *could* choose. You died while we were forced to live out our earthly life, waiting for the next round. But the last several lifetimes, when you remembered, you remembered your love for me. It stayed with you."

"So you thought I was her?"

"Yes." His brokenness filled the single word.

Emma lifted her chin and squared her shoulders. "So now what?"

Aiden laughed. "Always direct and to the point, Emmanuella. I love that about you."

"You don't know shit about me. What's to keep me from walking away from this entire fucking mess and never looking back? What if I don't want to choose either one of them? What if I've already chosen someone else?"

Aiden's mouth lifted into a wry smile. "Yes, Alex is right. That was a change that I hadn't anticipated until it began. But then again, you haven't chosen Will either."

His words were like a knife in her heart, twisting and slicing with her own treachery. He was right. She hadn't chosen him and she had a feeling it would now bite her in the ass.

"He should be joining us in a moment. Perhaps you will want to choose him then?" Aiden asked, a playful smile on his face

She didn't trust him. Didn't trust the smile spreading across his face. The man before her was a monster that wasn't a man at all.

CHAPTER TWENTY-SEVEN

WILL sped down the two-lane highway, searching for the gravel road that led to the house Emma had called from. He knew he risked getting stopped by the police, but it was a risk he was willing to take to reach her sooner. His arm tingled, but the feeling was only a slow burn, not an insistent need, so he had no idea what was wrong. It gave him little comfort that her terror hadn't risen to a level that she could contact him. At least this wasn't like earlier, when his mark was on fire and she refused to answer him.

A worn, whitewashed sign appeared on the side of the road. He flashed his high beams to make out "Martin" in faded black letters. He turned onto the gravel and cut his lights, letting the moon light the road. No need to announce his entrance.

He drove a half-mile before he smelled smoke. Slowing, he lowered the windows. The glow of a fire loomed through the trees. He stopped and listened to voices floating on the wind.

Will grabbed his shotgun and got out of the car. Emma was supposed to be waiting at the house, but something told him she was close. He made his way noiselessly through the trees, creeping closer to the fire. Voices grew louder, but he couldn't make out whom they belonged to until he heard her voice.

"So now what?"

He knew her well enough to read her voice. She confronted whomever she spoke to, her tone haughty and demanding, but he doubted anyone else heard the undertone of uncertainty.

Will approached close enough to make out figures by the fire. A man stood alone on one side of the fire. Another man, dressed in black stood in front of a woman in a long white gown. *Emma.* They both faced the man standing apart.

He crept closer and he saw a third man to the far left side of Emma. *Alex.* His grip on his gun tightened. Whatever Emma had got caught up in couldn't be good if it involved Alex. He raised his gun and watched through the magnified sight. The other man by Emma was the man from the bar in Joplin and the parking lot in Kansas City. *Raphael.* His chest squeezed with a force that caught his breath.

His attention turned to the man standing alone, who seemed to have the attention of the other three. He wore a long-sleeved button-down shirt and khakis, and looked completely out of place in the wilderness of Montana. Will continued to scan the area. He didn't see any other men, but a small bundle in the woods confused him. He began to make his way toward it, keeping his attention on Emma and the men. She didn't appear to be in immediate danger and seemed to be holding her own.

He watched her as he moved. Her feet stood shoulder distance apart, a defensive stance, yet her shoulders were raised and her chin lifted. While her exterior portrayed brave and strong, he recognized the fear hidden in her bluff. The mark on his arm only tingled, so she wasn't terrified. But it also meant he couldn't communicate with her.

"He should be joining us in a moment," the unknown man said. "Perhaps you will want to choose him then?"

Emma watched him, torment twisting her mouth. She lifted her chin higher.

"Come out, Will. I know you're there." The man turned to look directly at Will.

Will raised his shotgun tip and took a step into the clearing.

"Sorry I'm late. Maybe you can fill me in on what I've missed."

He scanned the faces of the people in front of him. The mouth of the man in charge lifted in a smug smile. He might appear unarmed, but Will didn't trust him for a moment.

Next was Raphael. His shoulders hunched in despair, his eyes dead in the firelight. Raphael looked like a defeated man.

Emma turned her eyes to his, and he locked on her for a split second. Bruises lined her cheeks. He gripped the shotgun tighter. "Who hurt her?" He turned to Alex, whose expression turned from a scowl to surprise.

"None of us, you idiot. She found us after she escaped from my father's men. They did that to her."

Emma took a step toward Will. Raphael swung an arm in front of her, blocking her path. "Not so fast. Where the hell were you when this happened?"

Will clenched his teeth in self-incrimination. “I left her for a short time. It was a mistake and it won’t happen again.”

“Didn’t you say that last time?” Raphael sneered.

Will’s arm muscles tensed. “How the hell would you know?”

Raphael’s eyes sparkled with an evil glint. “What? Didn’t Emma tell you about our late-night poolside chat in South Dakota?”

Will lunged forward and the fire exploded. The man by the fire looked annoyed.

“Now, now,” he said. “We have more important things to attend to than preening our peacock feathers.” He turned to face Will. “I think I should introduce myself. I’m Aiden. I believe you know the others.”

“Aiden? As in Emma’s father?” He swung his head to Emma, who nodded.

“You, Mr. Davenport, are sharp as a tack. Let’s get to business, shall we?”

“I don't know what you have planned,” Will said, walking toward Emma, shoving Raphael’s arm out of his path. “But I plan to collect Jake from Alex and pretend I never saw any of you.”

Aiden cocked his head with a grin. “Be careful what you wish for, William.”

When he reached Emma, Will stepped behind her and wrapped an arm around her waist, pulling her back into his chest.

"I don't have Jake," Alex said. "Someone stole him from me earlier tonight. Caused quite a mess, I might add. I suspect it was Raphael."

Raphael squared his shoulders as he glared at Alex. "If it had been me, he would be in his mother's arms already. I would never keep a mother from her child, you maggot."

Emma's eyes widened in panic. "Then where is he?"

"No need to worry, Emmanuella." Aiden said. "He is safe in my care."

"*You*?"

Will's arm tightened as she tried to lunge.

"Yes, he's my collateral."

"You fucking son of a bitch!" She jerked again and Will's grip lifted her feet off the ground. "Let go of me, Will!"

"Emma, calm down." He whispered in her ear. "I think Jake's here and I know exactly where he is. But don't let on to Aiden or we'll lose our upper hand."

Her body relaxed. He loosened his hold and she slid down until her feet touched the earth.

"Now Emmanuella," Aiden grinned. "That's no way to talk to your father."

"What do you want?"

"That's the crux of it, isn't it?" Aiden gloated. "What do *I* want? You all have bored me for so long, so many centuries. I'm tired of this game and I want it done."

"And you want your power," Alex added.

Emma lifted her head, the wind blowing her hair into her face. "Too bad because I don't choose either of them."

"Somehow, I knew you would say that, thus the need for collateral."

Emma's back stiffened against Will's chest. "You're using my son, your grandson, to make me pick one of them?"

"No," he scoffed. "What's the fun in that? I propose a new game."

Alex put his hands on his hips. "As long as it doesn't involve her picking Raphael or me because she will never pick me in a thousand lifetimes."

"What the hell are they talking about?" Will whispered in her ear.

"I'll tell you later."

"No, it doesn't involve that at all. In fact, Emmanuella is the strongest of my daughters yet. I might even go as far as to say her powers are equal to yours." Aiden looked toward the two men. "It shall be a challenge between the three of you." He turned to Emma and smiled. "See, you don't have to choose either of them."

"What do we have to do?"

Aiden's eyes narrowed. "First, we must even the playing field. You have to give up something you love."

****

Even as he spoke the words, Emma felt the trickle down her leg. She sank back into Will's chest. "No."

"Emma?" Will's grasp around her waist tightened, his voice anxious.

Pain gripped her abdomen, sharper than before and she doubled over Will's arm as she felt the gush of blood. He grabbed her arm and held her up.

"Emma, what's wrong?"

She looked into his face, hazy through her tears. "The baby." She choked on a sob.

He looked down. Scarlet drops splattered the white gown whipping around her legs. The ground darkened with the pool forming at her feet and his eyes widened with fear. "Oh, God."

He was terrified for her. "Will." She doubled over with another shot of pain. "I'm losing the baby. I'm so sorry." Her voice broke.

"No, no, no," he chanted. "It's okay. It's not your fault. As long as you're okay. I can't live without you, Emma."

"Do you intend to claim him, Emmanuella?" Aiden asked, his words mingling with her moans.

Will's face searched hers for reassurance. She hadn't even been sure she wanted this baby, why was it ripping her heart in two? *Will.* The man could drive her crazy, but she couldn't imagine living without him. The man who loved her so fiercely that its intensity scared her. The man who would give his life for hers, mark or no mark. Suddenly, she knew without a shred of doubt that she loved him. She needed him not just as her protector but as the other half of her. He offered her completeness, not Raphael. She grieved for the baby that bonded them together.

"Yes," she cried out in desperation, looking into Will's confused eyes. "Yes, I claim him. What do I say? I don't know the words. I only know that I love him."

"Perfect." Aiden's word filled the air and echoed off the trees.

The mark on Emma's back burned, causing her to cry out.

Will looked down at his forearm with a jerk. Emma's eyes followed. The mark on his arm began to fade.

"No!" Emma cried out in agony, gripping Will's arm.

"I told you that you had to lose someone you loved."

She shook her head. "No. You took the baby."

"The baby wasn't what you loved. The baby was what bound you to Will."

"Emma, it's okay," Will smoothed her hair and kissed her forehead. "I don't need a mark to love you, I told you that already. Now this just proves it."

But she knew there was something else, he said she had to lose someone she loved. "Please don't kill him, please. I'll do anything." Her words were wild and desperate.

Aiden chuckled. "Now, Emma, I never took you for the dramatic type. I don't plan to kill him."

She hiccupped a sigh of relief. "Thank you."

"But you have to let him go."

Will slid sideways to the trees, his left arm around Emma's waist, the other pointing his gun toward Aiden. "I've heard enough. I think we'll be going now."

"Your gun can't hurt me, Will," Aiden laughed.

Will pulled Emma along the tree line, behind Aiden. She struggled to keep up with him, fighting her cramps and nausea. Nausea.

Oh, God. No. "Will, they're coming."

His eyes widened. "Who?"

She fell out of his arms, vomiting onto the earth, adding to her sacrifice. What more would the earth claim from her tonight? She prayed what she had given was enough.

Will grabbed her arm and pulled her up. "Emma, we're close. Come on." He dragged her to a blanket-wrapped bundle that lay on the ground. Her heart leapt into her throat. Jake.

Oh, God. Jake.

Her breath came in desperate gasps as she fell beside it, her fingers fumbling with the wrapping.

"Looking for this?" Aiden asked.

Her head jerked up. Jake stood next to Aiden, his eyes glowing in the firelight. "Jake!"

He didn't answer, staring into the fire.

Another wave of nausea swept over her and she vomited again, cursing the stupid way her body responded to the threat. When she finished, she pushed herself off the ground. Will reached down and helped her to her feet.

"Jake! It's Mommy!" She leapt for him, but Will held her back.

Jake ignored her, lost in his daze.

"What have you done to him?"

Aiden put a hand on Jake's shoulder. "He's fine. He's under my control. I assure you he's not in any pain and he chose freely to go with me."

It all made sense now. "You were the one who visited him in his dreams before he was kidnapped?"

"Yes."

His tie to Jake ran deep. Her fury ignited, a burning ball of wrath spinning in her chest. She was only vaguely aware that her power grew.

"Emma." Will warned behind her.

Aiden's face beamed.

"What is your game, *father*?" she sneered, her hands stretching out from her sides. Electricity ran down her arms and lifted the hair on her neck. Will loosened his arm around her waist. "What do you expect of me? What am I and scores of others required to sacrifice for your entertainment? How do I get back my son?"

"You will battle each other to win, until one is left."

"And if I don't?"

"You have too much to lose."

She leaned her head toward Raphael. "How do you know they'll do it?"

"Because they are as desperate for this to end as I am."

"Wait!" Raphael called out, lifting his chin. "I want this clarified. There are four of us and only two will remain?"

Aiden gave him a sardonic smile. "Aren't you good with math?"

Raphael glared. "*The rules are there are four and only two remain*?"

Aiden's eyes squinted in annoyance. "You're not only becoming weaker but denser as well. Didn't I just say so?"

Raphael's face hardened, but a smile lifted the side of his mouth. "And this will be the end, you swear it?"

"Yes."

"So let's end this right now." Emma shouted, narrowing her eyes. The electricity in her body reached a fevered pitch and she released it, aiming at Aiden's chest. He held up his hand and blocked it, sending it into the fire. The flames shot twenty feet into the air, a deafening roar filling her ears. Weakened, she sagged to the ground, Will wrapping an arm around her waist and pulling her up.

"I'll let that go this time." Aiden's eyebrows furrowed as his mouth tightened. "Next time, I won't be so lenient. But one more thing before I go, Emmanuella. Time to say goodbye to Will. "

He and Jake turned, and walked into the woods. A massive wind howled and a cramp spread through her abdomen, followed by nausea. Hunched over, she looked up at Will. "We have to go, they're coming."

He looked at her with an expressionless face, his eyes empty.

"Will!"

His expression reminded her of Kramer's when she'd controlled his mind.

"Will?" she choked out.

He stared at her, his eyes clouded with confusion. "Who are you?"

Raphael ran to her side. "Your father has erased his memory of you."

"No!" she screamed and grabbed Will's face in her hands. "Will, it's me. It's Emma. I love you, Will. I love you. Please. *Please*, don't forget me."

He stared down at her, even more bewildered.

"Oh, God. Did he hurt his brain?"

"No, he's just momentarily confounded over the memory loss."

She grabbed his shoulders and shook. "Will! *Please*. Don't leave me. I love you!" She pressed her lips into his, wrapping her arms around his neck. Her tears fell onto his cheeks but his lips were unyielding and he gently pushed her away, a vacant look in his eyes.

"Do I know you?"

"No!" she sobbed. Turning to Raphael, she became frantic. "They're coming. Warren's men or the Cavallo are coming. We have to go. We have to take Will out of here."

Raphael shook his head, scanning the area. "Emma, I doubt he'll go."

"Please, help me. *Please.*" She wasn't beyond begging. She couldn't let them take him.

Raphael groaned. "Tell me why I'm helping you?"

"Because you lost your Emmanuella. Please help me save Will."

Raphael grabbed one of Will's arms and pulled. "Where are we going, Emma?"

"Will drove here in a car. If we can get to it, we can get away."

Will dug his feet into the ground. "I'm not going anywhere with you two."

Emma tugged on his arm. "Will, I know you don't remember me, but you're in serious danger. We have to run."

The sound of feet crashing through the forest made him straighten.

"Emma, you have to go. *Now.*" Raphael's insistent voice growled.

"No! I can't leave Will." She turned back to him. "Will. Please trust me. We have to go. They're going to capture you." Or worse. He no longer had his mark to protect him.

Will shook his head as though he tried to clear it. He scanned the trees then looked down at her, his eyes clearer. "Okay," he said. "What's the plan?"

Emma breathed a sigh of relief. "Do you have the keys to the car?"

He reached in and pulled out a set, handing them to her. "Why can't I remember how I got here?"

"I'll explain it to you later. Just trust me." She grabbed his hand and pulled as they took off running through trees. The anger built in her chest, not difficult to produce when she thought of all she had lost in the matter of minutes. And when she saw the first men creeping in the forest, preparing to attack from their right side, she released the energy, pushing it to them with a heart full of hatred. The ball glowed bright, an orange-red ball of hate that blasted into the trees. The ground shook and Emma fell, her legs weak from the lost of energy. Will's hand reached down to help her up but when she looked into his face to thank him, she looked into the eyes of a stranger.

"How did you do that?" he asked.

She stood and grabbed his hand again. Raphael moved in next to them. "You need to control your power."

"I don't know what the fuck I'm doing."

"No, shit. You're going to kill us all for eternity."

"So, you die, you come back. Big fucking deal." She yelled over her shoulder, running with Will beside her.

"No, Emma. You don't get it. This is *the end.* We die, we're done. We live as shadows. Forever."

The realization slammed her. This was it. Gunshots sailed past them and they dove for cover, Will releasing Emma's hand. He seemed to regain his senses as he swung up his shotgun and began to fire.

"Stay here," Will called out as he dashed into the trees, leaving Emma with Raphael in his wake.

"Where the hell is he going?" Raphael asked.

"He's protecting us."

"Why? He doesn't even know you now."

"Because that's who he is." It was true. This was the real Will, who was a hero at heart. She'd been lucky he chose to love her and now it was gone.

Raphael grabbed her arm. "We need to go."

"No! Not without Will."

"You're going to get yourself killed."

"What the fuck do you care? I die, you have one more chance of winning against Aiden."

Raphael knelt in front of her, his eyes full of anger. "No, Emma. We need each other. That's why I pinned him down. There are four of us, only two survive. He thinks he's an automatic winner. Together we might be able to defeat him, but separately we are doomed."

She stared at his dark face lit only by the moonlight.

"Emma, I'm your only chance to save Jake."

He was probably right. She needed him. "I won't leave Will."

He turned his head to the side. "Son of a bitch," he said, standing. "Come on." He led her in the direction Will had taken. Two armed men appeared from behind a tree. Raphael reached out toward the earth, releasing a green glow. The ground shook and separated, revealing a deep crevice into which the two men fell.

"Can you make your energy smaller, more controlled?" Raphael asked.

"I think so. I practiced before with fruit."

"Okay, a little bit more than fruit but not enough to blow us up."

When three men with guns appeared, she released energy toward each man. They fell onto the ground into a smoldering pile.

Her mouth dropped open in surprise and disgust.

Raphael grabbed her hand and pulled her away. "Better them than you. Let's find Will and go."

Gunshots echoed ahead of them. "Hurry," Emma shouted.

They found him surrounded by a group of armed men, laying face down on the ground. Emma sank to her knees in the cover of dense growth, Raphael kneeling beside her.

"Oh, God. They killed him." She choked back a sob.

Raphael put an arm around her head, covering her mouth. "Shh."

The men lifted Will and carried him toward a van several feet from the edge of the trees.

She struggled against Raphael's grip, desperate to get to Will before they tossed his limp body into the vehicle. Raphael held tight and as she struggled, a liquid warmth spread through her body, becoming alive with craving. Her body melted and molded into Raphael's. She watched the back doors close and the van drove away before Raphael released his hold.

The warmth slipped away replaced by the cold wind and the realization of what she'd just done. While men carted Will's body away, she yearned for Raphael.

She fell to the ground, sobbing her pain, frustration and betrayal into the damp ground, but the earth hadn't claimed enough from her yet.

It was greedy for more.

ABOUT THE MARKS

THREE intertwined symbols are on The Chosen Series covers: a trident, fire and water. All three appeared on Emma's shoulder blade at various times.

The trident was the symbol that Jake branded on Will's forearm as proof that Will was The Chosen One, the protector of his mother Emma. That mark was highlighted in *Chosen.*

In *Hunted*, the symbol for fire is highlighted on the cover and embedded on the title and chapter heading pages. Fire is the symbol that appeared after Jake was conceived and the symbol on the pendant Emma's father gave to her mother.

Water will be highlighted in *Sacrifice.*

ACKNOWLEDGMENTS

FIRST, I'd like to thank my children, as always, for not only tolerating Mommy's crazy work habits but respecting that this is Mommy's job. I love you guys.

Thanks to Scot Kraemer who was an indispensable resource during the writing of *Chosen* and parts of *Hunted.* Little did he know that a random tweet from me about researching South Dakota would get a character named after him that spans three books.

And little did my alpha reader, Brandy Underwood, know that she'd get a character named after her, too. Just goes to show you that you better be careful around an author.

Many thanks to Ken Hammond for his patience and expertise reviewing the airplane scene. He offered advice while I wrote the first draft then reviewed the scene and offered more suggestions after editing.

Thank you to my critique partner and best friend, Trisha Leigh. I couldn't do this without your support, encouragement and friendship. I suppose I *could*, but it would be ten times harder. And a whole lot lonelier.

Thank you to Eisley Jacobs, S. Frankie Blooding, Katrina Harris, Rhonda Cowsert, Anne Chilldon and Lissa Critz. Your critiquing and beta reading made *Hunted* so much better and gave me the encouragement I needed when I was sure it was the worst book ever written.

And last, but never least, thank you to my editor Jim Thomsen, who not only tolerates my moments of insanity but makes my books so much better.

ABOUT THE AUTHOR

DENISE GROVER SWANK lives in Lee's Summit, Missouri. She has six children, two dogs, and an overactive imagination. She can be found dancing in her kitchen with her children, reading or writing her next book. You will rarely find her cleaning.

You can find out more about Denise and her other books at www.denisegroverswank.com

Made in the USA
Middletown, DE
02 October 2016